Praise for *Daughters of Victory*

"A meticulously detailed, fierce, and often violent tale of two women with blood on their hands and the hope of freedom in their hearts, *Daughters of Victory* will leave you breathless."
—Kristin Harmel, *New York Times* bestselling author

"Gabriella Saab's *Daughters of Victory* is like a faded picture of a lost time coming back into brilliant focus: all at once vibrant, alive, and deeply emotional, leaving your heart pounding too fast as you breathlessly turn the pages to the story's stunning, surprising conclusion."
—Olesya Salnikova Gilmore, author of *The Witch and the Tsar*

Praise for *The Last Checkmate*

"With vivid prose and heart-stopping scenes, Saab unfolds the story like her protagonist plays chess, with cunning wit and brilliant strategy. Gabriella Saab's debut is immersive, smart, and haunting—a do-not-miss World War II historical novel."
—Patti Callahan, *New York Times* bestselling author of *Surviving Savannah*

"What's the best strategy to survive in a place as evil as Auschwitz? *The Last Checkmate* kept me turning pages long into the night. A fantastic debut!"
—Anika Scott, internationally bestselling author of *The German Heiress*

"Just wow! I was speechless when I finished reading this book. Raw and powerful in its humanity, *The Last Checkmate* will break your heart and stitch it back together again. Gabriella Saab has given us a rare and wondrous gift. A must-read for all historical fiction lovers."

—Sara Ackerman, *USA Today* bestselling author of *Radar Girls*

Daughters of Victory

Also by Gabriella Saab

The Last Checkmate

Daughters
of Victory

A Novel

Gabriella Saab

wm
WILLIAM MORROW
An Imprint of HarperCollinsPublishers

P.S.™ is a trademark of HarperCollins Publishers.

HarperCollins books may be purchased for educational, business, or sales promotional use. For information, please email the Special Markets Department at SPsales@harpercollins.com.

FIRST EDITION

Designed by Diahann Sturge

Library of Congress Cataloging-in-Publication Data has been applied for.

ISBN 978-0-06-324649-2 (paperback)
ISBN 978-0-06-329705-0 (library edition)

23 24 25 26 27 LBC 5 4 3 2 1

For MeMommy and Poppy; Auntie Niki and Uncle Simon;
Mama and Daddy: You encourage and inspire me, and I love
you all so much. Always keep a spot of blue over your head.

PART 1

*A man's eyes should be torn out
if he can only see the past.*

—Joseph Stalin

Chapter 1

Moscow, 30 August 1918

Svetlana

All day, I watched, and I waited, consumed by one certainty: The fate of the revolution relied on me and the bullets inside my pistol.

My grip on the gun remained steady, eyes trained on the crowd below, where the throngs gathered before the Mikhelson Armaments Factory in south Moscow, spilled across the street, seeped into the small square. A hot summer breeze drifted through the open attic window. Its efforts to ruffle my hair and skirt were futile, lost in a battle against the sweat plastering them to my skin. Neither the heat nor the filth deterred me; I had not spent hours hiding in this abandoned building on Pavlovskaya Street for my efforts to come to nothing.

Salvaging the revolution was never a matter of questioning my own ability. How could it be, when my Browning and I never missed our target? It was a matter of waiting. Waiting for him.

Stillness settled over the crowd; the same quiet found me inside this squalid attic. Perhaps the multitudes below sensed something monumental was coming. We were united, reverent silence tinged with anticipation—though I imagined our expectations vastly differed.

He condemned democracy for favoring capitalists and the bourgeoisie; though such claims held truth, he had blinded the working people by promising to free them from a government that had suppressed them. Did they not see that his party, too, would enslave them beneath its oppression, as imperialism had? I saw it. Understood where it led. The people had already overthrown the tsar, and rightly so; now it was up to me to prevent a new dictatorship before it began.

After he emerged from the factory, he stepped to the waiting podium and delivered his speech with a bravado that nearly made me shoot the bushy mustache and goatee from his face. Instead, as he concluded and a swell of commotion rose into the air, I suppressed the urge to act. Of all my self-appointed revolutionary missions, this was the most vital. Success would come, but not yet. Not until the proper time.

What would my aristocratic father say if tomorrow's headlines featured the name of the daughter he had likely spent over a decade trying to forget? Then a girl, now a woman defending every socialist belief he had tried to make her renounce.

The seconds were purposeful and concentrated, like the barrel of my gun as it shifted centimeter by centimeter, following my target's passage through the crowd, waiting for the best opening. For the proper time.

At last, it arrived. And I fired.

Three shots, each more accurate than the last, flowing from my gun as effortlessly as air from my lungs. One struck his coat, one his chest, one his neck. I was deaf to the screams of the crowd, immune to everything but the bright crimson pouring from the wounds and staining the pavement.

Another sound pierced through the uproar, that of the door to my hideout banging open. I whirled while someone entered—someone familiar. Someone aiming a revolver at my head.

It was the only thought I formulated before the crack split the air and the bullet struck.

I had no time to return fire before a strange, burning sensation spread across my scalp. Blood poured down my face and into my eyes, blinding me until my vision went white. Perhaps the bullet had lodged in my skull, perhaps not—either way, there was no use fighting it. But as my knees gave way and my pistol slipped from my grasp, I sought the windowsill, the wall, anything to keep me on my feet a moment more. I wanted to listen to the screams below, to wipe the blood from my eyes and relish what I had caused. No one could steal this moment from me.

Even my strongest desires were not enough to make my body comply. As I hit the floor, I lost all strength to rise. If the reason for this bullet was to prevent me from completing my task, it was too late. The screams of the crowd were proof; the bullet intended for me had not met its mark in time to stop me.

If I were to die, it was for my cause. For the revolution. For Mother Russia.

My blood surrounded me on this filthy attic floor—almost as filthy as the cell where I'd spent countless nights in the Siberian *katorga*—while I focused on the clamor drifting through the open window. The slick heat seeping from my scalp took all my energy with it; still, I strained my ears, waiting for someone to proclaim the news of the man's death. But his followers idolized him too much to pronounce him dead as he was, lying in the middle of the street. No, they would whisk him away to the Kremlin to fuss over fatal injuries; they would announce his assassination amid fanfare and mourning, as though his loss were some great tragedy.

Though my bullets always found their intended target, I needed to hear the words. The shouts and cries below grew more distant; I struggled to listen while the stenches of blood and sweat mingled with gun smoke.

Tell me I killed him.

Footsteps indicated my shooter was coming closer, followed by an unmistakable click, cocking the revolver. While I braced myself for the next bullet, something intense struck me, as white-hot as the whiteness blinding my vision, yet a different form of agony. One tinged with regret.

I would not live to hear the confirmation I sought: *Vladimir Lenin is dead.*

Svetlana

March–November 1917

Chapter 2

Siberia: Nerchinsk Katorga, 6 March 1917

S vetlana Vasilyevna Petrova, Socialist Revolutionary incarcerated for terrorism against the imperial government, the Provisional Government has granted you complete and immediate amnesty."

The guard's announcement echoed around my dingy Maltzevskaya Prison cell while the door swung open with a shriek, as if infuriated by the disturbance. Suddenly it was impossible to stand up from my small cot. Was the tsar attempting to portray himself as a benevolent, merciful ruler by creating a new governmental body—a Provisional Government—to extend amnesty toward political prisoners? Did he expect such a gesture to settle the rumored unrest sweeping the capital in Petrograd? But if my life sentence had truly been lifted, I could return to the same cause that had put me here.

"Did the baron procure a favor and buy his daughter's freedom?" came another woman's sneer from across the narrow hall. As the only hereditary noble among countless proletariat prisoners, I had spent over a decade bearing such jeers, regardless of my reasons for being imprisoned alongside the lower classes.

"Silence!" The guard passed one hand over a pitiful bit of

scruff—something of an attempted beard—and glanced at his document. "Fanya Efimovna Kaplan."

Before he launched into his speech, Fanya groaned. Eyes closed, she sat on the opposite end of the filthy cot, paying little attention as she pinched the bridge of her nose to battle one of her migraines.

"What is it this time? Insufficient labor again?" Standing, she let out a dry laugh. "I work as hard as I can, but it's incredibly dark in those mines." She rubbed her eyes, as though to ease the deteriorating vision that had plagued her throughout our time here, then grabbed her gray cotton gown to take it off.

While the guard motioned for her to desist, the reedy voice drifted from the other cell again. "What now, aristocrat? Will you lend your support to the tsar's senseless war against Germany? Suppress the protests in Petrograd? Deny my people a fair wage?" A clang of a palm striking the bars, mockery shifting to frenzied threats. "Enjoy your freedom while you can, because when we tear down the bourgeoisie, your kind will be—"

"*All* political prisoners have been pardoned," the guard interrupted, not masking his exasperation.

The voice across the hall fell into what I suspected was stunned silence.

I exchanged a look with Fanya, who seemed to have forgotten her headache. These were not the actions of a tsar who had never bothered to address any injustices toward the proletariat; rather, he had suppressed every attempt toward equality and freedom of political expression. And every woman here had been imprisoned for a crime against the imperial government.

"Shall I leave you to rot instead?" the guard asked when we

said nothing, but the contemptuous curl in his lip disappeared when I rushed toward him.

"What happened? Is it the revolution?"

At once, he pinned me against the wall, while his sweeping glance assessed me—small, slight, thin from years of incarceration, filthy from mining lead ore and silver, skin laced with cane stripes from the last time my prison gown had been stripped off for a beating. He leaned closer.

"Until you leave these grounds, I still have the power to put a bullet between your eyes." And perhaps he did, though I sensed this boy's uncertainty, his need to cling to whatever authority he had left for as long as he retained it; something unforeseen had indeed occurred. He tightened his hold. "Those who have overthrown the imperial government deserve to be locked away with vermin like you."

The breath that caught in my throat had nothing to do with his insults or threats. *Overthrown.* A pardon not from the tsar, but from the revolution. Forcing Tsar Nikolai into abdication was a step toward a progressive future; now we had our freedom and a revolution to finish to bring it to fruition.

The guard shoved me toward Fanya, tossed two parcels at us, and stepped back into the hall to wait.

I handed Fanya her parcel and tore mine open with shaking hands. A handful of rubles and kopecks. The blue dress and black wool overcoat I'd worn the day the Okhrana—the tsar's secret police—caught us after a failed attempt to bomb and assassinate a tsarist official in Kiev. But those were not the possessions I wanted.

I whirled toward the guard, who took a threatening step closer before I could demand an explanation. "If you cooperate, you will receive your remaining possessions outside."

* * *

Outside Maltzevskaya, a cold breeze whipped around me while sunshine glared against patches of dirty snow and ice. Narrowing my eyes against the painful brightness, I glanced at our surroundings. High white stone walls caging us in, the drab gray prison building, dirt paths leading to a series of log cabins marking the mines, endless stretches of scraggly trees and tired shrubs, a landscape as forlorn as the establishment it encompassed. Prisoners, once listless, now had a nearly palpable crackle of revolutionary fervor surging through them.

As Fanya and I joined the throngs of women awaiting their next packages, a guard stole discreet glances at the newspaper tucked into his coat pocket. I crept closer until I caught the headline—"Provisional Government and Petrograd Soviet: Can Two Govern as One?"

I nudged Fanya to share the news. If this new Provisional Government had joined forces with a workers' council, thus representing all classes, perhaps we could place our hopes in this establishment, after all.

After Fanya and I received our second parcels, I ripped mine open and let out a breath.

My FN Browning M1900. Despite sitting idle for over a decade, it remained in decent condition, requiring only a little cleaning of the black grips and silver barrel. I had spent so long fearing I would never know this feeling again—gun in my grasp, magazine loaded with cartridges, and soon enough, eyes on my target. I tucked the Browning into my waistband. Now I was truly free.

Freedom had disrupted my life the way a gunshot disrupted

the quiet—sharp, unexpected, piercing. As the gun settled against the small of my back, it was January 1905 again and I was eighteen, stealing this same pistol from my father's collection. Leaving his estate with no intention of returning. Seeking the only Socialist Revolutionary leader who might permit an aristocrat's daughter to join the people.

"Back to Moscow." I led Fanya down the muddy, icy road toward Nerchinksy Zavod. "We need to find Uncle Misha and—" I paused when she touched my arm.

"You've done enough for the cause," she said softly. "Go back to Kiev. Go to Tatiana."

My stomach tightened. How simple it sounded, as though dedication and passion alone were all it took to bring the desires of my heart to fruition. If such was the case, the revolution would have ended long ago.

But if the tsar had been overthrown, the Bolsheviks would surely attempt to establish one-party rule—another dictatorship to replace the one that had fallen. Establishing a right for all parties to vote—as the Socialist Revolutionaries intended— was necessary for this revolution to be a true success. My work was not finished. Not yet.

Blinking, I broke Fanya's wide, dark gaze and took the lead again. "This new government will be weak, so every party will try to take advantage of it. Uncle Misha and his contingent will need all the help they can get." I adjusted my coat as my pace increased. We had been away long enough. Soon our party members would realize political prisoners had been pardoned; every moment of absence would cause them to wonder why we had not returned. Would fuel suspicions.

"You don't want to take our chances with a group of Socialist

Revolutionaries in Petrograd?" Fanya asked, a strain creeping into her voice when a fierce gale swept over us. "That's where the heart of the revolution is."

"And if they discover you're a Jew with poor vision and I'm a former aristocrat?"

"My eyes might be bad, but I can still handle a gun, and the party recognizes that religion is a private affair. Despite what some might assume, my faith doesn't interfere with my party loyalty," she insisted. "Neither does your birth. Besides, your uncle won the people's trust, didn't he?"

Though I didn't respond, she knew the truth as well as I did; in my case, even more than hers, winning trust required far more than a convincing word or act. My blood meant privilege, oppression, the Old Regime, the life I had escaped, everything the people had just overthrown. My background put me—and anyone associated with me—at risk.

"The bomb plot in Kiev was supposed to change everything," I said at last. "It was supposed to be the proof Uncle Misha and the party needed to know that I was with them; now it will only prompt more questions. What happened, where have you been, did you carry out the plot at all, why did you never send word?"

"Then we will answer those questions."

"Why should anyone believe a nobleman's daughter?"

"He will let you rejoin, Sveta," Fanya replied gently, as if she knew what the rise in my voice meant. "Failure does not mean disloyalty."

Not for her, perhaps. For me, every moment was an effort to shed the perceptions of my birth, as my uncle had. To show where my loyalties resided.

As we reached the outskirts of Nerchinsky Zavod, dotted

with more log structures, I turned toward a sign indicating the railway platform, but Fanya continued walking without noticing.

"You shared a cell with me for eleven years, and now that the revolution is happening, you've lost interest in it?" I asked scathingly.

She whirled, eyebrows lowered into a fierce glare. "Can we not rest tonight and leave in the morning?" Then she winced before pinching the bridge of her nose—a sign the migraine from our cell was still plaguing her. "I can hardly see straight."

If I could have settled her into a warm bed with a steaming cup of tea, I would have, but we could not afford to delay. The revolution waited for no one. Neither did I.

Eleven years of political imprisonment had forged us together, unshakable and inseparable. I wrapped my arm around Fanya's waist, and we set off toward the railway, while snow crunched beneath my feet and cold air stung my lungs.

Chapter 3

Rays of golden sunlight stretched across the sky, painting color over the gray dawn while the Moskva River glittered below. Moscow was rousing. As Fanya and I passed shops and factories, drawing closer to the Red Square and the Kremlin, a sense of change overcame me, refreshing as the first gulp of air after holding my breath. A just future. I sensed it as surely as I sensed the crisp morning air against my skin.

Pedestrians sprinkled the sidewalks, automobiles rumbled along, and vendors offered their wares with a boisterousness too heavy for an otherwise tranquil morning. Fanya stifled a yawn. We had spent the better part of three weeks aboard a lethargic train and had arrived late last night; now we needed to locate our contingent. No other group would permit two women claiming to be recently pardoned political activists— one a former aristocrat—to rejoin the cause. If our headquarters was no longer in its original location, we had nowhere else to go.

I shook my head while the cold air chilled my lungs. Our party members would be there. They *had* to be there.

As we neared the Meshchansky District, signs of the revolution were everywhere. Stucco buildings riddled with bullet holes; remnants of shattered glass from storefronts glittering against the melting snow and crunching beneath my feet. The word *imperial*, its yellow flag, or its symbol—a double-headed eagle—defaced and destroyed wherever it appeared; billowing red banners with slogans draped across statues and streetcars, proclaiming *Long live the Republic* and *Land and the Will of the People.*

And the speeches! A man on a street corner advocated for reduced working days and improved salaries; another for the establishment of a democratically elected Constituent Assembly and for land to be confiscated from the bourgeoisie and redistributed among the peasants—a Socialist Revolutionary, judging by his views on land and Constituent Assembly support. Each man spoke without fear or reservation while cheers swelled from the onlooking crowds. It was unlike anything I had ever witnessed, giving a name to the sense of change: freedom.

I was admiring propaganda posters that studded the buildings when a piercing cry broke through the hum of automobiles and thudding footsteps. Reaching for my pistol, I located its source. Down the block, a woman approached a clothing storefront with keys in hand—presumably to open the shop— and fell to her knees beside the corpse propped against the door.

Based on glances and fervent whispers, the gathering crowd seemed privy to some secret. Tucking my weapon into my waistband, I pushed to the front while Fanya followed.

The dead man's white shirt and brown trousers were torn and bloodied, covered in slashes from a knife, perhaps a dagger. I counted at least six bullet holes, but what struck me were his eyes.

Though I was no stranger to gaping wounds or stiff bodies,

the sight of this man's eyes was even more unsettling than his injuries. Wide open, bright blue, and bloodshot, the results of an assault by some irritant—a chemical, even a poison. Whatever it was, I suspected it had blinded him prior to death.

"She killed him!" the woman wailed as she bent over the man, presumably her husband or lover, given the way she carried on. What made her so certain she knew who had done this?

"He was anti-Bolshevik?" came a man's voice; when the woman nodded, he shook his head. "Even with the entire Romanov family under house arrest at the Alexander Palace, you are not free to speak as you wish."

"Oppression under the tsar, and oppression now; it will never cease." The woman cast a frenzied glare at her onlookers. "If you support anyone *other* than the Bolsheviks, *she* finds out, and she does this." She pointed a dramatic finger at the corpse.

Little blood surrounded the man. Whoever *she* was, she had killed him elsewhere and tossed the body here for the woman to discover.

"Are you certain it was her?" someone asked.

"Who else would it have been?" another voice retorted. "Look at his eyes."

The crowd shifted to allow a man to pass, and when he extended his hand toward the dead man's open mouth, the woman held up a closed fist. By the time she opened her hand, I had already pushed ahead, close enough to snatch the item—a folded slip of paper. I turned my back to his bark of protest, heart thudding as I unfurled the note to reveal a single word written in elegant red script: *Orlova.*

A common enough surname, hardly a useful way to identify the person culpable for this attack. Surely the scrap had additional markings somewhere, more words—

A gloved hand caught my wrist, ending my search when the man seized the paper. After examining it, he paled. Perhaps the surname was a more certain form of identification than I had anticipated.

A gentler hand found my forearm—Fanya's, guiding me out of the throng. If not for the need to locate my uncle, I might have resisted, lingering to learn about this Orlova who blinded and slaughtered anti-Bolsheviks. As Fanya released me, my pistol pressed against my waist with every step. I had seen how this Bolshevik killer dealt with threats to her party; soon, she would see how I dealt with threats to mine.

Upon reaching Sretenka Street, the familiar redbrick building rose before us. Hotel Petrov was neither opulent nor squalid, though it was stately as it stood tall on the corner of the block. Familiar now, unlike the first time I had come here. Each step matched my breaths, as sharp as they had once been when this place had beckoned, daunting, intriguing, captivating a girl who had known only her family's grand estate outside Moscow.

* * *

IN JANUARY 1905, when I reached Hotel Petrov and introduced myself as the niece of the former aristocrat whose inheritance had funded the hotel's establishment, mine had not been the warm welcome I had anticipated.

"Do you know anything about the Socialist Revolutionary Party?" one man had prompted amid their barrage of questions and ridicule while I searched the hostile faces for my uncle's.

"Of course. The party was recently born of the People's Will, the organization that tried to—" Before I had finished with *assassinate Tsar Aleksandr III*, my interrogator scoffed.

"Our *views*, foolish girl. This is not the capitalist, bourgeois home you have known. What do you know of socialism? Of land reform? Of political terrorism?"

More questions, more jeers about my noble status, until both my hands and my voice were shaking. I refused to break, to let them win—

Then the face I sought emerged from the crowd, the one whose covert letters I had hidden from my parents throughout my childhood, ever since we had been forbidden to see one another. With a flick of his hand, Uncle Misha beckoned me and led me to his bedroom for a meeting. Once there, I paced back and forth across the Chelaberd rug while he sat on his four-poster bed, both among the few remaining pieces of finery from his old life.

Speech was impossible when my heart was still pounding, hands still trembling, hot blood running through my veins as every criticism filled my head. I met his bright blue gaze without slowing my pace. It had been more than a decade since I'd last met those sparkling eyes as my little hand found his to lead him into the gardens behind my family's estate. Cloaked in dusk, concealed behind verdant shrubs, trilling skylarks shielding our whispers from prying ears, I had spent endless hours with this man nearly two decades my senior. He had taught me everything about his political views on class struggles and women's rights, even how to fire a pistol, though I had been such a little girl.

"You resemble Vasya too much when you scowl," Uncle Misha teased at last. How clearly I envisioned my father's thick silver brows knit together—the look that had followed when he had discovered the outlandish views his little brother held, and that Misha had shared them with an impressionable child. When my mother had crossed herself and berated every servant for *leaving our daughter with a radical*. When Papa had banned my favorite uncle from our estate.

"To be a part of this cause, you must be committed to it," Uncle Misha said, all teasing gone when I stayed silent. "This party can only judge what they know of you—that you have come from the bourgeoisie. You must earn your place, like the rest of us."

"Your background is the same as mine," I replied with a huff. "Why do—?"

He cleared his throat, indicating what I had done wrong— spoken French, the language of the aristocracy, though Uncle Misha had addressed me in Russian. Another habit preventing me from earning my place. French still came more naturally to me, despite my efforts to resist it. I started over in Russian and finished my question.

"Why do they trust you?"

"I spent my years at university studying politics, listening to the lower classes, learning from them. Encouraging a little girl to fight for the most good for the most people," he added knowingly. "And then I showed the party that I was with them, starting with opening this hotel for us. How can you expect anyone to accept your word when you've given them no proof through your actions?"

"You said yourself that I've come from the bourgeoisie." My racing heart brought me to a halt this time. "I'm here. My parents will never forgive me. If those actions don't prove my words are sincere—"

"A first step," he conceded with a nod, his tone level to placate the rise in mine. "Not enough. Show us why you belong, Sveta; even then, you will not be accepted immediately. Trust is slow to win and quick to lose."

From that day onward, I kept his challenge as closely as I had once kept our shared secrets. Yet those who accepted my uncle rejected me for being the baron's daughter, for being a better shot than most men, for any number of reasons. Trust was a fickle thing, subject to change on a whim. In fighting to become a revolutionary, I fought against the blood of the nobility. A fight I could only win if my party members permitted it.

They had to grant me the same opportunity they had given my uncle. I had not come here to fail. I had given up my life, my status, my family's approval; I refused to give up the revolution.

Chapter 4

Moscow, 27 March 1917

When Fanya and I pushed through Hotel Petrov's oaken double doors into the plain, tired lobby with its black-and-white porcelain floors and dull white walls, I didn't care if it was as grand as the Kremlin or as dingy as the katorga. My eyes went to the woman sitting behind the dark wooden counter. Blond, younger than I—mid-twenties, perhaps—leaning closer as she regarded me, her striking hazel eyes flecked with gold.

"Mikhail Pavlovich Petrov," I said by way of greeting. "Tell him his niece is here."

Rather than fetching Uncle Misha from his room—fifth floor, room number twenty—the young woman stepped back from the counter and leveled a revolver at my chest. "Petrov's niece would know he's dead."

Though I had already drawn my own weapon, it almost fell from my grasp. "Dead?" I repeated shakily.

"For a couple years now. If you're going to attempt an in-filtration, you should come up with a better story," she said, a condescending glint in her eyes.

My dear uncle, gone. The only man who would have listened to me. Unless . . .

"Kazimir." I blurted it out before swallowing past the lump in my throat. "Is he still here? Kazimir Grigoryevich—"

"Weapons." Her aim remained steady, face betraying no answer.

Despite the interruption, I clutched my pistol tighter. "Let me speak with—"

She cocked the revolver, so I held the words back, avoiding Fanya's deliberate glance as she placed her Browning on the counter. My mouth tasted of his name: *Kazimir Grigoryevich*. A name that still created a knot in my stomach even as I longed to taste it again.

I surrendered my gun, biting the inside of my cheek when the young woman snatched it. She directed us into the sitting room, where various party members—mostly men—lounged in armchairs and rested coffee cups on small wooden tables. Some played cards and smoked, others engaged in fervent conversations, others read *Delo naroda*, the Socialist Revolutionary newspaper, or *Izvestia*, a new daily broadsheet publishing news from the Petrograd Soviet. At the sight of us, a few rose, already reaching for their weapons.

After instructing the men to guard us, the woman disappeared down the hall without explanation.

I exchanged a glance with Fanya, who stood close, brow furrowed. The woman had gone to fetch the contingent leader, presumably. If the position no longer belonged to Uncle Misha, his favorite niece would soon have a bullet between her eyes. Yet these men with their gun barrels pointed at my chest stirred nothing within me; I was hollow. This was my uncle's contingent, his life's work. He would never see the results of the revolution he had believed in with every breath.

"So it *is* you."

The boisterous voice made me swallow a sharp breath while my heart skipped.

Kazimir Grigoryevich examined me as if to confirm that the girl he had known had transformed into the woman before him. Perhaps he felt as if a lifetime had passed between us—and, in a way, it had. I, pale and thin after years of incarceration, lackluster honey blond tresses in a sloppy chignon, a faded dress that had last graced a nineteen-year-old body. He, a man grown from the dark, brooding boy thirsting for justice against the regime that, three decades ago, had executed his father alongside those condemned for Tsar Aleksandr's attempted assassination. The black scruff now a full beard, broad chest and shoulders thickened by muscle, eyes dark and unrefined. The leader of this SR contingent now, judging by the way all eyes focused on him.

When he paused before me, Kazimir straightened his brown leather jacket and crossed his arms over his burly frame, smirking.

"Welcome back, *dvoryanka*."

The term he had started using for me all those years ago, despite my hatred of it. While an almost visible bristle swept over the onlookers, my hand strayed toward my pistol, the dare for him to call me *noblewoman* again rising to my throat—but I was weaponless.

"That is *not* who I am." Too shrill, too flustered. It made no difference. Not when each hateful glare saw only the blood of the hereditary nobility. "Not anymore." Steadier this time, pulse thudding as his gaze challenged me to dispute him when no falsehood lay in the claim.

"We've come from the Nerchinsk katorga. Specifically, the Maltzevskaya women's prison." Fanya's assertion earned more dubious glances before she frowned at Kazimir. "Not the bourgeoisie."

Ignoring the remark, he turned to the young woman, whose narrowed eyes remained on me. "Vera Fyodorovna, take Fanya Efimovna for questioning." Then, looking to me, "I will take Svetlana Vasilyevna."

The way he said it made me want to slap the gleam from his eyes as much as to let it draw me nearer. I settled for a glower. After all this time, he was still infuriating.

* * *

DURING OUR MEETING when I had come to join his contingent, Uncle Misha had fallen silent, so I had resumed my pacing. Step after step, consumed by one thought: How to earn my place. To show this party I belonged.

"Few loathe the aristocracy more than Kazimir Grigoryevich."

The quiet pronouncement brought my pacing to a pause. On the bed, Uncle Misha sat taller; his eyes gleamed the way they had before he suggested venturing deeper into my family's gardens, an indication he was going to let me practice with my father's pistol.

"If you can win his trust, Sveta, you can win anyone's. He is one of my most dedicated."

If this Kazimir Grigoryevich hated the aristocracy so much, why had he joined a contingent led by a former nobleman? But Uncle Misha was already explaining.

"His father was part of the People's Will. I never knew him, but we had political connections in common." He proceeded to tell me all about his prized recruit, an ambitious boy fighting to topple the Old Regime that had torn his family apart. Then Uncle Misha summoned him.

When Kazimir entered the room, it was as if he had reached

out and caught me by the throat. His dark eyes raked over me, held me in place, crushed every breath. A single look, so guarded yet displaying such animosity even as something impossible to decipher caused him to hold my gaze too long. To linger over my lips. The same way I followed the curve of his stubbled jaw and the sweep of dark hair across his brow.

"Kazimir," Uncle Misha said without preamble, "you are assigned to assess Svetlana's loyalty."

A test, exactly the encouragement my party members needed in order to accept me. Already my fingers itched for the pistol at my waistband.

Kazimir stepped closer, his disdain evident. "If she fails?"

Was the underlying threat meant to frighten me? How disappointed he would have been to know it had only made my heart thud faster.

With a refined aristocratic gentleman, I could predict his every word, every look, every action, each dictated by the strict standards and etiquette established by our class. With Kazimir, I could predict nothing. His glances, clenched jaw, stiff shoulders, each stoking the flame burning inside me. I intended to prove I was trustworthy; perhaps he intended to prove the opposite.

I checked my pistol's magazine before holding his measured gaze. "Take me to someone who serves the imperial government."

Political terror was an integral part of this party. Those who had interrogated me upon my arrival had made it clear that they did not expect a young noblewoman to be willing to serve this cause in every way necessary.

I longed for the thrill that overwhelmed me in the moments before firing, the rush as I pulled the trigger, the satisfying hole through my target. I had never shot a man. But I had always known the time would come if I was to be a real part of this revolution.

A pleased smirk curved Uncle Misha's lips while Kazimir's guarded look never faltered, not even when I departed without waiting for him to follow, each pounding heartbeat urging me onward. Once I had fulfilled this mission, he would realize my loyalty was genuine. He did not have to be wary of me. Perhaps that was what I had sensed when he had assessed me, impossible as the look had been to decipher—he, too, had something to prove to himself and everyone else. What it was, I intended to find out.

He would realize who I was, why I belonged to this party; someday, perhaps he would show me the same. Someday, perhaps the guarded look in his eyes would disappear.

* * *

AFTER I PARTED ways with Fanya, Kazimir ushered me into a small interrogation room equipped with a table and two chairs. "Kiev," he announced, adopting an authoritative air. "You asked Petrov—"

"What happened to Uncle Misha?" I interrupted. "Was it the Okhrana, or the Bolsheviks?"

"—for permission to assassinate the governor-general with aid from Fanya." Kazimir glared to silence me. "You were stationed in Kiev in August of 1905. When your plot failed, we gathered from news sources that you were arrested in February of 1906 and incarcerated in the Nerchinsk katorga. True? Or misinformation intentionally publicized to mask the fact that you staged a fake plot and were never arrested, are working for the bourgeoisie, and have returned on their behalf to infiltrate?"

Doubts and accusations were what I had expected, though disappointment stabbed my chest. I lifted my skirt, exposing scars on my thigh—some from punishments, others from injuries, all from Maltzevskaya. Enough proof, surely, unless Kazimir accused a nobleman of beating me.

"Satisfied?"

As his eyes roamed over the marks, the muscles along Kazimir's jaw twitched, his careful restraint faltering. If that momentary change meant he believed me, I wanted to believe in him, too. But I knew better than to put all my faith in hope. Hope had disappointed me too many times. And he had already refused to tell me about my uncle's fate—though I would not let my curiosity go so easily.

I let my skirt fall and kept my voice level. "Give me my pistol."

"That can be arranged." The restraint wavered again, this time with the sardonic gleam I knew too well. "We earn our privileges here, remember? We are not born into them."

Whether or not he was my superior now, if this was the way Kazimir wanted to speak to me, this interrogation was over. I pushed past him toward the door, but a strong arm wrapped around my waist.

Cigarette smoke and leather washed over me, and I drank it in. I should have fought it; this scent—*his* scent—was my past, and now my present, one I knew better than to accept. But I failed to resist. A brief acceptance might stir what had been absent for so long. Absent, but never forgotten, never far, now drawing closer, awaiting my permission.

The arm tightened, pressing me into his chest. "Don't be angry over a little fun, Sveta."

His tone was low, lascivious, the one reserved for me. I could not afford to be that way again—that young, careless, stupid girl. Yet she rose to the surface, whispering for me to grant her permission now as I had then. To prove to him I was forging my own way, free of the expectations attached to my birth. To encourage him to push beyond that guarded look that had never fully disappeared.

The urge was fierce as the fire in his black eyes and the one he stirred inside me.

An unsteady breath passed between us before I stepped back.

"Have you heard of a woman called Orlova?" Her name alone set my heart racing again, pounding with every breath.

Kazimir passed a hand over his beard, all teasing gone. "We're not finished. Sit down."

"I saw a corpse. Blinded, tortured, and left with her name." I let the revelation sink in as Kazimir took his own seat. "Tell me about her, then I'll answer your questions."

Maybe we had been apart for years, but he knew me well enough to know my mouth would remain shut until he gave me what I wanted. And I wanted to know more about this woman who had sparked the old feeling inside me, a longing for what I had not felt in so long: My pistol in my grasp. My finger against the trigger. My sights on my target.

"Various underground activists have been circulating materials from Vladimir Lenin while he's been exiled in Europe, so he continues to influence the Bolshevik Party and act as its head," he explained. "The attacks from Orlova started a couple years before the imperial government was overthrown—

infrequent at first, then increasing over time. She's thought to be one of those activists, since she targets members of the bourgeoisie and parties that oppose the Bolsheviks."

A rogue assassin trying to secure a Bolshevik dictatorship and undermine my party. An excellent way to reaffirm my commitment to the cause.

"Her." I took my seat and leaned closer to him. "She's my target, and once I—"

"You can't kill Orlova," he interrupted with a scoff.

Can't? Maybe I was eleven years out of practice, but when I had my pistol in my hand, I never missed.

Kazimir lit a cigarette. "How do you expect to kill her when those who meet her don't live to tell of it? No one knows who she is."

More difficult, perhaps; not impossible. She killed those who opposed her party, so encouraging her to come for me would be too easy.

"You are not to target Orlova or anyone else without my authorization. Our position is too precarious for rash behavior to sabotage it." Kazimir took a drag of his cigarette. "Am I clear?"

Eliminating a major threat was far from sabotage. Orlova was an integral member of the Bolshevik Party. To make room for socialism was to destroy the existing system and take down those who perpetrated it; those attempting to establish another harmful government were not to be ignored, either.

I'd find out more about her—and about what had happened to my uncle—but this was not the time to fuel Kazimir's concerns about my loyalty. So I nodded and drew a slow breath, filling my lungs with his smoke.

Chapter 5

Moscow, 3 April 1917

A crisp breeze rustled through the towering birches and poplars as we waited. It had been hours; we had been on the outskirts of the city since dawn, but the waiting that came with our missions had always been one of my favorite parts. Moments building, anticipation growing, bringing me closer to my purpose.

The cluster of trees was perhaps a hundred meters from the road, where faint whirs and rumbles announced occasional passing vehicles. Fanya sat to my right, resting her back against a pine tree while she toyed with a cartridge. A few party members were scattered about our hiding place. One locked eyes with me. Rolan Glebovich, who had leaned close to Kazimir when we'd left the hotel, muttering about *when she flees back to her father's estate.*

As if my father would have accepted me if I returned. As if I knew whether my parents were at their manor house, country home, or somewhere else entirely now that revolution was brewing. As if I knew anything about them when I had not contacted them in over a decade.

A knot tightened in my chest. I held Rolan's gaze until he lowered it, though his hostility never wavered.

A week since returning to the party, and perceptions remained unchanged. No different from when I had been here as a girl, proving my loyalty only to be met with the same doubts and suspicions. How silly of me to have expected them to cease.

But today Fanya and I had our weapons back—for good, if all went according to plan. This mission was ours, the chance to prove we had returned with honorable intentions. After today, perceptions might finally change.

Kazimir had stationed himself at the forefront, behind the large poplar next to mine, gun in hand—directed at me. This was a test, true, but the implication that I might turn on my comrades was almost worse than being called a noblewoman.

He caught my bitter glance toward his weapon; rather than lower it to reassure me of his trust, he kept his aim steady. "Until you pass this loyalty test, only a fool would give you a gun and expect you not to use it against him. Proper precautions must be taken," he said, glancing from me to his weapon and back. "Am I to take your word for it that a handsome guard at Maltzevskaya didn't sway you politically? Or otherwise?"

Snide, provoking me as he always did so well, yet laced with the doubts he never seemed to shake. I stifled a sigh and closed my eyes, letting a cool breeze rush over me. Despite the warning Fanya had given me all those years ago, I clung to the belief that she was wrong about him. About the way he felt about me.

"One moment, you will win his favor; the next, he will denounce you before Petrov and the entire party," she had said late one night a few weeks after Uncle Misha had assigned Kazimir to work with me.

We had assassinated a member of the bourgeoisie, a true breakthrough—the way Kazimir had given me a small nod after I fired, even remarked on the accuracy of my shot. But my only friend sat across from me on her bed, giving one warning with her words and a stronger one with her dark eyes.

"Why would he have expressed approval of me today, if he sees me as an aristocrat?" I frowned as I pulled my quilt across my lap. "He's coming around, Fanya."

Though she sipped tea and consumed her last bite of bread and cheese before responding, the dubious look didn't falter. "When someone like him harbors such hatred for someone like you, don't expect it to change. Not permanently."

When instructed to share a bedroom with an aristocrat, this wide-eyed girl had not regarded me with the same hostility as the others; I had dared to believe she was different—bold, enthusiastic, not yet sixteen. Old enough to be infused with hatred for people like me, yet young enough to be impressionable.

I sipped my own tea, letting its heat mingle with the heat inside me. "Are you saying there can never be camaraderie between your kind and mine?" My hopes for convincing her I was not like other nobles began to dwindle.

Fanya set the teacup down. "I was born in Volhynia to a peasant family who supported the revolutionary cause. My birth name is Feiga Khaimovna Roitman."

Volhynia was part of the Pale of Settlement, a western region inhabited mostly by Jews, as they were rarely permitted to reside anywhere else. For those bound to the Pale, it was nearly impossible to escape.

"Jewish?" I asked, given the surname. She nodded.

"When I found work in Odessa as a milliner, I scraped together a convincing bribe and offered it to a man named Kaplan who had connections to different revolutionary groups, including your uncle's, and lived outside the Pale. Marrying him was the only way for me to escape. To have the chance to take a real part in this revolution."

"So you understand why I had to leave my family."

"I do," she agreed with a nod. "I changed my name on my papers to sever ties to the Pale, thanked Kaplan for upholding his end of our bargain, and came here a few months ago. Why put myself through that if my intentions weren't genuine?" So young, yet so sure of herself and her place. How I longed for that same assurance. "You left your old life, as I did. If these men had a hard time accepting me, finding acceptance here is ten times more difficult for you."

"And you don't think it will happen," I said softly, supplying the unspoken.

"You are the only daughter and youngest child of Baron Vasily Pavlovich Petrov, making you a hereditary noblewoman acting against her family's wishes." The titles that always made me grimace. "You were raised in the tsar's faith, in his world, in everything these men despise."

The Orthodox faith, one I had never accepted with as much fervor as my parents and had ceased practicing. A world of opulence and extravagance. Everything I had left behind, yet everything this party saw in me.

"I admire you for joining us," Fanya said when I stayed silent, "and I don't think you're serving the bourgeoisie. But men like Kazimir will always find reasons to doubt."

A tiny shred of reassurance, only to have it marred.

She had no right to make conjectures. I had won Kazimir's favor—not fully, perhaps. Impossible to be certain. But his fascination with me had always been evident, as though he were curious to discover whether I was the noble he expected. And

I would keep showing him who I was until he no longer had reasons to doubt.

* * *

THE HOURS PASSED as Fanya and I waited to complete our loyalty test. At last, Kazimir pulled out his pocket watch and checked the time. "To your positions."

His gun remained on me, Rolan's on Fanya.

I offered Fanya a tiny, reassuring nod, which she returned. This mission was not going to end as Kiev had.

On the horizon, the sun rested low. Light stretched across the ground, staining it blood-red, deep orange, and gold. A cool breeze filled my lungs with sharp pine and sweet grass— and the faint trace of Kazimir's tobacco. As if the wind were urging me toward him.

An automobile appeared in the distance, the setting sun glinting off its cobalt body and warming the tan canvas roof. Inside was our target: Zhukovsky, a member of the Bolshevik Party's Moscow Committee. This loyalty test had been too easy to develop after Kazimir overheard a man outside a café boasting about his son's committee membership and their efforts to establish a military organization and build up the Red Guards. It had not taken long to identify his son or the route he would take to today's scheduled committee meeting, and according to his father, Zhukovsky had commandeered a nobleman's Delaunay-Belleville after the imperial government was overthrown. This was a later model than my father's had been, but a car of such luxury was impossible to mistake.

Kazimir raised his free hand; Fanya struck a match. A sizzling fuse pierced the stillness.

I tightened my grip on my pistol as the car approached. A

committee of the Bolshevik Military Organization was not welcome here; neither were their Red Guards. My heartbeat pounded in my ears, keeping time with the fuse that had long since burned out of my earshot, but the crackle of its energy remained.

The car passed our hiding place; a moment later, the earth shattered.

A piercing crack and bang split the air when the dynamite detonated, throwing the car back. The vehicle struck the ground with a crunch, bouncing and skidding until it halted near our side of the road, overturned and aflame.

Stillness for an instant, then a rear door opened, and a man extracted himself with significant effort. Zhukovsky. He spilled onto the road, one arm across his face, shielding himself from the flames. The blast had not injured him as much as I had anticipated. I sensed his intentions immediately: Dart behind the car, stay low, break for the small cluster of trees on the other side of the street. We would lose our chance.

We had seconds, maybe less.

By the time Kazimir gave another signal, I had already pulled my trigger. My bullet hit Zhukovsky first, and the job was done. Over a decade since such exhilaration had last sparked through my veins, control and precision and success. Fanya's shower of bullets pierced the air behind mine and pummeled his body. He collapsed and lay still.

As we hurried to inspect our work, the stench of burning rubber, leather, and metal filled my nostrils. Zhukovsky was on his stomach, his back studded with bloody bullet holes. Mine was the one that had struck the base of his skull. I knew it, because that was where I had aimed. The old thrill raced through me; I closed my eyes for a moment to savor it.

Kazimir appeared beside me. Instinctively, I gripped my pistol tighter; I had already spent far too long without it, and Fanya and I had fulfilled our task. It was enough. It had to be.

Rather than demand my weapon, Kazimir gave me a small nod.

Another rush pulsed through me like a bullet splitting the air. Maybe Fanya did not believe he would ever fully accept me, but here was evidence. No animosity, no mistrust, simply respect and reassurance. This was the path I had returned to forge, one of loyalty and approval to lead me to the end of the revolution. To what I had left behind in Kiev.

And, along the way, the path was leading me steadily back to him.

An unmistakable engine whir broke through the crackle of the fire; a black car sped toward us while bullets showered around me.

Amid Kazimir's curses and orders to take cover and return fire, I shot one of the oncoming car's tires before ducking behind the burning automobile. The heat was suffocating. I shielded my nose with one arm, fighting the pungent stench of rubber. Even with its punctured tire, the car hurtled toward us and the destroyed vehicle. Not much longer until it collided with both.

Though the car drove in an erratic zigzag, making it a more difficult target, I narrowed my eyes against the heat, took aim, and fired.

On the driver's side, cracks snaked along the windshield, the fruits of my efforts; more bullets followed behind mine until the windshield shattered. The car skidded into the grass alongside the road, maybe ten meters from us, and we sent more bullets through the broken glass until we were certain no one would emerge.

When the shooting stopped, only gasping breaths remained. The air was hazy, tinged orange and gray. Three of our party members were dead; another held a hand against his shoulder, where his sleeve was stained red.

I approached the second vehicle, feeling as though I were still choking on smoke. They were Bolsheviks, surely, not tsarists. If they were tsarists, the blame for an aristocratic ambush would fall on me, without a doubt. After all I had done to prove my loyalty . . .

As Fanya joined me, unscathed, I counted three men and one woman. All dead and dressed in drab clothing with stacks of Bolshevik propaganda posters in the backseat. I breathed easily again.

The woman appeared a few years older than me and had a nasty head wound from the crash and a few bullet holes in her chest. Her eyes were still open.

Fanya scrutinized the corpses. "Do you think that's her?"

She didn't need to specify. Every time I came across a Bolshevik woman, I wondered if it was Orlova. But every time, another person eventually turned up dead and she claimed responsibility. Orlova was still fighting for her party as I was fighting for mine. I intended to be the one who emerged the victor.

Without taking my eyes off the dead woman, I responded to Fanya. "If she kills again, we'll know it wasn't."

After confirming there were no Bolshevik survivors, Kazimir directed one man to take photographs of the destruction. Meanwhile Rolan fetched Uncle Misha's Mercedes, a black touring car with a double phaeton donated to the party, from where we had hidden it behind the trees.

"Comrade Petrova," Kazimir called after me, adopting the authoritative tone that had become more prevalent as of late. "You didn't wait for my order before shooting Zhukovsky."

"Did I ever wait for permission from Uncle Misha? If I have a clear shot, I'm taking it."

"I never said I was surprised; I simply said you didn't." He raised a knowing eyebrow, cracking a bit of the formality before he continued. "I have to insist you follow my orders."

"And I have to insist you let me do what I do best." I allowed a coy smile to accompany the words as I closed the remaining centimeters between us.

His eyes fell to my lips before meeting my gaze. Perhaps he saw the noblewoman, perhaps the revolutionary; it was always impossible to tell. But I knew this guarded look from our youth, always prompting me to reach for him, to uncover what lay beyond it.

The car horn sounded almost as loud as the explosion, preventing me from reaching for him now as I had then. With a start, I blinked; when I looked over my shoulder, Rolan was motioning to us from his position in the driver's seat. Kazimir cleared his throat and led the way to the vehicle.

I delayed a second longer, unwilling to release the moment, unwilling for space to come between us. Then I followed him.

Chapter 6

Moscow, 3 April 1917

When we returned to Hotel Petrov, a crowd gathered outside, similar to the formation Fanya and I had encountered on our first day back in Moscow. In its center was a corpse.

My chest tightened. The victim was a woman this time, covered in slashes and bullet holes, eyes bloodshot, a slip of paper in her open mouth. Kazimir unfurled it to read the name written in red script: *Orlova*. When I extended a hand, he passed it to me. Still no markings, nothing beyond a single, infuriating name.

"She expressed interest in the Socialist Revolutionary Party and told me she planned to join this contingent," a young woman said softly, lifting a small handkerchief to her eyes. "We were going to meet here this evening for her to do so."

Kazimir stood in the center to address the crowd. "Be vigilant, but do not let this deter you from supporting your party or the government you wish to build. A Constituent Assembly will grant every citizen the opportunity to be heard, and every party has a right to representation—an opportunity the Bolsheviks aim to take away."

A few heads bobbed while most eyes returned to the

murdered woman. Mine stayed on Kazimir—assured, fearless, exactly the leader he needed to be.

He left the onlookers with a final word of encouragement. "We will not succumb to Bolshevik terror."

Zhukovsky had been dead a few hours at most. Not enough time for Orlova to torture this woman, kill her, and plant her body. This attempt to deter anti-Bolshevism was not retaliation for his murder. Something else had prompted this attack.

After instructing a few party members to bury the corpse, Kazimir wrapped an arm around my waist to lead me through the crowd. My heart was still thudding after his speech; now, with his familiar grasp holding me close, I nearly saw Uncle Misha's knowing smile, a look he had given me one evening while Kazimir and I field-stripped our pistols prior to a mission. As though my uncle knew how alike we were in our pursuit of our ambitions. As though he had seen the feeling that had stirred within me the moment I laid eyes on Kazimir— and he on me. The feeling that had strengthened over time and surged through me now.

How pleased Uncle Misha would have been with us both today: His recruit now a steadfast leader, and his niece reaffirming her place within the cause he had championed.

In the quiet entryway, Vera Fyodorovna sat behind the front desk, hunched over her typewriter, drafting articles for the *Delo naroda*. At once, she rose.

"Kazimir, I was told one of Orlova's victims was found outside, and—" She stopped, eyes on me. "A private word, please."

I was well accustomed to caution and judgment from my party members, but Vera regarded me as if I were responsible for every wrong the imperial government had committed. Even the gun at my waistband, a clear endorsement from

Kazimir, didn't seem to be enough for her. If only she knew I had spent my youth covertly reading articles like the ones she wrote, learning about the political changes sweeping the country.

I waited for Kazimir to assure her she could speak freely; instead, as our group dispersed, he led her down the hallway.

A knot tightened in my stomach. Had the nod I'd taken as reassurance simply been meant to acknowledge my ability? Had he permitted me to keep my gun because I was a good shot to use at his convenience, nothing more? He had given in to Vera's wariness; clearly, he did not have as much faith in my intentions as I had hoped.

Only Fanya and I remained in the empty lobby, and she muttered something about a migraine. When Vera and Kazimir disappeared behind a closed door, I started after them, hugging the walls close enough to count the flecks of chipped blue paint.

I was halfway there when a hand caught my arm.

"Eavesdropping, Sveta?" came Fanya's low voice. "If you're caught, passing today's test will have been for nothing."

"Which is exactly why I won't get caught." I tried to break her grasp, but she pulled me around to face her.

"*She* is in Kiev. Without you." When I sucked in a breath and looked away, she tightened her grip, so I met her gaze again. "Think about Tatiana."

A rush of heat coursed through my veins, prompting me to reach for my pistol—action I surely would have taken if I had been facing someone other than Fanya. Of course I thought about Tatiana. I always thought about Tatiana.

I broke her grasp, and she didn't interfere further. When I reached the door, I pressed my ear to it.

"You're certain?" Kazimir's muffled voice.

"My contact in Petrograd was among the crowd at Finland Station, saw him arrive this morning, and followed the procession to Kschessinska Mansion, where he will be headquartered," Vera replied.

"Did he address the crowd?"

"With an inflammatory speech against the Provisional Government. My contact believes that Lenin intends to oust them."

My breath caught. I didn't dare linger to hear more. I hurried to the cramped elevator, ducked inside, and listened to it groan and creak as it carried me to an arbitrary floor.

Lenin, back from exile with a plan to overthrow the Provisional Government—a bourgeois organization, true, but governing dually with the socialist Petrograd Soviet. The Bolshevik idea of socialism left no room for other parties—not even other socialist ones like mine. Without the Provisional Government's promise of a direct and secret ballot for all Russians to choose their Constituent Assembly representatives, we would be left with a Bolshevik dictatorship. And if Lenin had returned, Orlova likely knew about it.

No wonder she had killed that young woman. She curated fear, but surely the people would not succumb to it. Despite her efforts, they would reject the notion of another dictatorial government.

I had been raised under an oppressive government and an even more oppressive household. Tatiana would not be subjected to either.

But I could not involve her in a revolution against the upper classes, certainly not when my party members feared I remained loyal to the bourgeoisie. If they turned on me, she would be at risk. Her blood was as dangerous as mine. Better to keep her safe until the turmoil had settled. We would not be apart much longer.

Unless she was no longer in Kiev. The revolutionaries thirsted for bourgeois blood. The thought pierced to my core, chilling as the frigid gusts that had assaulted me and Fanya when we walked across the grounds of Maltzevskaya. No, surely not . . .

When the elevator gave a sudden, loud screech, I pressed my hand to my pounding heart. I had come here to explain my disappearance to Uncle Misha—now to uncover the reasons behind his death—and finish this revolution, but what if Tatiana had been jeopardized?

Somehow I needed to find out.

As my breaths steadied, I selected the main floor. If I returned to my bedroom, I'd risk running into Vera, the third member of Fanya's and my shared quarters. Thoughts of her ceaseless mistrust set my heart racing again, so I found my way to the hotel restaurant.

By no means was it grand—nothing like the places where I once dined as a child. Round tables rested atop worn oak floors. Wall sconces and table lamps served as lighting, their golden beams skipping across the crimson wallpaper. A lone, broad-shouldered figure sat at the bar.

When I took the barstool beside his, Kazimir crooked a finger at the bartender, who poured a glass of vodka and slid it across the counter. Kazimir caught and passed it to me, then we lifted our glasses in a wordless toast. I took mine in a single gulp, savoring the burn.

After swallowing his, he passed a hand over his lips. "Good work today, dvoryanka."

"I don't need your praise, certainly not if you're going to ruin it in the same breath." I lifted a hand to catch the bartender's attention. Another glass sailed into my waiting palm.

Kazimir grunted something unintelligible, though I didn't miss his amused sidelong glance. A small loaf of rye bread was at his place, and when he tore off a chunk and offered it to me, his hand collided with my glass. Gasping, I tried to stabilize it but succeeded only in grabbing a handful of vodka. By the time Kazimir snatched the glass, it was empty.

I flicked my hands and scattered a few drops as I flashed a teasing smile. "Well done."

"I don't need your praise." Smirking, he handed me a napkin and the piece of bread, then called for a refill and gave it to me as well.

We had known each other once—not simple familiarity, but true knowledge, recognition of what shaped and united us. The need that led us to one another. Perhaps the knowledge remained, or perhaps I was grasping at something that had slipped by as easily as the vodka passing through my fingers. Until I knew for certain, I grasped at the familiar hold, wondering if it endured.

After swallowing the last of my bread, I finished my drink. "You haven't told me why Uncle Misha left you to take his place," I said before continuing more softly. "Or how he died."

Kazimir lit a cigarette. "I'm in charge. What more is there to know?" The usual measured tone, igniting a sudden spark within me.

"Have I not done enough?" I slammed my pistol on the counter. "And even if I hadn't earned this today, or if you still believe I'm here under false pretenses, my uncle is the only family member who ever truly supported me. I deserve to know what happened."

In the ensuing silence, I put away my weapon and waited to be disappointed. At last he exhaled smoke, watched it vanish.

"It was 1915. I refused to fight the tsar's war, so I deserted at the first opportunity. When I returned, Petrov appointed me his second-in-command, then he was targeted by the Bolsheviks." He tore the remaining fragment of bread, letting each crumb fall and decorate the white porcelain plate, dark like tiny bullet holes. "I've led the contingent since then."

Blinking back sudden tears, I placed a hand briefly over his. It was all the gratitude I could muster before folding my hands into my lap. Of course it had been the Bolsheviks' doing. When I drew an unsteady breath, I nearly heard Uncle Misha's usual words—encouragement, even a challenge: *Show us why you belong, Sveta.*

Dedication was the code of this contingent. How fitting that he had left his work to the young man who embodied that code. The one who, one February night, had crouched alongside me in a snowy alley, waiting for a member of the local *zemstvo*, intending to ambush the provisional councillor outside the restaurant where he dined. I heard his breathless statement as clearly now as I had then: *After Petrov, I will lead our contingent. My father was killed for his attempt at revolution, and I will finish what he started.*

Something to prove. A longing I knew too well. I had seen the fire in his eyes, suspected he wanted more than to avenge his father's death; with his assertion, he had trusted me with every intention. But I had not responded, too intent upon what I needed to prove—that he had no need to loathe me as he loathed my kind. I stayed focused, breath forming clouds while the cold seeped into my bones, eyes trained on the restaurant door swinging open. The space between my target's eyes, squeezing my numb finger against the trigger, his blood black against the snow.

Kazimir had fulfilled every longing while mine continued to spark, growing brighter, reminding me that his party and cause were mine and I needed only to show him. His fire burned steadily, drawing me in—perhaps only to be warmed, or perhaps to be fully consumed.

"Uncle Misha helped us both immeasurably," I said after we had been silent for a while. "He gave me freedom from the aristocracy and you an opportunity for justice against the imperial government. Have you avenged him?"

Kazimir said nothing, but I knew who lay beneath this stoic, hardened leader—a youth grappling with loss, drawn to the allure of vengeance. While he tossed his cigarette into the ashtray, I leaned closer.

"I will help you. Who killed him?"

And when he brushed a loose strand of hair from my forehead, he was the youth I remembered—his touch light, his voice gruff. "Leave it to me."

Even as I instinctively neared, something unspoken lay between us. I drew back. He was not looking at me as if he had forbidden my participation because he believed I was an aristocrat. It was the same look he had given when he had forbidden me from targeting *her*.

"Was it Orlova?"

His jaw clenched. When he reached for his drink, I snatched it aside. Rubbing a hand over his beard, Kazimir conceded.

"Her first." His voice was unsteady for an instant. "He disappeared for a few days, then I found his body outside Hotel Petrov."

My next breath was sharp, nearly a gasping cry. My uncle tortured, slaughtered, left as a warning in front of the same hotel and contingent he had founded.

"You intended to keep this from me?"

He lit another cigarette. "I need you focused on what's best for the party."

Avenging the murder of our contingent's founder *was* best for the party. He had no right withholding matters concerning my family. I rose, but Kazimir caught my wrist. I whirled to face him; before I spat out an accusation or did more than glare, I found the ache in my chest reflected in his eyes. Something I had forgotten after all this time: He had loved Uncle Misha as much as I had.

When he pulled me into him, the urge to fight dissipated. My pounding heart slowed until it matched the steady thrum in his chest.

"The best way to avenge Misha is to win the revolution," Kazimir murmured. "We will get justice for him, Sveta."

Winning the revolution was a step toward vengeance. As was finding the woman who had murdered my uncle. Orlova was already a threat to my party; now she had taken the man who had allowed me to join his cause. I owed it to him to ensure her work did not continue.

Chapter 7

Moscow, 4 April 1917

U ncle Misha told me what the tsar did to your father," I
had said on the day Kazimir had been assigned to assess
my loyalty. I thought perhaps Kazimir believed I was ignorant
of the way the peasants had been treated by the upper classes;
if I expressed awareness of what the proletariat had suffered, he
might understand that my efforts to lend support were genuine. But as we stepped onto the elevator, his furrowed brow
silenced me.

"The blood of countless peasants is on bourgeois hands as
much as the tsar's, dvoryanka," he replied before lighting a cigarette. When I tensed, a flicker of cynical amusement crossed
his face. "Are you offended by what you are?"

"What I am is someone who wants justice for the proletariat." I crossed the elevator to meet him. "Does that make me a
noblewoman?"

"Make whatever claims you wish. No one is going to keep
me from fulfilling my father's intentions." He stood taller as he
looked down at me, so close I almost expected him to reach for
my throat. "Certainly not a member of the aristocracy." Though
the words were cutting, I didn't back away. A sudden glimmer
crept into his eyes. He blinked and rested his back against the

wall, then he tapped ashes from his cigarette, watching them descend to the floor.

My own anger turned as gray as the ashes fluttering from the orange embers, settling over his *bakhily*—soft leather jackboots like those I had often seen on peasants if I ventured beyond my family's estate or our country house and into a more rural village. I wanted to help this party, my country, perhaps even this boy whose life of loss had driven him here. We were bonded by our desires to prove ourselves to this cause and one another, despite the way he regarded me with contempt and how I resented his judgment. When I placed a hand on his forearm, he sighed and offered me a cigarette; I accepted it while something penetrated his contempt—perhaps the smallest flicker of hope that this girl was like her uncle, not like the nobility.

"It doesn't matter that Misha is your uncle. If you betray us, you will be dealt with accordingly." He allowed the warning to settle over me before continuing. "If you are with us, Svetlana, be fully with us." His dark eyes searched mine—almost drawing me closer with a look that sought the answer I hoped to give by proving myself to the cause. To him.

The answer I feared that, despite my efforts, he would never completely accept.

* * *

IT WAS PAST midnight by the time Kazimir and I finished a proper meal and a few more rounds of drinks. After bidding him good night, I stepped onto the elevator, sighing as the alcohol's warmth spread over me, then selected the fifth floor. The door had almost closed when it opened again, prompted by something outside.

Kazimir entered and leaned against the opposite wall. As the elevator began its ascent, the smell of tobacco filled my lungs.

The boy I had known, now this man, his eyes impenetrable. The ache of loss remained, no longer so exposed as it had once been but still present, fueled by fury yet contained behind barriers. Ones I longed to bring down; an ache I still longed to soothe.

Perhaps the vodka had loosened my convictions and allowed the young, careless, stupid girl within me to take control. Perhaps it was simply what I had wanted all along, whether I blamed it on the liquor or not. My opportunity to grasp at the hold between us, to see if it remained—and if it did, if it remained unchanged. Whatever it was, I forgot the resolution I made upon returning to Hotel Petrov, the one where I told myself to keep the careless girl in her place. I knew that girl; I *was* that girl. There was no holding her back.

I crossed to meet Kazimir, wrapped my arms around his neck, and pulled his lips to mine.

He caught my waist, kissed me with all the intensity and fervor I had once known so well. A sign that he had been expecting this moment, waiting only for my inability to resist it. How fiercely I had missed his touch, his hands tangled in my hair, lips against my neck, eliciting my little gasp. Everything remained, just as I believed it would.

Moments later, when the elevator door creaked open, Kazimir pulled me toward the room across from us—fifth floor, room number twenty. When his back hit the door, he didn't open it. Instead, he held me against his chest, his lips centimeters from mine. And when he said my name, he used the old, familiar tone, the one that sounded the way his tobacco tasted, robust and irresistible.

Then, with a little smile, he released me, opened the door, and disappeared inside, leaving it slightly ajar.

Eleven years since I had last felt that careless girl's prompting; now it was all-consuming, fueled by his touch. His mouth on mine, coarse beard against my skin, breathless voice forming my name, the smirk that recognized every desire pulsing through my veins—I hated how easily he drew me to him almost as much as I hated the way my lips tingled, needing his. My waist ached for his grasp, its strength and certainty; my ears clung to his gruff whisper speaking my name, communicating everything I had waited to hear. The pull between us was more alive than ever, sending me through the door, closing it firmly behind me, urging me into the waiting darkness.

* * *

PERHAPS I SHOULD have been alarmed by how easily we fell into our old ways. Prior to my journey to Kiev, we had bade one another goodbye—much in this same fashion—intending to reunite in Moscow once my work was finished. Due to my arrest, the reunion never came. Now I'd returned to Moscow, so we were simply reuniting.

I glanced at him, fast asleep beside me.

His touch was freedom from the shackles of birth and blood, from meddlesome eyes and scornful tongues. This bed was my momentary escape. After each escape I slipped from between the sheets, armored with proof that he recognized this was my cause, and my place was here, as surely as his own. Each moment left me with full confidence that these instances would build until they left no room for anything else.

Moonlight slipped through the window and fell across Kazimir's bare chest, sending blue-gray streaks through the web of curling black hair. I had stayed by his side, loath to bring our time to an end. His chest rose and fell in deep slumber; I'd risk falling asleep myself if I remained much longer. A moment more, savoring this night, then I got up.

In the dark, I scoured the floor for my clothes, tossed here and there in haphazard heaps. Once I pulled on my rumpled chemise, skirt, and blouse, I slipped out.

The dull thud of my footsteps interrupted the quiet until I reached my bedroom. Inside, the gentle glow of lamplight stretched across a relatively sparse room furnished with three small beds, nightstands, and a dresser. Fanya was asleep, having retired early with her migraine, and Vera's bed was empty—a sign she was working on her next article. Quickly and quietly, I donned a nightgown, then tiptoed toward Fanya's lamp to turn it off.

"Don't be an idiot."

At once, I reached for my gun, heart pounding; at the same time, I recognized her voice and knew exactly what was coming. Taking a slow breath, I relaxed my hand. "Don't startle me unless you want me to shoot you."

"I'd shoot you in return." Fanya sat up to face me. "Have him if you wish. I didn't stop you then, and I won't now. But don't drag me into your business a second time, because when I agreed to spend six months with you in Kiev, I didn't realize I was also agreeing to help you hide your pregnancy."

My stomach tightened. I gripped her shoulders and pulled her close. "If you've breathed a word to him—"

Fanya caught my shoulders just as tightly, keeping me at arm's length. "You know I haven't, so get your hands off me."

When she pushed me away, I released her, our glares tense and unwavering. I'd sworn her to secrecy all those years ago, and she wouldn't go back on her promise. She couldn't. Not when she knew what it would mean for me.

"Even if I'd known the whole reason behind your plans for Kiev, I still would have gone with you. And even if you hadn't asked me to keep quiet, I would have kept your secret. I have never questioned you or betrayed your confidence, Sveta, and I hope you know better than to question me."

I winced but held her gaze. "It's not *you* I question," I replied quietly. "You have been my friend from the moment I came to this hotel. But I . . ." My voice faltered.

One moment, you will win his favor; the next, he will denounce you before Petrov and the entire party . . . men like Kazimir will always find reasons to doubt.

Fanya pushed a lock of hair away from her face and softened her tone. "Be careful, that's all. You made a difficult decision once; I don't want to see you in that position again."

She waited, perhaps expecting a reaction. I didn't give her one. For an instant, we were back in Kiev. Two girls eager to serve their cause, one with a secret she entrusted to no one else, the other willing to help however possible.

With a small sigh, she rolled over so her back was to me and buried her head beneath her pillow. Maybe I was almost three years her senior, but she still saw me as a stupid girl, childish and impulsive.

After a few minutes, Fanya's breaths steadied, as did my own while I climbed into bed and turned off the lamp. Darkness washed over us.

Spending six months in Kiev to develop our bomb plot could not have fallen at a more opportune time. I had set the plan into motion before realizing what was happening inside me; by the time I discovered it, Uncle Misha had already granted permission to depart a month later, in August. It was the time I needed to decide what to do.

Should I see the pregnancy through? Should I not? If I did, what then? I never forgot how, in bed one night, Kazimir had sneered about a young woman in our contingent, Nina Semyonovna—how Uncle Misha had sent Nina away that same day, having discovered she had made such a foolish mistake, one that caused him to doubt her commitment. For all my uncle's talk of women deserving equality, loyalty to the party came first. No matter what Nina decided to do regarding her predicament, she had been careless enough to let it happen. Such carelessness had no place within this contingent. The situation occurred as I was beginning to suspect the same thing had happened to me.

So I withheld the truth from everyone except Fanya.

Finding a doctor willing to terminate pregnancy was the choice most girls made. Not the one I made. I had been granted the opportunity to bring a new life into a brighter future, one I was fighting to establish. This child was a part of me. A part of Kazimir. A part of what we might be together once the unrest settled.

Now I had a little girl in Kiev, waiting for the mother she had never known.

Sighing, I shifted positions and suppressed the tension in my stomach.

If Kazimir knew we had a child, maybe he would understand I was fighting to end this revolution and return to her; perhaps he might even help me and want to be part of our daughter's life. Or, more likely, he would treat me like Uncle Misha had treated Nina Semyonovna. The party mattered above all else. To him, a daughter was a distraction, an interference. More aristocratic blood.

I already had the stain of the nobility on my name. I could not add another stain, impossible to scrub out. My loyalty remained under constant question, and this held the power to break whatever fragile trust I had managed to gain. This matter could not come to light until the revolution was over.

* * *

IN 1906, ON the fourth of February, howling wind and heavy snowfall pummeled the windowpane of our filthy apartment in Kiev, the frigid single room warmed only by a small wood-burning stove. I had lain in bed for hours, drenched in sweat, crushing the hand Fanya had offered me.

Pain ripped through my body, sharp and fierce like the rip of each blanket fragment Fanya had shredded after my swollen belly had confined me to this bed. When it had become clear that the child inside me was coming.

She broke my grasp to remove the bloody rag between my legs. "Again."

Obliging, I gripped the sheets until my arms shook, encouraging my child to bring this agony to an end. Another cry emerged through my gritted teeth before I fell back, chest heaving.

"The baby?" I whispered, voice raw and aching.

Silence. More rustles of fabric and cups and bowls. "Not yet." A cool dampness found my forehead. "You must keep trying, Sveta. If the baby does not—" She broke off. Neither of us knew what to do if the baby did not come. We hardly knew what to do now.

I reached for her hand, then I poured all my energy, love, and desperation into the little one inside me, because if something was wrong, if my child did not come, there was nothing more Fanya could do. And I had not brought my dearest friend all this way just for her to bury me and the little one we had tried so hard to protect.

Fanya released me with sudden haste. A squeal joined my shriek, the sound of new lungs drawing their first breath, announcing entrance into the world.

I collapsed again before fighting to lift my head. "The baby?" I pressed amid the little one's wails. "Is it—?"

"Fine." Fanya beamed as she placed the tiny bundle in my arms. "*She* is fine."

She.

Her cheeks were aflame from her cries despite the cold in this room. A perfect little nose, ears, and mouth. A crown of light chestnut hair. A daughter. My daughter. For her my heart beat; for her my lungs drew breath; for her the blood raced through my veins. To her belonged every part of me.

As I held my little one to my chest, her skin warm against mine, I looked outside. The snow had ceased, leaving a heavy blanket over the building across the street—Saint Anne's Foundling Hospital.

Fanya followed my gaze. "You don't have to do this," she murmured, brushing her finger down the baby's soft cheek. "We can find another way."

I shook my head, blinking past sudden tears. I had already been accused of loyalty to the aristocracy countless times; if someone accused me of raising my daughter with aristocratic ideals, she would be endangered. If I brought a baby back to Moscow, Nina Semyonovna's fate would be mine, mistrusted and banished for carelessness. I could not have a life with her until it was safe.

After Fanya picked up a pencil and paper, I spoke slowly, fighting to keep my voice level.

"Today's date—the fourth of February, 1906. Born in Kiev."

Amid the scratch of Fanya's pencil, I studied the little face in my arms. Not long. A few months at most, surely. A few long, unbearable months away from these tiny toes, pink cheeks, little mouth slightly parted, until all classes existed in peace. I pressed my lips to her forehead. Then I finished my note, voice hardly above a whisper.

"Tatiana Kazimirovna Petrova."

Chapter 8

Moscow, 3 May 1917

Light fell across my eyes, rousing me. I rolled away, loath to depart from the haze of slumber, and had nearly settled again when the bed creaked. My eyelids fluttered open.

Beside me, Kazimir yawned as he ran a hand through his tousled hair. Sunlight stretched between us, guiding me closer. I brushed my fingers along the thin scar trailing beneath the dark hair covering his forearm—faded evidence after fleeing from a bomb we'd planted so long ago. When the factory exploded, the blast nearly caught us as it scorched the frigid March evening in 1905, but Kazimir shoved me down a dark, filthy alley for protection, colliding with me and throwing us to the ground.

We stayed there, stifling laughter and gulping deep breaths of cool air, letting it burn within our lungs. As a cacophony of footsteps, screams, and shouts filled the night, too close to our hiding place, he pulled me deeper into the shadows and placed a finger against my mouth. When the noise faded, he brushed the hair from my forehead, leaning closer as my lips parted in anticipation.

That day, I had succumbed to the inexplicable draw that held us together, prompting me to wrap my arms around the young man who vowed to avenge his father and lead this party after my uncle. To kiss him. To ignore every convention, every deterrent. To join him for the first of many nights in his bed.

As my fingers found the end of the scar, they fell to the mattress, following a golden beam stretching over the sheets. "Is it morning?" I murmured.

"What gave you that idea? The sunlight?" His voice was thick with sleep, despite its teasing edge, so like it had often been when we spent long nights and leisurely mornings together. Hours filled with whispers and laughter; my fingers trailing over his firm chest and abdomen; political conversations giving way to breathless kisses.

Clearing my throat, I pushed a few unruly strands of hair from my face and sat up, holding tight to the thin sheet against my bare body. I'd found myself here numerous times over the past month; I always slipped into my bedroom at the earliest convenience, though the careless girl inside me often urged me to linger. Last night I had succumbed to her persistence, foolish as it had been. Staying felt definite—a permanent, drastic certainty in an uncertain future.

Kazimir pulled my sheet away; though a little smile found my lips, I turned aside as he leaned closer.

"We need to leave for the café soon."

He glanced at the clock on the far wall. "Not for another hour." Then, as if that settled the matter, he brought his lips to mine.

Even his kiss held no power to distract me. Not when we had work to do.

I placed my hand on his chest and pushed against him. Instead of complying, his tongue probed mine, insistent, fingers trailing down my spine in the way that usually made me ease onto my back, melting into his caress. This time, it only ignited my impatience. When I managed to create enough distance, I gave him a warning glare.

The beam of sunlight stretched between us, a golden threshold not to be crossed.

With a heavy sigh, Kazimir fell against the pillow. "Are you always so disagreeable in the mornings?"

I nearly tore out his tongue.

Nothing ever changed between us. One moment drew us together, the next repelled us with the ferocity of a thousand explosions, yet we remained bound by that sizzling fuse.

No time to let him goad me into an argument; instead, I rose, deliberately forgoing the sheet. His jaw tightened, a subtle reward. I dressed while he watched with surly lines across his forehead.

Downstairs, the scent of hot tea and coffee lingered in the sitting area while a few party members consumed hard-boiled eggs and black bread for breakfast. When I joined Fanya on a small sofa, she mumbled a greeting and passed me her copy of *Delo naroda*. One of Vera's articles graced the front page, written under the pseudonym she used to protect herself from enemy parties—and, alongside her words, a photograph of a corpse.

ORLOVA: Pro-Lenin, Pro-Peace
by Arina Yakovlevna Drozdova

Hardly a few weeks since Vladimir Ilych Ulyanov, known as Lenin, has been back from European exile, and his influence spreads.

Lenin and the Petrograd Soviet continue advocating for Russia's unconditional withdrawal from the war while the Provisional Government pushes for a definitive

Russian victory, post-war annexation by the Allies, and reparations from Germany. This conflict has recently come to a head, as Lenin has incited a rise in soldiers' and workers' strikes in protest.

"The Provisional Government's views on the war with Germany are no different than the imperial government's," says Mikhail Andreevich Yemelin, member of the Bolshevik Military Organization. "We rebelled against the tsar, and we will continue to rebel until the bourgeois Provisional Government resigns."

Indeed, these rebellions have yielded results. The Provisional Government recently announced a revision to its position, stating any future peace treaty with Germany will no longer include annexations or war contributions.

Lenin has won a decisive victory for Bolsheviks and pro-peace Russians, but not all approve of his actions. Multiple witnesses claim an unidentified man stood outside the old Filippov Bakery on Tverskaya Street in Moscow, claiming Lenin's return to Russia was facilitated by the Germans, who permitted him to travel on a sealed train through Germany. The next day, the man (pictured) was found in the same location, tortured and blinded by Orlova, the notorious Bolshevik assassin, proving neither she nor her party will tolerate opposition.

What does this mean for the Socialist Revolutionary Party? Positions on the war vary—most in favor strictly as a patriotic and defensive measure, others opposed. No matter your position, I leave my SR readers with this thought: If Lenin has accomplished so much in so few weeks, what can we expect from the Bolshevik Party in the future?

True, many were tired of the war, but if withdrawal meant sacrificing land or appeasing Germany, we needed to fight against it. And if Germany had helped Lenin return to Russia, he could not be trusted. Still, what Vera had written was accurate. Lenin incited violence, drew power from the fear he cultivated, and Orlova was one of his many tools. Strikes and protests were visible, loud, often violent; an assassin was invisible, silent, always ruthless.

Beside me, Fanya passed a hand across her eyes and held the bridge of her nose before letting her hand fall into her lap. On the coffee table before us, a samovar, teapot, cups, and saucers waited on the tray, so I poured a cup and offered it to her. Tea always helped her headaches.

A flush rose to her cheeks while she pressed her fingers against her temple and settled deeper into her seat. "Is it that obvious?" She looked from me to the teacup.

"Only to someone who lived in the same cell as you for eleven years and watched you fight migraines the entire time."

"Not the entire time. The migraines didn't start until after our first year." She gave a halfhearted smile, then sat up, accepted the tea, and took a sip.

I stared into my teacup. If only Kiev had not failed—when Fanya had misjudged what time to detonate the bomb, prompting me to fire at the car too early in an attempt to salvage the mission, not realizing the governor-general, our target, had been inside the second car veering off to safety. The dark mines and strenuous labor following our capture had led to her migraines and failing vision. And if these episodes were still plaguing her, what if she compromised our work?

"You should rest, Fanya." When she didn't look up, I leaned

closer and lowered my voice. "It's for your own good. And the party's."

Her eyes narrowed. "Have you mentioned this to Kazimir?"

"Do you expect me to break your confidence when you haven't broken mine?" My frown softened as I recalled the newborn Fanya had placed into my arms.

"I'll be fine. The episode will pass soon enough." She finished her tea and returned the dishes to the tray. "They always do."

Perhaps, but if she developed a horrific migraine during our mission, Kazimir was bound to find out.

They had plagued her fiercely ever since the first onset when we had been stripped and shackled for another beating—whether for disrespecting a guard or a different transgression, I didn't recall. Heavy chains and tight cuffs bound my arms to a tall whipping post in the middle of the cell, Fanya beside me in the same fashion, cold stone beneath our feet.

The birch rod across my bare back and legs bit sharper with every stroke, but I bore it with little reaction until Fanya's cries shifted into terror. She cowered, screamed—*Stop, my head, please, I can't see, I can't think, please stop!* My bonds ripped my skin while I strained against them, demanding that the guard cease. He kept striking, while mine redoubled his efforts, to silence me. She was just a girl, only seventeen.

Neither relented until Fanya's limp form dangled from her bonds, body covered in furious red stripes. Mine mirrored hers, I knew. Rivulets of blood trailed down my arms, mingling with the rank scent of sweat and iron. *Do not leave me, Fanya,* I had whispered over and over, as if desperation held the power to revive her. *Please do not leave me.* Wherever this life sentence took us, whatever course the revolution took, we had to finish what we had started together.

Chapter 9

Moscow, 3 May 1917

Crumbling brick and boarded windows identified our target: a small café in north Moscow. Though the abandoned building required significant repair, Vera had learned from one of her sources that it had become a Bolshevik assembly space. After spending all day watching, ensuring no unforeseen meetings were taking place, we'd slipped inside at dusk and had dedicated the past hour to our work.

Compared to the exterior, the state of the interior was a slight improvement, though dust and mildew lingered in the air. Kazimir and Rolan had cut holes in the wall and floor and were burying a few sticks of dynamite. Sergei Markovich worked with them—a friend from Kazimir's time on the front, one of many soldiers tired of fighting the tsar's war against the Germans. After deserting, he had reconnected with Kazimir to join the revolution.

Fanya and I scattered guncotton to provide additional fuel. I pulled off a fluffy wad and offered the piece to her, then she stuffed it into the small hole in the floor. She had said nothing more of her headache, though this did not necessarily mean it had gone away; she had quickly learned how to mask her symptoms from our Maltzevskaya guards. Still, she knew how important these missions were for our party; if her condition had not improved, surely she would have said something to me.

We had a final stick of dynamite to bury, so we left the guncotton on an overturned table and knelt beside a hole in the far corner of the room. I stuffed the dynamite inside, leaving the fuse exposed.

As we stood, Kazimir approached, carrying a long fuse that extended from the opposite wall. "Light this and we'll have about a minute to get out before it detonates."

He tossed it at our feet before joining the men to gather our tools and materials. I examined the tables around me but found no matches. As Fanya collected our leftover guncotton, I was opening my mouth to ask if she had any when the room exploded.

It was as if someone had physically lifted me and thrown me with the full force of his strength. Pain was sudden, heavy, as I struck something hard—the wood floor, already hot beneath my cheek, the heat suffocating, pieces of wood and debris showering over me. Choking on smoke and ash, I slapped my skirt to extinguish a small flame. Beside me, Fanya raised an arm to cover her nose and mouth, gasping. Flames sprang up around us, encouraged by the guncotton, then another explosion shook the building and left us cowering beneath more fragments of wood and scraps of materials. No time to delay. I caught her arm and hauled her upright before staggering after the men rushing for the door.

We were halfway there when a body on the floor caught my eye, buried beneath splintered tables and chairs and shattered glass from the nearby window. Fanya and I pushed the broken furniture away to make sure he was dead; when we revealed his face, I forgot the fire drawing nearer with every second. I shoved her toward the door, knelt, and shook him by the shoulders.

"Kazimir?" Searing heat stole my voice. I shook him harder, the gash across his forehead black against skin glowing orange from the leaping flames. "Kazimir, wake up!" I slapped his face once, hard. He didn't move.

We had perhaps thirty seconds before the final stick of dynamite detonated. The one in the wall right beside us. He had to get up. This contingent needed him, *I* needed him.

"Get up!" Not a command this time, instead a plea. I slapped him again. A spluttering cough, a rattled breath, my own unsteady exhale as I wiped the blood dripping into his eyes.

Awake. Alive.

Fanya reappeared beside me. When we hooked our arms under his, he roused enough to help us lift him. We stumbled into the darkened evening, aflame with orange and red, and made it a few meters closer to the waiting car before the final blast split the air. Sergei grabbed Kazimir, and I was about to follow when a tight hold latched onto my hair and yanked me backward.

Scalp smarting, chest aching, I reached for my pistol while my cry gave way to a choked breath. My assailant had already snatched the gun from my waistband, and he tightened his grip to subdue my struggles.

Rolan held firm, eyes wild, veins popping out of his neck and face. His bellows made my ears ring almost as much as the blast had, nearly impossible to discern; then a few words broke through, unmistakable as the building turned to ash behind us.

"You treacherous bourgeois bitch!"

More hands gripped his forearm—Fanya's. She tugged, shaking her head but coughing too much to speak. He swung my pistol and struck her across the face, then she crumpled and lay still.

"No!" I lunged for my gun but only managed to knock it from his hands before another sharp pain forced my head back. I stared into his face, cheeks smeared with soot, one stripped raw from a burn.

"Lying about political imprisonment. Claiming to be one of us. All while serving *them*." Rolan caught my throat, pushed me back, closed the distance between us and the scorching heat. "And now your failed sabotage will be an example to the entire bourgeoisie."

I writhed, dug my heels into the ground, clawed the hands gripping my head and neck, the bicep where his torn sleeve was soaked crimson, but we had already reached the threshold. No words came to proclaim my innocence, only gasping breaths. Rolan pulled me close, his voice no more than a growl, flickering flames reflected in his eyes.

"Burn. In there, and in hell."

He shoved me into the café.

A crack split the air—perhaps a collapsing wall or shattering window—as I landed amid splintered wood and broken glass. Flames hissed, wood groaned, heat seeped into me, overwhelming and unbearable. Part of the ceiling caved, sending down a shower of debris; once the rest fell, it would block my path—or, worse, bury me beneath it. I was not going to die, not like this . . .

Covering my nose and mouth, I crawled toward the door, but I hardly made it a meter before a tight grip found my forearm, jerked me upright, and pulled me through the doorway.

Outside, I coughed and spat, blinking to ease my stinging eyes while groans and curses met my ears—Rolan's. He lay in a crumpled heap, blood seeping from his thigh. A gunshot wound, evidence of the crack I'd heard.

"Stop whining, you pathetic bastard. The bullet barely grazed you. And if I'd wanted to kill you, I would have." Kazimir's voice, raspy from smoke. His arm secured around my waist. His hands the ones that had pulled me out. The severity of his glower intensified by his jagged laceration and streaks of bright blood, soot, and sweat.

Rolan struggled up to his forearms; if not for the injury, I felt certain he would have gotten up and thrown me back into the building. "You should have let her die, Kazimir. There are plenty of other women who can warm your bed."

My mouth tasted of soot, impeding the number of retorts that rose to my throat. Instead I glowered; beside me Kazimir gave no reaction, a momentary delay that allowed Rolan just enough time for his sneer to falter and his eyes to brighten with sudden dread. Then, without losing his hold on me, Kazimir placed his boot against the gunshot wound and pressed down, extracting a cry through Rolan's gritted teeth.

"You work for me, and if you ever take action without my authorization again, I will shatter your fucking skull. Do you understand?"

"Enough . . . Yes, I understand," came the strained reply.

Kazimir held the pressure a moment more before releasing him. Ignoring Rolan's clumsy efforts to stand, we proceeded toward the car.

Deep lines remained across Kazimir's forehead. Not once had he looked at me. Had he overheard Rolan's accusations? Did he share those assumptions? When he extended his free hand to open the back door, I caught it.

"Kazimir . . ." Little more than a croak, but all my raw voice managed. I tightened my hold, stepped closer, anything to make him meet my gaze.

My efforts lasted a moment. He shook off my grip, opened the door, and shoved me inside. Before it slammed, I noticed a familiar item peeking above his belt, the item missing from my waistband—my pistol.

As I studied my singed clothing, streaks of soot and grime, minor scrapes and burns covering my skin, tension surged through my veins like the dynamite tearing the café apart. Beside me sat Fanya—lip split, still visibly dazed.

No one said a word during our drive.

Had Rolan caused the explosion in order to blame me? An effort to fuel mistrust and oust me from the party? But he had regarded me with such genuine fury, as if he truly believed that I was responsible.

I sighed and wiped blood from a scratch on my arm. If Rolan believed I was at fault, so be it. But the thought of Kazimir sharing those beliefs left my chest tight, as surely as if I were still choking on smoke.

When we reached Hotel Petrov and stepped out of the car, Kazimir wiped the blood dripping from his cut, ignored the arm Sergei offered him, and pushed ahead. Sergei transferred his assistance to Rolan. They hobbled after Kazimir while Fanya and I brought up the rear.

She shared a quick glance with me, the look in her eyes unmistakable. The one that followed every time her vision had impeded her.

Her headache. It had not disappeared as I had assumed. She must have heard Kazimir's order to light the fuse and had done so while I sought matches; her eyesight must have led her to mistake the long one for the short one I had planted.

When she reached for me, I turned from her, the heat inside me building with every step. Her carelessness had almost killed us, *Kazimir*, had led to Rolan trying to murder me. If she had compromised this mission, she would compromise more.

When we reached the door, Kazimir paused long enough to glower at our group. "None of you are going anywhere until I find out how this happened."

I didn't miss Fanya's small, unsteady breath behind me, putting a knot in my chest, subduing my fury. Her vision had been damaged by the katorga. By my plot. I had always done whatever I could to alleviate her suffering. If Kazimir threw out the friend who had always accepted me, how was I to endure without her?

Inside, crowded around the front desk, Vera sat with pencil and paper in hand, awaiting our return, while Yelizaveta Dmitrievna, another party member, clutched a stack of freshly printed propaganda posters. When they saw our disheveled state, their mouths fell open.

"What happened?" Vera asked, tossing her materials aside and hurrying to meet us. Yelizaveta rushed away, likely to fetch supplies, as she was our designated medic.

Kazimir was letting me get close to him again. To claim responsibility was to risk everything I had fought to rebuild.

"It was my fault," I said before Fanya could speak. "I accidentally lit the wrong fuse."

She stepped toward me, shaking her head until my discreet frown deterred her. Kazimir pushed away the handkerchief Vera attempted to press against his injury, then he met my gaze for the first time since the explosion. His hooded brows hovered above a fierce glare; I averted my eyes, afraid they might betray me.

Rolan leaned on the desk to take the weight off his injured leg but lifted his chin in triumph. "Tsarist," he spat as though it were a curse.

I bit back the urge to snap at him and caught Vera's accusatory scowl—followed by the gleam of satisfaction in her eyes when Kazimir caught my arm.

"Watch the others, Comrade Volkova," he said to Vera, then he dragged me down the hall.

I didn't fight him. Once we reached the interrogation room, he released me and slammed the door.

"An *accident*? That's what you call blowing up a fucking building with everyone inside?"

My heart was already pounding. An extensive explanation would seem overly eager, suspicious. "Yes," I replied instead. Straightforward, though perhaps too simple . . .

"You'll have to give better answers than that, because you are not leaving this room until you explain how this *accident* occurred."

Such contempt. Perhaps he had taken my reaction as impertinence.

He drew my pistol and brought it to my eye level. "This is supposed to be an indication of your loyalty. I will not have this party questioning my judgment."

Instinctively, I reached for my weapon, but he caught my wrist. He was looking at me as he had the first time we met. When he viewed me as a liar, a hypocrite, a fraud. An aristocrat.

I wanted him to accept my explanation, my intentions, *me*. I wanted our foundation to be sound enough to withstand even the most powerful of explosions; instead, it was a match held to a flame. One tiny spark was all it took to destroy it.

Everything in me longed to reassure him with the truth, as well as scream at him for so quickly losing faith in me; instead, I broke his hold with a harsh laugh. "If you believe my actions were intentional, why should I bother trying to change your mind?"

"Tell me I'm wrong. If you can honestly tell me that you are careless, then I will believe setting off the dynamite was a mistake."

I bit the inside of my cheek. Why hadn't I developed a better explanation? Kazimir had seen the care I put into my work, knew lighting the wrong fuse was an error I would not commit. I had never been negligent when it came to the revolution; when it came to him, on the other hand, the results of my carelessness waited for me in Kiev.

"Either you are lying to me about being responsible, or you lit the fuse on purpose. Which is it?"

I caught his face between my hands, forcing him to see the honesty in my eyes even if he refused to hear it in my words. "I have dedicated my life to the revolution and this party. And I would never sabotage either one." *Or you,* I refrained from adding. He would probably assume it was an insincere attempt to earn favor.

Perhaps he believed me; perhaps he wanted to, at least. As he began to turn aside, I tightened my hold; this time, he searched my gaze, his own wary but less hostile. When I brushed blood from his forehead, then a dark smudge from the exposed skin at the base of his throat, he stepped closer. The tang of blood, soot, and sweat rose from his skin.

"What am I to do with you, Sveta?"

Gruff and deep in his throat, part threat, part something else—longing, even a need, though tainted with reservation.

"You have three choices: kill me, throw me out, or trust me."

How easy I wanted that decision to be. Silence fell, thick and weighty. Considering his options.

"I should remind you, I *did* save your life." A halfhearted jest. All I had left.

"And I saved yours." He glowered again. "You are in no position to bargain with me, dvoryanka."

I had no anger left to rejoin; instead, I released him, pressed my back to the wall, and closed my eyes, feeling as if the explosion had torn through me and left nothing but destruction and ash in its wake.

"Is it so difficult, Kazimir?"

At my murmur, I heard him release a breath. When I opened my eyes, he regarded me with less hostility, though the old, impenetrable wall was there, never letting me see what lay behind it.

"I will accept your word. This time." A bit of the tension inside me eased before he continued. "And for the next month, you are forbidden from participating in acts of political terror."

A high price to pay for my own innocence, but not for sparing Fanya or remaining in Kazimir's good graces. I would spend the time roaming around Moscow, watching the strikes and fights encouraged by Lenin. Hunting for evidence of Orlova.

My sentence suddenly seemed far more bearable.

Countless Bolsheviks walked the streets or gave speeches every day. Easy targets. Dull. She was a challenge unlike any I had ever faced. Intentionally mysterious, maddening, yet audacious, as if daring me to defy her, taunting me for my uncle's murder, each corpse signifying her party's impending victory, the justice I would never attain. How wrong she was.

What started as a quest to avenge my uncle had transformed into far more than a simple task I needed to fulfill. I was bound to the faceless woman in my head who stared down the barrel of my pistol while my finger neared the trigger, waiting only for her face to take shape.

The urge was insatiable: to find *her*. Orlova was the Bolshevik whose blood would be mine.

Chapter 10

Moscow, 1 November 1917

Vehicles rumbled past while horse-drawn carriages trudged down the slushy, muddy streets. Ice caked the sidewalk and crunched beneath my feet like shattered glass after a riot. As a breeze swept over me, I strolled past an endless line of women waiting to purchase bread, milk, and meat, each four or five times as expensive as in the past. Autumn was proceeding into winter, but the early morning sun filtered through the clouds, warming my skin.

I sighed, my breath hovering in the air like cigarette smoke. The revolution was ever-fluctuating. Public opinion turned away from the Bolsheviks; then it turned back in their favor. Success never seemed to last. Though the Russian Army was crumbling on the front, I did not fear a German advance as much as I feared a Bolshevik uprising.

I reached my destination, thanks to a tip I'd overheard one of Vera's sources relaying in the lobby this morning. She would be here soon enough to investigate, so I would depart before she saw me, but I was not going to miss the chance to inspect Orlova's latest kill for myself.

It was the usual scene: The crowd. The mutilated figure sprawled on the ground. Bloodshot eyes. Open mouth with a tiny folded paper and surname in red scrawl.

One man held a Bolshevik propaganda poster, so I approached. "What happened?"

"I heard he was an ardent supporter of the Provisional Government." He nodded to the corpse. "As for whether someone gave Orlova his name or she chose him herself, I'm not certain."

Given the rise in Orlova's murders, I imagined those who tipped her off were well rewarded for their efforts, encouraging more and more to partake in such treachery. Still, I was no closer to finding her.

The man lit a cigarette before continuing. "It's no secret Lenin always wanted to remove the Provisional Government from power. Maybe this is a reminder."

I pretended to study the corpse to avoid giving a retort that would betray my party allegiance. Over the summer, rumors that the Bolsheviks had received funding from the Germans had been confirmed, so Lenin had fled from the public's disapproval. He was a coward. The Bolsheviks had a chance to reshape their party without his views, to support the Constituent Assembly's establishment, oust bourgeois policies, and work toward a government representing all; instead, Orlova continued reinforcing Lenin's influence. I nearly reached for my pistol, eager for the reassuring grip inside my palm.

I let out a breath to ease the tension in my chest, then left the scene to return to Hotel Petrov. If she wanted attention, very well. I'd give her a headline across every front page: "Orlova, Most Notorious Bolshevik Assassin, Dead."

As I pressed on, the crowd thickened due to a disturbance ahead. Shouts, thuds, and shattering glass, all sounds of looting. A group of men had torn a pharmacy door from its hinges and thrown bricks through the windows. I proceeded, ignoring them, stepping around the destroyed goods scattered about the sidewalk. Judging by their hearty guffaws and raised voices, they had already indulged in the cigarettes and alcohol they were passing around.

I had just passed the scene when something tugged on my skirt; one of those drunk men had chosen the wrong woman. I whirled, one hand on my pistol.

A little girl—no more than four years of age, I supposed— held tight to me, then released me, startled by my sudden movement. When she looked up, her face fell, obviously having confused me with someone else. Her lip quivered before she wailed.

"Maman? Elle est où, ma maman?"

At once, I caught her shoulders, pulled her close to the stucco bakery wall beside me, and knelt. This was no place for a child, certainly not an aristocratic one. Her plain brown dress would fool no one the moment she opened her mouth. She squirmed, sucking in a breath. The next shriek would surely follow.

"En russe. Il faut parler russe," I whispered fervently. My French calmed her; she bobbed her head, as though she had received the same instructions countless times. "Again," I said, this time in Russian.

She opened her mouth, then a crash sounded behind me. She flinched, eyes welling with more tears.

"None of that." I caught her cheeks, encouraging her to focus. *"En russe.* Say it again."

Another shaky breath, then she responded in kind. "Where is Mama?"

I offered an encouraging nod, then chanced a look behind me; we were next door to the looters, but the men did not appear to have overheard her initial cry. Such trusting eyes gazed at me, as if certain all would soon be well. I gently brushed a loose blond lock behind her ear, imagining it turned chestnut, softer than the finest velvet, crowning the head of the little one I longed for with every breath and every beat of my heart.

"Natasha? Natalya Antonovna, I told you to stay close!"

A woman hurried down the block toward us, clutching a baby and a valise with one hand and the shawl over her head with the other. Her shoulders were straight, her gait graceful, evidence of years spent at an institute for noble girls, learning the ways of high society. She reached for her daughter, her hand smooth and unblemished; a sign delicate gloves had once covered it. Her neck bare, once bedecked with gold and jewels. Her body dressed in borrowed rags, once adorned in fine silks and furs. This woman was exactly who I would have become had I not shed my old life.

Perhaps this was how I appeared to my party members—a noble trying to remain inconspicuous. Birth and blood were difficult to hide and impossible to change. This woman might have spurned the revolutionary cause, or she might have been ignorant of the damages inflicted by the upper classes; still, whatever her beliefs, she was a mother. For that, my heart twisted with a heavy ache.

The woman gave me a quick, appreciative nod, failing to mask the wariness in her gaze. It was a look I received when revolutionaries saw me as an aristocrat; this time, it was from a noblewoman who feared what this proletariat revolutionary might do to her and her children if their disguises failed.

She glanced at the looters. Motioned for Natasha to hurry.

My eyes fell to the baby in her arms. A newborn. My hand drifted to my midsection; for a moment, I swore I felt the tiny life that had once been inside.

"Natasha," I called as the girl scurried to her mother's side.

When I reached them, I lowered my voice. *"N'oublie pas."* Don't forget.

While Natasha nodded, the woman drew her daughter closer and opened her mouth, then closed it—shocked by my French, that I recognized their status, or both. I gave a single nod to assure her their secret was safe; the square, proud shoulders slumped in visible relief, then she hurried on.

I hoped they would reach their train, their car, whatever prearranged means of transportation they sought. I hoped Natasha would remember to speak Russian instead of French. I hoped they would find safety, wherever it was. Death was not a just sentence for a mother fighting to protect her innocent children. But it was a sentence many would be all too quick to enforce.

Revolution, for all its beauty, never came without tragedy.

Perhaps this noblewoman had felt lost without her daughter. Perhaps my daughter felt as lost as this little one had been. Though it was impossible to be together yet, her loss struck me anew, as surely as if we had been separated in a crowd as these two had, unsure when we would find one another again.

Since release, I had feared for her well-being; now the ache coupled with loss, consuming me. I needed to find Tatiana. Somehow I needed to go to Kiev.

Chapter 11

Moscow, 1 November 1917

By the time I returned to Hotel Petrov, the knot in my stomach threatened to overtake me, left by my inability to banish thoughts of what the revolutionaries might have done if they had discovered the aristocratic child alone on the street. Children had no control over their class or their parents. Yet if uncovered, my daughter, too, would face treatment according to her birth, to how others regarded her mother, to everything she had no power to change. And no matter our choices, little Natasha's mother and I carried the same fear: that our status might bring a horrific fate upon our children.

I made my way upstairs. Perhaps Fanya would have a suggestion regarding how to return to Kiev and eliminate this ache in my chest, unceasing until I knew the truth of my daughter's well-being.

A few months ago, the café explosion had nearly destroyed my friendship with Fanya as easily as the explosives had shattered the building. After Kazimir's interrogation, I had returned to our bedroom, the absence of my weapon stinging worse than the burns and scrapes covering me. When I opened the door, Fanya sprang to her feet.

"I thought it was the correct fuse, I swear—"

"You went on a mission even though migraines always compromise your vision." Though she flinched as if I had struck her, I didn't soften my tone. "You almost killed us. And you cost me my pistol for the next month."

"I didn't ask you to claim responsibility!" she snapped; then, as quickly as her anger had flared, she shook her head to prevent my retort, her voice quiet again. "When the headache didn't pass, I thought if I managed with them in the mines, I'd manage here. It won't happen again."

Of that, I would make certain. We had sworn to keep one another's secrets, but if those secrets came between us and the party, not even our vows were strong enough to see us through. This work was too important for anyone to jeopardize, friend or not.

Avoiding my scowl, Fanya proceeded to the door.

"Where are you going?"

"You took enough blame for me in the katorga and received countless beatings because of it. I'm not letting you do the same now."

I stepped in her path, letting my scowl go. "If Kazimir throws you out?"

"Perhaps it's for the best. If my vision continues to deteriorate, I can't stay."

Despite her set jaw, the words wavered. The work was too important to compromise, but neither could we abandon one another. Certainly not if her condition worsened; since release from the katorga, I had assured her that she could stay with me no matter where the years took us. A promise in which she seemed to find solace, particularly when her migraines were the shackles that clung to her even after imprisonment. Now I saw the combination of resolution and fear as she stepped around me, pausing only after I placed a hand on her forearm.

"We kept your condition from the guards for years, all while ensuring you were not a danger to yourself or anyone else," I said softly. "We'll do the same here."

She drew an unsteady breath and shook her head. "Your position is delicate enough. If I can't work, then I won't."

"If that time comes, then no, you will not. Nor will I let anyone send you away."

She held my gaze, as if confirming I was certain, then her shoulders heaved in a sigh of relief as she placed a hand over mine. Our party loyalty was strong, yet our loyalty to one another was just as unshakable.

And now that I planned to go to Kiev, Fanya would certainly help me.

As I stepped off the elevator, Kazimir's bedroom door was open. He sat at his desk with a few papers before him, then lifted his head. My feet carried me to him, powerless to resist.

Despite the café explosion setback, these past few months had gone well between us. Sometimes I found the old reservations; more often, he no longer regarded me as though he were dissecting every word, every action, every intention, assessing their validity. Now he caught my hips, pulled me close, looked up at me as if my presence were the comfort he needed. I brushed a dark lock from his forehead, though the ache in my chest intensified.

If only going to Kiev were as simple as telling him we had a daughter, thus gaining permission to ensure her safety. But it was not a subject to broach too quickly, not while our places in this new future remained uncertain. Until the revolution ended, I permitted faith to sustain me, reassuring me that our child might become just that—ours.

I glanced at the assorted documents before him. "What are you reading?"

"Insights from various Socialist Revolutionary leaders throughout Moscow, Petrograd, and elsewhere." He gathered the letters and papers into a neat stack before pushing his chair back. "Some require more attention than others."

As he stood, I picked up the first paper and read aloud. "'Rumors of Bolshevik activity in Kiev. Requesting a member of Moscow's Meshchansky District contingent to investigate and write a report for the *Delo naroda* detailing—'"

And then the paper rustled, snatched from my grasp. Kazimir moved the documents to a drawer and closed it. When he looked to me, a bit of the old barrier had returned, but my heart was already pounding. Though *Bolshevik activity* could have meant anything—the tips Kazimir received were never too specific—it was not the investigation that had seized my attention.

I chose my words carefully. "I know Kiev well enough."

His eyes narrowed. "You want to be sent away again? Shall I go with you this time, back to the estate?" He grabbed my hips to pull me close once more. "Tell the baron all about how the proletariat corrupted his daughter?" Lascivious, barbed, yet a momentary change crossed his face—almost pained, accusatory, yet too quick to decipher.

"You speak as if I only came here as a girl to create a scandal."

"Were your parents not scandalized when you went home?" He lifted my chin slowly, eyes falling to my lips; then he leaned closer. "What did they say when they heard about the men you'd killed? And that you'd given yourself to a terrorist's son?"

I pushed his hand away. "If I had wanted to go home, I would have asked Uncle Misha to send me home, and he would have. Instead I asked to go to Kiev, then I went to prison, and I am asking to go to Kiev again now." Though I broke his hold, I took a breath. Now was not the time to fight. "Please, Kazimir, I want to help you. Let me investigate."

Let me visit our daughter. The words danced on the tip of my tongue, eager and tantalizing. Withholding this from him was like my time in political imprisonment, torturous and agonizing, yet a necessary sacrifice for the future I envisioned. The truth held the power to save us or shatter us—a triumphant victory or a devastating loss, as volatile and unpredictable as revolution itself.

"If you know the area, very well," he conceded at last. "I'm sending Vera Fyodorovna with you."

My heart rose into my throat. Anyone was better than Vera.

Fanya had been through enough of my schemes with me; I did not want to force her into another, but Kazimir had left me no choice.

"I don't need help, but if you insist, I'll take Fanya."

He shook his head. "Vera made plans to investigate a lead in Petrograd. She can go with you, then you can go to the capital together and return from there."

This wasn't help; this was a guard. All the progress I thought we had made over the past months had been nonexistent. Did he not trust me now any more than he had when I first returned?

"It's been *months*, Kazimir."

"Eight months. Before that, eleven years." His eyes blazed oily black, matching the unexpected sharpness in his voice. "Eleven years without a single word from you—whether you had arrived in Kiev, completed your mission, were imprisoned, dead, or alive, or had returned to the estate."

I opened my mouth, but he wasn't finished.

"I'll never know what happened to you or what you've done this past decade, but I have been here, in Moscow, leading this party. And Vera is one of my most steadfast members."

If he had such faith in Vera—who remained no less suspicious of me than when I had first returned—how could I ever assure him of my intentions? A sudden tremble cut through my rage. "What more am I supposed to do?"

"Whether or not I trust you is irrelevant; given your volatile history, I can't send you away on your own." Kazimir was impassive again, guarded, unyielding. "Vera goes, or you don't."

My choice had been made for me, so it seemed. Every day, I waited for him to accept me; every day, it proved an impossible task.

Chapter 12

Kiev, 3 November 1917

Vera was no more thrilled to accompany me to Kiev than I was to have her; that much was apparent. When we left Hotel Petrov, she insisted on bringing Sergei along, the former soldier who had joined our party in the spring. We rode the train in overwhelming silence before reaching Kiev and settling on the second floor of a small hotel.

Vera settled on the single bed while I stood before the washbasin and mirror, splashing my face and hands after two long days of travel. Sergei was already sitting in the far corner, wrapped in his coat and hat and a few extra blankets, eyes closed as he rested against the wall. Our budget allowed for only one hotel room, and there was only one bed; he had insisted that Vera and I share it, saying he had slept in worse conditions than this while on the front. And indeed he did not seem bothered, his chest already rising and falling steadily.

"What do you know of these Bolshevik rumors?" Vera asked.

"Kazimir's letter included few details. We're supposed to wait here until his contact comes tomorrow morning to give us more information."

After drying my damp skin, I smoothed my hair away from my forehead—alarming gray strands mingling with my blond locks, as though every year in the katorga had aged me a decade. I was not in the mood for talking; instead, I turned to the window. Stared at the reason I had suggested that we stay at this hotel, a former apartment building.

Across the street, snow covered the cluster of buildings in the middle of the block, as it had when I had studied it more than a decade ago. A small school on one side; Saint Anne's Orthodox Church on the other, bedecked with lackluster stained-glass windows and faded blue onion domes topped with three-barred crosses. In the center, flanked by both, was the largest building. Where the children lived.

Within that structure of unimpressive crumbling stone was my daughter. If she was still here. Evening light tinted the sky with gold as employees gradually began to leave the foundling hospital. I memorized each face while looking for one burned into my memory—that of the woman who had picked up my baby.

Perhaps it was too much to hope she still worked at Saint Anne's. Even if the woman was not there anymore, someone would surely know something. The door swung open once, twice, three times, my breath quickening each time. On the fourth, the face appeared, perhaps a decade older than mine, framed by graying auburn hair. She wrapped her coat around herself the way I had once covered my daughter with my own.

I placed my hands on the windowsill, unable to remain upright without its support.

A chill rose from the pane and collided with the sudden heat upon my cheeks, seeping into me, as gripping as the February morning when I had ascended the icy steps at Saint Anne's Foundling Hospital. I had held Tatiana close to my chest, my coat wrapped around us, her skin so warm, so smooth.

This tiny heart that had spent months beating inside me,

now pressed against my own. This little body that filled my arms so perfectly, as if the space had always belonged to her and without her was incomplete. This little one born of a love that was certain to endure once permitted the chance. Her impending absence struck me like a fatal blow.

But I had to pour all my hope into the promise of our future, to let it heal the wound I would carry with me until I held her again, to do what was necessary for her protection even if that meant being apart for now. Only for now.

When I reached the top step, a pair of large eyes had peered at me from the depths of bundled linens. A folded scrap of paper was pinned to the outermost blanket, the note Fanya had written with my daughter's name and birthday, so I checked to make sure it was securely fastened. Then I knelt, smoothed my finger over the light dusting of chestnut hair, soft as down, and brushed my lips over the velvety cheek.

"Soon, my darling," I whispered.

For the first time in so long, I crossed myself as my mother had taught me. Begged God to watch over my daughter. Then gently, so gently, I placed her by the door.

She kicked and screamed, furious with me. I covered my mouth to stifle my own cry, each of hers like a noose around my neck and ropes around my body, strangling me, pulling me closer, preventing me from walking away.

But I had swallowed the tears and hurried to the alley across the street while snow trickled down around me and the ache in my stomach raged, fierce and unforgiving. Moments later, the door opened, revealing auburn hair twisted into a chignon. The woman's mouth dropped open while she scooped up the tiny bundle, looking around as if to see who had left a newborn in the cold.

My daughter had disappeared inside, cradled in another woman's arms. The echoes of her distressed cries remained with me, joining my own sobs as I sank to my knees in the alley, head bowed, tears falling, glistening like icicles against the filthy snow.

* * *

Kiev, 4 November 1917

Early the next morning, Sergei, Vera, and I woke before dawn. As we readied ourselves, a single thought consumed me: how to go to the foundling hospital. I had not come all this way to leave without knowing if my daughter was alive. Nor had I come all this way for Vera or Sergei to discover my purpose.

"When can we expect the contact?" Sergei asked after taking his turn at the washbasin.

"No time was specified, other than morning." Vera indicated the copy of the correspondence Kazimir had given us, laid before her on the bed, then looked to me. "Do you remember this area well enough to find food?"

I nodded, my heart suddenly racing. "I think so."

"Good." She reclined against the headboard. "Sergei and I will wait here."

She was probably hoping the contact would come before I returned, thus preventing me from listening to the conversation. Still, I was not going to dispute my good fortune. I tucked my pistol into my waistband, grabbed my coat, and departed.

The sun had hardly begun to lend color to the sky. Bowed heads and bundled figures hurried by, feet swishing through the snow as I darted down the alley where I had found refuge so long ago. From what I had gathered from the window this morning, the woman I sought had not yet returned for work; I would not move from this place until she arrived, no matter what excuse I had to give Vera and Sergei.

Moments later, I spotted auburn hair beneath a headscarf, waiting for a few streetcars to rumble past before she crossed the street toward Saint Anne's. She spoke to the younger woman beside her—another employee, if I recognized her face—so I hurried to catch them, the knots in my stomach clenching tighter with every step.

"I need to discuss a private matter," I said when I reached them, addressing the woman who had picked up Tatiana. "About one of the children."

She gave her wide-eyed companion a reassuring little nod before responding without hesitation. Without even looking at me. "We're late." With a little nudge, she urged her friend across the street. Away from me.

I was not blind to my ragged appearance, nor deaf to the frantic strain in my voice. Perhaps they thought me mad, or desperate, or attempting to win their trust in order to snatch their handbags.

"It is urgent." I reached for her before pulling my hand away, despite almost drawing the pistol pressed against my lower back, hidden beneath my coat. I left it there. Threats extracted answers but not always the truth. "A moment," I finished softly. "That's all I ask."

Agonizing silence. The younger woman looked to the other. "Olga, should I get help?" She did not bother trying to prevent me from overhearing.

Olga shook her head and waved the other woman along,

then conceded to me with a nod. Brow furrowed, her companion obliged while Olga stepped into the alley, away from the biting wind.

When I faced her, I held up a small pouch. With it came the unmistakable clink of the coins I'd spent these last few months collecting. "This is yours if you give me answers." If she planned on refusing to disclose private information to a stranger, this would encourage her cooperation; I gave her a moment to ponder the offer while she glanced uncertainly from the pouch to me. "Tatiana Kazimirovna Petrova, born in Kiev on the fourth of February 1906 and left at Saint Anne's the next morning along with a note stating those details. What do you know about her?"

"The same as you. We received no further information about the child, her parents, if they were dead or—"

"I asked about the girl, not her parents."

"She does well in her studies, keeps to herself most of the time . . . She's like any child, I suppose."

Confirmation at last. Tatiana was here, safe. My shoulders shook with a tremulous breath; I nearly smelled the newborn I had once cradled against my chest—like fresh, sweet milk, intoxicating. Somehow I had pressed a hand to my abdomen, the place that had kept her safe for so many months. And even after all this time, I had still managed to keep her safe.

When Olga met my gaze, her own shifted—curious.

I looked down, blinking past unexpected tears.

The alley was directly across from Saint Anne's; when chatter floated across the street, I turned. A middle-aged woman led a group of children to the adjoining school building, boys and girls trailing behind her like a tiny army following their general.

"At the front?" I whispered, picking a little girl from the crowd. Olga nodded.

Tatiana was small and slight, as I had been my entire life, her long hair nearly Kazimir's shade but with undertones like mine, golden as honey. She stood proud, shoulders back, footsteps quick and certain, leading the line of children with all the confidence and determination of the staunchest revolutionary. Sunlight stretched across the street, guiding my path to her, urging me to pull her into my arms and keep her there forever.

This time, I did not fight the single tear that escaped down my cheek.

When the children disappeared into the school, I steadied myself while Olga began to move past me. She hesitated when I offered her the bribe, then shook her head, as if to convince herself as much as me.

"No. No, I should not have—"

"We had an agreement. Take it," I said gently. "These are difficult times."

Olga's wary gaze drifted from the pouch to my face and back. Then she accepted it, shoved it into her handbag, and hurried from the alley.

Warmth filled my insides, bright and hot as fire. My daughter was alive. Her father and I were united in our revolutionary cause—even if I was also focused on bringing down my uncle's murderer, the woman he had forbidden me from targeting. When it was over, Tatiana would come home.

I had just emerged from the alley when a hand grabbed my collar and slammed me against the wall. My head struck hard, darkening my vision; I fumbled for my gun, but my assailant held me firmly, then cold metal pressed beneath my chin. I froze, blinking to make out the face before me.

Blond. Hazel eyes.

"This was a test, tsarist. You failed."

The emerald shade in Vera's eyes flashed brighter—mistrust and loathing, as always, joined by triumph. She drove her forearm harder into my chest, pressing against my racing heart. She had sent me on an errand only to follow me.

"No wonder you were so eager to return to Kiev. Tatiana, was it?"

I tensed involuntarily. She had overheard everything. "Please, you have to let me explain."

"You weren't in a katorga at all, were you?" She leaned closer, applying more pressure to the gun. "You've been here raising Kazimir's bastard child, then left her in a foundling hospital and returned to Moscow to destroy the revolution."

"No, that's not—"

"I told him not to let you stay. After he realizes you've been lying to him and working against us, he'll toss your corpse outside your family's estate."

Even if I went to Kazimir with the truth, all she had to do was make a different claim. How had I spent so long anticipating this day only for it to come to this, my future teetering on the cusp of ruin?

"I'm not with the aristocracy!" My voice was shrill as I strained against her hold, my heart pounding faster with every moment. "Do not lie to him."

"Do you expect me to believe a word you say? As for your little bourgeois brat . . ." Lips curled, she leaned closer. "You can watch while the revolutionaries shed every drop of her blood."

Fury struck, sudden and blinding. Surging forward, I grabbed the gun beneath my chin, simultaneously pushing

Vera against the opposite wall amid her startled cry. The impact knocked the revolver from her grip, then I pressed my Browning between her eyes.

I pulled back my slide and released it. *Snap*, sharp and satisfying, announcing a cartridge had slid from the magazine into the chamber. A momentary change swept over Vera's face—regret, perhaps even fear—before the mask of infuriation returned.

A beat passed between us, no sound but our heavy breaths, my rage building until I spoke, slow and controlled.

"Do *not* threaten my daughter."

I touched my finger to the trigger. Her breaths quickened.

Then I raised my pistol, struck her across the face, and watched her collapse at my feet.

Chapter 13

Petrograd, 6 November 1917

Much of my childhood had been spent in Saint Petersburg, strolling down the Nevsky Prospekt, frequenting luxurious French and English shops with Mama. We dined at extravagant restaurants like Donon's and purchased sweets from Papa's favorite patisserie. We attended Orthodox services at Saint Isaac's Cathedral, the bells tolling to accompany us into Divine Liturgy while sunlight glinted off the golden iron dome. But most of my time here had been spent without my parents, trapped behind the elaborate iron grille encasing the Smolny Institute for Noble Maidens.

My mother—Baroness Sofya Vladimirovna Petrova, eldest daughter of Baron Vladimir Vladimirovich Khovansky from Saint Petersburg—had attended Smolny. Therefore, she deemed it the only suitable option for her daughter's preparation for life in court among the ladies of society. I glanced at my skirt, envisioning the little blue uniform dress from those early years, days spent dancing in the grand ball hall, agonizing over penmanship, studying French, plucking harp strings, listening to lectures on antiquated literature and history. Days wishing I were home with Uncle Misha, learning about politics. Discussing the importance of equality and freedom, how wealth distanced us from the common man and blinded us to his plight. Stealing this Browning from my father's collection and practicing as my uncle had taught me.

That was the Saint Petersburg I had known, one of status, decadence, expectation. Now it was Petrograd, renamed following the outbreak of war to sound less German. As I walked with Vera and Sergei, the streets, caked with mud and snow, were crowded with refugees—Poles, Jews, Lithuanians, countless others who had fled the Eastern Front. As in Moscow, women stood in lines for food; men delivered political speeches. Pockmarked buildings lined the Nevsky Prospekt, chunks of brick and stucco stripped away by explosives and bullets; shop windows, if not destroyed or boarded, were dark. An automobile sat idle in the street, riddled with bullet holes; near it, a man's corpse, blood and entrails spilling onto the filthy snow.

The atmosphere was as chilling as the fierce wind that swept over me, yet it crackled with anticipation. These people were waiting for something; whatever it was, I sensed it coming as surely as they did.

A bedraggled little boy rushed by and bumped into me; another pursued him, brandishing a stick, mimicking the patter of machine gun fire. Laughing, the first ducked behind an overturned street vendor cart while Vera ushered us into a simple apartment building.

The single open room on the top floor was so cold I could still see my breath. I assumed it was a Socialist Revolutionary refuge where she stayed whenever she came to Petrograd. She often spent time away from Hotel Petrov, following revolutionary news throughout Moscow, the capital, or wherever it led. I strolled to the window and looked at the distant columns and Palladian front gracing the Smolny Institute—now the Petrograd Soviet headquarters, majority Bolshevik.

During my time at Smolny, I listened and read, uncovering the injustice toward the proletariat for myself, staying in touch with Uncle Misha, secretly attending political rallies whenever possible. None of my lessons had seized my interest as fiercely as the changes taking place outside those walls, changes no one in my family or at the institute acknowledged. No one but my uncle.

Sergei shoved his hands into his coat pockets. "I'll see if I can find food, coal, or wood." His tone indicated he did not expect success.

He departed, leaving me alone with Vera. She stoked what little coal remained in the stove. The flame brightened, illuminating the satisfying purple and green bruise my pistol had left upon her cheek.

Refraining from shooting her had been almost too difficult. She deserved a slow, painful death after threatening a child, *my* child. Shooting her would have kept her from harming Tatiana. From reporting my deception to Kazimir.

But the momentary look she had given me. As though the threat against Tatiana had been insincere, simply meant to intimidate me, and now she couldn't take it back and was preparing to die for it. It was the only time her typical disdain had ever faltered. The break was all I could trust with complete certainty. And killing her would have meant more secrets, more lies.

After she regained consciousness, I led the way back to the hotel, and we proceeded to Petrograd. Sergei did not reveal what he had learned from Kazimir's contact, though I presumed he told Vera; I had no idea if the information was connected to her mission here or something else entirely.

Now we were alone again for the first time since our

confrontation, so she turned to me, eyes gold against the gray dusk pouring through the window. "Why didn't you shoot me?"

Silence stretched between us. Hostile, expectant.

"If you want to tell Kazimir I lied about my purpose in Kiev and convince him that I'm a tsarist, I can't stop you." Unless I changed my mind about killing her, though doing so would hardly encourage Kazimir to find favor with me. "Regarding Tatiana . . ." I swallowed hard. "One day it will be safe for her to be with her parents. All I want is to give her that chance."

This time, her brow softened. Perhaps something about the girl resonated with her more than she cared to acknowledge.

"You and I are on the same side, Vera," I said softly.

Her eyes narrowed into slits.

"The same side?" she reiterated with a scoff. "After Tsar Nikolai's coronation, while he and his wife enjoyed their ball, do you know where I was? Khodynka Field in Moscow—my parents, siblings, and myself."

A pit settled in my stomach while Vera waited, perhaps to see if I understood how this story ended. And I did. The swarms of peasants and descendants of emancipated serfs surging to accept their commemorative cups, gingerbread, and other such meaningless gifts from the royal family. The ensuing madness. The panic.

She blinked, eyes glistening; the next words broke. "I was only a few years old."

"Don't." I shook my head. "You don't have to—"

"Papa scooped me into his arms," she went on, as if determined to make me aware of every horrific detail. "Assured me he'd keep me safe. And he did, while everyone around us screamed and bled and died. Most of my siblings were trampled or succumbed to their injuries."

So many lives lost in such a senseless tragedy. Even if I'd known what to say, I had no words to reply.

"Where were you, Svetlana?" Her voice rose as she stepped closer, then a sudden tear escaped, though her accusatory gaze did not falter. "Where were you while I was in Khodynka Field?"

I had been a child myself; still, I forced a response. "Smolny Institute."

A flicker of disgust—but not surprise—crossed her face, tightening the knot in my stomach. Vera turned away, brushing the moisture from her cheek. Silence fell over us.

When I'd heard whispered rumors of the stampede in Khodynka Field, claiming hundreds of peasant lives, I'd waited for news of the tsar's concern or sympathy. He did nothing. He attended his ball.

Such indifference from the man who was supposed to care for his people. From nearly everyone at the institute. From the upper class. Even while confined to Smolny, I was aware of the dissatisfaction brewing across the country. Change was needed; change was coming.

I learned about those changes throughout the next decade, then one January evening a few days after Bloody Sunday, I begged my parents not to send me back to the institute, as I always did when visiting home. Told them about the massacre that had just occurred in Saint Petersburg. Papa insisted on my return to Smolny, forbade political talk, while my mother lounged on the ivory brocade sofa, her heavy sigh of reproach breaking the tense silence: *You would be such a sweet, pretty little thing if you were not so difficult, my darling.*

The next morning, my parents sent me back; this time, upon reaching Saint Petersburg, I boarded the first available train to

Moscow. To Hotel Petrov, Uncle Misha, and his Socialist Revolutionary Party.

But my attempt to sympathize was not what Vera needed now. Not when my story was as simple as moving from one place to the next while hers was rife with suffering. So I stayed silent until she spoke again, her voice steadier now.

"Bloody Sunday. Where were you?"

Heat rose to my cheeks. "Smolny."

"You were there"—she pointed out the window—"and I was nearby at the Winter Palace with my parents and remaining brother. My parents argued over taking me with them, and I just wanted them to stop. To reach an agreement."

"They took you to the march?" I whispered, recalling the event and the ensuing conversation with my parents, both of which had prompted me to leave the institute. "Even after Khodynka Field?"

She placed her fingertips on the glass pane, staring outside. "All the crowd wanted was to present a workers' petition. Papa insisted it would be peaceful. That he would keep me safe. The Imperial Guard made certain he failed." Another unsteady breath. Another tear. "After that, I was alone."

I blinked back my own tears. If not for Uncle Misha, I never would have understood how broken our society was. While my family wallowed in opulence, the countrymen outside our estate struggled for rights, for their desires to be heard. Those like Vera's family.

No wonder she despised me. I represented a society that had taken a child's entire family from her.

She looked to me, eyes bright, voice shaky but sure. "While your kind enjoyed their privileged lives, mine were slaughtered. And now you think you have something to offer our cause? Something worth leaving your child without her parents?"

Heat found my cheeks, this time from fury. Protecting my child did not count as *leaving* her. The results of the revolution determined Tatiana's future; every decision I made was with her in mind.

I opened my mouth to retort, but Vera had already turned her back.

"Understanding is not as simple as professing the same political allegiance. You and I will *never* be on the same side."

* * *

VERA LEFT FOR the evening to investigate rumors circulating about the Bolsheviks. What those rumors were, she refused to reveal. And she refused to let me come.

"If Svetlana tries to leave, shoot her," she said to Sergei before the door closed. Apparently she didn't intend to reciprocate the mercy I had extended to her in Kiev.

I spent her absence pacing from the window to the opposite wall and back. "Either come with me or let me go," I said to Sergei for the hundredth time.

From his seat on the bed, he pulled his sheepskin *ushanka* lower over his short blond hair so the flaps covered his ears. "I'm not going anywhere, and neither are you."

With a huff, I returned to the window. Despite the distance, I picked out barricades of firewood surrounding Smolny, cannons, tiny dots indicating soldiers. There would be trouble tonight. I tasted it as surely as the sourness refusing to leave my mouth. Vera knew why Petrograd felt as if it were lying in wait. For what, I didn't know, but it likely involved the Bolsheviks. The thought made my hand stray toward my pistol.

I didn't draw it, so as not to give Sergei the wrong idea. No need to encourage him to take Vera's orders to heart.

Outside, a steady rhythm broke the quiet. The tramping of hundreds, even thousands, of feet. I opened the window and leaned out, ignoring Sergei's curses when an icy breeze swept in.

Even from this height, they were unmistakable. Soldiers— Red Guards—brandishing Bolshevik flags as proudly as their rifles. Some on foot, others on horseback, armored cars accompanying the ranks. They marched from every direction, setting up roadblocks, while others moved toward the railways, post office, banks, palaces, and government buildings.

By the time I slammed the window, Sergei had already reached me, blocking my path. "Don't, Svetlana." One hand rested on his pistol.

I didn't move. His hand fell, satisfied he had deterred me. I was nearly half his size; what I lacked in his brute strength, I outmatched in wits. When Sergei turned, I snatched his pistol from its holster.

He backed away hastily. "Don't shoot."

"A big soldier, afraid of a tiny bullet?" I lifted one eyebrow.

His throat bobbed as he swallowed hard, then he spoke softly, eyes on the pistol. "I saw what bullets do to men . . . that's why I left the front. I will do what I must for the revolution, but I don't want to die like that."

"Fair enough." Lowering the gun, I nodded toward the bottle of brandy he'd brought back from scavenging. "Drink that and let me go. If Vera finds out, we'll tell her I got you drunk and slipped out when you fell asleep."

He hesitated, then nodded, so I returned his weapon. As he accepted it, I caught his hand, prompting him to lift his clear blue eyes to mine. Anyone else assigned to guard a nobleman's daughter would have spent these last hours ridiculing me. Condemning me. Perhaps forcing himself upon me. Might have shot me, later claiming he had been doing his duty. Sergei had kept to himself, quiet and pensive, and now was permitting me to explore the unrest sweeping through the streets below.

As I let the gesture communicate my sincere gratitude, he gave another small nod, then I released him right as the door swung open.

"Let's go." Vera motioned for us to hurry, then proceeded down the hallway as we followed. "The Bolsheviks have already seized control of the railways, so we might need to find a car, but we have to get back to Moscow."

"What's happening? What have they done?" When she ignored me, I caught her shoulders and forced her to face me. "Tell me, Vera!"

Her eyes narrowed, but her tone was even. "Lenin is back in Russia."

It was like every time my bullet met its mark, when I witnessed my target's reaction—shock first, then understanding, then the pain set in.

It's no secret Lenin always wanted to remove the Provisional Government from power. Maybe this is a reminder. The observation made by the man I had encountered when I'd investigated Orlova's recent victim in Moscow.

The dead man had supported the Provisional Government, and Orlova had not targeted him to serve as a reminder; it had been a warning. A warning of what was to come and was now under way: Lenin's return was a direct threat against the existing powers, the balance between classes, everything.

Sergei found my forearm, urging me along. I stepped after Vera into the dark night, where the cold pierced me to my core.

Chapter 14

Moscow, 16 November 1917

More than a week since Vera, Sergei, and I had returned from Petrograd. Since then, the Bolshevik uprising had extended to Moscow and the streets had been overflowing with bodies and blood.

As I sheltered beneath a portico, I pressed my chattering teeth together. In the distance beneath the dull gray sky stood the redbrick walls and towers surrounding the Kremlin, its complex of soaring churches and grand palaces withering beneath heavy artillery fire. Clusters of Red Army soldiers spread across the Red Square, surging toward the crumbling brick and stone, holes gaping like empty eye sockets.

As a few White Army soldiers galloped by on horseback, I sank deeper into the shadows, then emerged from hiding. I had only paused to catch my breath; I would not go back to Hotel Petrov until I found him.

An impossible task, perhaps, considering the throngs of people, the casualties, the endless number of places he might be. But we had only been separated for a few hours; whether he was filling his enemies with bullets or had already given his life for the revolution, I would find Kazimir Grigoryevich.

My next breath shook; I clutched my pistol tighter to steady myself.

The repetitive whir of machine gun fire pierced the distant sounds of battle. At once, I darted behind an armored car, wincing when my knee struck a sheet of ice on the ground. I crouched low, breath forming clouds, then reloaded my magazine while I waited.

Snow settled on my dry, cracked skin, the car, the corpse beside me. A casualty from the earlier days of the fighting, I presumed, more preserved due to the cold.

A few sudden cries indicated the machine gun had located targets. I clenched my jaw but stayed hidden, examining the bayonet gash on my thigh. Bleeding again. One of my older injuries, the scab recently broken.

The gunfire ceased. I peered up the street, assessing the rest of my route—clear, though a few lingering flames licked a bookstore doorway while debris and still forms dotted the streets like empty bullet casings. Head down, I crawled toward the hood, found the machine gun on a nearby rooftop, straightened to shoot—but I slipped on a slick pool of blood and grabbed the car for balance instead. The steady *rat-a-tat*, bullets ricocheting around me, a sharp pain across my shoulder; cursing, I ducked, pressing my hand to my torn coat, where a vermillion stain seeped through. The bullet hadn't lodged, so I gritted my teeth, rose, aimed.

Two shots, and it was done.

Across the snowy, muddy street was a tobacconist shop; inside, a shock of tousled dark hair caught my attention. My heart leaped as I narrowed my eyes against the snowfall, trying to make out the figure.

Keeping low, shoulder throbbing, accompanied by nearby screams and gunfire, I dodged a corpse with a bullet hole through his neck. Another whose chest and stomach had been laid open by a bayonet. Near the bookstore, another covered in extensive burns—skin black, red, and peeling, hair almost completely singed, one hand all but charred. My eyes lingered only long enough to confirm none were the man I sought.

The shop door hung loose on its hinges; the windows were shattered. Shivering, blinded by sudden dizziness, I stumbled inside and leaned against the doorframe.

Kazimir—alive, pistol in hand, surrounded by ransacked boxes of cigars, cigarettes, pipes, ashtrays, and other merchandise—stood before the couple behind the counter. I wanted to collapse into his arms, overwhelmed by exhaustion and relief. I wanted his embrace, his care tending my injury, his assurance that he was unharmed. Instead, as I applied pressure to my wound, teeth chattering too violently to speak, not even Kazimir noticed me. He was dragging the man into the center of the room.

"We're not tsarists," the woman was saying as she trailed helplessly behind him amid the man's curses.

Blood seeped through my fingers. My relief vanished, replaced by a sudden chill. These people were simple shop owners, not wealthy aristocrats or government officials. If he saw me, focused on me, it might deter him . . .

"Take money, goods, anything," the woman went on. "What else do you want?"

Kazimir tossed an empty wine bottle aside; it shattered against the floor. He released the man but aimed at his forehead, slurring his words. "Bourgeois blood."

"Don't!" When he turned to the woman, she stepped back with a tremulous whisper. "Please, we have a son."

A son. Suddenly my heart felt like the wine bottle, shattered and in ruins.

The lines across Kazimir's brow deepened. "Did you ever write to the tsar, begging him to spare your husband's life for the sake of your three-year-old son?"

"Kazimir." I spoke cautiously so as not to startle him; only the couple glanced at me. He continued, oblivious to my presence.

"When you contacted countless members of the bourgeoisie, asking for help to change the tsar's mind, did each one refuse?"

"Kazimir, these people do not work for the imperial government." I took a tiny step closer, pleading for this family, for their child. "They were not involved in—"

"Did the tsar deny your request to see your husband in prison?" He was almost yelling now as he addressed the woman, his gun trained on the man, my heart pounding faster and faster. "And after your husband had been hanged, did your son ever forget the sound of his mother's weeping, or how the bourgeoisie had spurned her, or how he spent the next few years watching grief slowly kill her?"

Silence fell, broken only by distant gunshots and indiscernible shouts outside. My voice failed me, consumed by the pain in my shoulder and ache in my chest as I watched Kazimir, his steady aim. If he would look at me, just look at me—

The woman's eyes glimmered, then she bowed her head in resignation. "Lord, have mercy." She crossed herself while speech gave way to tears.

Kazimir's lips twisted with disdain as he looked from her to the man. "Neither your Lord nor your tsar had mercy on my family."

The gunshot coupled with her scream. The man collapsed, part of his skull ripped off by the bullet. Crimson blood seeped across the floor, fleeing from the destruction, the death, the sob piercing the quiet. Perhaps the woman's. Perhaps my own.

A flash of sudden movement toward the woman, then a cry sprang from my throat as if on its own accord.

"Kazimir!"

He spun, face and beard splattered in bloody droplets, pistol directed toward me. The ruthless gleam gave way to recognition. He lowered his weapon.

"Go," I said to her. She pressed shaking hands to her chest, tears streaking down her cheeks, and rushed past me through the ruined doors.

Kazimir glared while the knot in my throat urged me to curse him for what he had done, but it was useless while he was so enraged. Such rage was meant to be directed at the enemy, not innocents.

I swallowed, fighting to keep my voice calm. "Come back to the hotel. You need to rest."

"I don't take orders from the bourgeoisie."

So acrimonious, I nearly winced. The more time he spent among the fighting and pillaging, the more he gave me this attitude. And Vera hadn't even told him I'd lied about Kiev yet. Though he stashed his gun, I pressed my lips together while he crossed the room toward me.

He seized me so abruptly I gasped, fighting to loosen his grip on my injury while wine and cigarette smoke enveloped me, accompanied by his growl. "It is not your place to interfere."

No scathing rebuke was enough to distract me from his tight hold, the agony even worse than the bullet's initial strike. Trying and failing to pull his fingers away, I landed a kick on his shin with a furious yet desperate cry. "My shoulder!"

The fierce light vanished from his eyes. He let go as if I had scalded him, stared at my blood on his palm; with a sharp breath, I swayed. When I braced myself against the wall, his hands found me again, this time gentle, steadying. I pushed them away.

Pain flared, slicing down my arm the way a sudden ache sliced through my chest. The room swirled. This man, the father of my child; yet in his voice such fury, intensified by disgust, pain, even longing.

After a telltale rip, he eased my coat off. I had no energy to protest while he tightened a fragment of his shirt around the injury, creating a makeshift bandage. His hands fell to my waist; again, I pushed them away.

The couple had said they were not tsarists. Perhaps they supported the revolutionary cause, perhaps not. He had not bothered to find out. He had seen only their class. And if such bloodlust carried beyond revolution, beyond this moment, possibly over to me, to our child, then the future I envisioned for us was impossible.

"Their son," I whispered at last.

A heavy sigh—indicating slight remorse, I suspected, instilling within me a little flicker of reassurance despite the words that followed. "The boy will grow up without his father's bourgeois influence."

The truth I withheld from him burned my insides, its immense power threatening to spill over, to destroy us, hinging upon the answer to the question that now tore through me as easily as a bullet.

"Bourgeois influence?" I repeated softly. "If I had a child, is that what I would be?"

His shuddering breath fell hot upon my skin. "Would you

be, Sveta?" Quiet, unsteady. His eyes found mine—dark, raw, surrounded by crimson bloodstains.

The man blinded by fury was no more; instead, he regarded me with everything so often shielded from me, even from himself—sorrow, agony, hope, even fear. As though he expected me to walk away.

Was it my background? My decade-long disappearance? Both? Whatever was inhibiting him, surely the truth would eradicate his concerns. Once he knew what I had done to protect our daughter from bourgeois influence and proletariat hatred. Once we raised her together. The same dedication we had poured into vengeance and revolution, we would pour into each other. Our family.

Unless he rejected a life spent with a former noblewoman or a child with aristocratic blood. Unless the ruthless man I had glimpsed today returned to taint us beyond repair.

The truth wielded the ability to redeem or destroy; for now, we waited, washed in its shadows, anticipating its choice.

* * *

I left Kazimir among the carnage he had created and continued to Hotel Petrov alone. Suddenly I needed to be far from the hands that had sent a bullet into an innocent man, from the eyes that had regarded me with such fury, from the voice that had dripped with condemnation. He had watched me walk to the door, an almost desperate look nearly powerful enough to encourage me to remain. Perhaps I might have, if he had voiced the plea aloud or assured me of his faith in me. Instead, he said nothing. So I checked my magazine—one bullet left—before returning to the street.

Smoke clogged my lungs as I walked, then the crack of

multiple gunshots sounded behind me—distant, yet close enough to make me press against the nearest brick building for shelter. I adjusted my gun, turning, seeing no one; still, it had sounded too close to ignore. I proceeded toward the sound; the icy air eased my throbbing shoulder, where I'd bled through Kazimir's bandage. Then I adjusted my grip, rounded the corner, and tripped over the corpse propped against the building.

Blood spilled down his chest, blown open by multiple bullets; his eyes were not bloodshot, but there was a single, deliberate slash beneath each one. The paper in his mouth revealed her name in its usual red script. I crumpled it in my fist. Usually, Orlova killed her victims elsewhere and planted their bodies; this time, she had killed a man on the street, and I'd heard it happen. She was near.

The tracks in the snow were too muddled to follow, but I hadn't passed anyone on my way to the corpse, so she must have gone another way. A little thrill spurred me onward; I'd suspected she would take advantage of the chaos to stage an attack. All I had to do was find her.

When I rounded the next corner, I froze. Halfway down the street, a woman kept a swift pace, clutching a pistol, wearing a red armband. A Bolshevik.

Had fortune finally led me to the woman I'd longed to target since returning from the katorga? My final shot belonged to her; as Orlova went, so would a significant piece of Bolshevik influence. My uncle's murderer. After my mission was complete and once the Bolshevik uprising failed, I'd tell Kazimir about Tatiana myself; whatever Vera planned to tell him would cease to matter. Once this was over, surely the Bolsheviks would be suppressed. We could be with our daughter.

I drew a breath. Advanced a few steps. Took aim at the woman's turned back.

When a gasping cry came from the alley beside me, I stayed my hand. A Red Guard soldier held a young woman by the shoulders while she fought against him. A rifle lay idle at his feet and a revolver some meters away, evidently knocked from the woman's grasp. His voice carried to me.

"No money? Nothing?" He forced her face-first against the wall and pressed close. "Then you can give me something else." He brushed back the hair obscuring her face.

Vera Fyodorovna.

I looked up the street. The Bolshevik woman—Orlova, if my assumptions were correct—was about to round the corner. And I had one shot left.

"Don't, please don't." Vera's breathless voice rose as the soldier caught her skirt. "Stop, let me go!" She gasped when my only bullet tore through her assailant's abdomen.

He screamed, fell, and she stayed still, coat splattered in his blood, eyes wide. I tucked my Browning into my waistband, rushed to scoop up Vera's revolver—empty.

The soldier clutched his stomach, glaring at me, mouth twisted in agony before he managed a raspy jeer. "You missed."

"I never miss." Standing over him, I picked up his rifle. "Did you expect me to aim mercifully rather than let you die slowly?"

When I hurried back to the street, the Bolshevik woman was no longer in sight. She couldn't be far. I rushed toward the end of the block, checking the rifle as I went—nothing. And when I reached the corner, the street was empty.

My chance to eliminate Orlova, gone.

I threw the rifle with as much force as I could muster but

groaned when my shoulder protested. After the worst of the pain passed, I proceeded with unsteady steps. Not far to the hotel, and it was unsafe to linger on the streets without ammunition.

Footsteps sounded behind me. I gritted my teeth and reached for my pistol. Even empty, it could leave a few bruises. Before I drew it, hands found me. Vera pulled me along without slowing her pace but released me once I matched it.

"Keep up, tsarist. I may not have any more bullets, but if you give me a reason to need them, I will find someone who does."

Frigid air stung my eyes, carrying faint traces of gunpowder, smoke, and blood. "You question my loyalty after I killed a man to save you?"

"You're not a Bolshevik. Of course you killed a Red Guard soldier," she snapped, though her voice slightly wavered. Shaken more than she cared to admit, I suspected, but rejecting compassion or pity—especially mine.

I caught her arm, pulling her to a halt. Even if she never believed another word out of my mouth, she had to believe this: I shot the soldier for what he intended to do, regardless of his loyalties or my own.

Her resentment shifted as it had when I had pressed my gun to her forehead; this time the change was not regret or fear. This was simple understanding, gratitude for the woman before her in our world of blood and politics and men.

Vera broke my hold and pressed on. I wrapped numb fingers around my wound, cold and pain clinging to me while we trekked through slush and filth, blood and carnage. I kept my eyes on the path ahead, but Vera's remained on the ground beneath our feet.

* * *

BACK AT THE hotel, Vera and I stepped over a few corpses and let ourselves inside. Broken glass and furniture lay scattered about the lobby, where one man mopped blood from the floor while another staggered by, clutching a bloodstained thigh until others rushed forward to support him. The air was thick with chatter as party members tended to one another and cleaned up, then Fanya broke through the crowd, pausing before me. Perhaps it was my bloody arm that shocked her, or Vera at my side.

"Where is Kazimir?" Vera asked before she could speak.

"Upstairs."

Did she intend to deliver her report on Kiev? She set off, while Fanya and I followed; I clutched my wound tighter to prevent my hands from shaking.

"The Bolsheviks broke in, but they didn't get far," Fanya supplied for me as we walked. "We finished them off in the lobby."

"We?" I murmured.

She offered a half smile. "My vision doesn't prevent me from picking out a red armband."

Upstairs, Vera knocked on Kazimir's door and pushed it open. The harsh scents of disinfectant and antiseptic filled the room. Kazimir had cleaned up and now sat on his bed while Yelizaveta gathered bandages and medications. He met my gaze—without animosity. The tension in my shoulders lessened while he gestured from Yelizaveta to me, so Fanya removed my coat for her to tend my injury.

"Reports from a few different contacts," Vera announced,

easing my concerns slightly. "An uprising has taken place in Kiev."

That explained what had caused the rumors we had been sent to investigate. "It was successful?" Kazimir muttered while we traded places so Yelizaveta could treat me.

Vera nodded. "For the Bolsheviks."

"And in Petrograd?"

"Lenin worked with the Petrograd Soviet at Smolny to stage a coup d'état. They stormed the Winter Palace."

Her voice broke a little upon naming the place where the last of her family members had been slaughtered, now home to the Provisional Government's cabinet sessions. I looked at her to extend my sympathy, whether it was welcome or not. She met my gaze without as much hostility, then continued.

"After the Provisional Government surrendered, Lenin created a Council of People's Commissars, the Sovnarkom."

"He can't do that." I stood, dodging Yelizaveta's hand when she tried to press a cloth to my wound; she pushed me back onto the bed with a disapproving frown. "Moscow is not finished yet."

Kazimir offered a little nod, sending a rush of warmth through me. The uprising in Moscow had not been quick, nor bloodless, nor would we let Bolshevik victories deter us. Kazimir understood this, as did I; we were committed to victory, a commitment that bound us to one another, to our daughter, to the life we might have once I had the freedom to be honest with him. To make him fully understand.

"The Bolsheviks secured control of the Kremlin."

Upon Vera's quiet, heavy statement, I stood so quickly that I almost made Yelizaveta drop her cloth. I had witnessed the battle raging at the Kremlin today; surely it had not fallen. Kazimir froze for an instant, then shook his head.

"Sveta is right." He snatched his pistol from his desk and proceeded toward the door. "Moscow is still fighting, so—"

"Kazimir." Gentle yet firm, as Vera placed a hand on his arm. When he paused, I found the dread that pierced my insides reflected on his face.

My breaths quickened as Kazimir passed a hand over his beard. The pain from Yelizaveta's antiseptic was negligible compared to the sudden tightness inside me.

"It's done?" he asked wearily.

The pit in my stomach intensified.

"Aside from a few lingering skirmishes, yes. The Bolsheviks have taken complete control."

The report was a crushing weight, pressing down until I nearly gasped for breath. This could not last. My daughter was not going to live beneath the oppression of a one-party dictatorship. Such an existence would be wrought with persecution and bloodshed, little difference from the Old Regime.

Mila

June 1941–June 1942

Chapter 15

Vitebsk Region, 22 June 1941

All I knew about my grandmother was that she was blind. My grandfather directed the horse and wagon down the dirt road, approaching the small wooden fence surrounding the farmhouse; each jostle tightened the knot in my stomach. Why hadn't I been more persistent in my attempts to learn about Mama's parents? Dedushka seemed nice enough, but his wasn't the name that always brought a scowl to my mother's face. Still, even if I'd begged Mama to tell me about whatever had happened between her and her mother, my pleas would have been met with the usual response: *Stop prying, Mila.*

A gust of wind rumpled my skirt while Dedushka tucked the letter I'd given him into his pocket. Before I'd boarded the train from Leningrad, Mama had written to him and had given me a similar letter, proof of our identities. When I reached the station in Obol and found the white-bearded man holding Mama's correspondence, I hoped her letter had fallen into the proper hands. It was my only means of identifying the man taking me to my new—temporary—home.

The horse pressed onward while the rickety wagon groaned, as frustrated as I was. Of all the places in the Soviet Union, why Byelorussia—and, worse, why such a remote region? The wooden farmhouse was a brown speck in a vast sea of nothingness. No neighbors, no busy streets like Leningrad. Just grassy fields, a pale open sky, a dirt road, and the outline of a distant forest.

When we stopped, my grandfather tethered the horse to a tall wooden post. I followed him through the gate and across the yard while chickens squawked, annoyed we had disturbed them. Leningrad tugged at me, calling me back, and I would have answered if I'd had the means—with or without the rumor of advancing German soldiers.

When the door creaked, I followed Dedushka into a large open room as if we had stepped into the last century. Across almost half the back wall, from floor to ceiling, stretched the *pech*, a massive clay stove like something out of a folktale. A single painted tile rested within the white clay, perched above the arched hearth, drawing the eye to what lay inside. A wooden bench extended from the stove to the adjacent wall, wider than the small bench running around the perimeter of the room, where I set my valise.

I had no more time to take in my surroundings before she reached me.

Mama had referred to her mother as *that bitch* on more than one occasion. To my disappointment, the woman wasn't the towering, fearsome presence of my imagination. She was petite—slight build, sharp features, deep gray hair. Underwhelming.

Without greeting, she touched my forearm, presumably to locate me, then captured my cheeks between her hands. The unexpected gesture almost pulled a gasp from my throat. Despite the urge to cringe away from her touch, I held still while she explored my face with callused fingers. No bump or line or curve escaped her detection. Her sightless brown eyes didn't always focus on me, but when they did, they were so piercing I could have sworn her blindness was a ruse.

"Mila," she said after releasing me. That was all.

Her voice was strong, certain, yet barbed at its edges, as though already frustrated after knowing me for all of one minute. How she had earned the description as *that bitch* was starting to feel like less of a mystery.

"I'll send word that Mila arrived safely," Dedushka said before excusing himself to put the horse away, leaving me alone with the old woman.

My entire life, I'd known her only through occasional letters—ones my mother skimmed, discarded, rarely answered, never permitted me to read. Maybe she was glad to meet me. Maybe she'd felt coerced into accepting me as a houseguest per Mama's request, given the threat of a possible fascist takeover from Western Europe. Maybe she didn't want me here any more than I wanted to be here. It was impossible to tell—she was like Mama in that way. Her face betrayed little, her words even less.

She spooned loose black tea leaves into a chipped teapot that looked as ancient as she was and filled it with steaming water from the copper samovar on the wooden table. Near it was a small spread—black bread, strawberry jam, smoked herring, fresh tomatoes and cucumbers tossed with dill and sour cream. As she fetched plates and cups, my heart thudded while my mind silently cried out to my grandfather, imploring him to come back. His presence might ease the tension heating my insides like the water boiling inside the samovar.

"Sit," she said at last—so direct I nearly flinched as if it had been a reprimand. "The tea should be ready now."

As I sipped tea and nibbled a few bites, my grandmother's expression was so indifferent I almost would have preferred the look I'd found on my mother's face when she had announced she was sending me away. Like she considered me a child, an inconvenience, helpless and in need of protecting.

"If the Germans really do intend to break the Nonaggression Pact between our countries, I'll accompany Papa to Kirovsky Zavod in the morning," I had said, offering every possible solution to change Mama's mind while I paced around our one-room apartment. "The factory will need workers to aid the war effort, and I'm eighteen, so—"

"You will go to the Vitebsk Region until I say otherwise." Mama stayed seated on the small bed, Babushka's latest letter in hand. "It's already been arranged."

I paced, step by aggravated step. Cowards ran away. Not patriots. The Russian revolutionaries had fought against imperialism a few short decades ago, when Mama was a child; the German fascists would try to reestablish class structures like the ones our country had torn down. Did my mother not recognize the need to fight against oppressive powers once again? Revolutionary women had joined political parties and marched in protest across the Liteyny Bridge and along the Nevsky Prospekt; how could I walk those same routes every day without feeling compelled to defend all they had accomplished?

I sat, reached for my mother, but she snatched her hand away. Whether to prevent my touch or to keep me from the letter, I wasn't certain. "Please, Mama. Let me help. Let me stay." *With you,* I resisted including even as my chest tightened. Such an appeal never worked, certainly not when she was stiff, removed, as she always was when discussing her mother.

She pushed a lock of brown hair from her face and stood, taking the letter with her. "Pack your belongings. Your train leaves first thing in the morning."

It was our last conversation before a brief goodbye. The same tightness found my chest now, constricting more severely the longer I sat. As Babushka refilled her tea, I rose and strolled across the wooden floor. Near the far window, a radio faintly crackled—a small comfort, knowing a broadcast reached this area—and a flowering shrub grew in a large pot. The plant stood a few meters tall, wide leaves resembling stars, vibrant pink burs covered in spikes, though they didn't appear sharp at the ends.

"Well," I said, raising my voice so it carried while I reached for one of the bulbs to test my theory, "if you'll show me where to put my things, I'll—"

A firm hand latched onto my wrist when I was mere centimeters from the blossom, eliciting my startled cry as the hand jerked me back. Whirling, I found myself face-to-face with my grandmother's fury. Her free hand grabbed my other arm, capturing me in a shockingly strong hold.

"Did you touch the plant?" When I attempted to twist out of her grasp, she gave me a quick shake, her voice louder, sharper. "Did you touch the plant?"

"No," I said hastily, though my pitch sounded far too high; age failed to affect the tightness of Babushka's grip, one proving impossible to break. "How did you know?"

"From the location of your voice. Didn't your parents teach you to stay away from things you know nothing about?"

"It's just a plant!"

"A castor oil plant." Though the snap brought my struggles to a halt, my silence must have indicated the name meant nothing to me. "It's poisonous, stupid girl."

With that, she released me. I stumbled away until my back collided with the wall. My unsteady breaths pierced the thick silence while Babushka returned to her tea. Glancing at my wrist, I brushed my finger over the bright red marks left by her grip.

That bitch lurked in her depths; now she had risen to the surface. Mama and Papa had been desperate to save me from the impending German invasion, so they had sentenced me to this instead. My parents had delivered me into the hands of a lunatic. She'd poison me, and then they would be sorry, but it would be too late because I'd be gone. I would have been better off staying in Leningrad and taking my chances with the Fritzes.

"Castor oil itself isn't poisonous and has its benefits," Babushka said, her tone more even now. "I keep the plant inside most months because it thrives in warmer climates, but I never touch it without gloves. Some develop a rash from the leaves alone, and if ingested, the seeds are powerful enough to kill."

If she intended the explanation to be a comfort, she didn't succeed. As I swallowed to eliminate the dryness in my throat, the radio broadcast announced an interruption due to a special message from the Soviet foreign minister, Vyacheslav Mikhailovich Molotov. One stating that it was safe for me to return home, surely. I turned up the volume.

"Without a declaration of war, German troops attacked our country, attacked our borders at many points—"

I was so intent on listening that I didn't see the hand reaching for the radio until it clicked off. Scowling at Babushka, I turned it back on.

"The Red Army and the whole nation will wage a victorious patriotic war for our beloved country, for honor, for liberty," Molotov continued; again, Babushka silenced him.

With a huff, I flipped the switch and covered it with my hand, blocking it long enough to hear the end of the speech.

"Our cause is just. The enemy will be beaten. Victory will be ours!"

Amid cheers and fanfare, the broadcast ended. I had tried so hard to convince my parents the invasion wouldn't happen—whatever it took to persuade them to let me stay in Leningrad—but now it had. War had arrived.

Tightness returned to my chest. If the soldiers came—*when* they came—I'd do as Molotov advised and resist them, though this place was safe enough, I supposed. What would soldiers want with a tiny village? But Leningrad was a key industrial city. An obvious target. Leningrad, where my parents had remained.

My next breath evaded me before I drew a steadying one. With every Soviet rallying around Molotov's call to arms, a German defeat was certain. Maybe the Fritzes wouldn't even reach Leningrad. Maybe the war would end quickly, my parents and home would remain unscathed, and I wouldn't be trapped in this region long, after all.

A hand pushed mine aside—Babushka, seeking the switch, promptly turning it off. "Don't fill your head with such nonsense."

"Nonsense?" I repeated with a dubious laugh while she gathered the used dishes. "This is about our country's future."

"A future determined by the armies and no one else. You were sent here to avoid the conflict, not throw yourself into it."

"Did you avoid the conflict when the tsar was overthrown? Weren't you at least tempted to participate in the revolution?"

"The revolution is not your concern. Neither is this war." Measured but laced with warning, similar to the tone Mama used before a *Stop prying, Mila* followed.

Had my grandmother been a tsarist? Impossible. Mama wasn't—unless that was why she and her mother were at odds. Having lived through a civil war, born of a generation that had fought for rights and equality, surely Babushka had *some* political opinion, even if her visual impairment might have limited her involvement. But the more I tried to decipher her thoughts behind her stony exterior, the more I was convinced of her indifference. For whatever reason, she simply didn't care.

No wonder Mama had broken ties with this woman. How could she get along with someone who had no regard for government or country?

While she placed the dishes in the sink, grabbed a nearby pitcher, doused them with water, and began to scrub, I tried again. "Molotov said the *whole* nation. Everyone has a part to play in the war, even if not on the battlefront."

"Not us."

I directed a glower at the back of her head. "Maybe not *you*, but—"

Babushka slammed her hands against the counter, making a few dishes rattle. "Not. Us."

The words were so sharp they cut down any response I might have made. I stepped back. Though out of reach, I hadn't forgotten the tightness of her grip. Slowly, Babushka turned to face me.

"Do not get involved, Mila." Sharp but quieter, even strained. More of a threat than a warning.

My hands shook, whether from rage or fear or a combination of both, I didn't know. If Babushka didn't care about political news, fine, but she couldn't prevent me from staying informed. And the old woman was an idiot if she thought she had dissuaded me from joining the patriotic war. I'd fight the fascists when they arrived, one way or another. Even if I had been forced to live with the only Soviet who had no interest in her country's fate.

Whoever or whatever else she was, I had learned this about my grandmother: Svetlana Vasilyevna Petrova was no patriot.

Chapter 16

Vitebsk Region, 23 June 1941

C ome," Babushka said briskly the morning after Molotov's announcement.

I swallowed a groan. Dedushka had already gone into the fields; did she not have farmwork to do too? My time alone was my opportunity to listen to the radio without interference. As Babushka gathered a small woven basket, a knife, and rubber gloves, I rose from my chair. Maybe if I did her bidding quickly, whatever she had planned would end quickly.

With the basket in one hand and a long cane in the other, Babushka led me into the bright morning. I followed her behind the house, then down a dirt path toward the forest bordering the property.

Ahead lay thick, towering trees, mossy green mottled with shadows; behind, the farmhouse, a tiny beacon of life, shrank into the distance. I pressed sweaty palms to my skirt. It was like the start of every folktale meant to frighten me as a child. The unsuspecting maiden lured into the deep, dark forest, where witches and evil spirits lurked. Watching. Waiting.

"Keep up."

The impatient order broke the quiet tread of footsteps and set my heart pounding; Babushka must have sensed I was lagging behind. Narrowing my eyes at her turned back, I hurried after her. Despite relying on a cane to guide her path, somehow she kept a quick pace.

"Much here can help you, and much can harm you," Babushka said as we passed a small old shed bordering the property. From the dilapidated looks of it, no one went there. That was reason enough for me to return in the future. "I've found plenty of resources in these woods as well as poisons," she went on, capturing my attention again. "You need to be able to recognize what is and is not safe."

I glanced at my forearm, imagining her fingers wrapped around it. She kept a castor oil plant—supposedly for its benefits—and scoured the forest for toxins. Had Mama not felt the need to mention her mother's deadly hobby? But I couldn't join the patriotic war if I died by inadvertently consuming a poisonous berry, so recognizing them would be a useful skill.

"What kinds of poisons?" I hurried after her as we reached the cover of trees, where Babushka abruptly stopped. "More plants or—?"

"Hush!"

A simple question, and she was already upset with me. Next she would tell me to stop prying. Though I opened my mouth to retort, Babushka stood rigid, angled toward the distant road. I stayed silent, my palms sweaty again.

Something rumbled in the distance—thunder? No, the sky was clear; besides, this was a consistent rhythm unlike any sound I recognized.

"To the house." The tight edge in Babushka's tone indicated not to ask questions, despite the queries brimming on the tip of my tongue. My first forage would have to wait.

With each step, my heart raced faster while the space between the forest and the house seemed to stretch endlessly ahead. And with each step, the rumble grew louder. Closer. My breaths were sharp, shallow; above, the once-clear day began to turn hazy. As the smells of dirt and grass filled my lungs, a new smell joined them—like something burning.

"Upstairs." Without breaking her stride, Babushka gave me a little shove for encouragement. "Stay in the loft."

Though she had pushed me a few steps ahead, I slowed, glancing at her—brow furrowed, beads of sweat dampening a few loose gray strands along her forehead, pace as swift as visual impairment allowed. Did she want me to run the remaining distance? To leave her?

"Move, Mila!"

Babushka lifted her walking stick—whether to brandish it toward me or to indicate the house, I had no time to ascertain. She stepped onto an uneven pitch of ground, stumbled, and I caught her arm. As if by instinct, she clutched me in return. We stood still, our heavy breaths and the advancing rumble the only sounds.

I nearly did as she had ordered—fled to the house, far from this strange sound that had left a heavy pit in my stomach. But I was not going to leave her.

"There you are! Inside, both of you."

By the time I turned, Dedushka had already reached us. He wrapped his arm around Babushka's waist while I hurried to open the gate. Once inside the farmhouse, I rushed to the radio and switched it on—static. As I fiddled with the dial in a futile attempt to find a broadcast, my grandfather slammed the door while my grandmother sat at the table, where she propped her elbows and pressed her fingertips to her temples.

"Turn that noise off," she said through her teeth.

I leaned closer to the speaker to hear the garbled drivel through the static. "Maybe there's an update."

"Off!"

"No, you can't keep me from—"

"Upstairs," Dedushka interrupted, even yet firm. "You too, Sveta," he added, placing a hand on her forearm, likely to assist.

Babushka said nothing, nor did she react beyond covering his hand briefly with hers, as if to encourage him not to worry; I had already given up on the radio and moved to the window. Suddenly it was impossible to pull myself away as the source of the steady rumble came into view.

Columns of men marched in time down the dirt road. Round helmets, field gray tunics, trousers tucked into tall jackboots, pistols at their hips, rifles across their backs. A few massive tanks, some men on horseback, many on foot.

The German Army.

I pressed my fingertips to the cold windowpane while my shaky breaths formed hazy patches on the glass. The soldiers advanced, spreading like smoke across the ground, suffocating everything within reach. Another movement caught my eye—a middle-aged man coming from the opposite way, frantically directing his horse and cart off the road to avoid the oncoming masses. A few soldiers approached; they gestured to the man, who stepped down from the cart while the soldiers inspected the burlap sacks he was hauling—produce, maybe grain. One caught the horse's lead.

The farmer stood as if too baffled or stunned to react while they took his horse and cart after the marching men. One of the soldiers lifted his rifle.

A harsh crack, then the farmer toppled. I gasped, clutching the windowsill until my hands shook. If a man who had done their bidding had deserved death, what fate lay in store for those who resisted?

A gentle touch on my shoulder. Dedushka's murmur. "Come away, Mila."

But I could not.

A sudden orange flare rose from one of the nearby properties. Flames consumed the house and fields while smoke stretched up into the bright blue sky. I blinked, but the image did not disappear, was not a figment of my imagination. This was farmland, not a major city. If the army was passing through on its way to somewhere more significant, why destroy, pillage, murder? The only purpose it served was to inflict terror.

I bit my lip hard as men scattered, some armed with torches. None approached this property, so I unclenched my jaw a little. As they continued to pass, one man clutched three chickens by their snapped necks, bodies dangling limp in his grasp.

Hundreds of footsteps. What I could have sworn was a distant scream. More gunshots.

"What do we do?" I whispered, hardly able to speak around the lump in my throat. "If they come here, what do we do?"

Neither of my grandparents answered. Babushka sighed.

Surely she wouldn't disapprove of the patriotic war after this. But even if she did, I refused to sit idle while these men wreaked havoc on innocent people. And if they were treating these villagers so viciously, the same fate awaited the innocents in Leningrad. My parents.

Perhaps I couldn't accomplish much as one person, but after this, I suspected I would have little trouble finding others willing to join me in resisting the invaders. Even if my grandmother was not one of them.

Chapter 17

Vitebsk Region, 3 July 1941

Sleeping on a cot in the small loft upstairs had two benefits: First, I was secluded. Second, the dirt road was visible from my window. I could watch the Germans as they passed.

After the distant rumble had proven to be the army, I had thought we would endure that one horrific day and then they would be gone. I had been wrong. Over the days following Molotov's announcement, countless men had marched by, clad in field gray uniforms. So far, the Fritzes had spared this farm, but some mornings I woke to a sky turned gray from columns of smoke, air thick with ash. Others, to distant gunshots piercing the stillness.

This morning was quiet.

My grandparents had forbidden me from leaving the property until they were certain all the soldiers had passed through, so I surveyed my prison grounds. Expansive fields, a large stable. Behind it, a pen with a few fluffy white sheep, pigs, and goats. Beneath my window, chickens scurrying across the grass, and a garden, small but serviceable.

Downstairs, I poured tea while Babushka served bowls of kasha—a dull shade of brown to match the tangled locks I hadn't bothered to brush. Dedushka finished his porridge quickly and went outside; when he opened the door, I peered out. No Fritzes. Maybe they were gone and my grandparents would lessen their restrictions. I could go to the nearby village, Obol, and figure out how to join the patriotic war. No need to share that plan with Babushka, though.

Swallowing my last mouthful of breakfast, I studied the bright red skin along my forearms. A few days old, but the itch was still maddening. I dug my fingernails into the angry patches.

"Leave the rash alone." Babushka reached for the herbs hanging near the pech, presumably to see if they had dried to her satisfaction. "Didn't I tell you not to touch the castor oil plant without gloves?"

A simple *Water the plant, Mila* should not have required gloves, so I had left them off. And then, of course, the mundane task had turned into an incident.

"Would you have preferred I let the pot fall and make a huge mess?" I gave the rash a final slap, scowling. "Next time, I'll be sure to do that instead of grabbing an armful of those stupid leaves."

"Serves you right for knocking the pot over in the first place." Babushka adjusted the headscarf over her gray hair, then grabbed her long cane from its resting place near the door. "Water it today, then go to the forest and find death cap mushrooms. Otherwise, stay inside."

Confined to the indoors and the forest, as usual. Even the fields had been deemed too visible from the road, thus off-limits to me for the time being. But I'd find the death cap mushrooms even if it took all day. They had evaded me on previous hunts—perhaps because, according to Babushka, they were easier to find later in the year, yet still possible to locate now, especially due to a recent rain. Though the invasion had interrupted our first lesson, Babushka had spent the past week teaching me about foraging—an effort to distract me from the patriotic war, I suspected.

"How did you become so familiar with dangerous plants without—?" I stopped, but the intended word was clear: *sight*.

Too late to take it back, certain to set her off. I dug my fingernails into the rash again. Another attempt at conversation, another descent into argument.

Instead of snapping, she nodded toward the castor oil plant. "How can vision be trusted when your eyes perceive an alluring deception? Perhaps you learn after making a mistake once; perhaps it's too late."

"What can you trust, then, if not your senses?"

"Experience. Come to know what lies beneath what you perceive." She continued more softly. "Fall victim to a toxin, and it imparts a lesson you won't soon forget. Then you can trust what you know of it, but by then it's often too late."

She kept whey in ample supply and had explained I was to drink it until it forced the contents from my stomach if I ever consumed a poison. Maybe she knew what it was like to be deceived, unable to identify the poison until the only solution was to purge.

Outside, the sun was bright. A cool breeze tugged my hair over my eyes; I pushed it back and stood by the door, watching as Babushka made her way to the fields, her cane guiding her path. This was not a collective farm like many others, leaving my grandparents to work it alone, leaving me with no company but theirs. Thrilling as my dabbling in natural poisons had been, restlessness itched like the rash on my skin. I had to do something other than forage and sit indoors.

After watering the castor oil plant—while wearing rubber

gloves from Babushka, never again with bare hands—I found a woven basket and small knife. Since my arrival, Babushka had sent me to forage for both edible and inedible specimens, but since I'd failed to locate the death cap mushrooms yesterday, lessons wouldn't continue until I succeeded.

Behind the house, I followed the dirt path, then took a small detour to the old shed that had caught my eye on Babushka's and my first outing. When I pushed the door open, it squeaked as if it hadn't been disturbed in half a century. Inside was musty with patches of old hay scattered across the floor. A rusty rake, shovel, and rickety ladder were propped in the corner; a table was pushed against the far wall. The table had a deep crack through its wooden surface but hadn't split completely. A few more miscellaneous tools, broken items, and pieces of equipment decorated the space.

I went to the shelves to admire my specimens. Not many yet, just a few neat glass jars filled with castor oil plant seeds and baskets of various mushrooms—ones I'd be sure to study to refresh my memory of what Babushka had taught me. I gathered my notes from previous lessons and left them on the table, then I continued on my way.

Even now, the forest still struck me as unusual. Thick underbrush and towering trees were so unlike the stucco buildings and busy streets of Leningrad. I didn't exactly *dislike* the forest; it was quiet, beautiful, away from the farm. But it wasn't home.

I had established a usual route, sometimes straying but guided by landmarks—the massive oak with the thick, low-hanging branch curved into a perfect seat, indicating I was close to the old shed. Beyond it, a cluster of young birches. A tall pine with an eagle's nest. A patch of wild strawberries where a wolf had loped across my path one evening—prompting my hasty retreat. Not even two weeks of exploration, and the terrain was already familiar.

My hunt continued until the sun began to fade, then something caught my eye, nestled among fallen leaves a few meters from a young oak. Olive gray caps, white gills beneath; white stems with a pouch at the base. Death caps, exactly as Babushka had described them.

After wiping sweat from my brow and pulling on my gloves, I used the small knife to cut a few, then placed the mushrooms, knife, and gloves in my basket and retraced my steps. Success today meant Babushka would assign me a new specimen tomorrow.

The farmhouse was within sight by now, aglow in the setting sun. Its rays caught the thatched roof, spreading down to the thick wooden logs and over the decorative carvings surrounding the windows and doorframe. Beyond, approaching from the fields, Babushka led two cattle in for the night. But as she drew closer to the stable, she wasn't alone.

Four men. Unmistakable Wehrmacht uniforms.

She came to a sudden stop, indicating she had heard their footsteps or they had ordered her to halt—perhaps both. I had already dropped the basket and started sprinting across the grass.

When one soldier snatched her walking stick and tossed it aside, another shoved her away from the cattle, and a third grabbed their leads. She didn't appear to be resisting. I tried to pump my arms faster and lengthen my strides, wind whistling past my ears, gasping breaths slicing through my lungs. But not even my swiftest pace was enough to intervene before the last man raised his rifle, struck her head, and sent her to the ground.

"Stop!" An image clouded my vision, that of the soldiers seizing the man's cart, shooting him despite his compliance—his body shuddering, falling, unmoving. "Leave her alone!"

Babushka had propped herself up on her forearms, blood seeping from her scalp. Her head snapped in the direction of my cry while her usual fury met my ears, nearly a shriek. "Stay back!"

I was well past listening, and I lunged at the soldier who had struck her.

"Fucking Fritz!"

One hand found his chest, but a single blow was all I managed to inflict. Hefting the rifle in both hands, he used it to shove me down a few meters from Babushka.

Upon impact, the air escaped my lungs. I had no time to scramble to her side, no time for anything before hands caught my hair, my arm—my breast. A sudden chill joined the fury heating my insides. It was not enough to steal our livelihood, destroy our land, murder our people; they would steal *us*. Destroy *us*. Murder *us*.

No amount of writhing broke his hold. When the soldier flipped me over, my back struck the dry ground hard, then I was centimeters away from the lecherous glint in his gaze and the set of his mouth, screaming a protest as he held me down. The knife, why hadn't I kept the knife?

"*Allez, sautez-la!*" came a new shout—bold, almost like a challenge, even a warning, edged with mockery. "*Vous le regretterez quand vous serez aveugle comme moi.*"

When my grandmother cried out—in French?—the soldier paused. While two men restrained the cattle, another had pulled her upright and now held her securely, arms behind her back; she stood rigid, streaks of bright red blood gleaming against her flushed cheeks. Her lips turned with a devious curve, eyes sharp, chest rising and falling in rapid succession.

As I gasped for breath thick with musky odors of dirt and unwashed man, pinned beneath the Fritz, he glanced at her. *"Une paysanne sale qui parle français?"* he asked with a sneer while I thrashed, reaching for his uniform, round helmet, callous gray eyes, anything to stave him off. *"Vous m'embrouillez, vieille femme."*

He shoved my skirt above my hips. The others watched, eager, impatient. All four of them would do this to me, then to my grandmother. I had tried to help, tried to defend her, but I had only prompted *this*—hands forcing my legs apart, crushing weight, hot breath against my cheek.

"Cette jeune femme est une prostituée!" Babushka continued in that same tone, apparently deaf to her own granddaughter's shrieks. *"J'ai attrapé une maladie d'elle, et maintenant je suis aveugle."*

He pinned my arms above my head, and it was impossible to move, to prevent what would come next. But the moment Babushka finished, he froze; my near-sobs were the only sound.

"Mais . . ." He looked from me to her. *"Mais, elle n'est pas aveugle."*

She shrugged as much as her captor allowed. *"Non, mais regardez sa peau."*

When he lifted my arm, I resisted with what little strength remained; he held firm, looking for something—the red, scaly scabs left by the castor oil plant. With a disgusted cry, he released me and drew his hand back, then pain exploded against my cheek.

Bile and blood coated my tongue, sour and sharp, while he hissed something in German. An insult, most likely. His weight lifted, this time accompanied by poorly pronounced Russian.

"Filthy whore."

I hardly heard him. My mind swirled with the ache spreading across my face, the conversation, their voices—*her* voice, the way it had embodied flawless French, though edged with its usual asperity.

Every breath evaded me. I hugged my knees to my chest, pulled my skirt down with hands that shook so fiercely I almost didn't manage it. More German, more French, impossible to discern while my mind fought to clear. Adjusting rifles, Babushka's voice sharper, faster, a few more words in both languages. When I managed to lift my head, the gray-eyed Fritz was directing his companions onward, though his frown remained on me.

An ironlike grip caught my arm—this time, not a soldier's. "Inside," Babushka snapped.

She hauled me up and dragged me toward the farmhouse. While the German voices grew distant, I looked over my shoulder in time to see them disappearing down the dry, dusty road, cattle lumbering behind them in passive silence.

"What the hell is wrong with you, Mila?" Babushka slammed the door behind us and caught my upper arms. "Are you trying to get shot?"

My racing heart did nothing to quell a wave of sudden rage.

"Let go of me! They have no right to—"

"I don't care if they order me to dig my own grave. Stay away." She tightened her grip, eyes bright. "Stupidity is not bravery, and this is not your fight."

"Why not? Because by invading, enforcing their laws, persecuting us, and killing us, the conflict remains between the armies alone?" I pushed out of her grasp; this time, she permitted it. "During the revolution, did the women joining protests or spending hours in bread lines matter less than the soldiers fighting the Germans or the revolutionaries battling the imperial government? Those at home are as much a part of the fight as those on the battlefront."

Our arguments tended to take the same course, swelling and rising until we reached the apex. Nothing but our heavy breaths filling the room, our glowers holding one another in place, neither of us relenting.

And if refusing to budge would make her understand my position in this matter, so be it. I'd stand here all night.

"Enough," Babushka said to break the thick silence, but the word was tired and dull. She drew a hand over her eyes and across the bridge of her nose, where her fingers smeared the blood seeping from her head wound. She wiped her hand on her skirt in an absentminded gesture; I had already sunk into a chair, my legs too weak to stand.

I propped my elbows on the table and cradled my head. I still saw the rifle coming down on her. I still felt him everywhere. A shuddering breath shook me.

"None of that. You are all right." Direct but absent some of her usual tartness. A light touch found my shoulder; though I drew away, she pressed both palms against my cheeks, encouraging me to face her. "You are all right." Softer this time, assuring us both.

Babushka traced her thumb down to my lip, which was split from the soldier's blow. Her expression did not change, though a small breath betrayed her before her hands fell to my shoulders.

A lump settled in my throat. Swallowing hard, I covered one of her hands with my own.

Only a moment, then Babushka stepped toward the small hallway leading to her bedroom.

"Wait." I paused to clear the tremble lingering in my voice. "Let me see your head."

Once she'd taken my place in the chair, I gathered a few small cloths, a bowl of water, and antiseptic. The skin was broken on the left side of her head along her hairline. As I wiped away the blood and cleaned the injury, the laceration caught the lamplight, flaring crimson. Next to the fresh wound was another small blemish, mostly hidden by iron gray hair. The indentation was slight and the discoloration minimal, not much bigger than the new injury. Perhaps this one was from many years ago.

Once I had finished, Babushka picked up the bowl of water, now pink from her blood. I joined her by the sink, staring at my irritated skin. Imagining the bruises that would likely form due to the soldier's tight grasp.

"French?" I asked after a moment.

"I expected one or two of them might understand it more than Russian."

French, once prominent among Imperial Russia's aristocracy. Perhaps, prior to the revolution, a noble family had kept a country home in this region and hired her to tend their gardens or care for their children. My grandmother was keen, intelligent; it was easy to imagine her learning French by eavesdropping on her employers.

"What did you say? To . . ." My voice fell. "To stop him?"

"How could I have stopped him? I told him to do it." A heavy pit settled in my stomach, then she found my wrist and held it up, indicating the rash. "He lost interest when he learned you are a whore and your grandmother contracted an incurable disease simply from living in the same house as you, leaving her with impaired vision."

The weight in my stomach lifted while Babushka resumed drying the bowl. She had lied. To an enemy soldier. All to help her estranged daughter's child, someone she had known less than two weeks, though the invaders surely would have killed her if they had realized the truth. My mother viewed this woman as a heartless crone, perhaps for good reason. But perhaps that wasn't all she was.

"Make yourself useful, stupid girl."

When she said no more, I drew a slow breath and obliged. Those orders usually meant *make tea*.

* * *

Though we said no more of it, for the remainder of the evening, the incident consumed me. The soldier's body pressed against mine, the cattle following the men down the road, the crimson blood streaked across Babushka's gray hair and wrinkled skin.

I had witnessed such cruelty from my window. I'd seen Fritzes march by carrying sacks of confiscated potatoes, grain, fruits, vegetables. Pails of milk from Soviet cattle or buckets of water from Soviet wells. Leading horses, goats, or sheep meant to support an innocent family. I'd seen them harass those they passed along the road, heard gunshots during the night that led to still figures lying in the grass and dirt—or shallow graves, if Dedushka reached them before I looked out my window. Considering what might have happened, we had been fortunate.

But the soldiers had assaulted an elderly woman, a *blind* woman, who had not provoked them or shown opposition. One who shared my blood, different though we were.

The soup Babushka had been preparing for the last hour was nearly ready, while I had spent all my time staring at my cold tea. I'd told myself numerous times to get up and help her, especially considering her head injury, but movement felt impossible. And after I'd made our tea and retrieved my basket of mushrooms from where I had dropped it, she had not ordered me to make myself useful.

When Dedushka came inside, I finally rose to gather dishes. "Did any of the cattle wander off?" he asked as he closed the door. "We're missing some."

"Two are now property of the Reich," Babushka replied, accepting the bowls I offered her.

At that, he tensed and faced her; his eyes fell immediately to the gash on her head. After we had cleaned up, she had put a headscarf back on, and blood had stained it long ago. "The soldiers laid hands on you?"

"Did you expect them to politely request the cattle and then thank me for my trouble?" She handed me the bowls she had filled; as I carried them to the table, I kept my head down, though a split lip could not be hidden with a headscarf.

And when Dedushka looked at me, he found it. "Tell me what happened, Mila. What did they do?" The dread in his eyes revealed exactly what was on his mind. Everything that had nearly happened.

I lifted a hand to my mouth; if only covering the injury could prevent this line of questioning. "Nothing, I . . . I came upon Babushka with them, that's all."

"Meddling is never without consequence," Babushka said, maddeningly dismissive, as though nothing we had experienced today had been abnormal. Perhaps she hoped to placate Dedushka and spare me more questions; yet her tone was edged with a warning meant for me alone. *This is not your fight.* "Now sit, both of you, or keep talking and don't whine to me when your soup is cold."

Dedushka clenched his jaw but remained silent as he passed a hand over his beard. If Babushka closed a subject, we both knew not to press it.

After Dedushka washed his hands, my grandparents and I assumed our places at the table. The meal commenced in silence. My stomach churned while I swirled my spoon around my bowl. I didn't see the meal before me; I saw *him*. I didn't smell the potatoes, onions, carrots, or mushrooms swimming in broth; I smelled *him*.

"I'm sorry, I'm really not hungry." Without awaiting a reaction, I rose and left my grandparents and my untouched meal at the table.

Upstairs, I stared at the basket of mushrooms I'd fetched after the attack. They *were* death caps, according to Babushka.

Fall victim to a toxin, and it imparts a lesson you won't soon forget.

I pulled on my gloves and picked up a mushroom. It gleamed in the moonlight, gray as the German eyes that had stared down at me. Next time the soldiers confiscated what was not theirs, attacked innocents, harmed *my* family, I'd ensure they learned their lesson. I had been collecting poisons from my forages to help me remember everything Babushka had taught me; now I had a reason to put them to use.

Vengeance called to me, its pull strong and alluring. The

soldiers would be held responsible for the horrors they had inflicted. They would not harm me or my family again—not without repercussions. This patriotic war was mine to wage. To win.

For our beloved country. For honor. For *liberty*.

Chapter 18

Vitebsk Region, 6 July 1941

After the constant parade of Germans ceased, persuading Babushka to let me visit Obol had taken far more effort than it should have. It developed into one of our most spectacular arguments—culminating in me accusing her of holding me captive and Babushka threatening to show me *exactly* what life imprisonment was like—before Dedushka proposed a peace treaty. He said I could go to Obol when I wanted, as long as they were aware prior to my departure.

My grandparents lived a few kilometers outside the village, an easy walk. Tugging my shawl around my shoulders against the early morning chill, I trudged past a series of little log huts, a schoolhouse, and a small wooden church with a single dome, each aglow with early morning sunlight.

Obol was tiny, exceedingly dull—unpaved streets, a few shops stooping beneath the weight of passing time, the railway platform where Dedushka had met me, and near it, a massive gray stone complex surrounded by a barbed-wire fence. Once an abandoned factory, I suspected, now a Wehrmacht garrison. They had not been merely passing through as I had anticipated; they had settled here.

As I neared the railway, a few Wehrmacht soldiers stood on the wooden platform, waiting for a train. Perhaps bringing more soldiers, perhaps goods for the garrison. Beyond the Fritzes stood a small box office; I approached the ticket window.

Even if I'd had the means, I was not attempting to leave, though the temptation was strong. I wanted to go home, to get out of this region, to ensure my parents' safety; but the thought of leaving my grandparents left my lungs feeling like they were clogged with smoke from the invasion, thick and suffocating. Here, soldiers had assaulted my grandmother, me, perhaps would do so again. Here, I hoped, was a gray-eyed Fritz I intended to find before this war ended.

This place had to be safer than Leningrad, though not the refuge my mother had anticipated. If I couldn't go home, perhaps I could convince home to come to me.

The booking clerk had hardly looked up from behind his spectacles before I blurted out my request. "Are any trains scheduled to arrive from Leningrad?"

A different voice responded. "None, but the Fritzes are expecting a shipment—on schedule, isn't it, Yuri? And it had better include cigars. I'm running low."

The young man, perhaps three years my senior, indicated the cigar stub in his mouth. His eyes were a shade similar to my grandmother's, but his darkened near the edges, like a distant outline of trees bordering a thick forest, prompting me closer to uncover what lay beyond the complexity. It was as if his eyes had lived countless decades.

"What do you want with Leningrad when the German troops are swarming toward it?" he asked, removing the cigar as he strolled closer.

My chest tightened, though I snapped a response. "Why does it concern you?" I could have told him I hoped to bring my parents here, but I refrained. How fruitless the plan seemed now. Mama wouldn't come even if the trains were running. Not to her mother's. Not even if I made the request.

He let the cigar burn out while he looked me up and down. "You're clearly not from here, so you must be the girl from Leningrad. The old blind woman's granddaughter."

Was he judging me for not having dirt beneath my fingernails or grass stains on my blouse? And were the villagers already gossiping about me?

"My grandmother has a name."

Whether he knew or cared what it was, he didn't say. I pushed past him. I had no time for insufferable young men who cared only for cigars. If he knew I was building up my stash of toxins to use against the soldiers and planning to locate a resistance organization—if one existed anywhere in this village—he wouldn't have been so quick to make assumptions.

I continued down the road. How did one join a patriotic war? It wasn't as if I could ask where to go or whom to contact. And if that young man's attitude had been any indication, outsiders were not welcome here. These people wouldn't permit me to join their resistance organization even if one existed.

Sighing, I tucked a loose lock of hair behind my ear and meandered through the village, seeking any hints or clues to lead me to the group I sought. Others who felt as I did had to be here somewhere. Once I found them, then I'd worry about convincing them to accept me.

After more than an hour of wandering, I was nearing a small pharmacy when murmurs caught my ear. Pausing, I peered around the side of the building.

The young man I'd met at the railway platform stood with a woman perhaps my mother's age—close together, heads lowered, fervent voices drifting to my ears.

"If a soldier stops you, tell him your husband is suffering from typhus," he said as he handed her a brown bag. "The Fritz won't risk the possibility of contracting the disease."

"If that doesn't work?" the woman pressed, accepting the bundle. "If he inspects the contents?"

"He'll only see a few articles of clothing. The funds are sewn into the inseams—not much, but enough to sustain your family for a time while you repair the damages to your farm."

The woman nodded, then placed a hand over his. "You are a good man, Daniil Ivanovich." Even from my distant hiding place, I caught a little glimmer in her eyes.

Daniil offered a small smile in return, so different from the suspicion he had directed toward me. Maybe he wasn't as selfish as I had assumed. And maybe I had stumbled upon everything I was hoping to find. Daniil Ivanovich, of all people, might be my connection to the patriotic war.

As the woman turned to leave, I hurried a few steps back the way I had come, pretending to survey the surroundings as if deciding where to go. When her footsteps faded in the opposite direction, I rushed back to the pharmacy and nearly collided with Daniil as he emerged from around the building.

"Whatever you're doing, I want to help," I said, keeping my voice down.

"What I'm doing is going home," he replied without hesitation, so even and controlled that I almost questioned my understanding of what I had seen. "You should do the same. We have a curfew now, you know."

"Not until evening." I blocked his path when he attempted to step around me. His jaw clenched, then he moved around the building again, off the main street, so I followed. "You keep up with the train schedule to track the soldiers' shipments. You give funds to villagers. You—"

"Trains bring cigars and friends need help." He didn't even give me the courtesy of slowing his pace. Maybe he *was* rude, selfish, or just uninterested in permitting someone from Leningrad to assist him. With a huff, I caught his sleeve.

"You're part of an organized resistance group, aren't you?"

Daniil turned, regarding me with the same restraint as before, though I stood my ground when he stepped closer. "You shouldn't speak so freely of resistance, particularly to strangers. If I'm an informant, you have given me everything I need to see you executed. So unless you wish to return to Leningrad as a corpse . . ."

Perhaps it was a threat, but that wasn't why my heart was racing. "If you were an informant, you would be arresting me right now, I'd be doing the same for you if I were an informant. Now, have you had enough of being difficult, or should we keep this up until curfew?"

"Why are you so interested in resistance? This is my village, not your city."

"But it is *our* patriotic war." I grabbed the twine around my neck and pulled the attached vial from beneath my blouse. "I intend to poison plenty of Fritzes before I go home."

Daniil scrutinized the contents. Belladonna berry extract, a thin slice of death cap mushroom, a piece of a castor oil plant leaf, a vibrant purple wolfsbane petal, and a pellet of Dedushka's rat poison—containing arsenic. I had fashioned it and wore it always, a makeshift amulet to ward off the Fritzes. To remind me of what I intended to do to them.

"Your name?" he prompted, less hostile this time.

"Mila Lvovna Rozovskaya."

"You want your home back, and I want mine." A gust of wind ruffled Daniil's dark hair, and he passed a hand across his unshaven chin. A bit of suspicion faded from his eyes, replaced by a hint of intrigue that made me despise him a little less. "Perhaps we can help each other."

He motioned for me to follow him. As I did, I tucked the vial beneath my clothes, where the cold glass settled against my chest, next to my pounding heart.

* * *

LITTLE WOODEN HUTS lined the unoccupied road, each *izba* even smaller than my grandparents' farmhouse. Daniil led me to a door and ushered me inside. A cheerful fire blazed in the pech while a young woman, perhaps my age, turned to face us.

Dark hair swept into a tight bun, away from her broad forehead and square jaw; large, pale blue eyes on either side of a wide, flat nose. A commanding presence, one that nearly made me take a step back.

"I requested a private meeting, Comrade Tvardovsky," she said to Daniil.

"Believe me, I tried to get rid of her."

Before I could retort, the woman looked me over. "Well, if you annoyed Danya enough for him to bring you to me, I have a feeling we will get along. Your name?" Then, after I told her, "Go on."

Was I being recruited? If Daniil reported to this young woman, she held the power to dismiss me if she found a problem with me or my intentions. My resistance involvement relied on whether she saw me as he had: as an outsider. I swallowed hard, tempted to reach for the little amulet.

"My grandmother has been teaching me about poisons. It might be a useful weapon, one the soldiers won't expect."

"You wish to poison the Wehrmacht troops?" Her dark brow arched. "Why not shoot them?"

Because they had harassed a visually impaired woman. Because a pair of gray eyes had regarded me as if I deserved the punishment he intended to inflict upon me. Because I could not go home until this war was over, and meanwhile they would persecute innocents. Those who behaved in such deplorable ways deserved to suffer terribly.

But it was impossible to speak of what had happened only a few days ago, especially to strangers. "Everyone recognizes a bullet; few recognize poisons," I replied. "If I can get close enough to use them, the soldiers will assume illness, at least for a time."

She nodded. "Inside the garrison, perhaps. It would be an effective way to weaken their numbers." Her eyes brightened as she began to pace before me. "Such a mission would involve serious risk and require extensive training. A total infiltration."

I hadn't exactly thought of a specific way to fulfill my intentions, but the suggestion sent a thrill through me. Infiltration. Hours and hours with the Fritzes, examining every face until I found his.

Daniil passed a hand across the back of his neck. "Our numbers are low, and such a position is almost certain to get compromised eventually."

"Which is why I have asked you to gather more recruits and why I would assign only one recruit to this task. Would you be willing, Mila?"

I nodded without hesitation. Daniil looked past her as if something else were on his mind but said nothing.

"Daniil and I will discuss this further before any decisions are made. In the meantime, you will report to him for assignments." She stepped toward me, her sharp gaze holding mine. "If you speak of my organization to anyone, I will shoot you myself."

Without waiting for more, she placed a package in Daniil's hands and let herself out, closing the door firmly behind her. I stared after her while Daniil unwrapped the bundle. A package of Jakob Saemann cigars, which he promptly added to a cigar box.

"That," he said in the ensuing silence while my heart raced against my tiny amulet, "was Fruza, one of my dearest friends and the reason I've stayed off the front."

"Because you work for her?"

He nodded. "I was her first recruit after the invasion; now I oversee Obol. And you now work for her and the Byelorussian resistance."

Chapter 19

Vitebsk Region, 9 September 1941

"C an we forage this afternoon, Babushka?" I called out as I descended from the loft, having fetched my shawl after breakfast.

"If you don't come back too late." She gathered the dishes, so I joined her to assist, already imagining the new specimens we would find now that summer was fading into autumn.

Dedushka passed a hand over his white whiskers, peering outside at a sky that threatened rain. "Meeting friends in the village again, Mila?"

"That's right." Not a total lie.

Babushka made a sound close to a dubious scoff. I cast a sidelong glance at her—impassive, as usual. Impossible to tell what she was thinking. My grandparents asked surprisingly little about what I spent my days doing in Obol or in the old shed, though Babushka's feelings regarding the patriotic war remained unchanged. As did her belief that I did not belong in it. Maybe she thought I had heeded her warnings; maybe she feared—or knew—I hadn't. Still, if she wasn't going to ask what I was doing, I wasn't going to encourage otherwise. Even if she suspected more than she intended to share.

We placed the dishes in the sink; after stepping into his boots, Dedushka kissed Babushka's cheek before she shooed him aside, muttering that he was in her way, though I caught her brief smile. When he opened the door to depart, a cool breeze rushed inside, smelling of earth and impending rainfall, the promise of young mushrooms dancing across the forest floor.

While I fetched a towel for drying, a sudden clatter met my ears, then a splash joined by Babushka's curse. When I turned, the water pitcher lay on its side on the counter, its contents puddled on the floor.

"I'll refill it," I offered.

As I did so from the bucket of well water, I glanced at Babushka while she cleaned the spill. Perhaps it had been a simple accident, but she kept everything in specific locations and functioned with relative ease. A knot of tension formed in my chest.

When I joined her with the full pitcher, I chose my words carefully. "Should I make more tea before I go? Do you have a headache?"

"No." Not quite Mama's *Stop prying, Mila,* but close enough to make me obey anyway. If a headache wasn't behind the mishap, maybe I was overreacting. It had been just that—a mishap.

As we cleaned, silence fell until Babushka handed me a plate. Her sleeve pulled back slightly, revealing a purple discoloration on her wrist.

"When did you get that bruise?"

She hesitated before scrubbing the next plate. "I work on a farm. Do you expect me to remember how I acquired every bump?"

Though her manner was light, the underlying warning remained, as did the unsettled feeling in my stomach as I dried the dishes. A mysterious bruise from another mishap, perhaps?

Aside from now, I hadn't noticed her struggling; then again, I was often gone. Perhaps I hadn't spent enough time with her recently to detect a change.

Surely Dedushka would have mentioned it to me if a reason for concern had developed. Maybe he or I had left the water pitcher out of alignment, explaining why she had misjudged where to grab it.

But this feeling and I were well acquainted; it had recurred every time my mother told me to mind my own business, to stop asking why she never spoke to Babushka, to stay out of a matter that did not concern me. The feeling that this matter *did* concern me. Even if no one told me why.

* * *

A CRISP SEPTEMBER breeze swept across the open road, bringing scattered raindrops as I tugged my shawl around me and lengthened my strides. Fruza was expected at today's meeting. If I was late, both she and Daniil would have plenty to say about it.

My past months had been spent working for the All-Union Leninist Young Communist League, or the Communist Union of Youth; if I had known the Komsomol itself had charged Fruza with developing an entire resistance organization, perhaps I never would have approached Daniil asking to join. I had expected a tiny local resistance movement in which I worked against the Nazis, not one run by the Komsomol, where I worked for the Soviet. Intimidating though it was, a little thrill pulsed through me.

Only a minute or two late, I reached Daniil's izba and let myself in; to my great dismay, Fruza was already there.

"Sit." She indicated an empty chair beside Daniil, sparing

me a tardiness lecture. "Did you speak with Yuri Borisovich about the train schedule?"

I nodded. "Last evening. He reported no changes in troop movements and no railway delays, so all trains should be on time today. Medication is expected in the incoming shipment."

"Good. Katya, give me a list of items you've provided for us from your family's pharmacy, and I'll replenish your supply."

Katya, our makeshift medic and pharmacist, nodded and held up a folded piece of paper, likely a list she had already prepared.

"The fascist garrison?" Fruza continued, addressing Daniil.

"I delivered resistance pamphlets to partisans in the woods yesterday, and they reported sighting fifty more troops arriving. The partisans are developing a new plan of sabotage and will keep us informed if they need assistance."

Fruza nodded, smoothing a hand over her simple gray skirt and jacket. "Yuri is also NKVD. He remains our primary contact within the secret police and will provide us with their aid if necessary. We might need them sooner rather than later, given the report I received about the German advance."

I sat up straighter, gripping the edges of my chair.

"Yesterday, Leningrad fell under siege, and—"

My sudden, sharp breath interrupted her; I had no power to stop it. Her keen gaze fell on me, so I attempted an explanation. "Leningrad is where my parents—"

"Anyone who wants to worry can do that at home. To be here is to be fully committed to the work." Though she addressed the group, her eyes stayed locked with mine. "Is that clear?"

I nodded along with my companions, mouth too dry to reply. Babushka thought this wasn't our fight, yet each day it became more personal. *Siege.* The word sounded horrendous, like my parents crying out for the relief only freedom could provide. A freedom that felt further away than ever now.

"This blockade will cut off rail access and likely lead to terrible suffering in Leningrad," Fruza went on. I blinked and attempted to draw a steady breath, though it failed. "The harder we work here, the sooner we can help bring this war to an end."

She pulled a bundle from a brown bag, then presented it to Daniil—his cigars. Usually he promptly added them to his cigar box; this time he stayed seated.

Fruza grabbed her shawl. "Carry on, my Young Avengers," she called over her shoulder, utilizing her nickname for us, then she let herself out.

No one moved when the door closed behind her.

Perhaps my comrades didn't hear my shaky breaths, but they sounded deafening to my own ears. A few chairs creaked as people shifted. Someone cleared his throat. At last, a few rose, then others followed. One absentmindedly counted cartridges; another cast a blank stare over stacks of resistance pamphlets; another gathered parts to build explosives. My breaths only quickened. After rushing outside, I retraced my steps toward the farm.

Even if Mama rarely spoke to my grandparents, they needed to be made aware of what was happening in Leningrad. And I needed to forage for more toxic plants and have my lesson with Babushka. This war had to end now, before the siege worsened, before my parents sickened and starved . . . if a German bullet didn't end them first.

"Mila, wait." Daniil's footsteps pounded against the ground as he jogged to catch up. I didn't slow my pace.

"If you're going to tell me my parents will be fine, don't."

"I won't make a promise I can't keep." A strange tightness

found his voice as he matched my steps. "If Fruza shares more with me, I'll keep you informed."

The tension coursing through my body softened slightly. He was not a leader who regarded his recruits as tools to fulfill a duty; though the work came first, we, too, were people whose suffering he intended to ease, the same as he did the villagers.

By now we were near the railway station, where a small crowd had gathered. A handful of soldiers were barking orders. Daniil said something—low, insistent—but I kept my pace, eyes on my path. I had to tell my grandparents about Leningrad.

When he grabbed my forearm, pulling me back the way we'd come, I resisted, until a sharp German voice sounded too close. I froze. Daniil muttered a curse.

Two Fritzes approached, rifles in hand, gesturing for us to come nearer. By the time I looked to the grim set of Daniil's jaw, one soldier was already prodding him along with his rifle, directing him toward the crowd gathered around the box office. The other slapped a heavy hand on the back of my neck; when I flinched, he tightened his hold, ushering me after Daniil. Once they released us, bile rose to my throat.

A dead Wehrmacht soldier was propped against the building so he gaped at all who passed. The slashed uniform hung on his body in strips as ragged as the flesh beneath. Worst of all was his face—relatively untouched, aside from a few minor scrapes, eyes wide open and a fierce shade of red. Blinded.

These were signs of a kill I recognized from tales of an assassin active during the revolution. A woman. Now she was the most ruthless NKVD agent—or so we believed. Given that she was one of their most mysterious, effective tools, the NKVD might have simply adopted her methods to keep up appearances rather than admit she was dead or retired or any-where other than working for them. But I liked to think she was still involved. She had never struck this area before—not that I knew of, anyway. She tended to concentrate on Moscow, but her reach extended anywhere the NKVD could be found. Angering them meant the risk of incurring her wrath.

Clearly, she was not happy about the invasion.

One soldier had extracted a crumpled piece of paper from the dead man's open mouth and unfurled it. Given the frus-trated lines across his brow, I suspected he was having trouble deciphering the Cyrillic. He presented it to another soldier—one who presumably understood—and I knew the stories well enough to know what he would find. A single name written in red script.

"Orlova," the soldier announced before addressing the crowd in Russian. "Where is she?"

Beside me, Daniil's fingers twitched, as though pulling a trigger or perhaps curling around a cigar. Everyone stared at the ground. Shifted positions. Adjusted hats and shawls. I caught sight of Yuri fiddling with his spectacles.

A sudden crack shattered the quiet, then a cry, then a vil-lager collapsed. Blood spilled from a single hole through his neck.

The Fritz swept his pistol over the remaining onlookers. "Where is Orlova?"

A chilling breeze overtook the crowd. For an instant I swore it was the dead villager himself, sucking the life from us as his had been so suddenly and needlessly eradicated.

When the second shot split the air, I swallowed a gasp while a woman fell.

"You have one last opportunity to cooperate." The soldier

paused before a couple with their arms around three children. The eldest, a boy, appeared no more than twelve. "Where is Orlova?"

"We don't know," the man said hastily, helplessly, but the soldier was already lifting his pistol toward the smallest child.

"He's right!"

The cry broke free before I could stop it, and I wasn't certain when I pressed forward, only that Daniil caught my arm to keep me in place. His grip tightened when the soldier's bright blue eyes locked on me. I lifted a hand toward the amulet beneath my clothes before clutching my shawl instead.

The Fritz approached, his steady aim concentrated on my forehead. "Speak."

Though every pair of eyes focused on me, the only ones I felt were the dead soldier's. "Orlova kills and leaves her name to claim responsibility, but no one knows her face." I drew a shaky breath. "How can we tell you where she is when we don't even know *who* she is?" Another shot and strangled moan; the man beside me fell while I gasped and Daniil swore.

"How many bullets do I have to waste on you filthy peasants before you give up this story?" the soldier demanded, addressing the crowd before refocusing on me. "Lie to me again, any of you, and I will take this girl and kill her like your Orlova does, then I will leave her corpse to rot on this railway platform until one of you identifies the bitch who killed my soldier."

A stab of panic seized me as I looked away, unable to bear the sight of the corpse or the thought of enduring such agony. No one said a word. Then he fired at random into the crowd, shot after shot mingling with screams and agonized cries, while Daniil yanked me back, attempting to shield me. Though it ended as quickly as it had begun, I stayed close to him, heart thudding against my tiny amulet, until his tight grip found my shoulders, pulling me upright while his eyes swept over me. He relaxed after the assessment—perhaps because he had found no blood.

The Fritz lowered his pistol. "If she kills again, this entire village will burn." Then he waved a hand to his companions, who pulled a few from the crowd and issued orders to bury the soldier's corpse.

Everyone else scattered.

Daniil and I passed dead bodies and injured villagers, crimson ribbons streaming from arms, legs, heads, and stomachs. Another breeze carried the tang of fresh blood; I clenched my jaw against it. Death was our lives now. Here and in Leningrad. Murdered villagers, tortured soldiers, earth stained red, mangled strips of bloody flesh . . .

"To be here is to be fully committed to the work."

When Daniil echoed Fruza's words, I glared at him. "The Fritz was about to shoot a child."

"As they have shot other children and will likely shoot many more," he replied, though his brow furrowed. "I wanted to stop him as much as you did, but if I'm shot, where does that leave the Young Avengers?" He caught my arm, a sudden strain in his voice as he pulled me to a stop. "I have grown up with these people, Mila. I recognized every face that fell today."

"And I have known how much you care for them since the day we met." I broke his hold. "You don't have to convince me, Danya." I pressed on despite a little urge telling me to turn back, to ease the deep crease in his brow, to assure him he was doing all he could, and that it was enough.

"Our goal is to end this war as quickly as possible." His

footsteps sounded behind me. "If I die for the work, so be it, but the chance is high enough without encouraging it. Reprisals will fall on all of us, so if you—"

"Don't lecture me about reprisals!" I whirled to face him. "You know nothing of what I've seen the Fritzes do or the reprisals I've experienced."

He opened his mouth, then closed it, visibly taken aback by my surge of anger. If he managed a response, I didn't hear him; I had already started walking again, returning to that summer evening. Those soldiers so viciously targeting an elderly woman. My grandmother's shriek of protest joining the rush of wind in my ears. The soldier's weight rendering my struggles useless, suffocated by earth and sweat, screams tearing my throat raw . . .

A hand found my shoulder, bringing me to a pause. I met Daniil's measured gaze. He said nothing, simply looked at me as though he wished everything were different.

If only a look could make it so.

Daniil released me and went back the way he had come. Clutching my amulet, I pressed onward, past the garrison where the Fritzes lurked.

He had dispelled the summer day, the dead villagers, and the dead soldier from my mind, the bloodshot eyes that had felt as if they were following me at every turn. It was one of his most maddening qualities—the way he made me forget. He cast everything out and left me with nothing but the lingering weight of his hand on my shoulder, the memory of his dark eyes searching mine, the way he had attempted to shield me from harm.

I drew an unsteady breath for reasons I could not quite discern.

When I reached the farmhouse, Babushka was sitting at the table, fingertips pressed against her temple, indicating a headache. I gave her no time to acknowledge me before relaying the news.

"Leningrad is under siege."

She said nothing. I opened my mouth to demand to know why she remained so indifferent, especially with her daughter's life now at stake, but a faint crackle reached my ears, joined by a gravelly male voice. The radio delivering a report on Leningrad.

Babushka, listening to war updates? Was this what she did when I was gone?

"Fly agaric."

The soft statement broke through the haze surrounding my mind. "What?"

"Fly agaric," she repeated more emphatically. "Bright red cap with white spotted growths, concave as it reaches maturity. Cylinder stem with a ring, thicker at the bottom. Symptoms appear as early as half an hour after ingestion, with effects ranging from nausea to delirium and death." When I didn't react, Babushka stood with sudden speed, gripping the edges of the table as her voice rose. "Go."

The order propelled me into motion. I fetched my gloves, knife, and basket, then let myself out and found my path to the forest. As I walked, I held the image of the new mushroom in my mind alongside the echo of her tone, the unseeing eyes still sharp, as though to say, *Do you intend to poison the Fritzes or not?*

Chapter 20

Vitebsk Region, 11 November 1941

Most villagers stayed far from the Wehrmacht garrison on the outskirts of Obol whenever possible, avoiding the soldiers with their guns at the ready to eliminate the Jews they persecuted, resistance members, anyone who opposed them. I passed it every time I traveled to and from the village. I stared at the barbed-wire fence; ignored any insulting or lewd remark from those on guard; looked for the gray-eyed soldier even though the men were usually too far away to discern. I remembered every innocent victim they had slaughtered, longed for the day I would never see another field gray uniform here, in Leningrad, anywhere in the Soviet Union.

The morning was quiet, but as I trudged through snow and slush, a formation awaited me ahead, all too familiar after these long months of occupation. The crowd.

A frigid ache spread through me, more severe than a sudden gripping wind. If I hadn't had a meeting to attend, I would have turned around. If a soldier hadn't already spotted me and directed me to join the crowd, I would have fled. If I had been permitted any choice other than obedience, I would have made it. Anything to avoid witnessing whatever was coming.

A familiar figure appeared beside me, dark hair covered with a brown ushanka made of rabbit's fur—Daniil.

Before us, a group of soldiers stood with pistols aimed at a few villagers on their knees in the snowy, icy mud: a young couple and an elderly couple. Bloody, bruised. Trembling but not pleading. Heads lifted toward the crowd.

"Scheisse-Juden!" one of the Wehrmacht soldiers spat loud enough for everyone to hear.

A shower of bullets tore through the elderly couple, shook their bodies like tree limbs snapping in a fierce wind. They fell forward into the snow, surrounded by blood and fragments of clothing, skin, and hair. Somehow I had found Daniil's arm; I clutched it tight. And he let me.

"For sheltering Jews in defiance of the order for all Jews to report to the Wehrmacht garrison," the soldier continued, this time in Russian.

The order had been in place for some time; after a handful of Jews had reported and been massacred outside the village, others had tried to hide or flee to avoid the same fate. An icy wind stung my eyes; perhaps it brought on tears, or perhaps it was the sight of the elderly couple murdered only for being Jewish, and that of the weapons now directed at the two who had apparently been found guilty of aiding them. The guns sounded again.

Daniil and I were both shaking—outrage and grief, indistinguishable and fierce. When the young couple had fallen and the soldiers dismissed us, we pressed on in silence. I held tight to him, unable to let go. He didn't attempt to free himself, simply shoved his hands, which still trembled, into his pockets.

When we reached his izba, I released him. We exchanged a glance. Shared a steadying breath. Then I followed him inside.

Various Young Avengers were already hard at work, so I approached Yekaterina Stanislavovna and her assortment of medications and chemicals lined up in neat rows. Alongside those, Katya had various instruments and vials, all collected from her family's pharmacy. Behind a pair of goggles, her eyes were locked on a tiny scale. A thin slip of paper rested in the tray, and she carefully deposited small amounts of white powder from the beaker in her gloved hands. After each transfer, she paused, checking the weight, so I didn't disturb her until the scale read *300mg* and she set the beaker down with a satisfied nod.

"What are you working on?"

"Suicide pills." She gathered the paper and poured the measured powder into one half of a tiny capsule. "I heard the British and the Americans used them, so I thought I'd make one myself. When the Fritzes invaded and took over the pharmacy, I hid a number of our poisons and medicines before they checked stock."

I inspected the beaker's remaining contents, a powder resembling salt or sugar.

"Potassium cyanide," Katya supplied for me. She fastened both halves of the capsule, then pulled off her gloves and goggles and smoothed a few stray auburn hairs. "If the Fritzes catch you and turn you over to their secret police, you swallow this, and it only takes a few minutes to work. The Gestapo can interrogate or torture a corpse all they want, but it'll never talk."

"Or you could shove the pill down the interrogator's throat, and he'll never get the chance to ask you anything," I replied with a teasing smile, and she chuckled.

When I opened my palm, Katya dropped the pill into my hand. Such a simple, effective weapon if used against a soldier. One less Fritz, one step closer to the end of the war. To home.

* * *

No MATTER HOW much I argued, Daniil's answer was the same every time I begged for permission to test my knowledge of toxins on a soldier. *Not yet.* Today's resistance meeting had long since ended, but I had stayed, pacing and pleading. He watched me from his seat at the table, unbothered and infuriating.

"Not yet," he said again while I reached the wall and spun around. "Fruza agreed this will be a sabotage the soldiers won't expect—thus giving us an advantage—and feels this will be a successful mission, but her terms were that you dedicate yourself fully to it."

"I *am* fully—"

"You've only been preparing for four months."

"That's more than enough time."

"Not to learn all you'll need to know to carry out this mission effectively or to figure out a way to secure employment in the Wehrmacht garrison. And you can't rely on natural toxins alone." He rose and stepped in front of me, bringing me to a halt. "They're too unpredictable. What if you get the dose wrong and the Fritzes come for you?"

"Then I'll lead them on an outrageous manhunt through the forest behind my grandparents' farm." I stood taller to direct a challenging gaze at him. "They won't know those woods better than I do. They'll never catch me."

"Even if not, they will take out their anger on someone else."

Such was the price of resistance work. Over the past months, I hadn't forgotten Orlova's victim or the bullets that had struck the innocent crowd because of it. Yet it was not only those who rebelled that were targeted. For her compliance, my grandmother had been harassed and beaten; for my resistance to their cruelty, I had been assaulted. Our very existence left us vulnerable to punishment.

"They will take their anger out on us whether or not we fight them," I said, breaking the weighty silence that had fallen over us. "If I can contribute in a way that will shorten our suffering, let me."

Daniil caught the twine around my neck and pulled until he had freed the amulet. Taking it between his fingers, he held it within my view. "You can use these, but you have to learn about chemicals."

What fun was there in chemicals?

"Would you rather die by a few hundred milligrams of arsenic baked into your bread, or by eating a mushroom soup, where the toxin is clearly visible but you had no idea until it was too late?" With a sly smile, I snatched the vial back. "Which method would impress you more?"

"Nothing impresses a dead man." He smirked before sobering. "Katya has agreed to teach you what she knows, contingent upon her family's safety. If serious risk to them comes up, she will be out."

No wonder he had approached her for a whispered conversation following today's meeting. I didn't deny that Katya's work was fascinating. Everything I had learned through my resistance involvement was fascinating—how to build a bomb, shoot a gun, design compelling propaganda. Just not as fascinating to me as poisonous plants.

"Once you infiltrate, the villagers will find out. They'll think you're a collaborator. And we can't say otherwise in case there are informants in our midst."

"If that's what they think, let them. So long as they don't interfere."

Daniil fetched a cigar from the box. "For your sake, let's hope the siege lifts soon so you can go home."

Whether he meant due to the risks I'd face in the garrison or hostility from the villagers, I wasn't certain. Perhaps both. But those risks were not what plagued my insides now; it was the word *siege*, more deadly than any poison.

"Does Fruza have connections in Leningrad?"

He released a stream of smoke. "I imagine so."

"Do you think she—" I didn't hide the catch in my voice. No use pretending. "Can she get people out?"

"Of a city under siege?" Daniil clarified, though not unkindly.

It was foolish to consider the idea. But when every report mentioned the horrific conditions my home faced—starvation, meager rations, shortages, countless deaths, even rumors of cannibalism—and when it was nearly impossible to send letters to my mother, I always considered it. Some civilians had successfully evacuated, according to news updates. I had no way of knowing if my parents were among them. More than likely they were trapped.

Daniil looked at me—my superior, still not unkind yet measured and direct. "Young Avengers don't get to make requests. You follow orders, or you get replaced."

"Replace me, then." I nodded to the gun at his hip. "Find someone else to infiltrate the garrison."

"It seems a shame to take a bullet over a changed mind." He rested his back against the wall and toyed with his cigar, unaffected by my challenge. "Since the plan isn't very far along, you can be reassigned and Fruza can find someone else if she decides to move forward with the infiltration."

"That's not what I'm saying. You and Fruza don't owe me anything, and I will follow orders, but I need to ask this of you, so you can either replace me now or listen to me." I swallowed when my voice broke, then blinked past sudden tears. "If I'm going to undertake a mission that will in all likelihood get me killed, then let me die knowing I did everything I could to help my family."

Daniil watched the smoke curling from the end of his cigar, his expression unreadable. "Give me their names," he said quietly. "I make no guarantees."

I nodded and shuffled through materials from our meeting until I'd found paper and a pencil. I jotted down their names, home address, and the Kirovsky Zavod and its address in case the factory where my father worked was still operating. After folding the note, I pressed it into Daniil's waiting palm while he took a slow drag of his cigar. He made as if to pocket it, but I caught his hand in both of mine. He paused while I closed his fingers more tightly around the note.

"Thank you," I murmured, lifting my eyes to his. "Truly. No matter what comes of it."

He held my gaze, his own gentle yet almost agonized or perhaps frustrated, as though he wished he could do more. Change more. Then he blinked, chased the look away, and dipped his head in a brusque nod. "Any thanks will go to Fruza, not me." He tucked the note away. "Meet Katya at the pharmacy tomorrow morning."

Chapter 21

Vitebsk Region, 11 November 1941

After leaving my note with Daniil, I trekked through the frigid November afternoon, suppressing the flutter in my chest. In wartime, clinging to unrealistic expectations was as dangerous as assuming a position on the front lines. Still, Fruza likely had connections in Leningrad, ones that might be able to help or at least provide information about my parents. Information was better than nothing. Even if the information proved devastating.

Now as I reached the farmhouse, I wanted nothing more than a cozy fire and hot tea. But when I opened the door, standing inside was a German soldier.

He turned toward my involuntary gasp. Met my eyes with a gray gaze I'd never forget. The familiar surge of fury and terror coursed through me, heat and ice, leaving me unable to do more than stare.

Dedushka was somewhere on the property, working. I had been out most of the day. My grandmother was alone with a Fritz. *This* Fritz.

He approached Babushka with long, purposeful strides, one hand reaching for the rifle across his back. Before I could throw myself at him a second time, she muttered something hastily in French, then hurried to me while he paused.

"Come." She caught my arm in her fiercest grip. "Help me gather the eggs."

During colder months, the chickens stayed in a cozy space beneath the pech, but Babushka led me into the back garden. Once there, I wriggled against her.

"Why the hell is he here?"

"An old blind woman and a supposedly diseased prostitute who attacked a soldier? Did you think they spared us out of mercy?"

My head flooded with the voices from that summer day, the forceful slap that had blurred together the sounds of men checking their rifles and the sudden anxiety in my grandmother's voice, then no action taken beyond a parting glance from the soldier. Now the tension in my grandmother's hold told me everything I had failed to understand.

"They were going to shoot us, so you offered them food in exchange for our lives."

"Why kill us when given the opportunity to control us? The French speaker was the only one who understood me, so he called his companions off, gave some excuse in German, and now tells me when to expect him. Our exchanges remain secret so he can hoard the goods for himself." She released me, picked up a basket by the door as though we had come to fetch it, and shoved it into my hands. "Hurry. Reuter is an impatient bastard."

"You know his name? How often does he come here?"

"Often enough for me to know his name."

"Does he hurt you?"

"Only if my granddaughter spends all her time talking instead of doing what she's told."

Shuddering, I glanced at my arms, almost seeing the bruises

he had left. Like the bruise I had noticed on Babushka's wrist that September morning when we had been washing dishes. A shape I had recognized, unable to recall until now: finger-prints from a tight grip.

When I gasped, Babushka turned to me again. "Diseased thanks to you, remember? Get that notion out of your head."

Only a slight comfort; he had still grabbed her with enough force to leave a mark. I drew a trembling breath. "Does he know you lied?"

"You and I are still alive, aren't we?"

"Does Dedushka know about him?"

"No. I promised to keep you both out of the way."

Though she said no more, the words were heavy with im-plied meaning—that I had, in fact, gotten in the way. My heart pounded. If Reuter thought she had gone back on her word, I doubted he would see the value in sparing us a second time.

She picked up another basket and went inside, so I followed. There, Reuter was seated, helmet on the table as though we'd invited him to dinner. By keeping the chickens indoors, away from the cold, we gained a few extra weeks of production. Not many eggs, certainly not enough to waste any on him. But I knelt beside Babushka to gather them, if only to get rid of him.

Once finished, she spoke in French and set her basket on the table. I approached more slowly. Before I could place mine beside hers, Reuter rose, facing my grandmother.

I had no time to warn her. The slap knocked her aside, might have sent her to the floor if she hadn't caught herself against the pech; with a cry of protest, I hurried toward her until Reu-ter's sudden bark sent me back a few hasty steps. When Ba-bushka yanked off her headscarf and spat blood into it, my breaths sharpened.

"Was that because I'm here?" I demanded. "Does he think you broke your promise? Because you didn't, tell him you didn't."

"Keep your mouth shut," she snapped.

We had no control over this man or what he did to us; neither could I control the utter helplessness and rage that overtook me, swirling inside and emerging with a shriek as I threw my basket onto the floor. At the unmistakable sound of shattering eggs, Babushka pressed her lips into a hard line.

Only then did I realize what I had done.

Reuter picked up the only egg that remained unscathed. When he caught my chin, forcing me to meet his gaze, I suddenly felt his weight on top of me, his hands on my waist.

He placed a hand on my chest and shoved me back into the wall. I struck with a thud and a sharp crack—the egg, crushed between his palm and my skin.

Bits of shell, yolk, and albumen oozed down my chest, between my breasts, over the hidden amulet, all the way to my stomach. He kept his hold as though his open palm were absorbing each of my thudding heartbeats, likely would have done far worse if my grandmother hadn't convinced him I was a whore.

"Babushka!" he shouted, so loud I flinched, mocking me and my name for her, then he addressed her swiftly in French.

She cleared her throat and wiped more blood from her mouth. "I am to interpret," she supplied for me, her voice level, though tighter at the edges.

He continued, then she was silent for a moment.

"'If you destroy my property again,'" she repeated while the hand against my chest moved higher, fingers wrapping around my neck, thumb pressing to the base of my throat, "'you, and you alone, will hang.'"

The grip on my chin tightened while the pressure against my throat intensified slightly. He would leave Babushka alive, continue plaguing her, and I would die a death that accomplished nothing.

He grabbed my arm. At once I tried to twist away, but he would do it again, overpower me again—

He pulled up my sleeve, revealing smooth, unblemished skin. Not broken out in a rash like last time. I froze. He looked from me to Babushka. Uncertain, yet a look that said he would uncover the truth. All I could do was hope my face didn't reveal it.

Reuter released me, grabbed the other basket, and let himself out, slamming the door behind him.

My clothes stuck to the crushed egg, sticky against my skin as I waited for Babushka's inevitable *Stupid girl*. She stood rigid, a sign that always indicated she was too furious for words. My eyes fell upon the bright slash through her bottom lip.

"Babushka—" I fought to speak around a sudden break in my voice. "I didn't mean for—"

"I have been entrusted to keep you safe throughout this war," she interrupted. "How am I supposed to do that when you act like a child?"

Those words struck sudden and sharp like the eggshell's crack against my skin. She left me no time to reply before retreating to her bedroom.

I drew a steadying breath as I took in the mess on myself and the floor, then fetched a rag to start cleaning. If it was childish to resist the Fritzes, very well. I'd be a child, a stupid girl, whatever she thought that made me.

As for Reuter, I felt certain that he was determined to find out the truth behind the rash that was no longer on my skin. To catch Babushka in her lie. Once again, I had only made the situation worse. Because once he knew the truth, I was not the only one who would hang.

Chapter 22

Vitebsk Region, 30 April 1942

During the warmer months, belladonna grew wild and unabashed alongside the house. As the seasons crept by, I watched the flowers bloom into deceptively alluring purple bells while the berries ripened to shiny black. Thanks to my grandmother, I learned the pale, thick roots were the most poisonous part of the plant.

Wind swept over me, carrying the sweet scent of wet earth and sending ripples across my skirt as I took the root I'd just extracted to the old shed, where I experimented with my toxins.

A breeze cleared the musty air before I closed the door behind me. After depositing the root samples on the table, I fetched the belladonna berries I'd collected and stored, assorted dried mushrooms, castor oil plant seeds, and various tools—vials, beakers, chemicals from Katya, and other supplies—and carried them to my workspace. Using my small knife, I cut a piece of the root and transferred it to a mortar and pestle. After pulverizing it, I weighed the contents. A few milligrams— good, considering Babushka said even negligible amounts were toxic. I crushed the berries until they had been fully incorporated with the root. A wet, purplish mess of juice, skin, and fibers.

Babushka had taught me to use whey if necessary. I kept a

jar on my table during every experiment. She had also taught me about lethal doses, and I'd seen her taste various poisons to identify them. I dipped the tip of my knife into the belladonna juice and touched it to my tongue.

Bitterness, sharp and startling, spread across my taste buds. I spat onto the ground to clear it away. How could I force something so strong down a Fritz's throat without him noticing? Using poison meant getting close enough to transfer toxic levels of something like belladonna onto a man's skin or slip a suicide pill into his drink. Maybe I'd soak a knife in this crushed belladonna mixture. A quick stab, even a nick—but that would require hand-to-hand combat.

Worth a try if Reuter came back, messy though it might be. I hadn't seen him since the incident with the eggs, but he was still coming around. Some days, I'd return from a resistance meeting or foraging and notice items out of place—a chair pushed out, the water pitcher a few centimeters to the left of its usual spot, a sprig of dried herbs on the floor, the long wooden paddle used to pull dishes from the pech moved to the far corner. As though the items had been tampered with, intentionally and maliciously, to cause difficulty and confusion for my grandmother. That was how I knew he had come by. His schedule was unpredictable, making vengeance difficult, though not impossible.

Babushka and I had baked black bread this morning, so I pulled out the piece I'd brought with me and dunked it into the juice. Once it was saturated, I left it to dry and turned my attention to the small bottle of cyanide from Katya.

Our lessons had gone well these past five months. We met at her family's pharmacy, where she drilled me until I could recite her mantras in my sleep.

A lethal dose of sodium cyanide for an adult is typically between two hundred and three hundred milligrams.

Morphine is an opium alkaloid utilized for its pain-relieving benefits, least effective through oral administration.

The effects of arsenic on the human body include abdominal pain, vomiting . . .

And on and on. I had learned more about chemicals than I had ever cared to know. Daniil had to grant me permission to infiltrate the garrison soon.

After spending my night measuring cyanide to make suicide pills, the bread had dried. I pulled off a crumb, hardly as big as the tip of my fingernail. Enough to taste, not enough to kill. The instant I closed my mouth around it, bitterness rose to the surface. I spat it out. Not even bread was enough to mask the flavor. If I were to use belladonna in something edible, a lethal dose would have to be contained in the first bite—assuming the intended victim swallowed it.

I was sealing my first cyanide capsule when the shed door creaked. Snatching my knife, I whirled. The blade felt strange, fumbling with it this way rather than utilizing it for delicate cuts, but it was my only means of defense, inexperienced though I was. A figure stepped inside, washed in shadows. My fingers curled tighter around my weapon, bathed in belladonna. One scratch was all it would take . . .

"How many times do I have to visit before you stop reacting as if you're expecting a Gestapo invasion?"

The humorous remark settled the pounding in my chest. Sighing, I tossed the knife onto the table and glared at the now-familiar outline.

"How many times do I have to tell you to warn me before you visit?"

"And take away the fun of watching you jump out of your skin?" Daniil closed the door behind him and moved into the flickering lamplight.

Despite curfew, he had taken to visiting me on occasion to discuss my work with poisons. How he managed to keep the Fritzes from catching him as he came and went, I never knew.

As he lit a cigar, he strolled closer to my table, taking in the array of bottles and tools. "Are you prepared to decimate the entire German military?"

"I've been prepared for months," I replied, drawing the smell of smoke into my lungs. "All that remains is for you to let me."

"It's too important of a mission to rush. If you succeed, you have the potential to do a great deal for the cause. And a high potential for capture." He stepped closer, his prior humor gone. "Are you prepared for that?"

It was as though he had tossed me into a frozen lake, its icy waters seeping into my lungs, stealing my breath, chilling me to the bone until I no longer possessed the strength to resist. The little amulet felt like it was searing my flesh. Those women of my grandmother's generation who fought in the revolution had accepted that risk. Fighting against oppression was necessary no matter the cost.

I nodded. "Are you?"

He didn't respond right away, toying with his cigar. "I don't intend to lose anyone else to them," he muttered at last. Then he turned from me.

None of our recruits had died yet—not since I had joined soon after the invasion. The group had only existed for perhaps a week at that point. How could he expect to fight in the resistance without recruits getting killed?

Was he referring to civilians? Someone else? He wanted the Fritzes gone, as we all did; perhaps more lay beneath his reasons for hating them.

I swallowed against the lump in my throat, searching for my voice. He exhaled cigar smoke, tendrils curling around his dark hair like wisps of silvery moonlight seeping across the night sky. A wooden post stretched through the center of the room, connecting the floor to the beams; he rested his back against it. Facing me without seeing me.

To the untrained eye, he was the image of ease, the way his fingers curled around the cigar as though it were an instrument of his own design, one whose music only he coaxed forth; but my eye had been well trained. My eye caught the way his grip stiffened when he brought the cigar to his lips, a sign the notes were off-key.

"Last July, right after the Germans invaded," he said after a moment. "It was the first time I killed one of them. Once you do the same, everything changes."

Killing soldiers was expected in this line of work. But the strain that touched his voice was like the one I had heard when we had come upon Orlova's victim, as if these were his people and he could never do enough to help them.

I drew closer, waiting for him to elaborate. I wanted to ask what happened, *why* it happened, to reach for him, to erase the lines across his brow. The longing filled my insides as surely as the traces of smoke swimming within my lungs. But when he let the cigar burn out and brushed past me, I exhaled and refrained.

Growing up with my mother had taught me how to recognize when questions were not welcome.

I stayed where I was, halfway between my table and the

post, unsure what to do with the lingering ache in my chest. Certain something had just transpired, uncertain of what it was. Or if it would ever return.

"I left home to stay with grandparents I had never met. My parents are caught in a siege while I'm living under occupation, learning about poisons, and working for the resistance," I murmured at last. "You can talk to me about changes. Even if mine are different than yours."

He glanced at me, perhaps catching the unsteadiness in my tone; this time he was the one waiting for me to elaborate. So I did.

"A Wehrmacht soldier comes here to confiscate food from my grandmother. Give me permission to test my poisons on him."

Daniil sighed. "Mila, I've said—"

"It's been nine months of preparation. You've made me wait long enough."

"If the soldiers know this man comes here and he disappears, your family and the organization will be at risk."

"Am I supposed to do nothing, when it's my fault?" I rushed to him with such speed I nearly collided with his chest. Though he caught my shoulders, even his steadying hands didn't stop the fury surging through my veins. "It started during the invasion, and now my grandmother is paying for it."

"If all he wants is food—"

"She lied to him. To protect me." My fury ebbed and a gasping breath carried me on. "I think he knows. He suspects, anyway, and when he finds out the truth, he'll kill us."

When I succumbed to another choking breath, Daniil wrapped his arms around me. The first time he had pulled me close, it had been to shield me from bullets; this second time, to shield me from fear. He could not prevent the bullets, nor could he prevent the fear. But he could hold me against his chest, reassure me with the steady thud of his heart, strengthen me with the security of his grasp.

At last, he spoke in a murmur. "Don't do anything until you're certain he means harm."

"Don't they always mean harm?"

"If you kill him, the soldiers will enact reprisal."

"If they can't find a body, they can't accuse the villagers of murder. He might have deserted." Even to my own ears, it didn't sound convincing. I finished more softly. "Please, Danya. She's my grandmother."

He sighed—whether to grant permission or because he was grappling with his decision, I didn't know. Still, I tightened my hold to urge him to concede or communicate my gratitude, whichever was the appropriate response.

The little ache in my chest returned, preventing me from looking up. When his hands slid down to my waist, the simple gesture instilled in me the courage I needed. The smell of his cigar smoke lingered between us. I wasn't sure what I intended, only that I wanted to taste the sweet spiciness on his lips, to feel the brush of his stubble on my skin, to be near him. When I lifted my head, I found him waiting for me. My hands pressed to his chest, feeling the strong thud of his heart. Beat after beat, beckoning me nearer.

Then he straightened, released me, and stepped back.

The knot in my chest transformed into one of disappointment. It had no right to: We worked together. He was my superior. Was that why he had resisted? Or had something else brought the sudden tension between us even as I fought the urge to find his arms again?

He was like one of my poisons to be honed until it was just right. When working with poisons, one small flaw was all it took to destroy it; developing my creations required the proper care. The key element in my work was patience to ensure everything blended properly, that no flaws would disrupt what I'd taken such lengths to craft.

It seemed this creation would require more patience than anticipated.

Chapter 23

Vitebsk Region, 3 June 1942

C hanterelles."

At Babushka's remark, I adjusted my grip on the water bucket as we strolled from the well to the house. "Isn't it too early for them?"

The crease in Babushka's brow deepened, then she let out an exasperated huff. "I suppose, but I need fresh mushrooms for dinner, so bring me whatever you can find."

"If you want chanterelles, I have some dried ones."

"Why would I ask for fresh if I wanted dried?" Babushka switched her cane to her other hand and extended the closest one to me. When I passed her the bucket, she nodded toward the woods.

Very well, if she insisted on fresh mushrooms, I'd find some. I hurried inside to fetch my basket, which was waiting for me atop the wooden trunk at the foot of my bed. After twisting my hair into a messy coil at the nape of my neck and tying on a headscarf, I departed. Identifying which mushrooms were safe to consume was almost as thrilling as identifying those that were not.

As for poisoning the Fritzes, Daniil had never granted me permission to test my toxins on Reuter; neither had he forbidden it during our conversation in the shed five weeks ago. He had simply spoken of the risks to the organization—but if Reuter intended to kill us as I feared, that was another matter entirely. That was defending myself and my family. And once I had the chance to complete my task, that was the explanation I intended to give Daniil.

Halfway to the woods, I noticed the basket was empty. My gloves were still in my room. I retraced my steps; near the house, my grandparents' voices carried from the back garden.

"Now. My head is splitting." Babushka's usual impatience followed by Dedushka's reply.

"Do you need anything else?"

"The medicine and the items I asked Mila to write down this morning. The list is inside."

I went in through the front, up the ladder to the loft, and snatched my gloves, pausing at my window to watch Dedushka stroll along the dirt road toward Obol. If Babushka had a headache, she usually bore it with tea, rarely medication. From my window, I saw her in the garden, hard at work. Not moving like a woman whose head hurt badly enough to demand something to ease the pain.

First Babushka had sent me away, then Dedushka. And I knew what happened when she was here alone.

No wonder she had refused my offer of dried mushrooms; she wanted me out of the house, busy, distracted. That gray-eyed, French-speaking bastard had arranged a visit.

Outside, I crossed the yard slowly so as not to startle the chickens and betray my presence, then I eased the gate open and ran.

In the shed, my shelf was full of stored toxins, and I went right to the one I sought—death cap mushrooms. A recent heavy rainfall had led to a few early growths, so I had gathered them just this afternoon. I dumped the contents into my basket, then stepped outside to watch the house.

Moments later, a uniformed figure approached and went indoors.

When I had interrupted them, he had struck Babushka. Had threatened to have me hanged. But I couldn't let this continue, certainly not if our last encounter had led to him suspecting that Babushka had lied about me.

I pulled out my little amulet. Closing my hand around it, I sent up a prayer to any spiritual entity that cared to help me, god or devil. Then I proceeded. Every step down the path was like my feet racing across the grass to reach my grandmother and the four soldiers. An intervention that came too late, did no good. This was the chance I had awaited since that day, and if this Fritz took such pleasure in taking advantage of my grandmother, then that same arrangement was my opportunity for vengeance.

When I opened the door, I raised my voice. "Babushka, I found honey agaric, so—" I broke off, as though having noticed the Fritz with the rifle slung across his back and one hand gripping my grandmother's arm.

Reuter stood by the table, visibly angry about the meager offering Babushka had been trying to place in a burlap sack—a single head of cabbage and a few beets. He looked from me to her, brow furrowed. Though he released her, she stood stiff, not simply due to my unexpected return; I had named honey agaric mushrooms, ones that didn't grow until autumn. It was my way of telling her not to eat the ones I'd actually brought.

"Out, now!" Babushka crossed to me, seething with her usual fury—and something else. Fear.

Before she reached me, the Fritz shoved a wooden chair in

her way. When she collided with it, she grabbed the back for stability until he jerked it aside. Staggering, she found the table while Reuter approached me. His eyes fell to the basket, where the mushrooms were in plain sight. Before I had time to do more than stare, as if recalling our last encounter all too well, he caught my arm tight enough to make me gasp. The room stilled.

"Stupid girl," came Babushka's unsteady whisper. "After last time, I told him you'd gone back to your mother's in a nearby village."

I opened my mouth, then closed it. If he hadn't suspected the first lie, this one had certainly been exposed. And now, more than ever, he needed to do what I wanted him to do: Confiscate the basket of mushrooms along with what my grandmother had provided and leave. I had presented him with a new resource to acquire from us; surely he would see the benefit in leaving us alive to provide it for him. Then he would take the mushrooms back to the garrison and we would never see him again; if any of his companions found them among his belongings, they would assume he had foraged for them himself and made a deadly mistake.

Reuter looked at my face, then lowered his eyes, perhaps envisioning the egg he had smeared all over my exposed skin. Then he plucked out a few mushrooms and put them in his mouth.

Once, Babushka and I had tasted death cap mushrooms together—a morsel, quickly spat out and followed immediately by whey. They tasted as harmless as they looked. And a single cap was typically enough to kill.

I tensed as if he had just stolen something priceless. As if these mushrooms were the difference between our survival and starvation.

When Reuter pushed me toward Babushka, I caught myself next to her, then he slammed the basket in front of me and grabbed her chin. She sucked in a breath while he pulled her away from the table and pech until no support was in reach, nothing to allow her a sense of her bearings, just her hands around his wrist, desperate to alleviate the tight grip.

I bit my lip hard. But I did not interfere.

A rapid exchange—what sounded like a demand, then her strained response as she fought to speak around his hold—before he released her. One hand found her chest; the urge to shove a hundred more mushrooms down Reuter's throat almost overtook me. Instead, I shifted my weight, encouraging the wooden floor to creak, and drew a breath as loudly as I dared. She would hear both; she heard everything.

The smallest squeak, my inhale and exhale, then Babushka's head turned slightly toward the sounds. Though she was combatting sharp, heavy breaths, the tension in her shoulders eased while her chin lowered, a nearly indiscernible nod. She stepped toward me until she had located the table's weathered surface; then I, too, breathed a little more easily.

"He knows I lied, as I'm sure you've gathered," she said after regaining her voice. "While I bear witness, you can guess what he intends to do with you before killing us." She sank into a chair, as if too weary to stand any longer.

My stomach churned; Dedushka had probably reached the village by now, but he still had to complete his brief errand and walk back; even if he somehow returned within the next few minutes, he'd be killed too. Reuter clapped a hand across the back of my neck and pushed me down over the rough wooden table. My mushrooms might kill him, but not soon enough.

Instead of lifting my skirt, he spoke in broken Russian. "The forest." He leaned closer, bringing his lips to my ear. "There I have you. Then you and Babushka die." While his fingers tightened around my neck, I closed my eyes against a shuddering breath.

Now he was taking us into the forest, where there would be no risk of unexpected interruption, no one to hear or see anything. And he would not bring us back.

A firm grip tore off my headscarf, found my hair, and wrenched me upright, then he spoke to Babushka in French, likely ordering her to accompany us. Without a word, she rose while I fetched her long walking stick; when Reuter shook his head and reached for it, I stepped back, giving him my fiercest glare.

"If you want her to come, then one of us needs to guide her, or you need to let her use her cane. The choice is yours."

After Babushka interpreted, his jaw clenched, but he jerked his head in consent. I handed her the staff while he directed his rifle at us, then we walked toward the forest in excruciating silence.

My only reassurance was knowing he had consumed a lethal dose of mushrooms, but it would be hours before the poison took effect. And we did not have hours.

We ventured deeper and deeper into the forest until, beside me, Babushka stumbled and halted. At once I paused, ignoring a bark from Reuter, who followed a few meters behind us. Babushka held up a hand.

"A moment, please," she said breathlessly, not bothering to say it in French.

It hadn't occurred to me that the pace we were keeping had presented difficulty for her; a little pang struck my heart as she leaned heavily on her walking stick and reached for me, pulling me closer. But what Reuter did not notice was the way she wrapped my fingers around her cane before she held tight to me for support, blocking my hand from his view. The hand that now clutched our only weapon.

I gripped tighter as a sudden tremble nearly shook me. She had not needed to rest at all.

"Wait," she muttered, so calm, so quiet I hardly heard her over the blood rushing in my ears.

Overhead the leaves rustled, stirred by an insistent breeze; the forest itself sensed the anticipation coursing through my veins. I glanced at Reuter, who seemed to decide that this area would serve his purpose. He repositioned his rifle across his back and approached, his eyes on me.

Though she did not turn to face him as his footsteps neared, Babushka held up an imploring hand, convincingly defeated. "Do what you will, but let it serve as punishment enough and let the girl live. I give you my word, I will not interfere." Again she said it in Russian, then French as though realizing her mistake. To him a grandmother's desperation, to me a clear message: She was leaving the next part to me.

When he was nearly upon us, she stepped aside as if to prove her compliance. At the same time she released her staff.

I didn't hesitate. I clutched the solid piece of wood, spun around, swung it in a high arc, and struck him in the head.

A sickening crunch, his groan, my yelp, and he collapsed. I stared at the blood pooling at his temple, the cane in my shaking hands—then the wrinkled fingers pressed against his throat.

"Alive," Babushka announced. "He won't stay unconscious for long. What are you going to do with him?"

A challenge. The little curve of a devious smile. Almost as if she were enjoying herself.

Heart thudding, I looked from her to him, my fingers gripping my amulet, though I didn't recall clutching it. Sprawled on the ground, a Fritz. *The* Fritz. I had never been more terrified for my grandmother or myself than I had been almost a year ago. He had struck Babushka even though she had complied with him, had rendered me helpless, had regarded both of us as if we had deserved such punishments. Today, he deserved every agonizing moment awaiting him.

"Leave him here."

She jerked her head in a nod. "Get rope." She removed the rifle across his back, passed a hand from his chest to his neck and head, as if seeking a target, then stood and aimed at his temple. "I will hold him. But if he wakes and I'm forced to shoot him and another soldier happens to find the body, they will go in search of whoever fired the bullet, so I suggest you hurry."

I stared at her, at the rifle pointed so precisely, until she snapped at me to go. I sprinted to the old shed, my closest option, and returned moments later. A birch stretched skyward, its pale trunk covered in dark slashes like old wounds. Here we were too far from the road for anyone to hear. Too hidden for anyone to uncover.

"What kind of mushrooms did you give him?" Babushka asked.

"Death cap."

"How long before effects set in?"

"Approximately eight hours after ingestion, though it might take longer."

She dipped her head in a pleased nod, indicating I had re-called the lesson correctly. She adjusted her headscarf as if she were about to complete a task as simple as plucking potatoes from the fields, then she hooked Reuter by his underarms.

We dragged him closer to the designated tree. While I un-raveled the rope to bind him, Babushka knelt in the under-brush and grabbed a boot.

"Strip him," she ordered.

I cringed. "Is that necessary?"

"Our choices are to burn his uniform or let someone find it."

A fair point. She had already finished with his boots and moved on to his trousers, so I left her to it and began unfasten-ing his tunic. Once finished, we tied a gag around his mouth and propped his back against the birch. While Babushka bound his ankles, I pulled his arms behind the trunk and secured his wrists, then we stepped back.

His head slouched against his bare chest. A little groan emerged. At once, I stiffened while Babushka snatched the rifle at her feet.

Reuter lifted his head. Blinked. Focused glassy eyes on me.

"Interpret for me, Babushka."

He had already started tugging on his bonds, hurling what I expected were curses around the gag. When I reached him, I knelt so I was on his eye level. He paused, chest heaving as he fumed.

"You told me what you intended to do to me; now I will tell you what I intend to do with you. I intend to leave you here un-til you die, because you have ingested a lethal dose of poison-ous mushrooms. They *will* kill you." I leaned closer, holding his gaze. "Slowly and painfully."

While Babushka interpreted, I didn't break eye contact with

Reuter, though I swore I heard a little smile behind her words. But I watched him. The way his eyes widened, then glared, fear and fury mingling until he was left only with terror.

Hours later, after erasing all traces of Reuter's presence from the house, Babushka and I told Dedushka we were going on an evening walk around the property. Instead we returned to the forest to find the Fritz shivering, moaning, too weak to struggle against his bonds. The cramps and abdominal pains must have set in.

His gray eyes were nearly black in the increasing darkness, then his body shook violently. Vomit attempted to force its way around the gag while he fought against his bonds, choking, writhing. Then he shuddered, slumped forward, and lay still.

Quiet surrounded us. I waited for an indication I had failed—but no, nothing. It was done. And even if the soldiers sought vengeance for Reuter's unexplained disappearance, at least I had won my grandmother a reprieve. Had saved us from his intended evils.

"Son of a bitch," Babushka muttered. "A more merciful death than you deserved."

A cool breeze swept over us, and I swallowed the lump in my throat. "I owe you my life, Babushka, and much more."

She scoffed. "You aren't indebted to me, nor I to you. No person owes another anything, and it is an absurd, entitled notion to believe otherwise."

Perhaps it was. But neither was one person required to go to the lengths she had to protect another. Gratitude was never owed, only freely given. So I poured all of mine into her; she might not accept anything else, but surely she would accept that.

Chapter 24

Vitebsk Region, 3 June 1942

After burning Reuter's uniform and burying the body, Babushka returned to the farmhouse while I went to the shed, where I stashed a bottle of vodka for the occasional evening of indulgence. Or for times like this, when I needed something to calm me.

This bottle was almost empty, but there was enough to fulfill my needs. I guzzled what remained, walking across the fields and through the woods with no destination in mind, insides churning, head spinning. I had poisoned a Fritz. It was what I had set out to do, and I'd done it. Killed a man.

What if the other soldiers came looking for him? What if they found the body? No, impossible. Surely they would assume he had deserted before they assumed an old blind woman and her granddaughter were capable of killing him.

She had not killed him. *I* had killed him. A deserved fate. But tonight I could not be near the forest where he had suffered and died and now lay in the earth; in the farmhouse where I had watched him consume deadly mushrooms; in the loft alone with myself and the blood on my hands.

Shivering against the cool evening air, I finished the bottle, letting the fire purge my insides, then tossed it onto the side of the road.

I stopped. When had I found my way to the road?

Silvery starlight glinted above, while a distant owl hooted. Long after curfew. I'd already wandered past the garrison—without detection, it seemed, considering I had reached the railway station. Perhaps I had stayed in the forests and fields until I had safely passed, like the partisans often did. I had no faith in my ability to find my way back through the woods—not when encumbered by the thick haze that had seized my mind. If I used the road, I risked detection. A sudden wind swept over me, as chilling as a final breath leaving a body.

Daniil. His izba was closest. Maybe I had been seeking him all along; this report was urgent, then he'd help me find my way back or sneak me over to Katya's. Besides, his presence always helped me forget men like Reuter, the carnage, the blood. And I needed to forget.

When I found the little wooden structure silhouetted in the moonlight, I pounded on the door.

"Danya?" My attempt to whisper failed. As did my attempt to knock softly. "Are you there?"

The door flew open. A familiar hand shot out and pulled me inside.

"What the hell, Mila?" Urgent with a gruff edge, as though he'd been asleep. He scowled. "It's the middle of the night. You can't be here."

"I know, I know." I took a few unsteady steps farther into the room. "I won't be long, I promise, but I have a report. An *important* report."

The scowl softened. "You're drunk," he said slowly.

Was it that obvious?

"Don't chastise me, Daniil Ivanovich." I lifted my chin and

wagged a disapproving finger at him. "Don't I deserve a drink for killing a Fritz?"

Now that I was safe, I turned, seeking a place to sit, but he caught my wrist.

"What Fritz? Were you hurt?"

When I spun into him, I wrapped my arms around his neck for stability. His jawline was even more defined than I remembered. And his haphazard hair reminded me of the way it had looked that night in the old shed. When he had wrapped his arms around my waist. When I thought he was going to press his lips to mine.

"Talk to me, Mila." Daniil disentangled us. "What happened?"

I blinked, exhaled, smelled the alcohol on my own breath. If only my head would stop whirling. "The Fritz who kept coming to the farm. You didn't exactly give me permission to poison him, but I wanted to tell you now in case they enact reprisals for his disappearance." A sudden unsteady breath interrupted me. "I wanted it to appear as if he had mistakenly gathered poisonous mushrooms, and he ate them like I hoped, but then he took me and Babushka to the forest."

Daniil tensed. Everyone had heard stories about what the soldiers did to women in the forest.

"No, he didn't . . . I hit him before he could, but given the head injury, it no longer looked like an accidental poisoning, so—" I faltered. "We destroyed his uniform and buried him."

As I waited for his inevitable disapproval, Daniil pushed the hair away from his forehead. "You saved your grandmother. And yourself."

My thudding heart slowed, though his words weren't

enough to erase the gray gaze burned into my memory. And I just wanted it gone. Daniil passed a hand across his jaw, then suddenly we were close again. It was his eyes I saw, the only ones I wanted to see.

"Kiss me. Make me forget all about him."

Had I said those words out loud? Had they sounded the way they had felt, somewhere between a demand and a plea?

I *had* narrowed the space between us. I *had* wrapped my arms around him. But he didn't react, giving me no indication as to whether I had voiced the urge or kept it contained. We were just there, close to one another. His hands along the small of my back. My arms around his neck. Neither of us moving.

The last time I found myself in his arms, he had stepped away. Why had I sought the same arms that had released me? And if they ever were to remain around me, I did not want it to be on a night like this.

Cheeks aflame, eyes suddenly smarting, I drew back. I'd wander through the village all night, find more vodka, whatever it took to erase the tightness of Reuter's grip on my neck, holding me against the table, telling me exactly what awaited me.

When I found the doorknob, a hand reached over me to hold the door shut. I tugged on it anyway. "I can't stay here."

"It's not safe for you to leave. Not with curfew. And not like this."

Protesting required too much energy. I let my hand fall. Daniil wrapped a sturdy arm around me and I leaned into him, losing myself in the lingering spiciness of cigar smoke on his clothing and skin. He led me to the adjoining room, where next to the wooden bed an oil lamp rested on the dirt floor. He released me long enough to light it, its flame winking in the darkness.

After offering me a glass of water, he settled me on the bed, then he drew the blanket over me and leaned closer. The lamplight reflected in his eyes. "I'll be on the pech."

I would be here while he stayed on the stove's warm, flat space utilized for sleeping. If I had wanted to be by myself, I would have stayed in my loft on the farm.

It was the first time I killed one of them. Once you do the same, everything changes.

Daniil's words from the night in the shed echoed in my mind. He knew what it was like to stare into a man's blank face. The scent of freshly overturned earth, the feeling of dirt beneath fingernails, dragging a limp corpse to the grave.

I brushed my fingers over the stubble along his cheeks, accentuated by the lamp's golden glow. "Stay," I whispered. I wanted to forget everything else I had done this night. Everything except coming here. Seeking him.

He took my hand away, though with gentle care. "Get some rest." He released me and turned to go.

I wanted him near, nothing more. He was going to leave me alone, my only company the memory of the Fritz's final choked breaths.

"Wait." I reached after Daniil, my hand trembling now, but he was already too far away. "Don't leave, I didn't mean . . ." I paused, swallowing hard as he faced me. "Stay, that's all. Please. Just until I fall asleep. It's the only way I'll stop thinking about—"

"Killing a man." Blunt yet somehow soft. He nodded.

He climbed into bed next to me—hardly enough room for two, but I didn't mind. After extinguishing the lamp, Daniil drew me nearer, as though to ensure that I wouldn't fall off; I nestled close to him.

The warmth from the alcohol and his presence settled over me.

His murmur broke the quiet. "Even when your actions are justified, it doesn't feel better. Fresh wounds feel the same no matter how you earn them—painful, all-consuming. But wounds heal."

It was true; wounds did heal in time. But wounds also left scars.

"Has it gotten easier for you since last July?" I asked softly, recalling his words from the night in the old shed. The first time he had killed a man. "After the soldiers invaded."

He didn't say anything. Perhaps I had upset him.

"Yelena Agafonovna and I had been seeing each other for about a year." He spoke quietly but resolutely, the vibrations in his chest tickling my ear. "Her family lived on a farm outside Shumilino, so when the invasion struck, I planned to stay with them for a time."

Yelena Agafonovna. I had never met her, and Daniil had never spoken of her. And at the mention of her family, it occurred to me that I knew nothing about his.

"Your family?" I prompted. "Did they go with you?"

"When I was small, my mother died giving birth to a stillborn daughter. At the time of Molotov's announcement, my father hadn't come home in months. He's a drunk. Was. I'm not sure anymore."

If he expected a response, I didn't know what to say.

"I wanted to help Lena's family protect themselves and their land in case the Fritzes came here," Daniil went on. "When I arrived, the soldiers had already come through. The livestock had been confiscated and the fields stripped bare or destroyed." A pause. He cleared his throat. "And the house was burning."

Sudden tears pricked my eyes; I blinked them back. My grandparents' farm had been spared the destruction, but I remembered those first weeks confined to the property while the soldiers passed. Dedushka assessing every farm between ours and Obol, desperate to shield me from the violence. The same soldier I had just murdered stealing from us. Then, walking past ruined fields on my way to the village, mounds of earth betraying shallow graves. Each horror as raw and unexpected as the last, now a common occurrence. Now, similar to what was happening to my parents in Leningrad.

I closed my eyes for an instant, then stole a peek at Daniil. He stared at the wall across from us, gaze distant yet glimmering through the darkness.

"The soldiers were already gone except one who came from behind the house. He had hardly noticed me before I shot him and threw his corpse into the flames."

Quiet settled over us.

"And Yelena?"

"Behind the house, barely breathing. He had slit her throat." Another pause, the silence indicating what else the soldier had done to her, followed by a trembling breath. "She died in my arms. When the house had burned down, I found the rest of the family's remains inside. I can only hope they were dead before the fire started."

The obstruction in my throat left words impossible. Tentatively, I brushed an escaped tear from his cheek, the moisture glittering gray in the darkness, then reached for his hand. When I found it, he didn't pull away.

Moonlight stole through the window, slipping between the open curtains. Soft beams stretched over the bed, gathering their courage to come closer and sweep us away into the night, into darkness and slumber and peace.

I listened to his heartbeat while he traced his fingers up and down my back, gentle as the whisper that slipped from my lips. "You loved her?"

He brushed away the stray hairs that had fallen over my face. "Very much."

The silver moonlight crept closer, falling across the peaks and valleys our bodies created beneath the bedding. My breaths slowed until they matched Daniil's.

"Very much," I repeated. Guileless, candid, yet severe, the embodiment of a passion struck by utter desolation. Though I intended to say more, the words slipped out of reach. The fog in my mind overtook me, and its warmth carried me away.

* * *

WHEN MORNING ARRIVED—BRINGING my scattered memories from the previous night—I bade Daniil goodbye and left, nearly in the same breath. Perhaps it should have been a more meaningful goodbye, considering I didn't imagine I would live to see him again by the time Babushka was finished with me.

The sun had hardly embarked upon its tentative exploration of a sky layered in shades of heather, indigo, and cobalt. A few stars lingered, loath to depart until their next welcome, while I walked as quickly as I could manage. Given the lingering queasiness in my stomach, a splitting headache, and a mouth that was as parched as a desert, I felt as if I'd swallowed death cap mushrooms myself.

With any luck, my grandmother hadn't noticed my absence;

when it came to her rules, she still treated me like a child. As I eased the door open, luck wasn't on my side.

"You'd better have a damn good explanation for where you've been."

Babushka could tear me apart with nothing but the intensity of her glare; today was no exception.

"Sit down." Two words yet enough to make me wince.

I obliged, launching into my defense. "I drank too much after—" I lowered my voice. "What happened."

"You're lucky you weren't shot for wandering around after curfew." She lifted her coffee cup, though I wondered if the beverage could get past the hard set of her mouth. "Wait until they find the body."

Even if it was a jest, I tensed. Why had we left such obvious evidence? Only one assassin got away with leaving her victims for everyone to discover. Even then, the rest of us suffered.

"We have to dig him up and burn him," I said. "The Fritzes shot a number of people and threatened to burn down the village when they found the soldier Orlova killed, so if—"

Babushka stiffened. I had never mentioned Orlova's victim; apparently, it had been wise to keep it secret. Though I got up, her grip found my arm, forcing me to remain in place.

"Explain yourself this instant, Mila, or you will never set foot off this property again."

Who threatened a nineteen-year-old with punishment? "It was a long time ago, last autumn."

"And you never mentioned it?"

"Why mention it when you told me not to get involved? She was active in the revolution, so didn't you expect her to fight the Germans, too? Resistance comes with risk, but it *can* work despite what you claim, and if Orlova—"

"Not another word!"

The order was so fierce it silenced me. Babushka's heaving chest steadied when she took a slow breath. Her next words fell on my ears like a perfectly measured milligram of cyanide for a suicide pill—specific, balanced, purposeful.

"You killed that man, and you are done." Each word settled, milligram after milligram into the capsule. "This is not your fight."

It felt as if she had shoved the cyanide down my throat.

I had no chance to retort—which was for the best, since she didn't need another reason to be angry with me. Babushka released my arm, collected the breakfast dishes, and began washing them, mouth closed, indicating this conversation was over.

I went outside and closed the door harder than necessary behind me. Along the path to the shed, I lifted my face toward the sun and let its heat absorb my lingering fury.

Babushka didn't know about all the good the Young Avengers had done for the cause, or Fruza's plan to station me inside the Nazi garrison. This *was* my fight, and I would see it through until it was safe to go home.

PART 2

We shall destroy everything, and on the ruins we shall build our temple.

—Vladimir Lenin

Svetlana

December 1917–August 1918

Chapter 25

Moscow, 6 December 1917

I n the Nerchinsk katorga, winter had been bleak; in Moscow, overtaken by Bolsheviks, winter was merciless. Every Bolshevik flag and propaganda poster gleamed as bright as the welts and bruises that had once laced my skin; every bellow condemning opposition and suppressing free speech sounded as harsh as those from men who had once cursed me, taunted me, called me by a prisoner number.

Gray dawn stretched across the sky, forlorn and timid. A sliver of pale yellow light attempted to breach it, faint as the hope keeping my spirits alive—that of the Constituent Assembly elections.

For the past few hours, Vera, Fanya, and I had been putting up posters campaigning for the Socialist Revolutionaries. After the coup, I had lost all hope for the elections, but a few weeks had passed and they were carrying on. Were the Bolsheviks so delusional that they expected the people to support a party that had forcibly taken control? Whatever their reason for permitting elections, it gave the Socialist Revolutionaries a chance to secure a majority vote. To prevent a dictatorship.

Cold air stung my nostrils like the frigid winds that had carried the pungent perfume of revolution—fresh wounds, burning wood, singed flesh, smoke, and gunpowder. On our way back to Hotel Petrov, we traversed streets once glistening with blood. Graffiti and posters covered a pharmacy's boarded windows; we were adding our final pamphlets when a piece of Bolshevik propaganda caught my eye.

The image depicted a nobleman's corpse, his decorated military uniform torn, covered in bloody slashes, eyes too large for his face, bulging and bloodshot. A woman's shadow stretched across the poster and fell over the victim. Above, on a banner made to look like a slip of white paper, written in red script were the words: *Those blinded by bourgeois deception shall not see the Soviet triumph.*

I ripped it off the wall.

After the poster landed on a pile of fresh snow, Vera picked it up. "I hope you're not fond of your vision."

"Afraid Orlova will come for me?" I asked scathingly.

"That can always be arranged. My sources tell me informing on anti-Bolsheviks is a lucrative business." She addressed Fanya with a devious glint in her eye. "Care to turn Svetlana in with me and split the reward?"

Ignoring the jest, Fanya slapped paste over a few posters and waved a hand for us to resume our work. She frowned the way she often had in the katorga—an attempted deterrent, expecting me to defy an order, argue with another prisoner, chase the excitement that had been absent ever since a man had seized my gun and sentenced me to a lifetime of beatings and hard labor.

Vera scrutinized the Orlova propaganda before letting it fall. "What do your sources say about her?" I asked.

"Don't you read Arina Drozdova's articles?" Vera lifted a

brow, referring to her journalistic alias. "My sources give me everything they know, and I report anything worth mentioning."

"Do they know who she is? Does she intend to discourage anti-Bolshevik votes during this election?"

She scoffed. "Don't put much faith in the elections. As long as Orlova holds significant influence, so will the Bolsheviks. Would you vote against a party if doing so and getting caught meant a death sentence?"

"Should I let Bolshevik attempts to crush free speech deter me from supporting our party?" I pressed my final poster against the wall, wincing when the movement aggravated my shoulder, where my gunshot wound from the uprising was still healing.

Vera stood straighter, eyes gold against the gray morning, perhaps expecting me to continue. Instead, I drew a slow breath, letting the lingering ache from my injury quell the heat brewing inside me. Killing Orlova was not enough to destroy the Bolshevik Party, but it would damage them while giving the people more opportunity to express their political views without fearing repercussions.

The satisfaction of stopping her was most irresistible of all.

Vera already knew too much; I had spent the last month agonizing over when she would reveal my affairs in Kiev. If she discovered my plan after Kazimir had refused to let me target Orlova, it was another secret to share with him. More fuel for his mistrust. Deception was a serious transgression; defying a direct order was certain to seal my fate.

Every secret she collected was another bullet sliding into her chamber. She retained the power to fire on a whim.

* * *

BACK AT THE hotel after we shed our coats, boots, and shawls, Fanya fetched tea while Vera and I remained in our bedroom. Though I'd coaxed warmth back into my limbs, my hands hadn't stopped trembling. Since we'd discovered Orlova's propaganda, Vera had been tense. The time had come; she was ready to use everything she had against me. I felt it as surely as I had felt the bullet ripping across my flesh.

The moment the door closed, she sat across from me—jaw set, grim. "When we first met, all I saw in you was Khodynka Field. Bloody Sunday. A class that never cared for mine."

I shifted in a futile effort to banish the discomfort prickling across my skin. If she was determined to convince Kazimir I was loyal to the bourgeoisie, so be it. But let her dare to touch my child; then she would know what it was to make an enemy of me.

She continued with an unusual lack of animosity. "During the uprising, you prevented a soldier's attack. Perhaps saved my life." Her voice quavered as a little shudder escaped. "Since then, I haven't seen the massacres as much anymore."

I knew this battle well—wrestling with change, straying from a place once known and familiar into one entirely new. Such a journey did not occur without confusion, uncertainty, struggle. Different though our experiences had been, this one we shared—I by leaving my class for hers, she by reconsidering her opinion of an aristocrat, and everything we had endured to reach these points. Suffering had forged us into unbreakable casts, yet inside these molds lay the fragility and brokenness left by that same suffering.

"People judge only by what they know," I said, breaking the quiet that had settled over us. "Uncle Misha told me that, when I first came here. I know what you and your family have suffered, and I've seen your dedication to this cause."

"And I know your class, your history with this party, and that you are keeping your daughter from Kazimir."

Not accusatory, simply observant; still, I flinched. I felt the warm newborn against my chest, her little legs curled up as though she were still tucked inside, her tiny clenched fist gripping a lock of my hair.

"I want the timing to be right, that's all," I said softly. "You lost your parents, Vera. My daughter deserves a chance to be with hers."

She said nothing, impossible to read; perhaps her opinion of me had not changed after all. Whatever she chose to tell Kazimir, he would believe. If she convinced him and the party that I was working with the bourgeoisie, she would shatter my chance to be with him and Tatiana. To destroy Orlova. To avenge Uncle Misha's murder. My bomb plot in Kiev had failed, but I could not lose this, too. Failure was not a notion I intended to revisit.

"Your uncle shared an interesting observation." Vera spoke without hostility, surprisingly forthright. "I won't tell Kazimir about Kiev unless you give me a reason to do so."

A sudden swell formed in my throat; I looked to her to communicate my gratitude, so she offered a small nod in return. Suddenly I felt my daughter's presence again, this time as the little girl I had seen in Kiev—her arms around my waist, my lips pressed to the crown of her head, her father's secure arms around us both. My little whisper of reassurance that Mama and Papa would never, ever leave her again.

* * *

Moscow, 10 December 1917

A few days after establishing my newfound friendship with Vera, I joined Kazimir in his bedroom for a glass of wine and what was supposed to be a night alone. But when Vera stopped by to ask him about our party's depleting finances for the article she was drafting, her brief question developed into a discussion. Now we reclined on his bed, watching his incessant pacing.

Kazimir ran a hand through his disheveled hair, his eyes rimmed by dark circles. "We can't acquire funding from the banks now that the Bolsheviks have seized control of them."

I finished my wine and placed the empty glass on the nightstand. "We can breach their forces and take what we need."

"Not likely, with each bank so heavily guarded."

"And since they have also encouraged the proletariat to steal back private property, the surrounding estates in Moscow are being pillaged," Vera added, turning to me. "Has the same happened to the Petrov family estate? If not, what if we went there?"

A knot tightened in my stomach; pillaging estates was never without violence if the aristocrats had not yet fled. I knew nothing of my former home or my parents' fate, only that I hoped they were unharmed, alive, safe. Did Vera expect me to target my family? Kazimir stopped pacing while I crossed my arms to hide a sudden tremble in my hands. I needed to continue spreading propaganda for the Constituent Assembly elections, hunt for Orlova, and work toward the end of the revolution.

Still, if I tried to dissuade her, she might take that as a reason to reveal my secrets to Kazimir.

Though she had suggested *the Petrov family estate*, the threat I heard was *Kiev*.

But my family did not deserve to die.

"Let me speak with Kazimir," I said at last. "Alone."

Chapter 26

Moscow, 10 December 1917

I had to tell Kazimir the truth. If Vera had mentioned my family because she still resented me and planned to reveal what I had hidden in Kiev, I needed to tell him before she did. Surely he would listen to me, welcome our daughter, and leave my family's estate in peace.

But the truth was beyond my control now. No matter what I claimed, Vera held the power to accuse me of spending the last decade in Kiev working for the bourgeoisie. And if Kazimir believed her, he would hold me captive. Interrogate me. Perhaps even execute me. And then what if he never accepted Tatiana, or if harm befell her?

As the door closed behind Vera, my voice fled—whether due to this conversation or the possibility of directing my father's own pistol at him, I wasn't certain. The only way to ensure Tatiana's safety—and my own—was to do as Vera wished.

My shallow breaths pierced the stillness. Kazimir's cigarette flared orange, then his exhaled smoke wrapped around me. Normally, it might have drawn me nearer to him; not this time.

I managed a whisper. "Confiscate funds from my parents, but you can't ask me to shoot them."

"One doesn't often come without the other." He took a slow

drag. "My contingent has no place for those who take pity on the bourgeoisie."

"This has nothing to do with my opinions on the bourgeoisie. These are my *parents*, Kazimir."

That day in the tobacconist shop filled my head, as excruciating as his grip on my gunshot wound. Yet despite the blood he had shed that day, I had seen the struggles of the man who lay buried beneath this leader. And I needed to find him.

"Do not expect this of me." Desperation turned my voice shrill, pleading as I had for the shop owners whose sole crime had been their birth. "Take money, valuables, everything else. Not their lives."

A nauseous turn gripped my stomach while the blood rushed in my ears. I craved that rare look of his, intensity mixed with passion, frustration, agony, as though his heart had been laid bare and had led him to me. Not the look I feared I would find from the tobacconist shop, when he had said it was not my place to interfere.

Kazimir finished his cigarette, then closed the distance between us. His light touch brushed a lock of hair from my face. "I won't force you to hurt them, Sveta."

A little sob bubbled in my throat. I wrapped my arms around him, pouring all my gratitude into my touch. He held me close while every fear slipped away, banished by his words, the heartbeat in his chest, his strong arms enveloping me. When I lifted my head, he guided my lips to his, gentle and reassuring.

If Kazimir refused this suggestion, Vera would not dispute him. No reason to destroy the peace between us, no reason to tell him about Tatiana.

"We will leave tomorrow night."

I stepped back. "Leave?"

"For the estate."

When I opened my mouth, no sound came. Kazimir regarded me without concern despite claiming no harm would come to my parents. How quickly he had forgotten that assertion.

"The Bolsheviks control most of our former resources, so we have little choice. If land and wealth are being confiscated from the bourgeoisie and allocated to the proletariat, what better way to use your family's than in support of our cause?" He placed a hand on my cheek. "I have to do what's best for the contingent."

"No." I jerked away from his touch before digging my fingers into his forearms. "*No*, Kazimir, you said you wouldn't make me hurt them!"

"And I meant it, so I'm ordering you to come." His voice was level, his hands certain and steady as they found my waist. "No need to worry, Sveta. Someone else might shoot them without a second thought; you can give your family a chance to be reasonable. With you present, I expect they will agree to whatever you demand."

His logic did little to ease the knot in my throat. Perhaps they would concede. Or perhaps they would not.

* * *

Petrov Manor House, 11 December 1917

In the distance, my family's estate lurked in shadow. Down the long flagstone road to the wrought-iron gates stretched an avenue of lindens, thick branches draped in icicles glittering like the jewels that had once glistened against my skin. The last time I traveled down this road, I expected not to return.

This estate, where I had dressed in elegant silk gowns to attend my parents' balls and danced with my father and three elder brothers. All three in military service under the tsar before I was old enough to attend Smolny; perhaps they were alive now, perhaps dead. I swallowed hard.

I still tasted the countless feasts in the dining hall. Roasted lamb, pork, smoked salmon, black caviar, vegetable soups, assorted breads with jams and butter, fine cheeses, fresh fruits, chocolates, pastries, wine, liqueurs—each delicacy the best that could be acquired. I still envisioned the sparkle in my mother's emerald eyes as she gushed about literature, poetry, art, opera, and ballet. I still smelled fresh earth and grass as I fled deep into the back garden, ducking behind thick hedges to hide from my governess. Usually Uncle Misha found me and promised to give me another lesson with my father's pistol if I emerged and obeyed her for the rest of the day. Disobedience, he said, would get me confined to my bedroom as punishment, interfering with time I might have spent with him, so it was best for me to do as I was told now and have my secret lesson with him later. And finally, he concluded, it was not fair to bring my parents' wrath upon my governess for her inability to make me behave, because it was not the poor woman's fault that my parents had entrusted such a wayward little girl to her care, at which I always giggled.

This estate, where Papa had condemned my political leanings while Mama listened in silence. Then she placed a hand over mine before shaking her head wearily, her voice carrying as she followed him out of the room: *Vasya, darling, the revolutionaries will be suppressed soon enough. Sveta will become a fine young lady, marry well, and forget these silly notions.*

This estate, unjust and broken like the government itself, yet the landscape of my childhood. The family of Baron Vasily Pavlovich Petrov, my own blood, impossible for me to spill.

Kazimir and I stood near our parked automobile. My shallow breaths pierced the stillness. He motioned for our companions to get out of the vehicle, then led our small group—Rolan, Vera, and myself—toward the manor house. I watched them go, unable to follow, until my gaze fell upon Vera's turned back.

Kiev.

With a shuddering breath, I drew my pistol and pursued them. I'd find my parents first, usher them to safety or into hiding, tell everyone they were gone. But if I failed, or if they did not concede as Kazimir anticipated, this night would end in bloodshed.

When I was first to reach the gate, I stopped. It was ajar; beyond, the house was dark. No guards or staff in sight.

I hurried across the frozen, snowy ground, up the wide stone steps, through the unlocked double doors. Stale, frigid air greeted me. I switched on the electric lights, revealing parquet floors, a massive chandelier overhead, and a grand marble staircase.

A rush of familiarity brought me to a sudden halt. I was a little girl again, perched at the top of the stairs. Listening while Mama ordered the servants to prepare for the evening's party. Catching snippets of Uncle Misha's and Papa's voices floating from the parlor where they drank and played cards, getting along rather than arguing over politics. Watching servants carry trunks and luggage to the automobile waiting to chauffeur us to our country house, where we spent the summers.

Summers of picnics and parties, music and laughter, frolicking through our gardens, the fields, and the forest, foraging for mushrooms and wild berries and presenting my finds to our cook.

"Mama? Papa?"

Silence greeted me. I rushed to their chambers, breaths sharper with every step down the long halls, past the library, parlors, ballroom, dining room, and bedrooms. Voices rose behind me; the others were inside, about to tear through my family's collections of ancient tomes, fine china, silver, and antiques. Now I was running—faster, faster, anticipating my mother's startled cry, my father's enraged bellow, Kazimir's furious shout, then gunshots.

And yet, I preferred that vision to the one I saw more clearly with every step. The one where, following the raised voices, instead of gunshots I heard silence while I hurried back toward the entryway, but Vera intercepted me in the hall, pulled me close, murmured for my ears alone: *Kiev*. An indication I had to do as she wished, whatever it was. Then she followed me as I found my parents at the foot of the stairs, on their knees in surrender, gaping when they recognized their daughter, while Vera told Kazimir that I had decided to give them what every aristocrat deserved. Mama, Papa, their looks of blank horror as my trembling hands aimed, each sharp crack tearing through me as though the crimson blood splattering the white marble were mine. Vera's threat reverberated with every aching thud of my heart, *Kiev, Kiev* . . .

I stumbled into my parents' bedroom.

The wardrobe doors were open. One valise was missing; another lay open on the bed with a few clothes tossed into it. From the icon corner, decorated with icon lamps and religious images gilded in gold, the Madonna was missing. Draped over Mama's jewelry box was her sapphire-and-diamond necklace fashioned by Fabergé, the same jeweler who designed Easter eggs crusted in gold, silver, enamel, and precious jewels for the royal family. The jewels had been plucked out. On the mantel over the fireplace, the silver crucifix was missing from its usual place beside the ormolu clock with a patinated bronze eagle, wings outspread.

These, all signs of a hasty escape. My parents were gone.

A fierce tremor seized me while the gun fell from my grasp. Somehow I ended up on my knees, too weak to stand, to face what had almost been.

Once the tension in my stomach eased, I picked up my weapon with shaking hands, then the necklace, fingering the empty places before something else caught my eye—a slip of paper wedged between the velvet lining inside Mama's jewelry box. After opening the compartment, I extracted a note written in French.

28 March 1906

Dear Mama and Papa,

I write from Maltzevskaya Prison within the Nerchinsk katorga in Siberia. For terrorism against the imperial government, I have been sentenced to life imprisonment.

Perhaps this does not concern you; perhaps you forgot me the moment I defied your wishes and joined Uncle Misha. For our differences, I do not ask pardon, nor do I renounce my beliefs or regret my decisions. For the grief I have caused you, however,

I beg your forgiveness. My intent was never to disappoint or cause distress, simply to create a future of equality and fairness for all.

Should this letter encourage you to correspond, I will write when permitted. If you wish to forget me, I will respect your choice. However, I ask that you do not forget. I ask you to listen. To think. Most of all, I ask you to try to understand.

If you have forgotten me, perhaps someday you will remember.

Your daughter,
Sveta

Once I returned the paper, I placed both hands on the vanity table. Steadied my breaths. Wiped sudden dampness from my cheeks. My chest ached as it had while writing this letter; I'd spent weeks awaiting a response before concluding one would never come, though Fanya futilely encouraged me to be patient. Someday, after the revolution, I had hoped my parents and I would find peace. Their silence had taken my last hope as surely as the imperial government had taken my freedom.

It was done, unchanged. The urge to establish peace no longer plagued me, nor would I be disappointed again when it never came. But Mama had kept the letter. Perhaps she had listened, thought, tried to understand. Perhaps she had remembered.

"They've been gone for a few weeks, it seems. Probably since the uprising."

As I faced Vera, I left my pistol on the table to resist the temptation to use it. "Disappointed?"

Vera's brow furrowed. Uncle Misha had been right: People

judged by what they knew. But people also reserved the right to accept or reject such knowledge. And Vera rejected everything she saw in me except the aristocracy. What I truly was or wanted to be made no difference. I was Bloody Sunday, Khodynka Field, the bourgeoisie.

"Tell Kazimir about Kiev, if that's what you've decided," I snapped. "This is between us, not my family."

"I told you, I'll stay silent unless you—" She paused while the lines across her brow eased. "Coming here sounded reasonable and enabled us to get the funds we needed. That's why I suggested it." Vera placed a tentative hand on my forearm in attempted reassurance. "I never intended for you to feel threatened, Sveta."

My breaths trembled too much to respond; her hazel eyes brimmed with sympathy. So much churned inside me, it was impossible to make sense of it all—fury, terror, relief. My family was safe. My friend was still my friend.

Vera gave me a little squeeze, then she released me and circled the room, past the oil painting of ballerinas *en pointe*, an original Degas commissioned by my grandmother; the double-armed golden wall sconces with ivory-winged cherubs supporting each slender candle, one of Mama's purchases from Saint Petersburg. Finally, she paused by Papa's Boulle desk, passed down through generations of firstborn Petrov men, and ran her fingers over the *première partie* red tortoiseshell, intricate brass lions' heads, curling leaves and vines, rabbits, dogs, snakes, and birds.

His desk was where Papa always summoned me after our disputes. Once, when I was fifteen, home from Smolny Institute for a few days, I made my usual request not to return. One of our most heated spats followed, then I found him seated with neat stacks of papers before him, spectacles perched on the end of his nose. My eyes roamed over the intricate piece before settling on my father while I waited in obedient, if sullen, silence.

At last, he passed a hand over his silver mustache. "Your uncle Misha's ideals have driven him to squander his inheritance with his anti-imperialist friends. That is not the life our father would have wanted for him, nor is it the life I want for you, Svetushka." Gruff yet endearing, the caring father I loved coupled with the baron fighting to keep his family name from ruin. "Perhaps I cannot control my little brother, but it is my responsibility to help you understand your place. Someday you will teach your children the same." He removed his spectacles, straightened his navy necktie, and looked to me, eyes rich brown, matching mine. "You see? You and I are no different."

The warmth in his gaze indicated he truly believed those words, felt certain I required only a little guidance to reach the same understanding. And I *did* understand; my place and the one my father expected of me would never be the same.

* * *

HEAVY FOOTSTEPS BROKE the quiet long after Vera had left; I had stayed beside my mother's vanity, staring at my father's desk. I snatched my pistol and spun around, aiming at a pair of glittering black eyes.

"Expecting Mama or Papa?" Kazimir nodded at the gun. "Your change of heart suits you, dvoryanka."

"And a bullet between the eyes suits you."

When his jest went unappreciated, his smirk faded. Lowering

my weapon, I marched toward the door until he blocked my
path. Though he opened his mouth, words were already spilling from mine.

"If they had been here and had resisted, would you have
shot them despite my wishes? Is that how little I mean to you?"

He stiffened but did not waver. "The bourgeoisie—"

"Yes, I know, they're all the same. Aristocrats, capitalists,
tsarists, the bourgeoisie . . . to you, they're no different." My
voice caught, then fell to a strained whisper. "*I* am no different."

I longed to break the tension in his gaze, for him to insist he
did not see me as he saw them. Nothing changed—neither the
look in his eyes nor the expanse of space between us.

But my father and I *were* different. He accepted a life of nobility; I did not. He had power, influence, rights; I did not. He
saw my ideals as a girl's fleeting whims; I did not.

His blood was noble, his politics imperial; my blood was noble, my politics proletarian. I put my faith in our differences
as proof we were not the same, yet perhaps our differences
meant nothing when we were bonded by blood. I could change
my mind, my politics, my views; I could not change my birth.
Too often, I was reminded I was the only one who saw and accepted those differences between myself and my father; most
never saw beyond our shared blood.

I lifted my eyes to Kazimir's. "Even when I wrote to tell them
I had been imprisoned, they never wrote back." Admitting it
now felt almost worse than the day I finally acknowledged no
letter was coming. "I will never agree with the aristocracy. I
will never become the woman my family expected me to be.
But I will always care for my parents."

Stillness followed, pierced by his unsteady exhale. "If you
were permitted to send letters from Maltzevskaya, you could

have written to Misha to explain what had happened. Instead, we were left wondering if the arrest reports were true, or if you had returned home. Why did you never write to him?" A pause, then in hardly more than a whisper: "Or to me?"

He was looking at me as he had so often during our youth, seeking confirmation that I was with this cause, with *him*. An almost desperate hope tainted by doubt.

"I did not intend to leave you, Kazimir, nor did I return to the aristocracy," I murmured. "If my word isn't enough to convince you, would a letter have been any different?"

How was I to make him understand that my second letter would have been his, would have explained everything if I'd had the chance to send it? Faced with life imprisonment, I had little choice; Kazimir was all Tatiana had left. My parents would never accept their disgraced daughter's child; once he realized my fate, I had to believe Kazimir might find it in his heart to care for her. But my fellow inmates discovered my first letter had gone to a noble family. That an aristocrat was in their midst. Their persecution led to countless spats between us followed by punishment from the prison authorities, and the first was having my writing privileges revoked.

I had written to my aristocratic parents. Not to the man I loved, my daughter's father, the one whose revolution was mine. In attempting to win my parents' forgiveness, I had left Kazimir to draw his own conclusions about my loyalty. The conclusions he had spent over a decade believing, perhaps would have always believed no matter what I said.

The crease in Kazimir's brow was deep like an old wound. He narrowed the distance between us, then his eyes lowered to my lips.

Suddenly I needed the heat of his fingertips against my skin, the taste of tobacco on his lips, the thud of his heart in time with mine. Our love was a bullet leaving a pistol, unstoppable as it sought its target, heedless of the destruction, the torn flesh, the blood.

The pull between us urged me to shatter his perceptions, to banish all doubt. But how, surrounded by the girl I had been and the woman before him, did he still need reminding?

I stepped past him before his hands found my waist, before his dark eyes urged me nearer, though not before his familiar murmur found my ears.

"Sveta . . ."

I kept walking. The last time I had left my family's property, I had looked back only once, to remind myself why I needed to leave it behind. This time, as I returned to the car to wait, the estate loomed behind me in the darkness. I kept my eyes forward. My feet pattered against the icy flagstones, the sound a former signal of the new life I had hoped to create, now a reminder of the one some would never permit me to leave.

Chapter 27

Moscow, 20 December 1917

Vera, Fanya, and I had spent a leisurely morning in our bedroom, drinking tea and reviewing the latest issue of *Izvestia*, from which I had just read a portion aloud. As Vera pushed aside a pile of notes for her next article, she extended a hand for the paper. I passed it to her, swallowing the sour taste this latest piece of information had left in my mouth.

"At least the Socialist Revolutionaries won a majority in the Constituent Assembly elections," Fanya said with a reassured little sigh. "Surely Bolshevik power will be checked once the new constitution is drawn up."

"And since the constitution hasn't been defined, no need to fret until we're certain of what to expect." Vera gave me a pointed look, knowing I didn't share their optimism.

Thick silence fell while Fanya sipped her tea. The elections had been my sliver of hope; when the Socialist Revolutionaries won the majority, the sliver had expanded, only to be diminished by the reality that weighed constantly on my mind. Even when the revolution seemed to be in my party's favor, it never lasted. Winning an election was not enough to ensure anything.

"Should Fanya and I leave you alone, Sveta?" Vera prompted,

solemn though the teasing edge betrayed her. "You look as if you're ready to shoot someone, and we're the closest targets."

Amid their shared chuckles, I snatched the paper, ignoring their attempts to summon me back. I walked to Kazimir's room, heat building inside me with every step. Order needed to be established—one with rights for all parties.

"What can we do to ensure this new constitution is defined properly?" I asked when I handed it to him. "The Socialist Revolutionaries can't stand by if the Bolsheviks attempt to retain the power these elections have taken from them."

"Neither can the Socialist Revolutionaries assassinate every Bolshevik who attempts to define the constitution in terms that favor them alone—if that is their intention at all." The paper fluttered to the floor when he tossed it aside. "You're not shooting anyone."

I pressed my lips together. "You haven't given me an assignment since the uprising."

"Decisions regarding the revolution are mine to make." He stood above me, shoulders stiff. "Now is not the time for you to be rash."

I stared in response to this unwarranted outburst, but Kazimir had already found the bed. He sat, silent, a clear dismissal.

For the past week—since leaving my family's estate—our interactions had been stiff, formal. The risks our visit had almost posed to my parents were still too raw, as was the uncertainty he had shown toward me. Now I saw a man at a loss. A man . . . afraid?

The lines across his forehead struck me like slashes upon my skin.

The thought of my party losing political influence left a heavy ache in my chest. Too often, I forgot it left the same in his. He was the boy desperate for justice, I the girl longing for equality; now he was the man seeking victory, I the woman fighting for our child. Failure was the knife at our throats, striking constant fear into our hearts. To succumb to its unceasing attacks was to lose ourselves. The foundation upon which we had built our politics, our lives, and the bond that held us together was only as strong as our ability to overcome this most relentless enemy.

When I sat beside him, he said nothing. When I touched his forehead scar from the café explosion, he turned aside. But when my fingers dropped to the exposed skin at the base of his throat, he drew nearer.

"Sveta . . ." A halfhearted deterrent. Kazimir narrowed the distance between us while I wrapped my arms around him.

"We won the elections. Once the constitution is established properly, we will be in a stronger position than ever," I murmured, touching my thumb to the hard set of his mouth; his lips parted. "You can finish this."

"I will," he replied without hesitation. "But I need you to do as I say. Especially now." Another attempted warning, more emphatic but only hastening the eager thud in my chest. His hand curved along my neck, lifted my chin, rough fingers sending heat through my aristocratic blood as surely as they would have spilled another's.

He brought my mouth to his—deep, urgent, desperate. All too soon, he drew back and tightened his hold on my chin, prompting me to look at him.

"Do you understand?" Kazimir pressed, his voice gruff. "You must be fully committed to this revolution. To us."

I pressed my palm to his bearded cheek. "Us?" A question I had never dared to ask. Not when the answer was so delicate.

Perhaps the *us* he had in mind did not include a child. Still, if he was considering our future, that conversation could come in time.

He softened at my touch. "We can't be certain of anything until the revolution ends. And then . . ." His thumb trailed down my neck to the base of my throat, so light against my pulsing heartbeat. "Perhaps."

More certainty than I had ever dared to expect from him. We were rivalry, animosity, defiance, vengeance, yet everything that might have forced us apart had drawn us together. Had developed into a mutual recognition of that which bonded us.

A sudden swell filled me, threatening to spill over, urging me to tell him everything though it was not yet time. Before the impulse overtook me, Kazimir shook his head in mock admonition. "Countless proletariat women throughout Moscow, yet I find myself with you, dvoryanka." He leaned close, the next growl rumbling in his throat as one hand slid down to my waist. "It would be far simpler to put a bullet between your ribs."

I tangled one hand through his hair, tightening my grip just enough to hold him in place while our eyes met. "And if I shoot first?" With a sly smile I pulled his lips to mine. A single, slow kiss, infused with all that we were and longed to be. Then I broke away before succumbing to the urge to spend all day in his bed.

He wanted my loyalty to the revolution and to us—and once he learned that *us* included Tatiana, he would understand why I had to defy his orders regarding Orlova. It was more than what she had done to my uncle, more than reminding the Bolsheviks that this revolution was not over yet. It was a final achievement before my daughter became my sole focus, the act to crown my revolutionary involvement, the success I had envisioned ever since returning to Moscow.

* * *

OUTSIDE, COLD BIT through my coat, and I wrapped it more tightly around me while my footsteps crunched against the ice. Somewhere in the distance, a car horn blared. Somewhere else, a dog barked. Otherwise, silence settled like the blanket of fresh snow over the ground.

I had volunteered to stand in a bread line; it seemed like the most logical place to spend hours talking to other women, finding out if Orlova had struck in response to the elections. If so, I'd investigate before returning to the hotel.

I didn't even make it to the bread line before I found the information I sought.

After I pressed through the crowd gathered around a tavern, the sight banished everything but the surge of rage sending fire from head to toe. Two men, two women, all mutilated and gawking at me with bloodshot eyes. And one of those women was Yelizaveta Dmitrievna, an SR in my contingent who had recently attended an anti-Bolshevik rally outside this tavern.

I extracted the paper from her mouth. "'Orlova,'" I read aloud, then I scrutinized a second word I didn't recognize. "'Cheka.'"

Confused murmurs swept over the crowd before a man stepped forward. "The All-Russian Extraordinary Commission. Cheka, for short," he explained. "The Sovnarkom just established it."

"Its purpose?"

"To suppress counter-revolution."

The fire coursing through my body intensified. *Counter-revolution* clearly meant *anti-Bolshevism*, considering the Council of People's Commissars—comprised exclusively of Bolsheviks—had established a new secret police force. Orlova had spent so much time defending Lenin's ideals; now, through the Sovnarkom, he had established the Cheka and named her one of its members, granting her a formal position beneath him.

I'd heard enough. I spun on my heels, shoved the crowd aside, and marched back to Hotel Petrov.

Blind rage drove me to my empty bedroom long enough to pull off my coat and hurl it onto the bed, then I paced up and down the hall. Back and forth, back and forth.

When I had returned to Moscow nine months ago, Orlova had been one woman working toward unrestrained Bolshevik violence. Each day brought her outrageous vision closer to fruition. First she was an assassin, now a member of the secret police, judging by her Cheka claim—and something more. She was a symbol of her party; a warning that pressured the people into succumbing to the fear of who she was and what she had created.

Those who succumbed to fear did not win a revolution.

Kazimir's voice carried down the hall. "What the hell is wrong with you? Did you get bread?"

Without slowing my pace, I made my way to the ashtray near the elevator, where he was tossing a cigarette. His jaw tightened when I ignored him. When I passed, he followed.

As we neared my bedroom, my mind refused to comprehend what I had uncovered—or, worse, how to tell Kazimir. The possibility of a constitution that favored the Bolsheviks—despite our party's electoral victory—had shaken him enough.

"Comrade Petrova, I asked you a—"

I caught him by the lapel of his leather jacket, crushed my mouth to his, and pushed him into my bedroom. Vera was out conducting interviews for a story, and I'd passed Fanya in the lobby, where she was deep in a conversation about propaganda designs; this bedroom was all mine for now, and this was not the time to dwell on what I had seen. I didn't want to talk about Yelizaveta's assassination, I didn't want to talk about the Cheka, I didn't want to talk about Orlova. For a time, brief as it would be, I wanted to forget.

Sometimes I found it impossible to cast everything from my mind; this time, forgetfulness was easier to achieve than I had anticipated, light and freeing. From the moment we fell onto my bed, everything melted away, and I happily succumbed to the respite. The careless girl embodied me, the one who directed me to my escape each time I needed it, who kept me coming back to it.

To him.

I savored every instance, every breath, every touch. Then Kazimir rose, dressed, and left without a word.

Alone on my bed, I clung to bliss until reality returned, crushing me with despair and disappointment. I remembered again, this time with no hope of forgetting.

I nestled deeper beneath the bedding and reached under my pillow, where I'd stashed my Browning after removing it from my waistband. I pulled out the magazine and stared at the unused cartridges. Each one at the ready, waiting for a target.

It was impossible for my party to gain proper support when the threat of Bolshevik reprisal impeded it. I needed a suitable way to attract Orlova's attention, to lure her out of hiding. To force her to come for me. Then I would rely on these bullets, this method that had never failed me; after her death, the fear she instilled would dissipate. Even if the Bolsheviks continued suppressing the opposition, they would have lost a significant piece of their influence.

Except now the Bolsheviks had a secret police force. One the people would fear as much as they had feared the tsar's. Even if Orlova was gone, I felt certain that the terror she had started inflicting so long ago would continue.

Chapter 28

Moscow, 21 January 1918

For each head of one of our leaders, we will demand the heads of a thousand others.

The words that concluded the article floated across the page no matter where I looked. I stood a few meters from the newsstand, having been sent from Hotel Petrov to find a Bolshevik paper to read the report containing their latest threat against those who killed their party members. My insides burned despite the January chill, while another man stepped away from the stand with his own paper.

He held up the headline for the vendor to see, another piece of news that sent heat through my veins. "There, did you hear? We have declared the elections to the Constituent Assembly invalid." He smacked a hand against the paper with a triumphant grin. "And that, comrade, is excellent news for my party."

His face was one I recognized: Mikhail Andreevich Yemelin, part of the Bolshevik Military Organization. Perhaps Orlova had suggested declaring the elections invalid; she remained the most prominent Cheka agent. Perhaps it had been Lenin's decision; either way, public threats were not my concern. The Bolsheviks had undermined my party, so I had a job to do.

Fate had sent me Yemelin. A chance for reprisal.

As he left the newsstand, I followed.

Night descended around me, quiet as the gentle rainfall. In my coat pocket, the weight of my Browning steadied my breaths, preventing fury from blinding me. It channeled the rage, providing me with clarity and focus until the rage found its outlet: My hands clutching the pistol. My finger squeezing the trigger. The cartridge emerging from the barrel and taking my fury with it.

Ahead, his long leather coat snapped in a frigid breeze. Though my fingers itched for my pistol, I drew a deep breath of cold air to settle myself, nearly tasting the gun smoke that would soon linger in my wake.

The future of our government lay in such a precarious balance.

When Yemelin stopped, I rested my back against a dark store window for shelter. The streets were empty, likely due to the rain and frigid temperature, and dark from another Bolshevik-mandated power cut. At the end of the same block, Yemelin prepared to cross. After adjusting the shawl over my head, I sank deeper into the shadows and slipped my free hand into my pocket. My fingers united with my pistol. We remained the only two on the street, but I had to time it perfectly.

Proper timing had been ingrained within me from the moment I fired my first bullet under Uncle Misha's watchful eye. It was a subtle prompting, the smallest nudge; once it came, I never hesitated.

I fired and ducked around the corner of my building, despite the urge to observe the impact. Better to ensure that any unexpected witnesses who glanced toward the shot found nothing but an empty street.

Silence. I should have fled the scene right away, but eventually I deemed it safe to evaluate the results of my work. I peered around the corner and found the figure lying in the street, head surrounded by darkened snow and ice.

I strolled the way I had come, the frozen Moskva River glimmering still and tranquil in the night. Though my pistol held no power to change the decree, it had done enough for now. The Bolsheviks were not the only ones who could make a statement.

* * *

BACK AT HOTEL Petrov with my impromptu mission complete, anger returned; this time, it had no outlet other than a glass of wine.

I sat at the hotel bar with Fanya while my party members pored over the papers I'd brought back. Every issue of *Izvestia* included calls for people to join the Cheka, to cooperate in overcoming lawlessness, and discussed news of Bolshevik terror, but the announcement about the elections had left us in silence—heavy, cold as the pistol tucked into my pocket.

"How can the Bolsheviks do this?" Fanya muttered. "Then to disband the entire assembly and render the Socialist Revolutionaries insignificant . . ." She didn't finish. There was nothing more to say.

I clutched the stem of my glass so tightly it felt as if it might snap. Now my party needed to regain public support. A feasible task, surely, considering the people had voted for us and not the Bolsheviks. It would take more than a supposedly invalid election and party dissolution to end this battle.

Let the Bolsheviks demand a thousand heads for every one of their murdered party members. I would not rest until the lives they had sworn to claim in retaliation had swelled so much that the number was no longer attainable.

But they had already started claiming some of those lives. Innocent ones. I stared at the article before me, discussing the workers who had gathered in Petrograd to peacefully march in favor of the Constituent Assembly. And how this peaceful demonstration had ended like the march on the Winter Palace in 1905—with the streets swimming in blood.

"The Bolsheviks had no right to massacre them," I said. Fanya sat with her head in her hands, likely combatting a migraine; her wine was untouched, though it was a full-bodied Merlot brought back from my parents' wine cellar after looting my family's estate.

When I shifted in my seat, a loose lock of hair fell over my eyes—such pronounced gray streaks against the blond.

At a small table against the far wall sat Vera, Rolan, and Kazimir. They read the papers while Kazimir nursed a beer, brooding.

Despite the little whisper urging me toward him, I resisted. The Constituent Assembly demonstration was a peaceful protest that developed into a massacre, just like Bloody Sunday. We needed to link Bolshevik violence to the violence of the Old Regime. As I left Fanya with her wine, I traced my finger along my pistol's smooth barrel. The Bolsheviks had issued an unmistakable challenge, a direct threat. It gave me no choice other than to respond in kind. Yemelin's was the first of many heads, the start of turning the tide back in my party's favor. Perhaps targeting every Bolshevik was not feasible, but I intended to try. Whatever it took to bring her to me.

When I reached the elevator, Rolan followed me inside, regarding me with his usual spite. I ignored him. As the elevator began to move, he held up a newspaper.

"The Bolsheviks have been drawing media attention away

from the Constituent Assembly demonstration shooting. Instead, they have stirred up rumors about the SRs. Claiming we've been conspiring with the bourgeoisie to oppose them."

I said nothing in response to his accusatory glare. Even after all this time, to him I remained the aristocrat. I nearly felt his tight grip forcing me toward the burning café after the explosion. My skin prickling with heat, lungs clogging with smoke, Kazimir pulling me to safety even as he grappled with my perceived betrayal.

When Rolan punched a button, the elevator screeched to an abrupt halt; I nearly lost my footing, then his fist slammed into my stomach.

Air rushed from my lungs, my insides twisting and aching like they had every time I'd been dealt this same blow in the katorga. When my hands and knees hit the floor, he snatched my gun and tossed it aside. I reached for it, still coughing, but Rolan had already caught my shoulders. He pinned me against the wall, glowering as he had that day outside the café.

"Did you think I'd forgotten how you tried to sabotage us?"

"If my intent had been sabotage, I would have succeeded. When I kill people, I do it properly." Not quite the intended forceful statement as I fought for breath, but I still managed a taunting smirk. "You cannot say the same."

A sudden sting on my thigh pulled a gasp from my throat. Rolan held up a dagger, its edge tinged red with fresh blood. He brought it to my neck, halting my struggles.

"If you never fail, then explain Kiev all those years ago— unless that entire plot was a lie."

I owed him no explanations, particularly not when he wouldn't believe them. I stayed still, unblinking. He leaned closer.

"Now that the Bolsheviks are making false claims about the Socialist Revolutionary Party, you are an even bigger liability. And there's far too much at stake to let a liability break the people's confidence in us."

He watched my chest rising, falling. Touched the dagger's pointed tip to the base of my throat. Drew a straight line down, slow and light, not breaking the skin, until the blade rested between my breasts.

"Soon Kazimir will tire of his tsarist whore."

I pressed my back harder against the wall. Was that all I was to this party? An object of Kazimir's use? Was that all I was to *him*? Impossible; if seeking only pleasure, he could have found it in countless women. Yet Kazimir continued finding his way to *me*, and I to him. He had spoken of *us*. Surely there was more to *us* than an occasional shared bed.

When the doors opened, having returned us to the main level, Rolan released me. As he stepped back, I sank to the elevator floor, the pain dull, the air too hot and stifling.

Rolan shoved past a waiting figure while a gasp met my ears. "Sveta?" At the familiar voice, I blinked; Vera crouched beside me and caught my shoulders. "What happened? What has he done?"

"Nothing that hasn't been done to me before." A slight rasp edged the words, my chest and stomach still tight from his blow. To ease her concerns, I relayed the incident and showed her the cut on my leg—shallow, in the same place Kazimir had shot Rolan, punishment for acting without orders when Rolan had thrown me back into the burning building. Now this wound served as a reminder of what Rolan had said then and repeated now: Kazimir wanted me only for pleasure, and when he lost interest, no one in this party had any need for an aristocrat's daughter.

"That's the second time he's attacked you and acted without authorization," Vera said, eyes alight with sudden fury as she helped me to my feet. "With your statement and me as a witness, Kazimir will—"

"Give Rolan the satisfaction of believing he sent me running to Kazimir for protection."

"He deliberately defied orders."

"Even if I say something and he's killed for it, Rolan dies confident that he successfully frightened me and proved to everyone I'm helpless without Kazimir." I shook my head, though I squeezed her forearm in gratitude as we stepped into the hall. "I won't do that; he knows I won't. This stays between us, Vera."

Without awaiting her reply, I made my way outside. Frigid blackness swept over me, sucking the heat from my skin, steadying my pounding heart. The glowing ember of a cigarette cut through the dark, bright as blood gleaming against silver metal.

"You're scowling, Sveta."

I sighed, fighting to release the lasting memory of Rolan's blade against my skin. Steady rainfall surrounded us, though Kazimir hardly seemed to notice.

"What's wrong?"

I shook my head. Threats and attacks had been a part of my life for so many years; it was not as if I were unaccustomed to them, even if they were never easier to bear. But it had passed now; I was here, with him, letting his presence settle me.

"Is this about the Constituent Assembly elections?"

I offered a half smile. "If I'm upset, does that mean I have politics on my mind?"

He chuckled. "Usually."

The timbre of his voice, the rumble of laughter in his throat, all of him sent my heart racing with a new urge, sharp as the dagger that had pressed between my breasts. I plucked the cigarette from his mouth, luring him closer. When my back was against the building, his body overshadowed mine, so close he might have been preparing to press his lips to my neck or slip a bullet between my ribs. Raindrops thumped against the ground, keeping time with my heart. He seized the cigarette. Took a final drag. Released a slow exhale.

Wisps of smoke danced between us. As Kazimir pressed his hands against the wall on either side of me, I drank in the scent of rain mingled with tobacco. Crystal droplets glistened against his dark beard. Anticipation built, as in the moments before pulling the trigger, swelling until it reached the apex, a crescendo of bullets piercing the sky.

When I sensed his lips were centimeters from mine, he stopped. Was that all my efforts had earned me—teasing? In response to my frustrated frown, he flashed a wicked smile and traced the back of his finger down my cheek. Before I could slap his hand away, the taunting glint left his eyes.

"The Bolsheviks are much stronger than they once were. If you truly want what is best for the revolution, do not do anything rash in response to their decree."

I had already responded through Yemelin. If he had been with me, surely Kazimir would have agreed to the reprisal; still, better to keep it to myself.

His hand found my cheek again, lingering this time. "Promise me, Sveta." So soft, nearly lost in the rain.

Was work carried out with precision and care still considered rash? Perhaps the assassination of Yemelin had been, but now I had established my plan. Plans were not impulsive; each future assassination would be completed in accordance with it. That, I could promise.

So I nodded. Whether or not that was the promise he was asking for was another matter.

Chapter 29

Moscow, 8 May 1918

On my walk back to the Meshchansky District, armed with a meager bundle of near-spoiled herring after hours in line, the gray sky burst. Fat drops pummeled the streets while I sidestepped puddles, bumped into impatient passersby, and wrapped my shawl around the thin paper to prevent it from getting soaked. Despite the rain, I maintained my leisurely pace, my thoughts on Kazimir. On his lack of retaliation following the Constituent Assembly disbanding.

"We cannot afford to be rash," he said every time I urged him to let me carry out reprisals. Instead, he focused on propaganda or reaching out to peasants and workers for support.

Perhaps my rogue assassinations defied his orders, but he knew what it was like to be seized by a mission, consumed with purpose. Surely Kazimir would understand, once it was safe for me to tell him everything. During my efforts to coax Orlova out of hiding, why not eliminate threats to my party as she eliminated threats to hers?

It was an easy method: Go on an errand, target the most prominent Bolshevik I saw. Sometimes they were giving speeches; other times putting up propaganda posters; or sometimes it was simply a face I recognized from newspapers or a name identified by a bystander. I followed them, found a quick opening, and finished the job.

A sudden gust stirred my sodden clothing; on the corner ahead, a newsboy pulled his hat lower over his face and adjusted his thin coat over his remaining papers. When I glimpsed the headline, I paused.

Once I had paid for the paper, I ducked beneath the nearest portico, wiped rainwater from my eyes, and read the headline that had caught my attention: "Four Bolshevik Leaders Dead." The article went on to discuss the mysterious murders—a single bullet each, individual corpses found on various streets along the Moskva River.

Last night had been a resounding success.

My search for medication to help with Fanya's headaches had taken me farther than intended. Past the Cathedral of Christ the Savior, its four columns topped with golden domes while its fifth dome, the largest, towered in the center, gleamed in the moonlight. Down to Ostozhenka Street, following the water's curve. Fog curled over the Moskva River, tendrils reaching for the sky above, luring the stars closer, swallowing them into its depths.

My route led me to four different Bolsheviks, each alone. So I took each opportunity fate presented.

Nothing ostentatious like Orlova. Just one simple, effective bullet.

A rush coursed through my veins, the feeling that always found me when I pulled my trigger. If my actions had been deemed newsworthy by someone other than Vera—who had started reporting the mysterious Bolshevik murders even though no one knew I was behind them—surely Orlova had noticed too. Not much longer until we faced one another; until then, all I had to do was provoke her, encouraging her to put a stop to this threat against her party. And the day she tried could not come soon enough.

* * *

AFTER MY ERRAND, Kazimir called everyone into a meeting room and droned for what felt like hours, holding us captive around a large oak table. The ban on our publication had come as a shock to everyone. First the destruction of the Constituent Assembly, now the *Delo naroda*. The Bolsheviks were stripping everything away, tearing my party apart and scattering the shreds until nothing remained.

As he rambled, I sat straight, my insides hot as the weak, untouched coffee before me. I wanted our next step. An assassination. An act of terrorism to carry out in retaliation. Anything but meetings, speeches, propaganda posters. To get Bolshevik attention, we needed to act.

Beside me, Fanya's eyes met mine. Usually her pointed looks contained a warning; this time I found curiosity. I had been silent this entire meeting.

I had told no one of my reprisals, not even Fanya. I was not going to ask her to keep another secret for me. Yet, the look she gave told me what, deep inside, I had known all along. She had been by my side for over a decade; it was no surprise she had realized I was not sitting idle. Still, I merely sighed and shifted positions. Even if Fanya suspected me, neither she nor Vera needed to know the truth. My friends were not going to be held responsible for awareness of my actions if I was caught.

"We must keep the Cheka in mind as we proceed." Kazimir stood at the head of the table a few seats away from me, addressing the onlookers. "Between their agents and organized combat units, they will be prepared to suppress opposition."

"What if we targeted the Cheka headquarters?" Rolan offered—perhaps the only reasonable suggestion I'd ever heard emerge from his mouth. "It's not far, over on Bolshaia Lubianka. If we planted explosives—"

"An attack of such magnitude will take months," Kazimir interrupted, shaking his head. "Even then, more local soviets spring up every day, and new recruits continuously bolster the Cheka's numbers. By the time we managed such a feat, the impact would be insignificant."

I had endured this long enough.

"Insignificant?" A few people jumped, perhaps due to the force in my tone, or the fact that I was already crossing toward Kazimir. "Speeches and propaganda pamphlets are *insignificant*. Give me the name of the man who runs the Bolshevik press. He'll be dead by this evening."

"And so will you when the Cheka and Orlova realize what you've done," Kazimir said with a laugh.

How little he knew of my activities these past months.

"If you're too afraid of Bolshevik reprisal, I'll do it myself."

Challenges were the best way to win his attention. I had learned this useful tidbit upon joining this contingent, when Kazimir assessed my loyalty and I suggested the assassination of a member of the imperial government. The challenge had worked then. I needed it to work now.

Before Kazimir responded, Rolan scoffed. "Send *you* against the Bolsheviks? They've already spread lies about our party being hired by the bourgeoisie. If you attack, you'll provide them with more ammunition."

How I hated that my fellow revolutionaries knew exactly

where to land their blows. I grabbed my gun before a hand clamped around my wrist, preventing me from drawing it. A thick beard brushed against my ear. "Shooting a party member, dvoryanka?"

I entertained the idea of swinging the gun at Kazimir. Instead, I broke his hold and left the room.

Cowards, every single one of them. Cowardice was no way to win a revolution. Actions were necessary, actions only I wanted to take. Not even a challenge had tempted Kazimir enough. Once in my room, I collapsed on my bed. My heart raced, leaving emptiness behind, a gun with no bullets in its chamber.

"Kazimir has been a part of this cause for a long time. He knows what he's doing."

At the sound of the gentle voice, I sat up, glaring as Vera closed the door behind her. "Does he? His methods clearly aren't working. And I don't wait for orders."

Vera stiffened, while I began to pace. My heart was pounding too much to care that I had just implied everything I had promised myself I would keep from her. The trigger had been squeezed, the bullet set free. The mission possessed me, bending me to its will as if it knew I was powerless to resist, did not *want* to resist.

"She's one of the most powerful Bolsheviks, my uncle's murderer. I can't wait for orders, Vera, I *can't*."

She stepped in front of me to block my path. "Orlova?" she asked incredulously. "Do you intend to kill her?"

Hearing it aloud sent another surge through me. Surely my assassinations over the last few months had captured her attention. It was time to find a more direct approach. Time to end this.

Vera was already shaking her head. "Kazimir has forbidden anyone from targeting her, and if he finds out, or if the Cheka catches you, or if *she* catches you, you know how this will end." Her voice broke, then she gripped my shoulders. "What about Tatiana?"

My heart twisted, though with it came a little flare of warmth. Not much longer. But not until this was done. Vera released me and wrapped her arms around her waist. Suddenly she looked so young, like the little girl alone in the aftermath of a bloody massacre, surrounded by corpses, among them those once dear to her. No one left to care for her, to love her, to save her from a life of loss.

Perhaps I should have offered reassurance; once I located Orlova, this would be no different than the past missions I had successfully carried out. No need for Vera to worry about my safety. Instead I fought to steady my voice while my pounding heart refused to slow. "Ask your sources to find out whatever they can about her."

"No." She shook her head vehemently. "If you want to defy orders, that's your choice. Leave me out of it."

"You've already been reporting the recent Bolshevik assassinations, so in a way, you're already helping me." She stared, this time with no need to ask a question; of course I was the unidentified figure behind the attacks. "And after I confront Orlova, you can break the news through the *Delo naroda*. This will benefit our party, Vera, you know it will. Help me prove it to Kazimir."

Vera sank onto the bed, staring at the floor as if attempting to grasp everything she had heard. When I joined her, she didn't look up. "It's too dangerous," she murmured at last.

My hopes deflated; still, I was accustomed to working alone.

Her concerns would cease following my success, then perhaps she would write the report. When I rose, a gentle touch found my forearm.

"Change your mind. Please." Despite the plea, the increasing tension in her grip told me that she already knew it was useless. She stood to face me. "If you pursue this, I won't approve of it. But I will do what I can to help, only because this is not something you should be doing alone."

Before I overcame my surprise enough to thank her, Vera released me and closed the door behind her. I drew a breath, letting relief and excitement rush over me. Maybe she didn't approve, but she was still my friend, and a journalist. Friends helped one another, and no journalist would have resisted the opportunity to break such a story.

I had little time to entertain thoughts of my future success before the door swung open. Kazimir's frame took up most of the doorway. "Did you expect me to permit you to go on a rampage over a setback as minor as a publication ban?"

"Censorship is not a—"

"Furthermore," he interrupted, raising his voice over mine, "you are not to leave a meeting prior to dismissal."

A bitter laugh rose to my throat as I closed the distance between us. "You're angry because I didn't ask for permission? If that concerns you more than the opposition's attack on our party—an attack you referred to as *minor*—then you have no business leading us."

His relaxed jaw tightened while his chest swelled. I stood my ground, watching him fume. This, the deepest chord I could have struck: Criticism of the leadership ability he had sought to prove since his youth.

"I will decide what is best, and you will listen. Is that clear?"

The words were tinged with something indiscernible, but I was too furious to care. When I spoke, my voice shook with rage.

"Get out."

Kazimir did not move. His eyes swept over me—slowly, the way that usually set my heart thudding faster. This time, those eyes roamed not in anticipation of our lips meeting, but to assess me, defy me. Challenge me. And indeed, my heart pounded in response.

Such was the caveat; challenges worked on him, but they worked just as well on me.

Something inside seized hold, drove my hand toward my pistol, closed my fingers around it.

Then he caught my arm and forced the barrel beneath my chin.

A moment came in every challenge, one that presented the ultimate test. The choice was simple: succumb to failure or overcome and emerge victorious. Never once had I succumbed; I did not intend to start now. Rather than flinching, I met and matched the fire burning in his eyes. We remained centimeters apart, the cold metal against my skin, faint traces of cigarette smoke and leather filling my nostrils. I took in the faded scar on his forehead from the café explosion.

"Never turn your gun on me, Sveta." An order, yet the salacious growl I knew so well.

Kazimir pressed the barrel into my chin, guided it higher, brought me closer. Then he kissed me and the careless girl embodied me, yielded to the touch she craved.

As he parted my lips, I was aware of nothing but him. His firm grip on my arm; rough beard brushing my skin; solid chest against my pounding heart. A sound low in his throat;

his tongue sweeping over mine, tasting of smoke, then faintly of metal when he slightly intensified his pressure on the pistol.

It was the way he knew I longed to be kissed—unhurried, deliberate, all-consuming. This, my sole vice. If resisting him was the test following his challenge, I had failed miserably.

One kiss was all he offered, though it left me gasping for breath. A reminder of what I risked losing if we destroyed everything that held us together. The fire in his eyes had shifted, gleaming as it did every time he rendered me speechless.

"You can't solve every problem with a pistol."

So he thought.

I grabbed the gun and twisted, regaining control and breaking his hold, then I pushed him away and stepped back. We studied one another, heavy breaths mingling.

When presented with a challenge, victory and I were well acquainted with one another; yet, on occasion, victory evaded me. This time, I was not certain which outcome I had achieved.

* * *

Moscow, 12 June 1918

Vera had agreed to keep Kazimir busy for a few days—another benefit regarding her awareness of my plans. With him distracted, I had a mission to complete. Though not my usual sort.

As I walked, the sun glared gold in a pale blue sky while a hot breeze stirred the stagnant air. Cheka agents were never hard to find. Despite being *secret* police, they were everywhere. Ahead, a young man was reaching for the door to an apartment building when three men called out to him. One held something in his palm—the silver badge with a large red *V*, a sword plunging through its center, and a hammer and sickle.

The victim's face went white. Before he could react, two of the Cheka agents drew Nagant M1895 revolvers, while the third traded his badge for a long dagger.

As they ordered him inside, I hurried to meet them. "A word, comrade?"

One Cheka agent waited for me. When I reached him, a scream pierced the closed door.

I waited for him to suggest we go somewhere more private, quieter, away from the young man's suffering. He didn't. The familiar weight of my Browning pressed against my lower back, urging me to use it.

"I have a message for Orlova," I said. "About a Socialist Revolutionary."

The man glowered. "Long live the red terror against the hirelings of the bourgeoisie." A quote from the article burned into my memory, the Bolshevik call for heads and blood after the Constituent Assembly disbanding. "Tell me what you know."

I held his gaze, unflinching. "What is my help worth to her?"

A flicker of annoyance crossed his face. Perhaps he had expected to wheedle the information out of me without a bribe, but no informant would give knowledge away for nothing. I waited. Besides, I needed funds for my eventual return to Kiev.

He held up a small pouch sagging with the weight of its contents. "My comrades are inside with a man accused of being an anti-Bolshevik," he said without offering it to me. "He is being suitably punished, as you will be if you are wasting my time with a report that is of no use to Orlova."

On the contrary, my report was exactly the kind that would be of use to her.

"The Socialist Revolutionary is a young woman, part of the Meshchansky District contingent." I paused, interrupted by another of the young man's cries. "A former aristocrat with possible remaining ties to the bourgeoisie."

The Cheka agent handed me the bribe. "Her name?"

I delayed until the man's next shriek had ceased. "Svetlana Vasilyevna Petrova."

Chapter 30

Moscow, 28 July 1918

S ilence spread like a disease, eradicating those in its wake until it had stolen their voices and left them gasping for breath. Tinged with suffocating tension, irrepressible and ruthless, it had overtaken the entire hotel for the past few weeks.

The silence felt particularly weighty this morning as I found Vera behind the front desk. "It's been over a month," I said as I reached her. "Do you think she received my message?"

Vera finished jotting a note before setting the pencil down. "Orlova and the Cheka have been busy, it seems."

I clenched my jaw. The publication ban had been lifted—much to Kazimir's smug satisfaction, since he had claimed it would never last—but the Cheka grew increasingly relentless. Dead bodies were their favorite form of propaganda. Each day brought raids, arrests, and murders, including the arrests of Rolan and Sergei the day after I had given my name to the Cheka agent. Both were imprisoned for illegally distributing Socialist Revolutionary newspapers during the ban.

When Vera bent over her notes again, I moved them aside; this conversation was not over. "Anything from your sources? Can't one of them direct me to her?"

"Don't you think Orlova's identity would have been revealed

by now if those who worked with her weren't sworn to secrecy and likely threatened with death if they betrayed her?"

"When has Arina Drozdova ever let confidentiality keep her from her journalistic duty?" I raised a teasing eyebrow. "I'm sure you can persuade anyone to tell you anything, Vera."

She flashed an amused smile. "Believe me, I've tried. My sources aren't foolish enough to compromise their positions, and I don't think they receive information directly from her, so they probably don't know who she is anyway." She picked up her pencil again and freed the papers I had held captive between my palm and the desk. "Give it time."

It had been over a year since my release from the katorga. I had already given it plenty of time. My blood was irresistible bait; how was it not enough to attract Orlova's attention?

I paced from one bare wall to the thin, low table on the wall parallel to it. Above the table, a painted landscape depicted a river rushing through a thick forest and emerging into a bright meadow while a white-tailed eagle soared overhead. The calming scene did little to settle me. With each step, the weight of my pistol grew heavier.

I had enacted my own reprisals since the arrests, of course, but the effort was beginning to feel futile. Until Orlova targeted me, there was little more I could do to locate her or convince her to come for me.

As I paced, Kazimir and Fanya entered, so I hurried to meet them.

"If we retaliate in response to these increasing arrests, we risk the Cheka executing our party members as punishment," Kazimir said before I could ask my usual question.

"A risk each party member willingly accepts, imprisoned or free," Fanya spoke up, and I nodded.

Whatever the risk, we had to take it. The Bolsheviks grew bolder each day; I had even heard rumor that, a few days ago, the Whites found the Ipatiev House in Yekaterinburg empty. No sign of the imprisoned Romanov family, only bloodstains and bullet holes. Had the Bolsheviks made innocent children pay for their parents' incompetence?

Before anyone said more, the hotel door swung open. I turned toward the sound while a thin, haggard man shuffled inside. Beneath the disheveled appearance and dingy clothes, I recognized him; Fanya's sharp intake of breath confirmed my suspicions.

As I drew my pistol, Kazimir was the first to reach him, though Sergei raised both hands in response to everyone's weapons, assuring us he wasn't armed. After Kazimir nodded, Fanya pulled a chair from behind the desk. Sergei sat while we crowded around him.

"They pardoned me this morning," he said.

A claim that the Bolsheviks had ordered him to give us? I exchanged an uncertain glance with Kazimir. Sergei accepted the glass of water Vera offered him, sipped it, and passed a hand through his tangled blond hair.

"I realize it sounds unusual," Sergei went on, perhaps sensing our doubts. He cleared his throat and scrubbed a smudge of grime from his cheek. "Orlova thought it might help win support from other deserted soldiers."

This time, I exchanged a glance with Vera, who looked at me as if to say *Don't start*; I still turned to Sergei. "Orlova pardoned you? Did you speak with her?"

He was already shaking his head.

Though I had expected disappointment, it was like every bit of fury and frustration inside me had been ordered to aim and fire. But that would have to wait until tonight. The Cheka had my name, and they knew an assassin was targeting them; tonight I had a plan to connect both. I'd find a reason to go out, locate a target, and remind Orlova I was tired of waiting for her.

"You are either a liar or a fool," I said through my teeth, though Sergei refused to look at me. "To have been in Cheka custody, pardoned by Orlova, yet to come back with nothing useful—"

"I will tell you all that I can."

Far from reassuring. Information never came freely; from the katorga, I had learned the art of acquiring such knowledge. Find someone willing to give it. Give him whatever he demanded in return, no matter how detestable. Accept every risk that accompanied the arrangement. And Sergei was not a man to risk worse punishment if he were caught trying to uncover Bolshevik secrets; of course he had come back with nothing.

"While I was imprisoned, they asked us if we knew who was behind the assassinations against them that have been occurring these past months. No party has claimed responsibility."

At last, some good news. My efforts continued to garner Bolshevik attention. Though frustration lingered, I stood a little taller.

"Rolan?" Kazimir asked.

Sergei shook his head. "Dead."

Vera let out a little breath, while Fanya pinched the bridge of her nose. Kazimir sighed and passed a hand through his hair. I watched Sergei. And the look on his face told me he was about to reveal the worst news of all.

"Kazimir." He gripped the desk for support and used it to pull himself upright. "After these arrests, executions . . ." He glanced at Fanya, then me, then Vera, then back to Kazimir. "It's time we stop fighting the Bolsheviks."

The words fell on my ears like the crack of a pistol, sharp and deliberate. More than ten years in a katorga hadn't stolen my fighting spirit. A few weeks in a Cheka prison cell were all it took to destroy Sergei.

When I opened my mouth, Fanya caught my arm and pulled me a few paces away. "Don't. He's been through enough, and your criticisms won't help."

"Neither will giving up." I broke her grasp, but not her glare. "This party has no room for cowards."

With that, I paced; Kazimir said something about taking Sergei for further questions. Vera volunteered, leading Sergei away, while Fanya offered to assume Vera's place at the desk.

If Sergei had told the truth, he hadn't been strong enough to resist the Cheka; they had convinced him they were too powerful to dismantle. But my chance to do so was closer than ever. Orlova had noticed my actions, likely had received the message I had sent with the Cheka agent, perhaps was already looking for me. She was angry, as was I.

A revolution had no place for two angry assassins. Not for long.

I'd only made a few passes when a tight grip found my forearm, pulling me to a halt.

"This is not the time to forget what you promised." Kazimir, a tone that said, *Do as I command, dvoryanka.* I returned his warning glare. Whatever promise he thought I'd made, how did he not realize the foolishness of it now?

"If you stop fighting the Bolsheviks, you will make a mockery of us." I clawed his fingers, attempting to pry them loose; instead, his grip closed around my shoulders and shook me so hard it halted my struggles. My head swam; I blinked to clear my vision. He drew me close, then enunciated each word, slow, measured.

"Do not be rash."

We remained centimeters from one another, chests heaving as I assessed the challenge in his eyes. It was different, heavier.

No, not a challenge.

A warning.

* * *

THE RULES FOR our contingent were clear: Never act without authorization. Still, I wished Fanya hadn't overheard Kazimir's reminder in the lobby, an indication he had specifically forbidden me—only me—from lashing out. A direct order to reinforce a direct order.

I had never admitted to my outright defiance, but the look she had given me during the publication ban discussion had indicated Fanya had guessed my activities. After Sergei's report, I suspected she had little doubt that I was the one behind the Bolshevik assassinations. Still, Kazimir's warning had left her withdrawn, silent. Unsettled. Her concerns remained unspoken, a wall between us as impenetrable as those surrounding Maltzevskaya.

"Do you intend to go through with this?" she asked at last, reclining on her bed while I field-stripped my pistol in preparation for my evening mission.

"It's working, isn't it? You heard Sergei."

"And you heard Kazimir." Fanya sat up, frowning. "He hasn't been reminding *me* not to be rash, so clearly he must not expect you to listen. Were you ever going to tell me you're acting against direct orders?"

I glowered. "Was it not obvious he never consented to targeting Orlova or assassinating Bolsheviks behind his back?"

"Exactly." She approached, shattering what remained of the wall between us. "Of course I know that, yet you still withheld the truth from me."

How could I give her the full extent of my plans when that meant involving her in whatever repercussions followed? I could not change what the katorga had done to her—what my bomb plot had done to her—but I could keep her from suffering on my behalf again.

When I said nothing, Fanya sighed and passed a hand over her eyes. "You'll never be honest with me, will you, Sveta? Not when you asked me to go to Kiev. Not even after all these years. All we've been through." She turned to the door. "And if you can't trust me, then—"

"Vera is already helping me, and if something goes wrong, I won't let both of you be held accountable."

It sprang free before I realized what I had done, pulling her into the depths of this plot alongside me. First Vera, now Fanya.

She faced me, all hostility gone, voice soft. "You told her? And not me?"

Of all the secrets I might have revealed. For an instant I saw her bound to a whipping post, only this time it was my own hand that brought the cane down. "Only because Vera's contacts have information. She doesn't like it any more than you do and is afraid Kazimir will—"

"Kill you?" Fanya demanded, glaring. "If he's going to retain the party's respect, you've left him little choice, haven't you?"

I scowled. "When it's done and he hears the truth from me, Kazimir will understand, but I—"

"Do not pretend this is for your uncle Misha, or for Tatiana, or for anyone other than yourself. You won't stop until you kill Orlova because you don't *want* to stop." She took a shaky breath without breaking my gaze. "No matter what happens to you or anyone else."

The silence was thick, accusatory. Perhaps she was right; perhaps I didn't want Kazimir to know until it was over. Until he had lost his chance to interfere.

I picked up my coat, pistol, and the note I'd written—three words in black script.

Svetlana Vasilyevna Petrova.

This note, to be left with whichever Bolshevik I found and shot tonight. This note, tying me to the recent Bolshevik assassinations and reminding Orlova that she had been warned about me. This note that would surely force her to take action.

It was impossible to stop. Not until after I had faced her.

I tucked the note into my coat pocket. "I have always trusted you, Fanya. Please trust me when I tell you that I will be finished after I find Orlova."

She looked as if she wanted to believe me.

* * *

AFTER I PARTED ways with Fanya, the knot in my stomach settled as I walked to Kazimir's room. He had asked me to visit him this evening; perhaps he believed I had taken his threat to heart.

When I entered, he was sitting at his desk, dressed in dark trousers and a white undershirt, a bottle of wine beside him. He poured a second glass. As I accepted it, his fingers lingered against mine, all hostility from the lobby gone. I nearly lifted my chin, inviting him closer.

Instead, I sat on the bed. The red wine was warm and rich

on my tongue, and I savored it in silence while Kazimir lit a cigarette. He offered one to me; again, I accepted. The sweet wine cut through the acrid smoke, eliciting a little sigh as I exhaled.

When the glasses were empty and cigarettes snuffed in the ashtray, Kazimir brushed a lock of hair from my forehead— graying quicker each day, it seemed. Wine and smoke mingled, relaxing and decadent. I brought his lips to mine, pulled him down with me as I reclined, focused on the steady build of my heartbeat as his touch brought me to life.

While I teased my tongue over his, Kazimir wrapped his hand around the small of my back to remove my pistol, as he usually did. Instead of placing it on the nightstand, he lifted his head. Held the gun before me. Waited.

I glanced from his face to my Browning, heart thudding faster. I reached for the pistol, but he caught my arm, forcing it down, pinning me back against the bed. After an instant of unsuccessful writhing against his crushing weight and impossibly strong hold, I settled for a glare.

"The recent string of Bolshevik assassinations. You are behind them, aren't you?"

This, the reason for his invitation. "How did you find out?" It wasn't as if I were the only sharpshooter in Moscow. Vera had not betrayed me, she wouldn't . . .

The lamplight lent a vicious curve to his smirk as he leaned closer. "You can't stay guarded, Sveta. Not from me."

Did he truly believe he had the ability to decipher all my secrets? How little he knew. Such arrogance deserved rebuke, but he had already pulled away and leveled the pistol at me, his smirk gone.

"Before I shoot your pretty head off, you're going to explain why you acted without direct orders—or, if you were following orders, whose they were."

Suddenly I forgot the loaded gun, forgot the little whisper cautioning me to deter him from pulling the trigger. A wave of heat surged inside me, clashing with the icy darkness in his eyes.

"Why explain that I made my own decision to act on our party's behalf? That I was under no influence from the bourgeoisie or anyone else? You won't believe me."

"I told you not to—"

"I'm not going to follow an order that damages my party." I shifted beneath him, fighting for breath. "If my uncle were here, he would be ashamed of your lack of leadership, but he would not accuse you of betrayal the way you have accused me. Uncle Misha never lost faith in you, even though your father worked alongside Lenin's brother."

At once, he pressed the gun to my forehead, but my heart was already pounding too fast.

"My father was a revolutionary, not an aristocrat," he snapped. "And if my father had met yours, he would have tossed a bomb into the baron's carriage, just like he planned to do to the tsar's."

"I am not my father!"

I waited for him to argue, to tell me I would always be my parents and my blood, no matter what I did. This battle never ended any differently. But this time, perhaps this one time, it might. Perhaps he would see beyond birth and titles until all that remained was what had always been right in front of him.

He did not dispute me. He did not concede, either.

The stony eyes holding mine were like the pistol's cold metal seeping into my skin, turning the fire inside me to ash.

"Why won't you trust me, Kazimir?"

At my whisper, his hardened gaze wavered for an instant. Or perhaps I fooled myself into believing it, the same way I fooled myself into believing he would ever view me as more than a dvoryanka.

He removed the gun without releasing me. "Comrade Petrova, you are indefinitely forbidden to engage in acts of political terrorism."

My heart surged, and I strained against him. "Bastard, give it to me!" When the effort to overpower him proved exhausting, I wrapped my free hand around the back of his neck; though he stiffened, his unyielding gaze met mine. A tremor stripped my next words raw. "Please, you can't do this."

To me. To our daughter. He had no idea the extent of the damage this caused. If he took my gun, imprisoned me, worse, Tatiana would be alone in Kiev.

Not a word. Not even a flinch.

When Kazimir rose, pulling me to my feet, I twisted, desperate to face him. "Wait, we have a—"

"Another word, and I will shoot you." He pressed my pistol to my chest, emphasizing the threat.

The truth had always held the power to shatter or save us; now it had been rendered insignificant. The true power lay within the secrets, lies, deception, a power grown so strong it was impossible to eradicate. No matter how I tried to explain.

He tucked my Browning into his nightstand drawer before drawing his own weapon. He was holding my gun hostage, tossing my revolutionary plans away as easily as the tsar's guards had tossed me into the katorga.

Kazimir directed me into the empty bedroom next to his. Better than an interrogation room, but still a cell. After he slammed the door behind me, the lock clicked from the outside.

The ache settled in my stomach, nearly broke me. I pulled the tiny note from my coat pocket and tore it to shreds. Pale white pieces littered the floor like unrecognizable remnants of something long dead and forgotten.

I pressed my back against the wall. Fighting tremulous breaths, I wrapped my arms around my waist while I sank to the floor, combatting the tears on the brink of spilling over. The ghost of a tiny body shifted inside me, a memory of what had once been. Of what may never be. Absence and loss mingled, sudden as a bullet to the heart.

He had stripped me of my weapon, of my plans, of my revolution. Of my very soul.

Chapter 31

My body was in a small, sparse bedroom in Hotel Petrov, but my mind thrust me back into solitary confinement in Maltzevskaya. I had been isolated for—what was it for? Cursing the tsar? Inciting rebellion among my fellow prisoners? A physical altercation with another inmate? I failed to remember.

Two guards gripped my arms, heedless of fresh welts and lacerations, and dragged me down the long, damp corridors to that horrible cell. I struggled, dug my heels into the ground, but they forced me toward the open door, a gaping maw eager to swallow me whole. They tossed me into the cramped space, then my prison gown after me. Cold stone against bare skin still hot with slick blood, beads of sweat on my brow, breaths shallow as though breathing the thick, dusty air in the mines.

The door screeched shut, footsteps retreated, then nothing.

Hunger, filth, silence, cold, pain, and beatings. So many beatings. Stagnant air reeking of piss and decay; bloody red streaks across gray skin, jagged like cracks snaking across stone; thick, inky darkness.

Fanya. I needed Fanya. But she was in our cell, and I was here, alone. My only visitors brought stale, moldy bread, jeers, shackles, and thick birch rods.

I gasped when the door swung open and a man stood in its

frame—a guard come to beat me again, surely. When I found the wall, my knees buckled. I drew them in even as a brittle laugh sprang from my throat.

"Have you not shed enough of my blood yet?"

I clutched my head, gripped the hair turning gray as my skin, writhed when I felt his hands about to hoist me up. Perhaps I never won this battle, but I never succumbed without a fight.

"Svetlana, stop!" Loud, insistent. Odd; the guards never used my name, only a prisoner number. His grasp relaxed. "No one is hurting you, Sveta."

I sucked in a shallow breath. This was Moscow, not Siberia. Kazimir had not been back since he had put me into this room more than a week ago, though it felt far longer. Now he crouched before me, brow creased.

If I hadn't known better, I might have called it surprise, even concern. He had no right to regard me with either. He was the one who had put me here, had sent others to bring me food or check on me, had not come back himself. Had confiscated my pistol.

During my years of political imprisonment, every day of sacrificing freedom came tinged with my weapon's absence. A sacrifice nearly too difficult to bear, one I shouldered for my cause. This was different. This was not a sacrifice for my beliefs; it was an attack. Upon me, my plans, everything.

For that, more than anything else, I wanted to reach for his throat, grip it tight, refuse to let go. Instead, my shaking hands clutched his forearms.

"Fanya," I said in a reedy voice. "Please, take me back to Fanya."

"You're alone so you won't attempt to conspire with anyone. It's a different bedroom, nothing more."

"Let me go back. Have Vera watch me if you wish, but let me go back." My breaths stilled as I looked up at him, earnest, entreating, while sudden tears threatened to overtake me. The gaze I found in return had suddenly hardened.

Kazimir broke my hold. "Do not try to gain sympathy when I should kill you for what you've done."

I sprang to my feet as he neared the door. "Shoot me now, then. *Please*, Kazimir." When he turned, I caught him in my arms, pressed into his chest. "Please, don't leave me here."

The shaky breaths returned; I closed my eyes to fight them, to ward off the guards' voices echoing in my ears as they abandoned me to solitude: *Go mad, filthy anarchist. No one who comes here keeps her wits.*

Kazimir's deep breath dispelled their jeers. At last, he grabbed my shoulders, prompting me to lift my head.

"I will permit Vera to supervise visits between you. That is all."

I drew in a breath as I had when he had pulled me from the fire, cleansing my lungs of soot and ash, this time of total isolation. As long as I knew Fanya was coming, it helped. With a grateful nod, I stepped away, but he tightened his hold.

"Do you have no regard for your own life? For the decisions you are now forcing me to make?" His voice shook with rage, perhaps with something else. "Whatever your reasons, they cannot have been worth this."

Without awaiting a reply, he released me and slammed the door behind him.

Though the feeling of Kazimir's hands lingered on my arms,

it was not his threat that settled over me. It was the odd strain that had touched his voice, his eyes dark as the mines that had once enslaved me.

* * *

THE DOOR SWUNG open again—hours later? Minutes? I didn't know. This time, when I lifted my buried head, the two new-comers had already reached me.

Fanya folded me into her arms. Our past dispute forgotten, I clung to her as tightly as I had after returning from solitary confinement, as if her embrace extracted every horrible mo-ment and banished it from memory.

"Get me out," I said when we drew away, looking from her to Vera. "Get me out so I can find her."

With a huff, Fanya turned away and pinched the bridge of her nose. "I told you, Vera. I told you she would ask us that."

Vera glanced around the sparse room before settling on me—unkempt, in dire need of a proper bath, sustained only by the urge to finish what I had started. "Please, Sveta. You must give it up."

"So I can sit in this hotel waiting for whatever Kazimir will do next?"

Silence wrapped around us. Imprisonment was only a set-back. I was not one to back down from a fight, nor one to settle for a loss. And this fight to locate Orlova, then return to Kiev, was not over yet.

"If you help me and anyone questions you, blame me and the bourgeoisie. Say that I must have been loyal to them all along, so with the support of the nobility I broke out of the ho-tel and acted on my own. Point all responsibility to me."

They said nothing. What argument did they have? My blood was an indisputable excuse.

Completing my scheme meant reclaiming my weapon without authorization and, once again, defying Kazimir. He had made it clear I was out of second, third, fourth chances. But that no longer mattered.

Was it possible to break a trust that had never fully existed? All these months, I had entertained the hope of a future with him and our daughter. Neither would happen now. We were so broken, not even the truth could mend us.

Perhaps the careless girl inside me had been wrong; perhaps the hold between us no longer existed. Or it had never been there at all—she had simply found what she wanted to find. What she perceived as a connection, an escape, was nothing more than a delicate scale tipping with skill and leadership, blood and party, nobles and peasants, challenges and proof, never reaching equilibrium.

"You agreed to help me." All vehemence was gone now as I broke the quiet, glancing between them before settling on Vera. "Please get me out."

The little girl in Kiev flashed inside my mind as they looked to one another. Then Vera's sharp hazel gaze met mine and she dipped her head in a single nod.

* * *

Moscow, 9 August 1918

A few days later, I remained in my makeshift prison, though with permission from Kazimir, Vera and Fanya paid me occasional visits, bringing food, much-needed company, and smuggled papers. This morning we poured over today's *Izvestia*.

"Hasn't this gone on long enough?" As they looked up, I pointed to the list of recent Cheka arrests, executions, and fines. New ones had been reported almost daily since the end of last month. "Why is no one putting a stop to it?"

Fanya trailed her fingers across the small tea cart she had brought into the room until she found one of the delicate porcelain teacups, then sought the rim. "I certainly would not want to fall victim to Iron Felix."

I scoffed. "Dzerzhinsky should have been eliminated long ago. What better way to make a statement than to assassinate the head of the Cheka?" I rose and picked up the teapot; she stepped back with a nod of appreciation, then sat on the bed and rubbed her eyes with a little sigh.

After I had served our tea, bread, and a link of sausage Fanya had found among the provisions in the hotel kitchen, we ate in comfortable silence. Once we had finished, Vera returned the dishes to the tea cart.

"You have one bullet and two people before you: Iron Felix and Orlova," she said, turning to me. "Whom do you shoot?"

"Orlova, of course, but I line up the shot so the bullet passes through her and hits Dzerzhinsky next."

She smirked while Fanya departed to take the cart downstairs. In silence, I flipped through the rest of the papers until a headline caught my attention. It publicized an event taking place at the end of the month, and I gripped it tighter. Of course. Why hadn't I realized it from the start? Until now, my assassinations had been far more insignificant, meaningless. He was the one I needed, the one I should have been seeking all along. The one she shielded.

"Here." I passed the paper to Vera. "This is how I'm going to get Orlova's attention."

As she glanced at it, her brows lifted. "I don't have to remind you what this will mean if you're caught."

"Nor do I have to remind you that she won't ignore this."

"Fair enough." Vera passed the paper back. "If anything is going to draw Orlova out, that is certain to succeed."

I stared at the headline, heart thudding in my chest: "Vladimir Lenin to Give Speech in Moscow."

I needed to assassinate the leader of the Bolsheviks himself, the face of the party, the man Orlova had defended long before anyone else. To take down Lenin was to take down the party, and her along with it. Not even Kazimir could fault me for this; it was exactly what my party needed to regain the influence we had lost.

The Bolsheviks were a festering wound, infectious and destructive. Once that wound was cauterized, this revolution would heal. And once it was healed, I could be with my daughter.

As a girl, my bomb plot in Kiev had failed simply because Fanya had set off the explosive too early and I had fired at the wrong target; now I was a woman who would carry out every step of this plan with meticulous care. I knew my target. I would not fail again.

Orlova would come for me once it was done. And I would be ready.

Mila

— · —

August 1942–March 1943

Chapter 32

Vitebsk Region, 17 August 1942

Report to the garrison, Mila. Now."
As Fruza burst into Daniil's hut, bringing the command with her, I nearly dropped the suicide pill I was making alongside Katya. Summer was nearing its end, and I had been working with the resistance and preparing for my garrison infiltration for over a year. I held my breath while she continued.

"Yuri just notified me. Yesterday, the Wehrmacht caught their kitchen aide sheltering Jews, so they need a replacement. Should you secure the position, *Oberstleutnant* Hans Alscher will serve as your supervisor."

The kitchen aide had certainly been executed for her actions. Beside me, Katya let out an unsteady breath, a newfound heaviness in her green eyes. If I were caught, the former employee's fate would be mine.

I placed my completed pill in Katya's palm, closed her fingers over it with a little squeeze, and rose. I had used my poison on Reuter over two months ago. I had seen its success. Fruza had entrusted this mission to me, and I would ensure its success, too.

And then home. A rush of warmth washed over me even as the usual ache twisted my heart. Did home exist anymore?

"I won't remind you of the risks you will face, but I don't expect them to be in vain," Fruza said. As I nodded, she handed Daniil a fresh stack of resistance papers. "Bring me Mila's report as soon as you receive it." Then she made her way to the door.

The knot in my heart twisted tighter. Though Fruza's visits were infrequent, each time I awaited the results of the note I had asked Daniil to give her containing my family's information. And each time, nothing.

"Fruza?" When she faced me, her clear blue gaze suddenly felt impossible to meet. "Any word on Leningrad?"

"I will communicate when and if I receive information. I expect you to remain focused on your mission, Comrade Rozovskaya." So stern I held back a wince. "Understood?"

"Yes." All I managed without risking a break in my voice, then she closed the door behind her.

Of course I was focused on the work; the implication that I was preoccupied with other matters stung worse than the antiseptic Katya used when I returned from missions with minor scrapes. Months had passed since Daniil had given Fruza my note, and I'd heard nothing more; was it wrong to be curious?

One steadying breath, then my pounding heart drove me to the door. I had a mission to fulfill.

Daniil followed me outside. My skirt swished across the dry, dusty road as the midafternoon sun swept over us, its warmth urging me on with each eager step. As we walked, Daniil's was the concerned look I had come to recognize so well now—as if no matter what he did, he was bound to lose something. To fail.

"Are you thinking the better of this plan?" I asked to break the silence. "You knew I wanted to work with poisons. Isn't that why you introduced me to Fruza in the first place?"

"Yes, but I hoped she would think it was a terrible idea and find a way to send you back to Leningrad." Despite the jest and my teasing nudge, he sighed. "I thought the war would end before it came to this." A strain touched his voice, similar to the way it did when he spoke of his worries for this village and, even more, its people.

"I've been well prepared." I longed to reach for him, to reassure him with my touch as his reassured me. "You, Katya, and Fruza have done all you can."

"When you step behind that fence, it will be you and the Fritzes. Our best efforts can never be enough for that." He faced me, his eyes burning with sudden fury. "Prior to the invasion, I thought I was prepared for whatever it might bring. I was wrong. Preparation means nothing."

Without saying more, he retraced his steps, leaving me alone on the road. Suddenly I felt as if I had just witnessed the devastated guilt-ridden young man walking away from a farm in Shumilino, its charred remains, and the young woman he had once loved drenched in blood.

Still, not even Daniil's fears were enough to dull the spark inside me as I drew closer to the massive stone structure ahead.

After fumbling attempts to communicate with the men on guard, they brought me to a small office, where I sat before a dull garrison commander whose name, as Fruza had said, was Hans Alscher. And who spoke Russian, fortunately.

"Nadezhda Olegovna Kharitonova." I handed him the papers identifying me by the alias, hoping my racing heart wouldn't force a tremble into my hands. "Nadya."

He studied the documents and rubbed a hand over tired eyes. At last he smoothed his gray uniform, drawing attention to various insignia that, I suspected, were meant to remind me that he was a Wehrmacht officer who had better things to do than interview village girls. "From Shumilino?" he asked in a monotone.

I nodded. "A farm." Daniil's idea. A good one, despite how I nearly choked on the word. It felt too authentic, as though I'd plucked myself from the city as easily as I plucked potatoes from the soil when harvesting with my grandparents. Once extracted, they never returned.

Mila Lvovna, no longer the young woman from Leningrad, just a local farm girl. A girl who foraged for mushrooms, wild strawberries, and blueberries, harvested cucumbers and turnips, milked cows, collected eggs, plucked rogue strands of hay from her unkempt hair, and futilely attempted to scrub mud and grass stains from her skirt hems.

After a few more minutes of discussing my qualifications, Alscher leaned across his desk toward me. "The girl who held this position before you has been executed. Do not give me reason to award you the same fate."

I swallowed hard, nearly reaching for the little amulet beneath my clothes before shaking my head earnestly. "I won't, Herr Oberstleutnant. I want to work, I *need* to work, and I'm not fit for much else. Please, I don't want to—" I broke off before *die*, but the completed statement hovered between us.

My frantic plea had been enough, I suspected. When Alscher looked me over, I knew what he had decided: I was an ignorant villager terrified of the invaders but desperate to support herself, willing to comply with them, eager to keep her life. No such girl would work for the resistance. Or be brave enough to poison his men.

He jerked his head in a single nod. "Be here in the morning at first light."

* * *

I ENJOYED MY walks to and from the village, accompanied by the uneven road, the occasional passing wagon, and distant trees climbing toward the expansive stretch of sky. A chilly edge nipped the late afternoon summer air, signs of an impending transition into a world of drifting snowflakes. A screech pierced the quiet. An eagle soared across the darkening sky, dove toward an open stretch of farmland, then rose clutching an unsuspecting victim in its talons, carrying the tiny creature away into the night.

Not even the weight of my mission was enough to keep my heart from soaring, as purposeful and powerful as the eagle gliding above. Though my footsteps on the road were the only sound, I nearly heard the roar of streetcars, cries of vendors, clatter of feet against cobblestones, all sounds of the Leningrad I had left behind. Not for much longer.

As I neared the farmhouse, I caught sight of my grandparents coming in from feeding the animals—she with her cane in one hand and her free arm intertwined with his. I hurried to meet them.

"You said you'd be home by early afternoon," Babushka said by way of greeting.

"The Fritzes stopped me. They need someone to work in their kitchen and ordered me to do it." Convincing enough. Was I supposed to defy a direct order?

And yet Babushka still said, "I hope you refused."

"Of course I did, I have a noose around my neck and a sign that says *for defying the Reich* to prove it."

My attempt toward levity went unappreciated, considering the way her glower deepened. Her grip on my grandfather's forearm tightened—uncertainty of her footing, or perhaps a reaction to my news. The loose hairs that had fallen from my chignon stirred when a breeze swept over us, as though attempting to usher the uncomfortable silence away.

Dedushka passed a hand over his beard. "For how long?"

"Until they tell me I'm dismissed, I suppose." Or until they caught me poisoning them and shot me.

My grandparents said no more. If they weren't going to badger me, then this mission was already progressing even better than I had anticipated.

As we reached the house, Dedushka rubbed his beard again, an indication that something weighed upon his mind; Babushka muttered for me to make myself useful—as always, meaning to make tea. So I did, while Dedushka went back outside to fetch more wood for the pech, then I offered a cup to my grandmother.

"They will torture you. Then they will kill you."

The quiet statement nearly made me drop the cup. Had my actions against Reuter led her to assume my purpose? Or was it my sneaking suspicion that she did indeed know that I had not respected her wishes about my involvement in the patriotic war? Perhaps she knew exactly what I intended to do inside the garrison.

I gave her forearm a reassuring pat. "It's a kitchen position, Babushka." I poured my own tea, then sliced the last of the rye bread. "All I have to do is follow orders."

She sipped her tea, her expression unreadable. Maybe I had convinced her, or maybe she had realized the truth and conceded to it. Maybe she had finally learned this *was* our fight.

Chapter 33

Every time I harvested alongside my grandparents, I heard the conversation between myself and my mother when she had informed me of her plan to send me away from Leningrad.

"A *farm*?" I had demanded, looking up from the skirt I had been hemming. "You grew up on a farm? And you're sending me there because of rumors?"

"In times of war, all rumors must be taken seriously," she replied, sewing a new button onto my father's shirt. "If the Germans come here, you'll be much safer there."

We sat on a small sofa by a single window, where golden streaks fell through the thin curtains and over Mama's sewing basket. Sunlight glinted off my needle as I drove it into the skirt, then a sudden prick of pain went up my finger. Blood bubbled on the end of my fingertip.

Muttering a curse, I sucked the wound before continuing. "I'm not a child."

"But I *am* your mother."

"Have your parents agreed to let me stay with them?"

"When I finish this, I intend to write to them and find out."

"Well, then," I said, seizing my opportunity, "if you're going to make me live with your mother, tell me what to expect. I know she's blind." One of the few pieces of information Mama had given me. "What is she like?"

"You'll find out for yourself when you're living on a farm outside Obol." The usual stiffness yet edged with humor at my expense.

My friends and I frequented restaurants, taverns, museums, the old palaces and gardens, busy squares, political speeches, everything city life had to offer. I was *not* a farm girl—and I had never imagined my mother was, either. She embraced city life, moving to Leningrad at sixteen and securing employment at the Kirovsky Zavod, stationed on an assembly line next to a handsome young man—resulting in my parents' first meeting, and me not long after that. But Mama never spoke of her childhood. Where her childhood was, so was Babushka. The topic that was always off-limits.

Sighing, I put aside my sewing. "Why send me to live with someone you hate, especially if you won't tell me why?"

She pushed a lock of dark hair from her face, then inspected the button. Her reluctance was no surprise, this time accompanied by something indiscernible. Something that made her hands tighten their grip on my father's shirt.

"Please, Mama, all I'm asking is—"

"Stop prying, Mila."

And that was that.

Now I could almost hear my mother laughing, realizing I was indeed laboring on a farm. I spent my days driving a spade into the ground to extract potatoes and beetroots—with minimal damage—and plucking zucchini and squash from the vines. Not as satisfying as working with poisons, but I came to appreciate the dirt beneath my fingernails, the scent of fresh earth carried on a cool breeze, the ache traveling down my neck and shoulders to my back, arms, and hands.

Working in the fields didn't prevent me from missing Leningrad—sometimes I missed it more. There, life was evening walks through Ostrovsky Park, bustling cafés on Nevsky Prospekt; here, life was sweat upon my brow and clucking chickens around my feet.

The afternoon sun fell across my basket, coloring the potatoes crimson and amber until they resembled autumn leaves. A few meters away, Babushka worked at twice my speed. A crisp breeze wrapped around me, carrying Dedushka's voice.

"I'll finish here," he said, meaning it was time to go in for the evening.

Babushka and I emptied our baskets into the wagon with the other potatoes and harvested vegetables, then she caught the horse's reins and beckoned him with a click of her tongue. As we trudged on, she navigated the terrain with ease, every bump, rock, and uneven stretch known to her sure-footed step. She held her cane without relying on it, whereas I had worked these same fields countless times and still had difficulties.

As we walked, tiny mounds of dirt lay scattered about like those from the invasion betraying bodies. Like those who had been hanged or shot and buried in shallow graves in reprisal for partisan attacks or resistance activities. I shivered against a cool breeze. Sometimes it was difficult to feel as if our work was saving lives or shortening the war when no act of resistance came without suffering or death.

I cleared my throat. "I have to return to the garrison in the morning. The Fritzes only permitted me this week to harvest so I can continue providing for them." Once Alscher learned I was living on a nearby farm—though I had falsified the location, claimed a couple had simply permitted me to stay with them, and kept our familial ties secret—he had demanded food in addition to my employment.

Babushka remained impassive, head forward.

I had killed a soldier who had confiscated goods from my grandmother, only to forfeit them myself. Now I went to work occasionally armed with burlap sacks of produce, jars of milk, butter, or cheese, or baskets of eggs, then I passed through the gate accompanied by hateful glances from any villager who happened to see me. People like Anton Maksimovich, whose property had been severely damaged during the invasion, leaving him struggling to support a wife and small child. I passed their land on my way to the village. He had seen me enter the garrison countless times; each time, he sent a vicious glare after me.

I didn't blame him; my actions *did* look treacherous.

A cool gust teased my skirt as Babushka and I drew closer to the stable. Inside, we worked in silence, transferring produce to empty burlap sacks or baskets. Despite having lived here for more than a year, something always interfered with my ability to adjust to these moments of camaraderie, something that robbed the moment of its authenticity. It was as though camaraderie were a task at which we would both ultimately fail. And we both knew it.

While I closed the horse into his stall and rewarded him with an apple, Babushka tied off her final sack and placed it with the others. "Don't be late tomorrow."

"I won't. After work, I need to stop by the post office so I can mail a letter to Mama, then I'll be home." I wasn't certain if any letters reached my parents, but it didn't prevent me from trying.

The ease in Babushka's eyes vanished and took the moment with it. Just like that, we had failed again.

With an incoherent reply, she set off toward the house. This, the reason those rare moments of camaraderie never lasted. I'd spent my entire life obeying every *Stop prying, Mila*, but I had a right to know what had fractured my family. If Mama refused to fill in the gaps, maybe Babushka would.

When we reached the fence, I held the gate closed, my face and neck hot despite the evening chill. "She's your daughter, Babushka. Why won't you talk about her?"

Her mouth tightened at the corners. "What is there to say?"

Just like my mother. Body rigid and unrelenting, the unspoken warning.

Stop prying, Mila.

"You're worse than she is." Though I attempted to speak with conviction, my voice broke. "Mama will admit she hates you, but you don't have the courage to do the same."

The words felt as though they could undo all that had been done. If I struck far enough, I could find the seed that was buried deep, poison it, and let it die. Poison it as it had poisoned everything else. But her expression remained neutral, impassive. I had struck and found nothing but silt and endless earth.

Rather than snapping at me in her usual fashion, Babushka chuckled. "If I hate your mother, why did I let you come here?"

A question I pondered every day. After living here all this time, I felt no closer to the answer, but hearing my grandmother acknowledge it was like hearing the question in an entirely new manner. One that still made no sense but provided an inkling of some sort.

Part of me dared to hope she would elaborate. When she didn't,

I shouldn't have let the stab pierce my gut. Disappointment—familiar, yet more painful each time.

My eyes smarted, though not from the chilly gust sweeping over us. Combatting the sensation with a sharp breath, I released the gate and found the path to the shed.

As my feet crunched against dry leaves and gravel, I took a few breaths to regain control of myself. *Useless tears*, Mama always called them. Tears never changed anything.

Perhaps the differences between here and Leningrad were figments of my imagination. Was it possible for two places to be different when both left me hollow, aching for something impossible to uncover on my own? Something others refused to give. If what had happened between my mother and grandmother was drastic enough to keep them apart, how could I belong with either one of them?

Inside the shed, I fetched my kerosene lamp, set it on the table, then found an empty wooden crate to use as a stool. Flipping it over, I set it by the shelves to help me reach the top, where I stored the dried fly agaric and sulfur head mushrooms next to a few old boxes and crates. My time before dinner would be much better spent experimenting than sitting inside.

When I stepped on the crate, the slats groaned in protest. I reached for the mushrooms—nearly there. If I moved closer . . .

As I stepped to the edge, the crate tipped.

My cry mingled with significant clatters and crashes as I struck the ground, taking some items from the shelf with me. A dull, heavy pain spread across the back of my head while the room spun. Gingerly, I pushed myself up, then touched the source. Tender, but no blood.

Broken glass and scattered mushrooms surrounded me, as did a solid wooden box from the shelf—one I'd never touched.

Most of the items in this shed looked as if they had been here far longer than I cared to know.

With painstaking care, I salvaged every fragment of dried, sliced mushrooms and stored them in new jars. They were going to the garrison eventually; if they had a little dirt or broken glass on them, it was just what the Fritzes deserved. Once the mushrooms were safely stored, I swept the shards, buried them in the woods, and returned to clean up the wooden box I'd knocked off the shelf.

One item had fallen out and landed about a meter away. Buried in shadows, difficult to see; still, unease rose in my chest. I fetched the lantern and brought it with me for a closer look.

Once I'd illuminated the space better, I set the lantern down. The item was unmistakable now.

A pistol.

My breaths rattled, crackling in my chest like radio static. With hands that suddenly felt clumsy and unnatural, I picked it up. This was a Browning, older than any of the ones my fellow resistance members used. A few cartridges and magazines lay scattered around me, so I scooped them up and shoved them into the box.

Dedushka kept his guns inside. He had been a young man during the revolution, so he had probably carried a gun for most of his life. Maybe this was one he no longer needed.

With gentle care, I placed the gun inside the box, then returned it to the shelf. I put out the lamp—now that I was probably late for dinner—but as I hurried from the shed, another little inkling nagged me. This pistol had stirred a memory, hazy yet getting closer to the surface, clearer . . .

Then it emerged: The way Babushka had handled Reuter's rifle with such ease.

I spun around to face the shed, heart pounding. If she had a hidden weapon—

No, an absurd notion. My grandmother had never breathed a word of knowledge about guns. She had no use for them and no reason to hide one. She didn't even approve of resistance, even if she had possibly conceded to my involvement. And all she had done with the Fritz's rifle was point it at him.

There was a simple explanation for the gun: It had been Dedushka's a long time ago.

Releasing a slow, calming breath, I continued toward the house.

Babushka didn't shoot guns. The only weapon my grandmother wielded was her tongue.

Chapter 34

Y ou're certain you don't need help?"
The last time Zinaida Viktorovna asked me that, I threatened to hit her with a spoon. The kitchen staff consisted of myself and Zina, who seized any excuse to talk about her four sons but never remembered our roles: cooking was my job and serving and cleaning was hers.

As I bent over the assortment of potatoes, beef, onions, and carrots I'd thrown into a pot, I waved the spoon for emphasis. "Fetch the dishes."

Next time, I'd threaten her with something worse than a spoon. Maybe a fork. A quick jab would teach her.

After Zina offered me the bowls, I portioned out the stew, then she took the servings to the table. Once she was out of my way, I pulled the bread from the oven.

Outside the kitchen was the dining room where the soldiers ate. Often, their voices reached my ears—particularly after they had guzzled a few pints of beer—but Zina alone mingled with them when she served meals. I stayed behind closed doors, exactly where I wanted to be. Waiting for the right moment to utilize my poisons.

The urge consumed me more each day, but the time didn't

feel right yet. I had spent my last weeks obeying orders, establishing trust, ensuring Alscher knew I was a perfectly obedient employee. One who would never dare defy him.

Soon enough, the right moment would come to me.

The evening progressed without disruption until Zina was putting away the last of the utensils. "Do you need help checking stock?"

Another of my tasks, not hers. "No, it never takes me long." We had been working together for nearly two months and she still posed the same questions.

With a nod, Zina departed for the evening. Her work was done, and I preferred checking stock alone. In silence, I went through the pantry, noting the items while muffled chatter sounded in the other room, indicating a few Fritzes lingered at the dinner table. I had just finished my task when one barged into the kitchen, his empty beer mug in hand.

"You are not the old woman," he said in heavily accented Russian.

"I should hope not."

He stared at me, as though unsure what to make of my response. "You are . . . ?"

"Nadya. You?"

"Friedrich." Green eyes, dark blond hair, perhaps my age. Handsome, though it pained me to admit it.

When Friedrich handed me his empty glass, I tried not to accept it too eagerly. Zina was gone. The soldiers in the other room sounded drunk, which meant Alscher wasn't around to rebuke them for indulging. Perhaps the moment I had been awaiting had come.

Alone in the pantry, where the excess beer was stored, I pulled arsenic from my pocket, poured the white powder into the glass, and refilled it. An exhilarating pulse surged through my veins when I gave it back to Friedrich, who took a deep gulp as he departed. Arsenic mimicked the effects of a stomach illness; no one would suspect poison. And if this method worked, this was the start of what was certain to be a success. Today, one less Fritz inside this garrison; by the time I was finished here, hopefully none would be left at all.

* * *

Vitebsk Region, 27 October 1942

First Zina cut her hand on a knife after I had explicitly stated that *I* would slice the bread; then, while I sought a clean blade and a bandage, I left the onions unattended on the stove and burned them. And serving the soldiers a late dinner was not an option.

Zina pressed a rag to her palm while staring at the charred mess in my pan. "You can salvage them."

"I don't have much choice, do I?" Scowling, I chopped another onion so at least one would be edible, then added cabbage and sausage. All it needed was the ground castor oil plant seeds in my pocket.

Two weeks had passed since I had poisoned Friedrich, so I was itching to increase my efforts; but Zina was watching, making my task impossible even if I completed it quickly. And if I delayed until she was distracted, it would put me even further behind schedule. Poisoning required precision, not haste.

As the mixture sizzled, I refrained from reaching for my vial and gathered plates instead. Faint German conversations floated from the other room, certain to shift into impatient grumbles soon. I hurried back to the stove, served a meal that looked as unappetizing as it smelled, then placed plates and silverware on trays.

"Can you lift those?" I asked Zina, who was fashioning a clean rag into a makeshift bandage.

"Yes, I'm fine now." She reached for a tray, but a crimson stain was already seeping through the cloth.

I caught her wrist. "Alscher will hang us both if you get blood all over their dinner." Without awaiting her reply, I hefted the tray myself and pushed into the dining room, where a series of long tables stretched across the space. If any of the men noticed that it was not Zina who had entered, no one seemed to care. Not until I had served the last dish and was about to return to the kitchen for the next round, when a grip found my arm. I froze.

"The other woman." Alscher, his usual measured tone, yet it sent the blood rushing in my ears. "Where is she?"

"The kitchen, Herr Oberstleutnant," I breathed. "She cut her hand, so—please." My voice rose when his hold tightened. "Please, I can show you."

Another agonizing second, then he released me. "Move."

This was exactly why I always insisted that Zina and I keep to our roles. Alscher was a man who disliked unexpected change.

I had only led him a few steps when frantic shouts disrupted the chatter, prompting us to spin around. A young soldier with dark blond hair stood at the opposite end of the room, gesturing to his companions.

Friedrich—except he was supposed to be dead.

It took all my willpower not to gape. How had I gotten the

dose of arsenic wrong? If I had failed to poison one Fritz properly, I sure as hell couldn't poison hundreds.

As he shouted, I caught one of the few German words I recognized, the one for *partisans*. I swallowed hard. The partisans must have staged an attack. After a command from Alscher, soldiers rose and rushed to the door, checking weapons as they went.

"A guard will escort you off the premises," Alscher said to me, then he followed them as they swarmed out of the dining room, leaving only a few remaining troops.

I stared after Friedrich's retreating figure.

Mila, you stupid girl.

What I had considered a success had developed into a spectacular failure. Friedrich was still alive, and now he had uncovered some sort of partisan attack and had alerted the garrison to it. If I had succeeded, perhaps that attack would have gone undetected until it was too late.

No more mistakes. If I were going to continue making mistakes like this one, I might as well swallow poison myself.

I intended to finish what I'd started. To prove to Fruza my heart was with this cause, to fight the patriotic war, to go home to a Leningrad free of siege and suffering.

But if Friedrich knew what I'd done and had alerted the entire garrison to my intentions, I would eliminate as many Fritzes as possible before my time was up. Let them waste their time with interrogation and torture. I guarded my resistance secrets as closely as my poisons, and I refused to give up either one.

Chapter 35

Vitebsk Region, 27 October 1942

W hen the soldiers led me outside the gate, I hurried toward the village, seeking Daniil's hut. For this report, the only thing on my mind was Friedrich. Still breathing.

I left the barbed-wire fence behind, sensing the guards' eyes on me as the distance stretched between us. Dusk settled across the sky—violet, azure, streaked with auburn. My stomach clenched, aching for the tomatoes and onions I had delivered to the garrison today. Life on a farm was unbearable when almost everything we produced was confiscated—or forfeited, thanks to me—while our rations dwindled. Sighing, I stared at the footprints my feet left in the road, muddy from recent rain. A chilly breeze lifted its faintly rotten scent to my nostrils.

More footsteps sounded behind me—others walking back to Obol before curfew—while distant figures came from the opposite direction, presumably on their way to the outskirts of the village. As a cluster of men neared, though, they weren't walking past me; they were walking toward me.

No, I was wrong, surely. Paranoid after today's discovery of my failure. Daniil's izba was in the distance; I was nearly there—except now those men *were* approaching me, brows furrowed.

If they followed me, I'd go to the pharmacy, as if to shop; then, if necessary, Katya could sneak me into her family's apartment above the store, and I could stay there tonight. Holding my sheepskin coat from Babushka tighter around me, I glanced over my shoulder. The footsteps I had heard behind me proved to be more men, a horse and cart, and a few women fanning out until they had created a barrier impossible for me to pass.

I froze. I was surrounded by villagers. This was an ambush. In a place as small as this, everyone recognized the outsider. Everyone knew the young woman from Leningrad who worked for the invaders and took them food from her grandparents' farm.

Once you infiltrate, the villagers will find out. They'll think you're a collaborator.

This throng of hostile glares, clenched jaws, and stiff shoulders brought Daniil's warning to life. Panic wrapped around my throat. Professing my innocence was useless. Besides, telling the truth would compromise the resistance, especially if those quick to join this crowd proved as quick to share information with the soldiers.

A few paces ahead of the others stood a glowering young man, burly despite gaunt features—Anton Maksimovich, who lived near my grandparents.

"If you have something to say, say it quickly, unless you want to explain to my grandmother why I've come home late," I said, voice level, though I gripped my coat tighter to steady the tremble in my hands.

His eyes raked over me, likely aware my ease was a front. "Treachery is a serious offense. Serious offenses require serious punishments."

Rapid strides approached behind me, then a strong grip found my shoulders, so tight I sucked in a breath. No one was armed, as far as I could tell; rather than lingering to find out, I drove my heel into my captor's shin, broke his hold, and fled toward a gap in the throng. More hands caught my arms, waist, and hair, rendering my attempt useless, stripping off the thick coat. When they had me restrained, they turned me to face the cart, where a few men were lifting a large sack. No, not a sack. Something wrapped in a cloth. It already resembled a form I recognized, leaving a heavy pit in my stomach; they propped it against one of the wheels, blocking my view as they uncovered it. And when they stepped aside, I gasped.

A young woman, pale skin bright with fierce slashes that were red as her bloodshot eyes. Jagged remnants of skirt and blouse covered her, while her mouth hung slightly agape, a sign that a slip of paper had rested there. As a burst of wind assaulted me, filling my lungs with the putrid earth beneath my feet, I swore the stench was stronger now, intensified by blood, decay, death.

"A collaborator." Anton nodded to the murdered woman as he strolled closer to her. "I saw her speaking with a soldier, then he handed her a piece of bread and she went on her way. I made sure her treachery wouldn't continue."

Whatever she had exchanged for food—information, goods, her body—had sentenced her to a brutal death. And my perceived offense was far greater. Still, I didn't look away. Threats were not footprints in the mud along this village road, leaving a lasting impression; they were dust dissipating on the breeze. If this crowd planned to sentence me to this woman's fate, why frighten me first? Surely that meant their threats were empty. They were making a point, nothing more; then they would release me.

Anton made a dramatic show of rolling up his sleeves.

My theory withered. Perhaps they intended to do more than frighten me, after all.

"Do not touch me," I said through my teeth, if only to delay the inevitable a few seconds more.

"Scream all you want," he replied as he approached, clenched fists corded with veins. "Your fascist friends won't hear you."

Then he swung a fist into my ribs.

My knees buckled against the overwhelming pain, while another blow found my stomach, another my jaw. The hands released me. Cold, wet mud squelched beneath me as I gasped for breath, then a kick struck my shoulder. I shielded my head from the onslaught, while voices rose—some cursing me, others reminding their comrades not to finish too quickly, and to get off the road.

The blood in my mouth tasted rancid. They wanted to drag me into the woods, beat me, slaughter me, leave me until the worms had picked my bones clean.

Or, worse, turn me over to Orlova, as they had apparently done to that woman.

I swung my legs at the nearest set of feet, earning a startled cry as the man collapsed. If I got up, if I could run—but another series of blows sent me back down.

More hands brought me upright; Anton gripped my chin. "When we're finished with you, you're free to go, then we will contact the local NKVD and have them send word to Moscow." He pressed his free thumb to my eyelid, forcing it wide open as he lowered his voice. "Orlova will be eager to make an example of an anti-Soviet."

A tremor broke what remained of my resolve. Whether Orlova came here, they took me to her in Moscow, or she instructed one of her agents to carry out the task for her, the other woman's body was proof this was no empty threat. Even if I swore my garrison involvement was a resistance scheme, she would consider me a liar, a cowardly fascist desperate to save her own skin. Yuri would vouch for me, surely, but if Orlova received reports about me from dozens of loyal Soviets, would she take one NKVD agent's word over theirs?

And, if Orlova killed me, who would poison the soldiers in the Wehrmacht garrison? Who would help my grandparents on their farm? Who would listen for reports on Leningrad, hunting for ways my parents might escape the siege? Fruza was doing all she could, I knew, but the tides of war could shift at any point. If a change occurred, one that might alleviate my parents' suffering, I needed to know and share it with her.

A dead girl could do none of those things.

Neither could a Young Avenger tell the truth to this mob without jeopardizing her mission.

As the crowd swarmed toward me, a gunshot broke through the uproar, accompanied by an unmistakable voice.

"Lay another fucking hand on her, and the next bullet is yours."

When they let me fall again, I blinked past the mud obscuring my vision while Daniil shoved the crowd aside, pistol at the ready. Most dispersed; others lingered to see the next spectacle.

"Have you been drinking like your father, Daniil?" Anton asked with a sneer. "Why else would you be interfering with summary justice?"

Though I drew my knees closer to defend myself from the next blow, Daniil had already stashed the pistol, punched Anton across the face, and caught his collar with both hands to keep him upright. "Is it justice to attack an unarmed woman?"

Daniil tightened his hold, suppressing Anton's struggles and lowering his voice to a growl. "Coward."

The other man's glare abruptly shifted, blood streaming from his nose. He glanced from me to Daniil, as though he had uncovered something unspoken.

"Are you fucking a fascist?" This time, he regarded Daniil as though *he* were the treacherous one. "What a way to honor Yelena's memory."

The pain coursing through my body faded, pushed aside by the fury twisting my heart. Whatever they assumed about me, about us, did not warrant this for Daniil, certainly not for Yelena.

Tense silence fell while his eyes ignited with pure, deep rage. Then he shoved Anton into the filth and fell upon him. A few shouts, muffled curses, and though Anton managed to strike once, it only took Daniil a few more blows to render him unconscious. When Daniil stood, he turned at once to me.

While he helped me to my feet, some remaining crowd members left me with hateful glances; others directed a few at him. With his support, I stumbled toward his izba, every breath aching, mind thick as the mud caked all over me.

Inside, he settled me in a chair by the warm pech, returned the coat he had picked up, and gathered a bowl of water, clean rags, and antiseptic. Anton's blow hadn't drawn Daniil's blood, so he had fared much better than I had. I shivered despite the fire's warmth while his eyes swept over the filth covering me.

"Take off those clothes."

Of all the ways I had imagined such a conversation between us, following an attack from an angry mob was not one of them.

Daniil offered me a spare dress from the trunk of clothes

the Young Avengers kept here, since most missions took place outdoors and often led to torn, stained, bloodied clothing. "Change while I find Katya. You need medical attention. The crowd will know better than to come here for you, and I won't be long, then I expect a full report."

When I extended a hand to accept the dress, a sharp pain stabbed my chest. Wincing, I shook my head.

"Katya will have to help me."

Daniil brought the kerosene lamp closer. He touched a muddy patch on my sleeve, assessing how damp the garments were, then knelt and began unfastening the buttons on my skirt. "Tell me what happened." Direct, focused. Leader and Young Avenger.

"They think I'm a fascist and they intend to give my name to Orlova." Straightforward, clipped, matching him. "I didn't reveal the truth."

The lines across his forehead deepened. "I'll have Yuri draw up a report for her to explain your infiltration."

As his fingers found my shirtwaist, one I'd purchased from a shop in Leningrad, I drew an uneven breath. Button after button sprang free until the lamp's orange glow fell across my pale skin, my slip, the twine around my neck. The little amulet had guarded me from so much, yet failed to protect me from the need for him. But if I whispered for him to come nearer, I knew where such prompting led: to his arms releasing me, to the distance that always remained between us. Instead, I stayed silent. Exposing one's body was far less dangerous than exposing one's heart.

This was our work. I had a report to give.

After the final button, Daniil helped me to my feet. I braced myself against the pech, hoping to steady my balance as well as my breaths.

"A soldier I poisoned isn't dead."

"A Fritz survived your toxins and an angry mob attacked you and threatened your life?" He passed a hand over his beard, then sighed in resignation. "I'll tell Fruza the operation is over."

"No, I don't want out. The mob won't . . ." I paused. Would they come for me again? Daniil had scared them away for now, but I doubted their fear would last. Not if they thought a traitor remained in their midst. Another breath. Another stab of pain through my chest. "If the Fritz is aware it was poison, he's given no indication," I said instead.

"Do you want to go home after the war or not?" Unexpectedly sharp, prompting me to meet his glower.

"Of course," I snapped, then gritted my teeth when my aching ribs protested.

"And I intend to send you there, which will be much more unlikely if you stay at the garrison. The chance of Gestapo capture was already high, and now the villagers want your blood, too."

I had no time to retort. Daniil eased the skirt and blouse away with painstaking care, leaving me in the old, tattered slip I had brought from home.

"When risk transforms into death sentence, it's become too dangerous." Gentle, softening my own stiffness in turn. He caught the twine around my neck, running his fingers over it until he cradled the vial, tracing his thumb over the smooth glass. An unsteady breath, matching my own. "I can't leave you there." Gruff, hardly a murmur.

I covered his hand with mine, tightening his hold on the vial, holding both to my chest. "If I want out, I'll tell you."

His eyes lifted—dark, intense, as though seized by a sudden longing, yet something interfered. Something always interfered.

Daniil broke my hold.

The pech's fire crackled and popped, jeering at me for almost believing that, this time, something would *not* interfere. While he doused a rag and squeezed excess water from it, I focused on the blood and muck staining my skin, fetid and thick.

When he returned to my side, Daniil draped his own sheepskin coat across my shoulders, large and heavy and warm, then dabbed a cut on my cheek. "If the soldier has realized he was poisoned, you might walk into arrest tomorrow." His touch remained light, his voice husky.

"If I try to quit, they won't believe whatever lie I tell them. Let me stay." I placed a hand over his, encouraging him to meet my gaze. "Trust me. You'll be the first to know if I don't feel safe."

Since I had stayed the hand holding the rag, Daniil brushed his free thumb over my lip. His eyes searched mine while my blood on his finger turned burgundy in the lamplight. "Do you feel safe, Mila?" he murmured. "Do you really want to stay?"

Ignoring the stab of pain in my chest, I reached for his cheek in return, as if wiping away mud—though nothing was there—and responded in a whisper. "Very much."

Chapter 36

Vitebsk Region, 12 January 1943

Over the past months of working in the garrison, I'd poisoned dishes without Zina's knowledge, making it appear as if illness had struck and resulted in a few deaths. My system was simple and effective: Lace a few dishes, spare others. Give some men a full dose, others half, others less. Each time, I observed my work from the security of the kitchen.

One January evening, Zina returned from serving the main course, adjusting her headscarf over her graying auburn locks. Often a sign of nerves. "Many empty seats," she said. "And this morning, my son Viktor—the one home from the war after his back injury—woke complaining of a stomach ailment."

"The same one that has struck the garrison?" I asked, knowing very well that it was not.

She said nothing, though her mouth tightened with worry; the one plaguing the garrison had killed a few. I resisted a smile. Since failing to poison Friedrich—a mistake that had since gone undetected—I hadn't failed again.

As the night neared its end, I tossed the last of the dirty dishes into the sink and grabbed a bottle of vodka, preparing to ask Zina to offer a final round of refills, but I had no chance before the kitchen door burst open and ten soldiers flooded inside.

Amid Zina's startled yelp, I spun toward the back door

while the Fritzes swarmed toward us, yelling in German. If a guard saw me running, he might shoot, might spare me from whatever was about to happen if I stayed.

Hands caught me, pulled me back with such force that my feet left the floor, then slammed me face-first onto the counter.

It was like swallowing poison myself, pain splitting across my head and dancing before my eyes, robbing me of breath, twisting my stomach into knots. The room spun until a sudden jolt of pain demanded my focus when the soldier forced my arms behind my back. With a cry, I struggled to alleviate the agony, but he pulled me upright and dragged me toward the remnants of prepared food.

Only then did all the shouts fall silent, aside from my shuddering breaths as I stood before the hostile crowd, pain coursing across my scalp and down my shoulders and arms.

Zina had also been restrained, her chest heaving in panicked breaths.

Alscher stepped forward. "You are to be questioned," he said to us, then he jerked his head at Zina's captors. They led her from the room, though she left me with a final glance, her eyes wide.

Questioned. Was this to do with our employment? Had something happened in the village? After five successful months, surely they didn't suspect my poison.

"Why did you try to run?"

"Because I'm unarmed, facing the armed men who barged into my workplace." Not the most respectful answer, given Alscher's frown, but the pain swirling through my head prevented me from caring.

He picked up a bowl of kasha and brought it beneath my nose. "These dishes contain poison."

Silence met this pronouncement. Perhaps I'd gotten a little overzealous with the arsenic. Why did I continue using arsenic when I had much more faith in mushrooms?

True, I had laced the rye bread as well as the porridge, but I had distributed carefully—two different batches of porridge, one with arsenic and another without. I varied the proportions in each serving so none of the soldiers would be affected in the same way, and I had been using arsenic this entire week so they would get sick on different days, as though infecting one another. My usual process, one that had always yielded satisfactory results.

As Alscher set the bowl down, I put on the appropriate mask of shock before scowling. "Poison? That's a rather weighty insult to my cooking."

Another unappreciated response, judging by the severity of Alscher's glare. Even if appeasing him with respect had been my biggest concern, I had no time before one man pushed forward, assessing me with heavily guarded eyes.

Friedrich, naturally. My failure would haunt me for the rest of my days, limited as those might be now that I had come under question. I hadn't laced his dishes yet, afraid of a second failure and drawing his suspicion—much like I had anyway. My caution had amounted to nothing.

"The night we met, I suffered from stomach pains," he said. "You poisoned me."

They were convinced I was guilty, every one of them. If I didn't figure a way out of this, my sentence was certain. But another thing was also certain: Nadya had made it clear to Alscher that she did not want to die.

This was my weapon, my fight, my patriotic war. And there was only one way to win this battle.

"No, I didn't do anything wrong, I wouldn't!" I shouted, resorting to the frantic desperation I had presented to Alscher upon our first meeting, struggling as my guard began ushering me to the door. "Please, Herr Oberstleutnant, let me show you the food is safe!"

Alscher held up a hand. My captor paused, then released me.

Arsenic. One of the first poisons I studied with Katya. I would have about thirty minutes before its effects set in. Before my body absorbed a lethal amount if I consumed too much.

Whatever it took to protect the mission.

I tore into chunks of bread, then inhaled a few mouthfuls of kasha—the safe batch, thankfully, since it was closest to me. Once finished, I grabbed the bottle of vodka from the counter and lifted it to them in salute.

"Pròst," I said, utilizing one of the German words I'd learned from eavesdropping on many dinner conversations. I took a sizable gulp and slammed the bottle onto the counter. Let them challenge me now.

As long as they did so before my thirty minutes were up.

After a moment of bewildered silence, they started talking and gesturing to me, likely convinced this had been a misunderstanding. Alscher nodded to the door. One by one, they began to leave while a rush of relief coursed through me.

But Alscher remained. Staring at me. "Many of the men say illness set on quickly, so I will wait here to observe you."

Once again, I had lost the battle. In proving I was trustworthy, I had signed my own death sentence.

I assumed the appearance of calm, as though certain I had done enough to avoid the fate that would have awaited on the other side of interrogation and torture. I lifted my shoulders in a nonchalant shrug and grabbed the vodka. "Do as you please." I brought the bottle to my lips again, but he confiscated it—and with it, my plan to drink myself to death before the poison killed me first. The clock hanging on the far wall ticked in ominous warning; I glanced at it. Six minutes gone.

Babushka's familiar whisper echoed in my ears—*Mila, you stupid girl, what the hell were you thinking?* Her scolding was not what I needed to escort me to the afterlife.

"May I have the vodka back?" I asked. Based on his scowl, I gathered the answer was no. I stole another peek at the clock.

Fourteen minutes gone.

At least my crossed arms hid my shaking hands.

Panic served no purpose. This was a noble death, after all. A death for my cause. Such a shame I wasn't going to take more Fritzes with me first.

Though I fought to breathe evenly, I already felt the poison's impact on my stomach. What had started as a few milligrams of white powder was now pummeling my insides without mercy.

Not much longer.

Alscher watched me like an eagle preparing to swoop down on its prey, making it even more imperative to mask my symptoms. How had I not convinced him? I imagined Babushka at my funeral: *Stupid girl, of all the idiotic ways to die . . .*

A soldier opened the kitchen door briefly to shout something—another partisan attack, perhaps? Daniil had mentioned a plan to bomb a power plant; I held my breath while Alscher muttered what sounded like a curse, then looked me over with disdain.

"I have more pressing matters to attend to than peasants."

As if it were my fault he hadn't ordered someone else to observe me. "Do not give me reason to suspect you again, or I will see to your execution myself."

Alscher's threat upon my ears was as beautiful as a chorus of Soviet voices singing "The Sacred War." Was he truly letting me go? Had I won this battle, after all? And Zina was ignorant of my actions; when he questioned her, surely she would convince him of her innocence.

I bobbed my head, while he spun around without waiting for me to leave. Definitely a partisan attack; nothing else ever made him this anxious. When the door closed behind him, I checked the clock one last time.

Twenty-six minutes gone.

I tore through the refrigerator and snatched the whey. The sight of the watery, milky substance with little white curdles floating in it was almost enough to do what I required, but I had no time to rely on sight or smell alone. I rushed to the sink, tipped my head back, and guzzled it until my stomach rebelled. The creamy sourness of the whey mingled with acidic bile. I drank more, vomited more, until the jar was empty.

The poison descended upon me, harsh and unforgiving. My stomach felt like it was tearing itself apart. I staggered through the back door, where a guard waited. Suddenly I was grateful for the soldier who had thrown me against a hard surface with all his force: He had given me an explanation for my unsteady steps.

Not even the frigid January gusts alleviated the drops of sweat forming against my skin. The arduous walk resulted in a kind farmer offering me a ride on his wagon when he saw me stumbling down the road. After he dropped me off, I kept going toward the farmhouse, a hazy speck in the distance. Urging me closer, promising relief from the biting cold, rest from my aching insides, yet fading alongside the evening light.

My gray *valenki* reached my knees, but the felt boots sank deeper into the snow with every step; perhaps the snow would soak through into the lambswool interior, chill my toes, spread upward, eradicating the heat surging through me. About ten meters from the door, the searing pain brought me to my hands and knees. I retched, vomited, collapsed in the snow, lying in my own filth.

You cannot go on, the arsenic whispered. *You have failed, Mila Lvovna.*

True, though not a total failure. Not like before, with Friedrich. Surely Mama would be pleased to learn her daughter had been so devoted to the cause—or maybe that devotion was the very thing she despised in me. Persistence, relentlessness, each accompanying my quizzical glances and repetitive questions until each *Stop prying, Mila* presented me with another failure.

I had lost this time, this final time, but I wasn't going to die at a Fritz's hand. Didn't I deserve credit for a minor victory?

The poison merely sliced through my insides, giving me no credit. Neither did the icy wind or the snow holding my vigil.

Once the snow had buried me, snowflakes would soothe my parched throat and cover me in a blanket to cool my burning brow. It would save my grandparents the trouble of a funeral, trying to dig into frozen ground. I imagined Babushka's cane sweeping through the snow and ice, on her way to visit my final resting place.

A gale tore across my skin, but the sound of my grandmother's cane remained. It hadn't been inside my head. When I opened my eyes, the increasing darkness failed to shield the familiar figure moving toward the house.

"Babushka." I meant to yell but only whispered. "Babushka." Though my voice remained faint, she stood still and turned in my direction.

"Where are you, Mila?"

She didn't sound worried, but of course she wasn't.

Another retch overtook me. When it passed, everything I intended to say condensed into one small plea. "Help me."

She found me in seconds. "What happened?" The sound of more heaving coupled with the stench around me revealed the answer. "What did you take?"

I shivered with cold and heavy terror. "Arsenic."

She muttered a curse. "Get up."

Her voice was difficult to discern through the haze of pain, heat, cold, trembles, shallow breaths. When I realized what she wanted me to do, I shook my head slowly, though she couldn't see the gesture. "I can't."

"Then I hope you're comfortable out here. I'm sure the wolves and bears will take excellent care of you." Babushka crouched beside me, wry humor gone. "Get up, Mila."

Even now, I lost the courage to disobey that tone. I pressed my palm into the snow and managed to push myself into a sitting position. Once I was there, Babushka drove her cane into the ground with one hand, gripped my upper arm with the other, and brought me to my feet in one smooth lift.

"You have to walk," she said as she wrapped her arm around my waist.

Despite the agony ripping through my body, I turned an incredulous glance upon her. "How did—?"

"You're not so heavy, and I'm not so old."

After a few moments of shuffling through the snow, I was faintly aware of Babushka pushing the door open and calling to Dedushka, telling him to fetch buckets, blankets, wash-cloths, cups, water, and whey.

She deposited me onto a bench, stripped off my soiled garments, then dressed me in a clean nightgown. A large, warm hand found my cheek—Dedushka. One arm slipped around my back, another beneath my legs, then I was pressed against a broad chest smelling of earth and wood. I closed my eyes, feeling small, fragile, wishing to be held like this until the poison inevitably stripped me away.

Gently, he placed me upon the pech's wide, flat space used for sleeping due to its warmth. As pain overtook me, I clung to every folktale I had ever heard of the stove's healing powers, every household spirit said to live around it; if any cared to cure me now, I would devote the rest of my life to ceaseless gratitude.

Chapter 37

Vitebsk Region, 13 January 1943

I propped myself up as far as the space between the pech and
the ceiling allowed, watching as the morning sun stretched
across the fields. Vomiting and dizziness had overtaken my
entire night. I remembered little—only Babushka by my side
through it all. This morning, though my insides were still
churning, the pain had considerably lessened. And I was due
at the garrison soon.

If only I could get a message to Daniil. I had promised to
stop by on my way home last night to deliver a report; since I
had failed to do so, he was probably convinced the Fritzes had
thrown me in prison.

As I tucked my blankets and furs more securely around
me, trapping the warmth, the front door swung open. "More
alert this morning?" Babushka called as she stepped across the
threshold, shaking snow off her valenki.

"Much. I might be able to keep some tea down."

She didn't fetch the samovar, though; instead, still clutching
her cane, she approached until she stood beside me—eyes like
twin dark rings, an indication she had hardly slept last night.
"Mila, get out before it gets worse."

Her voice was not its usual snap, a bullet leaving a pistol; it
was belladonna seeping into the bloodstream. Slow. Deadly.

No longer did she question what I spent my days doing; perhaps it had been a long time since she had last questioned it. When I responded, my voice matched hers. Unrelenting.

"And if I refuse?"

She knew I was determined to see this fight through to the end. Our differing opinions and family secrets were the constant divide between us.

"If it goes too far—" Then she stopped, her face drawn, oddly stricken. Though we had endured nearly two years of foreign occupation, I suspected her life prior to this had been quiet, untouched beyond the hardships of farming, despite having lived through a revolution. Perhaps this war and seeing her granddaughter on the cusp of death had struck her more than either of us had expected.

Babushka returned to the door, calling over her shoulder as she went outside. "Your young man has requested a word."

I opened my mouth, but Daniil was already entering.

I had given him strict orders to stay away from the house, even when he visited me in the shed. Babushka disapproved of the resistance enough as it was; the last thing I needed was her meeting those I worked alongside. She would spare me no questions, draw conclusions like *your young man*—

"What are you doing here?" I asked, keeping my voice down.

"When you didn't stop by, I had to locate you." He fetched a small wooden chair from the table, pulled it closer, and sat. "Svetlana Vasilyevna told me it was arsenic, and that you are an idiot."

"You can ask Svetlana Vasilyevna what she would have done if her choices were eat the food she poisoned or give away her entire operation," I replied bitterly, slumping against the wall.

"You want to go back, don't you?"

I nodded. I hadn't swallowed poison just to quit. "Alscher never saw me get sick, and I'm well enough to work."

"Still, if you've been accused of poisoning them . . ." Falling quiet, Daniil removed his ushanka and toyed with it. An indication that a plan was coming. "What you're doing is already collaborative on its surface—a Soviet working for the fascists. We might be able to use that to draw suspicion away from you."

Though I resented the word *collaborative*, falsified or otherwise, he had a point. It *was* part of my infiltration. But I didn't need reminding that I looked like a traitor. The mob that had attacked me last October had made that very clear—as had Babushka when I had come home that evening, battered and bruised. I tried to hide it, considering her inability to see the wounds, but her ears heard my shuffled steps, sudden winces, until she demanded the truth. She shook her head, cursed my stupidity, muttered that she knew my role at the garrison would lead to assumptions, then consequences.

Daniil leaned closer, eyes bright. "Even the Fritzes can't resist a bribe. One accepts them from me in exchange for information; I'll convince him to sneak me into the garrison tonight. After you leave, I'll leave a threat against you outside the kitchen door—maybe a cartridge and a note saying this is what Soviets who collaborate deserve."

Let Daniil put himself at risk for my safety? That sounded even worse than swallowing arsenic.

"Once I've done that and my contact has gotten me out, a few Young Avengers and partisans will fire on the garrison, as if attempting an attack before retreating. Then, tomorrow morning, you can find the threat and show it to Alscher. He'll assume someone from the attack got in and left it."

My chest tightened. "Can't you bribe the contact to plant it for you?"

"He wouldn't be stupid enough to take on that risk no matter what I offered. And what kind of outraged patriot would let a Fritz do his work for him?"

"Why not give me the note and let me plant it? If your contact betrays you, or if you get caught—"

"I won't have you getting caught with it. Not after you were nearly caught poisoning them."

"Can your Fritz be trusted?"

Daniil gave a dry laugh. "Can any Fritz be trusted? He's paid well and hasn't betrayed me yet."

That was the problem: There was always *yet.*

Daniil passed a hand over his beard. "The contact will believe I'm planting a legitimate threat against you. He won't know that you and I are working together, so you won't be implicated."

"And if *you're* implicated?" Glaring, I swung my legs over the side of the pech; with Daniil's help, I eased myself down. "I knew the risks I was taking on with this infiltration. I've accepted them, so why can't you let me?"

"What would Fruza say if I sent you back to your death? It's my position I'm protecting as much as yours." Daniil glared in return as he watched me take cautious steps to test my strength. "I'm not forbidding you from going back. But if you *are* going back, it will be under these terms."

I let out a huff. The risks I had accepted were not ones I wanted Daniil to take, certainly not on my behalf.

"Fine. Carry out your plan, but I don't agree with it."

"It's not your job to agree with it." He caught my shoulders as his voice softened. "It's mine to keep the work safe. To keep *you* safe. I told you, I don't intend to lose anyone else to them."

Those words he had said so long ago, in that strange tone—
tight, weighty. He wasn't naïve, knew death was a risk that
came with this work. Other than various resistance members
who had given their lives to the cause these past months, the
only other person he had lost to the Nazis was Yelena, the
young woman who had been slaughtered alongside her family
during the invasion.

But he had loved her. Not so with us, despite those moments
when my heart had driven me to him, longed for something
more meaningful. Yet, as he met my eyes, I found no words to
respond.

Daniil released me, closed the door softly behind him, and
left me with the infinite darkness of his gaze, a sea of a love
and loss he couldn't bear to repeat.

Chapter 38

Vitebsk Region, 13 January 1943

Please, Katya." I followed her up and down the pharmacy aisles. "What if I trade you money instead of produce and take just arsenic, not cyanide?"

All this time she had been silent, jaw set, eyes narrowed as they roamed the shelves and checked stock against the list in her hands; now she rounded on me with finality. "No. I told you, my father said the Fritzes are getting stricter about inventory. If I keep supplying you, they might notice."

Sighing, I followed her to the front counter. The soldiers had seized control of countless businesses like this one, permitting Katya and her family to continue doing all the work while the Fritzes reaped the benefits. But our arrangement had never been an issue before.

"You've been covering it up all this time. Can't you continue?"

Katya glanced toward the door, probably to ensure no customers were entering, then caught my arm with sudden speed and pulled me close. "My mother's brother married a Jewish woman and moved to Taganrog," she began, her voice sharp. "The fascists rounded up my aunt, uncle, and their four children alongside thousands more, took them to the Gully of

Petrushino, and massacred them. Young and old, men and women and children."

She fell silent, perhaps giving me a chance to answer. I had nothing to say.

"If the soldiers are watching us more closely now, adjusting the numbers would be reckless," she went on without loosening her grip. "I'm not afraid to die for this cause, but I *am* afraid to be the reason my family is sentenced to death."

She swallowed hard, the intensity leaving her eyes, and she released me. She turned back to her list, staring at it while I pictured my own family sentenced to death because of me. My parents in Leningrad. My grandparents.

"I'm sorry about your family in Taganrog," I murmured at last.

Katya responded with a small nod, eyes on her list.

When she was adamant, I knew better than to pursue the subject. I had various mushrooms and plants tucked into my pockets as well as some chemical poisons. I would have to make do with those in the event I needed them tonight.

Katya would change her mind when the Fritzes relaxed. She had to change her mind.

Mumbling a farewell, I departed. The morning was as quiet as the snow cascading around me. Still, I had to hurry; I had spent more time at the pharmacy than intended, and it wouldn't do to be late to the garrison.

A sharp wind gripped me, powerful as Katya's hold, the vehemence in her eyes. I increased my pace along the bare dirt roads, past the railway platform, where Daniil and I had come across Orlova's victim nearly a year and a half ago. The image of the mutilated body filled my mind. I almost wanted to find more soldiers' corpses there, a warning powerful enough to

scare the Fritzes away once and for all rather than prompt reprisal. Then there would be no need for Daniil to carry out the
plan that had left an ever-present ache in my stomach.

When I reached the garrison, the guards seized me at once.

It was so abrupt, so unexpected, that I forgot to struggle.
Surely they didn't suspect me. Not when I had taken such
lengths to prove my innocence and had dragged myself back
this morning, despite spending an entire night writhing in
agony. Each step across the snowy grounds intensified the lingering ache in my stomach.

When they pulled me into the kitchen, Zina was there—
unharmed—gathering pots and pans, as was a familiar figure
in a spotless Wehrmacht uniform.

"Do you remember what happened to the girl who held this
position before you?" Alscher demanded; I bobbed my head
vigorously. "Tell me."

"S-she . . . she was . . ." I let my voice tremble even as my
heart thudded against my chest. My mission and my life de-
pended on these next few moments.

I poured all my trust into my tiny amulet, begging it to ward
off these demons who surrounded me, feeding off my fear as if
sucking the blood from my veins. Then I bowed my head and
sank to my knees, voice rising, breaths sharpening.

"I told you the truth last night, I swear, I—"

Alscher's firm grip caught my chin and forced my head up.
"What happened to the other girl?"

I took a moment before answering in an unsteady whisper.
"She was executed."

He nodded, then lifted my chin higher. "And I do not think
you would face death as defiantly as she did, Nadya."

With that, Alscher and the guards released me. I stayed

where I was, heart racing. My actions last night coupled with my presence this morning must have convinced him of my innocence; it was the only explanation for why I was still breathing. Even so, Daniil's plan was the reinforcement my story needed.

As the day progressed, Zina and I worked in overwhelming silence. I gathered some soldiers had recovered from the supposed disease, others had died, and some carried lingering traces. Despite Alscher's threat occupying my mind, the news made me want to open a bottle of vodka or fill a mug with German beer and drink to my success. Perhaps I would lace a handful of dishes tonight to let a few others catch the disease before I permitted it to leave the garrison for a time. Best to make the most of the false illness.

Daniil planned to slip into the kitchen once I was alone. Then, after I left safely, he would plant the false threat against me, escape with help from the bribed soldier, and stage the false attack. It was to mask my resistance involvement, to ensure the continued success of this mission; yet, he had been so insistent. So determined not to *lose anyone else*. But what if that determination had led him to trust the wrong man, to breach the barbed-wire fence for my sake, only for his plan to go terribly wrong?

I lifted a hand to my chest, pressing it against the amulet hidden beneath my clothing. Too late to stop him now.

The closer we came to the end of the evening, the more my heart raced. Every sound, every man's voice, every footstep turned into Daniil's. Perhaps I would feel better once I laid eyes on him, saw the contact had let him get this far—unless the contact let him come to me so the soldiers could ambush us together.

Once dinner ended, I sent Zina to the pantry to check supplies, silently imploring her to hurry so she would leave. I wiped lingering grease stains from the stovetop and brushed wine off a tiny corkscrew, hands already shaking. A few minutes more, only a few . . .

"Missing something?"

Gasping, I whirled toward the accusatory voice. Friedrich stood in the doorway. One hand leveled a pistol at me; the other presented me with a vial—empty aside from a small amount of white powder.

I gaped at the label: arsenic.

"After we confronted you last night, I came back to search the kitchen and found this." He waved the vial; it must have fallen from my pocket during the scuffle. I bit the inside of my cheek to suppress a wave of panic.

"Did you tell Alscher?"

"If I had, you would be dead." Not the answer I expected, though I masked my surprise while he strolled closer. "I'm the one you tried to kill, so shouldn't I get to decide what to do with you?"

"You withheld evidence from your superior." If I kept him talking, maybe I'd have time to figure out what to do next. "Won't Alscher be angry?"

"I'll tell him I went to the kitchen after dinner tonight, caught you with the poison, and interrogated you, then I will present him with my evidence and your confession." He looked at the tiny vial. "That will earn me a promotion, don't you think?"

Well, at least his arrogance had led to a foolish mistake. If Friedrich was the only one aware of my guilt, he was the only one I had to worry about for now.

And then Zina emerged from the pantry.

"Everything is in place, so I—" She stopped, staring at the pistol while I muttered a curse.

Friedrich showed her the arsenic. "I don't think this is yours, but you are going to be my witness, and I will tell you exactly what you are going to tell Alscher during interrogation." He waved his gun toward a pile of twine and butcher paper from the sausages I'd unwrapped for dinner, then nodded to me. "Bind her."

Zina grabbed the thin string in shaking hands and brought my arms behind my back. She wrapped the twine around my wrists, cutting into my flesh, then stepped away from me. I kept my back to the stove and swallowed past the sudden knot in my throat.

"On your knees," he ordered.

Zina reacted with a sharp intake of breath. Meanwhile, I obliged.

I had to break through my restraints. While Zina and Friedrich had been distracted by the butcher paper and twine, I'd swiped the little corkscrew from the countertop and hidden it in my fist. Now I gripped its wooden handle and worked my fingers up the spiraled iron until I located the pointed tip. Carefully, I sawed through the twine. Back and forth, fiber by fiber.

Toying with the vial, Friedrich strolled closer. Zina's eyes darted from him to me, her breaths shallow. My hand moved little by little, pressing the tip of the corkscrew into the twine and pulling it away.

"Do you work for the partisans?"

I said nothing, though I swallowed a rise of panic. Panic wasn't going to break my bonds. I needed time.

"I can kill you slowly or quickly. That depends on how much information you give me."

Somehow I had to keep him occupied without betraying the resistance, without prompting him to take action.

When he raised the gun, Zina shrieked.

"Don't!"

Friedrich drew back, then a gunshot rang in my ears, eliciting my automatic cry. With a moan, Zina fell to the kitchen floor, blood pouring from her chest. She gasped, clutching the wound as if desperation alone held the power to extract the bullet.

"I was going to let you live," he said while she writhed. "Now I have to tell Alscher you interfered."

She looked at him with unmasked hatred and managed a gasping claim. "The vial is mine."

His lip curled in contempt. "Liar."

Perhaps Zina was a partisan, or had realized what I'd been doing these past months, or was simply one woman defending another. I stared at her, hoping my eyes communicated my gratitude, and how much I wished the price of her efforts had not been her life. Then her hand fell and she lay still, drenched in blood, wide eyes locked on mine.

Friedrich pressed the gun to my chest. I pulled my shoulders back, though perhaps he felt my heartbeat pulsing, making its way up the gun barrel and into his steady hand.

"You aren't going to tell me anything?" He stepped back, evaluating me before settling on my knees against the hard floor. "A slow death it is."

He angled the gun toward my left kneecap.

"Wait, I'll talk, I'll talk!" As he paused, glancing at me with renewed intrigue, I combatted unsteady breaths. "I . . ." Another little shudder as the twine broke with a light snap. Then I lifted my head and flashed a devious smile at him. "I *did* poison you, you stupid Fritz."

I drove the corkscrew into his wrist and knocked his hand aside, loosening his grip on the gun amid his furious shout. When both my corkscrew and the weapon clattered to the floor, I sprang to my feet, grabbed his arm, and held with all my strength.

He turned back to me, eyes wild, free hand reaching for me. His fingers closed around my throat. Gasping, flailing, I sought something, anything, to use as a weapon, clawing at his grasp while he squeezed tighter, tighter. As my vision darkened around the edges, my fingers found something next to the stovetop. I gripped the object's handle and drove it into Friedrich's stomach.

With a choked cry, he released me and staggered back, leaving me coughing, spluttering, clutching a butcher knife.

I stared at the red streaks against the gleaming blade, then looked up when a sudden thud reached my ears. Friedrich had collapsed, blood seeping from the hole in his stomach. He twitched one last time, then no more.

Friedrich and Zina, surrounded by crimson pools. A bloody knife in my stained hands. I, Mila Lvovna, already accused of poisoning the Wehrmacht soldiers, had now stabbed one.

What the hell was my plan now?

The back door creaked open. I spun around, still clutching the knife.

Daniil rushed to meet me; I stood in dumbfounded silence, while his incredulous gaze roamed from the arsenic vial to the corpses, settling on Friedrich's.

"What the fuck happened, Mila?"

My hands shook, unable to loosen their grip on the knife. New plan, we needed a new plan. A way to explain to Alscher how a dead soldier ended up in my kitchen . . .

All at once, the solution fell into place, as perfectly balanced as one of my experiments.

I placed the butcher knife near Zina's bloodstained hand, then kicked Friedrich's gun closer to him. Once finished, I assessed my clothes. A few marks, but not many, since Friedrich had fallen so quickly. A little blood was easy enough to justify.

I returned to Daniil's side. "Hit me."

He narrowed his eyes in dispute; before I could urge him on, he found his voice with a little bark of incredulous laughter. "No, absolutely not."

Fine, I'd do it myself. I grabbed a metal measuring cup and smacked it against my cheek—enough to leave an impact but no lasting damage. When I yelped, Daniil ripped the cup away, while I blinked to clear my vision. Gingerly, I touched my face; my lip and cheek were cut. Glancing down, I watched a drop of blood fall to my chest, joining the other stains. Exactly as I had intended.

"What the hell are you doing?" Daniil tried to wipe the blood trickling from my mouth, so I pushed his hand away.

"The Fritzes know I'm the last to leave the kitchen at night. If they find one of their own dead in my space and a supposed partisan threat against me, it will look like I killed him and planted the threat myself to make them believe I'm innocent."

"We can clean up before morning. Toss the bodies, get you somewhere safe, carry out the original plan, and—"

"If someone comes looking for Friedrich as we're wiping his

blood off the floor? I don't think anyone heard the gunshot, but they could walk in at any time."

"They already suspected you once. If it happens a second time, you won't fool them again."

"I'm not running. And if I come back tomorrow as if I know nothing, they won't believe me." I presented the lacerated skin on my wrists, a sure sign of my involvement thanks to Zina's bonds.

Daniil's eyes fell to my neck; he brushed his fingertips over the marks Friedrich had left. At his light touch, I reached for his hand, but he let it fall before drawing it across his face.

"You want them to find you here. With the bodies."

Despite an unsteady breath, my voice was sure. "It's my best chance if I'm going to convince them I'm not involved in the resistance. Call off the Young Avengers and the partisans. Will your contact get you out safely?"

"If not, and if Alscher doesn't believe you, then this time tomorrow will see us both in interrogation."

After I reviewed what had taken place, followed by my more detailed plan, I scrubbed the blood from my hands, then Daniil bound my wrists the same way Zina had and followed me to the pantry. Once I stepped across the threshold, he closed me inside. I allowed my eyes to adjust, then I pressed my ear to the door, listening as he slipped out through the back entrance.

I had forgotten to ask him to tell Babushka I wouldn't be home tonight. Maybe I would be better off remaining locked in the pantry forever. Twenty years old now, yet my grandmother's chastisements still held the power to make me feel like a little girl—even if they held no power to change my actions.

Now I had one more step to complete my story. Blinking

through the darkness, I stumbled over a sack of potatoes, turnips, or something of the sort, then located a lower shelf, sat, and lined up the back of my head against it. I took a deep breath, gathering my courage. This was going to hurt much worse than the measuring cup to the face.

I threw my head back and slammed it against the shelf. Heavy pain surrounded me while everything slipped away, but not before one paralyzing whisper seized my thoughts: This was all for nothing. The most incriminating piece of evidence was still out there. The one Friedrich had used to confirm my guilt.

Neither Daniil nor I had picked up the vial of arsenic.

Chapter 39

Vitebsk Region, 14 January 1943

Maybe the splitting headache roused me. The numbness spreading from fingertips to shoulders. The scuttling on the shelf beside me, a sound I often heard in the stable, right before Dedushka advised me to spread rat poison. Perhaps all three took turns, poking and prodding me even though the darkness refused to relinquish its firm hold. I slipped in and out of a heavy sleep, conscious of little more than drowsiness and pain.

At last, I tried to rock into a sitting position, but abandoned the attempt when my stomach gave a nauseous turn. Instead, I remained on the cold concrete floor, cheek and lip covered in dried blood, head pounding, surrounded by the smell of burlap sacks, wooden crates, and spices. Opening my eyes required too much effort, so I kept them closed, focusing on my prepared story instead of the cords cutting into my wrists.

Startled German cries sounded from the kitchen. My original plan had involved yelling to get their attention, but no sound came.

The arsenic. Had they found the arsenic yet? To think I had gone to all this trouble just for one misstep to lead to my downfall. Even if I convinced them it wasn't mine, they would figure out the vial had come from the pharmacy. Neither Katya nor her family would be spared.

When the door to my prison burst open, I squeezed my eyes tighter against sudden light. More exclamations fell on my ears, then various hands picked me up, cut my bonds, supported me as I staggered out of the pantry. The room spun. My stomach jolted as the soldiers ushered me past the bodies.

After the men led me to a stool, something wet splashed my face, leaving me gasping and coughing, then a rough cloth followed, smothering me as it wiped the dampness away. Another hand found the back of my head, holding me still even though I yelped as his fingers pressed against the knot left by the shelf. When the cloth released me, my blurry gaze focused on Alscher, who set a dish towel beside an empty glass on the counter. He reached for me again, this time smacking my cheek—not hard, but hard enough.

"*Wertlose Sau,*" he muttered—*Worthless sow,* so I had learned. A phrase he used often when referring to me. "Wake up."

I imagined shoving arsenic down his throat as payback for his methods, and for the way he and his men equated women to farm animals. As the pain dulled and my arms returned to life, I took in the gruesome scene, trying to come up with an explanation for the poison.

But the vial was nowhere to be seen. Neither were the bonds I had originally broken with the corkscrew, or the bloody corkscrew. Either the Fritzes had already found them—probably not the case, considering I didn't have a noose around my neck—or, before leaving, Daniil had staged our scene one last time. Gathered any evidence that pointed to the Young Avengers or discredited my story. Ensured the Fritzes would never suspect me, Katya, or her family.

A savior, Daniil Ivanovich was.

"What happened here?" Alscher demanded.

"I . . . I think it was her all along." I met his gaze with wide eyes before dropping my voice. "Zina."

Alscher sat in rapt attention while I fed him my story. That I had confronted Zina last evening, suspecting she had been poisoning the meals without my knowledge; it was the only way to explain why the men had gotten sick after she delivered the plates I had prepared, but I had been fine after eating the same unserved food. That I had intended to gather proof before taking my theory to Alscher, but she had struck me. Said she hated the soldiers; called me a traitor for my planned report. Knocked me unconscious and tossed me into the pantry. And when I roused, it must have been a few minutes later and Friedrich must have overheard the commotion and come to investigate, because I heard his voice, then startled cries and a gunshot.

When I finished forcing my way through the lies, silently assuring Zina it was noble of her to take the blame to protect my work, Alscher spoke with another officer, presumably relaying my story. I waited, hoping he would draw the intended conclusions: Zina had stabbed Friedrich, then he had shot her before both succumbed to their injuries.

I stared at the glass of water in my tight grip—one I was permitted to drink after Alscher had doused me with the first. Were my hands still red, coated in hot, sticky blood? When I looked again, the glass was the knife, my hands tinged crimson.

"Clean yourself up."

I nearly jumped at Alscher's order, while his eyes roamed over the bloodstains on my clothes. To poison a man was one matter, but to kill him with my own hands left my mouth tast-

ing like belladonna, its bitterness coating my tongue and sliding down my throat.

The bodies. Was I supposed to remove them? I resolved not
to ask. No need to put ideas in Alscher's head.

I wet the cloth but had no time to wipe the blood from my
clothes before the kitchen door swung open again, then German voices broke through the rush of water pouring from the
faucet.

Two soldiers entered, dragging a tall, dark-haired young
man between them. Handcuffed, blood pouring from a gash
on his forehead and into one eye; he looked to me, but I was
too busy swallowing a gasp to read what I found in those rich
brown depths.

My fear all along: betrayal.

When Daniil's captors pulled him to a halt, his gaze darted
from me to the corpses before he fixed Alscher with a deadly
glare. "Nadya didn't come by last night. Why didn't she come
by?" He drew a sharp breath and took a forcible step closer,
despite his guards' resistance. "Son of a bitch, answer me! Why
did you keep her here?"

No, not betrayed, not if he was using my alias and attempting a ruse . . . Had he come back?

His voice trembled in a way that nearly had me convinced—as
though he were truly furious, truly terrified of the unspeakable
reasons I might have been detained—before he looked to me.
All eyes followed.

"Nadyushka." Strained yet softer around its edges as he
took in the cuts on my face. "What have they done?"

So sincere. So concerned. A most convincing act.

Before I could attempt a response, the Germans started prattling, then Alscher addressed Daniil. "Sneaking around the

perimeters, were you? Not a bright decision if you wanted to stay alive."

"I was trying to find someone to ask about her whereabouts."

"Is that so?" The words weren't mocking, simply observant, which was almost worse. Alscher looked him up and down. "Do you know what we do with Red spies?"

Daniil's lips quirked into a little grin as he dipped his head toward the corpses. "Let me guess: spies?"

He probably expected the blow as much as I did; when Alscher's fist met his jaw, he responded with nothing more than a little grunt. As Daniil spat blood from his mouth, Alscher crossed toward me in a few strides and grabbed my arm, drawing a gasp from my throat. He hauled me off the stool while Daniil strained against his captors; they held him securely until I stood before him.

"Her name?"

"Nadezhda Olegovna Kharitonova," he responded without hesitation.

"And his?"

"Aleksandr Stepanovich Averin." I named his alias with just as much assurance, despite a slight strain. Then, softly, "Sasha."

Daniil held my gaze, tried to move closer again. Whether for the ruse or involuntarily, I wasn't certain.

Alscher spent a few more minutes quizzing us until he finally shoved me away. "While you're here, you can make yourself useful," he said to Daniil, jerking his head toward the corpses. "Give my soldier a proper burial. The woman will be a reminder of what awaits those who defy the Reich."

Daniil gave no reaction, though the eye unobscured by blood glistened with hatred.

"And you." Alscher took my chin between his gloved fingers—firm enough to make me tense. "I can find any number of peasants to take your place. Shall I make an example of you, too?"

My terror, my ignorance, my desperation, always what he sought to reassure himself of my obedience. He pressed his pistol between my eyes, eliciting my gasp.

"Please, I've done nothing wrong."

"See that you don't. If you or your lover give me any more trouble, I will put a bullet right here." He pressed harder, making me flinch, emphasizing his next words. "Am I clear?"

"Jawohl." Yes, sir. The one German phrase he required me to use. And when the gun's pressure intensified again, I quickly supplied the part I had forgotten. "Jawohl, Herr Oberstleutnant."

After he released me, it took me a moment to breathe normally again while the soldiers removed Daniil's handcuffs. When they departed and the door closed, he stared after them.

Everything I wanted to say nearly poured from my mouth—thanking him for removing the evidence last night, asking why he had returned this morning. Stronger than that, so strong it was almost startling, was the urge to act. To wrap my arms around him. To press my lips to his.

He crossed to the sink and bent over it, so I let the urge slip away.

In silence, we bathed our injuries, though I cast the occasional sidelong glance at him, wondering. Wondering if, when his eyes met mine again, I would find the same look, the one he had used to reinforce his ploy of concern. The one that had placed this strange lump in my throat.

At the sound of approaching voices, Daniil stepped away

and I grabbed the first pot I found, while his two captors stalked inside. One held a shovel. Both sets of lips were curled with nasty delight.

As I pretended to focus on my work, they barked orders in German, gesturing to the corpses, so Daniil opened the back door. Beyond a small walkway that had been cleared, I glimpsed walls of snow, at least a meter high. Daniil stooped and caught Friedrich's body by the ankles, then dragged it to the door. Once there, he hefted it over his shoulder to transfer it outside while one officer encouraged him with a shove. He stumbled but maintained his footing.

Before the door closed, a biting wind swept inside and across my skin, carrying with it the sound of a solid object striking something—the shovel's long wooden handle against Daniil's back, judging by his effort to suppress a cry, then muffled sniggers. I didn't realize how hard I had bitten my lip until the metallic taste of blood filled my mouth.

The soldiers came back inside, shaking snow off before gesturing for me to make tea. I nearly threw the boiling water on them instead.

They stayed in the kitchen, sipping the warm beverage, conversing, smoking, every now and then checking on Daniil, hauling him back in only once to fetch Zina's body. Hours later, when they pushed him back inside, they threw a clean rag at his feet and gestured to the bloodstained floor.

Teeth audibly chattering, hair and beard covered in ice and snow, he knelt slowly, reaching for the rag with trembling hands while I poured a fresh cup of tea and approached him. I only made it a few steps before one of the Fritzes smacked it out of my hand. It fell to the floor and shattered.

This time, I nearly threw the jagged edges of porcelain at them.

Armed with a rag, pan, and broom, I knelt to clean the mess but chanced a quick look at Daniil, his hands blistered and bloody from shoveling through the frozen earth, cracked and raw from the unforgiving cold. The sight put a new lump in my throat and tightness in my chest, stronger than any I had felt all day, while I swept my shards and he drew the clean rag across the bloodstained floor.

* * *

WHEN THE SOLDIERS escorted us from the garrison, Daniil and I walked toward the village in silence. A gentle snowfall descended as I waited for Daniil to speak, to look at me, to do *something*. But he just walked. The tension in my throat had remained all day and showed no signs of departing.

If he wouldn't bring up what was certainly on both our minds, I would.

"Why did you come back?"

"When I left the garrison last night, I told my contact that I'd almost gotten caught planting the threat against you, so I didn't get a chance to do it; that way, he wouldn't be suspicious when no one found it. This morning I wanted to find out if the Fritzes had believed your story, so I returned to ask him if I could try again tonight, and he would have told me what happened to you."

"You would have gotten your answer when I stopped by this evening—or when I didn't."

"Better to know sooner. But I didn't see my contact and the others caught me." Daniil shoved his hands into his coat pockets. "It would have been foolish to wait. If we were compromised, I needed to make Fruza aware."

The tightness moved to my chest as I whirled to face him. "Compromised? You expected me to break during interrogation?"

He shrugged, then pushed a lock of hair from his face before adjusting his ushanka. "The best of us do."

Heat raced through my veins. Would someone who didn't have the strength to withstand interrogation be willing to infiltrate the garrison, where the risk of capture, torture, and death lurked in every corner? "You're the idiot who got caught trespassing. If the best of us can break, how do you know you wouldn't have?"

"I don't."

"Then why come back, especially if you suspected my story hadn't worked and I had been arrested? If you were anticipating betrayal, why not contact Fruza and protect the organization as much as possible before the Gestapo came for all of you?"

"I needed to know," he said, tone barely audible. Avoiding the question.

I wanted the truth. If he doubted me, I wanted him to match my outrage and say so to my face. Most of all, I wanted him to look at me.

"What if we had carried out your plan last night and it had gotten us arrested, or your actions today had? If you don't trust me to protect us, why put yourself and the entire organization at risk instead of staying away and preparing for what you thought I—?"

"Mila!" The interruption came in an urgent, angry breath,

and then he looked at me for the first time since Alscher had forced us to face one another.

It was back. That look. The one that had lent authenticity to his professed fears, to his desire to help and protect me. The one that startled me now even more than when it had been for show. Because, this time, he had no reason to put on an act.

Chapter 40

Vitebsk Region, 9 March 1943

Babushka hadn't masked her disapproval when I came home after locking myself in the Wehrmacht garrison pantry all night. I didn't explain my absence; for once, she didn't ask. Maybe she didn't want to know. She knew I refused to give up the patriotic war, and I knew she would never approve. So we simply carried on as we always had.

Blaming the poisonings on poor Zina had diverted suspicion away from Nadya. I had spent the last seven weeks being perfectly obedient despite the incessant urge to act, one that intensified after a new group of men had moved into the garrison last month. The urge gnawed at me more each day, tearing through my insides like arsenic, forcing me into submission.

Raucous laughter and chatter sounded from the dining room as the soldiers waited for me to serve them. The air was thick with steam while the familiar scent of borscht permeated the kitchen. I stepped away from the hot stove long enough to wipe the perspiration from my brow, then sliced rye bread and fetched bowls. Since Zina's murder, the Fritzes hadn't hired a new assistant—Alscher's idea to minimize the civilian staff given Zina's supposed infiltration on behalf of the partisans. I was on my own.

I had to stage my attacks carefully; Katya still refused to

supply me, so my stash of chemical poisons was running low. And though new men had come, Alscher had remained along with his suspicions, watchful eye, and meticulous records of Zina's crimes. The next time an "illness" came to the garrison would likely be my last; even if Alscher fell victim, the remaining soldiers would examine the reports and realize I had been the perpetrator all along.

As I ladled portions of soup, my eyes drifted to where Zina had sprawled across the floor, blood seeping from her chest. No one deserved to have her corpse stripped. Bound to a post in front of the garrison. Left on display for weeks before the soldiers finally permitted her family to take the decomposing body. No one deserved to die by a Fritz's hand.

Like Daniil might have if Alscher had not believed his reason for coming to the garrison.

I took a steadying breath as I transferred the remaining borscht into the last bowl. He had risked capture, likely followed by interrogation, torture, and death. Because he had *needed to know.*

I had gone over our conversation endless times, poring over every detail. Each time left me more confused. Maybe he truly was afraid I didn't possess the strength for interrogation. Maybe he wanted to be certain of my fate before preparing the Young Avengers for the worst. Or maybe the look in his eyes had told me everything his words hadn't.

Since he had left me standing in the middle of the road, baffled and unable to continue our conversation, he hadn't paid one of his occasional visits to spend time with me in the old shed. Whenever the Young Avengers gathered for meetings or missions, he kept busy. He hardly glanced at me. We rarely spoke.

If he resented me, I didn't blame him. Because of me, he had been forced to desecrate one corpse and dig a grave in the middle of winter to bury another—well, that wasn't completely my fault. He came here of his own accord. If not for him, I would have desecrated Zina's body and dug Friedrich's grave. We would still be on speaking terms. The knot in my chest wouldn't form every time I saw the jagged pink scar on his forehead, a remnant of that long, bloody gash. My breaths wouldn't stop when I pictured the torn, blistered flesh on his hands as he scrubbed bloodstains from this floor. I wouldn't be wondering. Always wondering.

If not for him. If not for the way he had looked at me.

It had been nearly two months; I had spent too long wondering. When my workday ended, I went straight to Daniil's izba and burst inside without knocking. He sat at the table, cigar in hand, untouched plate with a few small potatoes and a scrap of meat before him.

"You came back for me."

Wax dripped from a candle stub near his plate while its flame cast tiny golden beams across his face and over his beard; he did not acknowledge me, not even as I continued.

"That morning in the garrison, after you helped me cover up the murders. You came back." My voice was nearly shaking. "You can't do something like that only to resent me for it."

Daniil's shoulders heaved in a little sigh while I waited, washed in a combination of candlelight and shadow. "I always resented my father for the way he started drinking after my mother and sister died." He took a drag of his cigar. "It went on for years until he left home and never came back, shortly after Yelena and I started seeing one another. I thought him weak. Cowardly." He watched the little tendrils of smoke curling up from the ash, the next words more unsteady. "After Yelena. That's when I started smoking."

He placed the cigar in the ashtray and shoved it away with sudden force. I said nothing, cheeks hot though my chest tightened. As he rose and crossed to meet me, he looked so apologetic, almost pained.

"I do not resent you, Milushka." Gently, he brushed a few stray hairs away from my forehead. "But if I can't guarantee your safety, and if you were to—" A break swallowed the words.

I hadn't decided if I was prepared to forgive him until I heard the inflection in his voice. The way he said my name. And, as I recalled the night I had spent here, learning about the love this war had stolen from him, I finally understood. All these months, I had not fabricated those moments when I had felt drawn to him, and he to me; yet this barrier remained, keeping the distance between us.

He walked slowly to the far window, where a faint beam of moonlight spilled into the room. I joined him. Placed a hand upon his forearm.

"Look at me, Danya."

He did, eyes bright as I drew him closer until I had pressed my back to the wall. All I wanted was to soften the hard set of his mouth, to steady the pounding of his heart beneath the palm I pressed to his chest. I placed my free hand upon his cheek, brushed a sudden escaped tear. If only a gesture held the power to absorb such an intense ache, I would erase all the pain that the past had burned into his heart.

I pressed my lips to his. I wanted to alleviate the torment, the fear—even if his heart remained torn beyond repair and we never became more than we were in this moment. As I wrapped my arms around his neck, he pressed closer, seizing control as he kissed me more deeply, smoke and spice.

Intense, urgent, everything I had always imagined and more, as if we had finally been granted the permission we had both craved yet never dared to request. Another moment, then Daniil drew back. At last, he spoke in a voice like the whisper of a final breath.

"I can't do it again."

Very much, those broken words said.

You loved her?

Very much.

Suddenly I had no idea why I had come. Why I had longed for this when I knew he was coping with a devastating loss. Why I had kissed him. His heart was a risk I couldn't bear to take. If this war took us from one another, shattered him again, how could I be so selfish as to demand that from him?

And, after the war, he would be staying here. And I would be returning to Leningrad.

I placed a hand on his cheek to assure him I understood. Daniil held me a second longer, as though wishing for the impossible. Then he released me.

As I walked home, the evening chill settled into me, stabbing my heart with every aching breath. This loss was of something I never truly had, far less severe than the one Daniil had suffered; yet, now I understood why he refused to risk such a loss again.

* * *

THE NEXT DAY at the garrison, I stayed as busy as possible. Anything to keep my mind off Daniil. His arms around me, lips pressed to mine, the depths of his gaze, *Milushka* . . .

As I served dinner, the clamor of German voices and clinking glasses met my ears. Alscher approached the head of his usual table, where the empty chair waited for him. Entering alongside him was another man, who removed his leather trench coat, revealing a different uniform. And not a German one.

I stared. This man wore *galife* trousers tucked into tall jackboots. A khaki-colored wool *gymnastyorka*. A thick brown leather *portupeya* belt, holster, and shoulder belt. A *kartuz* cap with a shiny black visor, maroon band, and cornflower blue top.

My heart lurched. He was NKVD. A member of the Soviet Union's secret police force, surely sent here thanks to the mob that had threatened to give my name to Orlova.

No, this man had come with Alscher; an NKVD agent sent to arrest a Soviet traitor would not do so here. Nor would he be having dinner with the fascists. I swallowed hard.

This NKVD agent was a collaborator. And I had to put a stop to this treachery.

When I fetched more bowls of soup, I searched my pockets for a vial of death cap mushrooms, dried and sliced into small, thin pieces, and left them in a bowl of warm water to reconstitute. Then I sprinkled lethal doses of arsenic—almost all I had left of it—into two dishes, stirring quickly to incorporate it. Only two contained lethal doses. To those, I added death caps for good measure, disguised alongside the non-toxic borovik I had included in my original recipe. I tossed poisonous mushrooms into as many bowls as possible. If this was my last attack, it needed to count.

I served the remaining men, saving the lethal doses of arsenic for last. One for Alscher, one for the traitor. When I placed the bowl before the NKVD agent, it hit the table with a clatter, nearly sloshing soup over its side.

"*Wertlose Sau!*" Usually Alscher voiced it as a lazy complaint, as though my every move inconvenienced him; this was charged with irritation. "Apologies, Commissioner Sokolov."

He was hoping to impress his guest. Anticipating the secrets this man was preparing to spill—and, considering he held one of the highest rankings, he probably had many. Alscher feared my clumsiness would upset this Commissioner Sokolov and ruin whatever alliance they had forged.

As I adjusted the bowl, Sokolov lifted his empty glass, expectant. Alscher, too, curled his mouth into an impatient frown, silent chastisement for not bringing drinks alongside dinner. I hurried back to the kitchen and returned with vodka. Once I'd filled both glasses, Sokolov downed his in an expert gulp, set the glass down, and caught my wrist.

Gasping, I jerked away, but he tightened his grip and pulled me nearer.

He was perhaps my grandfather's age. Dark hair and thick beard, both streaked with silver. Skin leathered. Impossibly strong, as indicated by his hold. His eyes were so dark they were almost black, evaluating me—first my face, then from head to toe and back.

When a man grabbed a woman to bring her closer, one certain look typically followed. This look was different, more difficult to decipher. Studious, memorizing everything about me. Somehow it felt more violating than anything else he could have done.

At last, his deep voice broke through the flurry of my thoughts.

"Leave the bottle."

The vodka on his breath mingled with another faint smell, sour and ashen. Cigarettes, perhaps. Resisting the urge to cringe, I set the bottle down. One more glance, as though his curiosity had been satisfied, then Sokolov released me.

Shivering, I retreated to the kitchen. He would not be returning after tonight, and neither would I, yet his presence had taken root deep within my bones, terrifying for reasons I did not entirely understand.

After I'd spent a few minutes washing dishes, the door creaked behind me—probably Alscher armed with another reprimand. Shaking water from my wet hands, I turned.

Not Alscher. Commissioner Sokolov.

I gaped as if his presence alone held me in place. He strolled closer, offering the vodka bottle to me. With a nod, I accepted it and set it on the counter, my heart in my throat. He could have left it for me to clear along with their dinner dishes. The vodka was not why he had come.

Even after months spent among hundreds of Fritzes, being alone with a collaborator felt most dangerous of all.

"Will there be anything else, Commissioner?" Unsteady, but all I could manage.

Anticipation was like a nick from a belladonna-soaked blade, letting the poison into my veins to seize control of every muscle and nerve. Sokolov regarded me almost as if he recognized me. A look that told me I needed to leave this room immediately.

Muttering an excuse about cleaning the dining room, I dipped my head in another respectful nod, then rushed past him.

Until his familiar, painfully strong grip caught my upper arm. "Let go of me!"

His other hand covered my mouth, heavy and stifling despite my efforts to twist aside. No weapon was within my reach, not a knife, not a ladle, nothing. He pinned me between himself and the countertop in a hold impossible to break.

He made no efforts to do more, simply watched me struggle, held tight. And when I ceased, he lifted a dark brow, a little warning gesture, then removed his hand from over my mouth. I stayed quiet, fingers gripping the countertop behind me. Alerting Alscher would do no good, anyway. They were on the same side.

Something pressed beneath my chin—cold, unmistakable. His pistol barrel. A strangled sound emerged from my throat before he intensified the pressure. He was a collaborator, he knew I worked for the resistance, and he was about to kill me; I was sure of it. My chest heaved in shallow breaths; his steady gaze held mine. Then he spoke, unhurried and weighty.

"Leave this garrison. If you come back, your death will be slow. Excruciating. As will your family's. And you will die with their blood on your hands." Sokolov watched my chest flutter in response, then lifted his eyes to mine and used the gun to draw me closer. "Mila Lvovna."

I stiffened, impossible to prevent even if I had tried. He regarded me with such a strange look. Part warning, part something indistinguishable. It stole any fight I might have had, any brazen retort I might have made, any movement toward the poisons buried deep in my pockets; then he removed the gun and released me.

When the door closed behind him, I clutched my amulet with shaking hands, consumed by the threat, by this man who knew me. A man soon to be dead.

* * *

After dinner, I hurried home, though I considered stopping at Daniil's to inform him that returning to the garrison would be impossible now that my culpability for the poison-ings would be evident. Instead, I pressed on. Better to be as far away as possible when they discovered what I'd done. I'd spend the next few days in hiding while the soldiers searched for Nadya—whose residence on my false papers had been listed nowhere near my grandparents' farm. The Fritzes wouldn't trace anything to them; even if interrogated, my grandparents knew little, though Babushka probably knew far more than she revealed. Their ignorance would be legitimate; surely the soldiers would recognize that.

I drew a steadying breath while the air chilled my lungs. Once the search calmed down, I'd report to Daniil to tell him about the treacherous NKVD agent. His threat. If caught before I had a chance, maybe it meant death by a Fritz's hands, but I would die knowing I had taken plenty of soldiers and one traitor.

When I reached the farmhouse, I shook snow off before pushing the door open. Inside, my grandparents sat around the table, Dedushka with a letter before him and a pencil and paper in hand. Sometimes I found him here or outside, writing—usually to Mama, he said, updating her on my well-being. Between the two of us, maybe one day a letter would reach her and we'd receive a response.

The sight on the table was promising. He was staring at it, brow creased, but looked up hastily when I entered.

"Is that from Mama?" I asked as I removed my coat. "Did a letter actually get to Leningrad? Did she respond to mine, too?"

"No," Dedushka said gruffly. "Not from your mother. From another farmer." He tucked both letters into their envelopes and shoved them into his pocket. "I'll finish my response later."

"Something wrong?"

"Must you always meddle?" Babushka snapped—the equivalent of a *This is not your fight* or *Stop prying, Mila.*

"Enough, Sveta." The closest Dedushka, always so even-tempered, had ever come to outright chastisement. She didn't retort, but Babushka's hands strayed toward her forehead in their telltale manner while he turned to me, softer now. "Worries about the crops, that's all."

"We'll need you here to help," she added, her voice tight. "Effective immediately."

I paused in the middle of kicking off my valenki. "If you're trying to keep me from the garrison—"

"Mila, you can't go back there with—" She stopped abruptly, fingers digging into her temples, then finished through her teeth. "Them."

I approached the table, ready for a dispute—though after his unusual outburst, Dedushka might stop us before we began. She remained as she was, elbows propped, head in her hands, before she drew one hand across her eyes.

"It's gone far enough." So shaky, so soft. So unlike her.

I cast a helpless glance at Dedushka. He was looking at the dirt beneath his fingernails. And both of them looked so utterly hopeless.

"I want to help, and I'm sorry I haven't been around as much to do so," I said gently. Babushka kept her head lowered, so I reached for her forearm. "I promise I'll—"

The moment she felt my touch, she jerked aside and stood so quickly her chair nearly toppled over. She marched to her bedroom, where the door slammed, then we were left with silence.

Combatting a sudden, trembling breath, I stared after her before Dedushka's leathered hand covered mine. He gave me a little pat before standing and letting himself outside.

Then I was alone with the pech's crackling fire, watching as the flames lashed the logs, whittling them away one by one.

Chapter 41

Vitebsk Region, 13 March 1943

S eated at my table in the old shed, I brought the lamp closer, its warm glow chasing away the evening darkness, and pulled the letter from my pocket—the only one Mama had sent, just before the siege. I still had no word on how my parents were, so I had taken to rereading this letter instead. As I unfolded the worn paper, Mama's familiar hasty scribble greeted me.

Dear Mila,

All is well at home, but I've told you not to ask me when you will be able to return because I don't have an answer. Until the threat subsides, it's outside our control. In the meantime, stay well.

Mama

P.S. You know better than to pry. Ask your grandmother your questions if you must, but if you mention her again, I won't write back. Do you understand?

No different than our usual interactions. Why did I ever expect different? Maybe because all I had asked was whether or not Mama and her mother had squabbled as much as Babushka and I did.

To be fair, my grandmother hadn't brought up the garrison since her fit a few nights ago. Every day since, I had pretended to leave for work but instead had kept to the woods behind my grandparents' property. No soldiers had come to the farm yet, but I'd give their fruitless search another day or so before reporting to Daniil.

Sighing, I folded the old letter, returned it to its envelope, and left it on my table. Even if my recent letters were reaching her, maybe there was no point in continuing to write.

Next to the letter, my poisons were spread across my workspace. A little arsenic. Some cyanide. A few remaining grams of morphine. A few belladonna roots and castor oil plant seeds. Various dried mushrooms. But I had no interest in working with my poisons tonight.

Instead, I moved to the pallet I had created on the floor—a thick pile of hay, empty burlap sacks, worn quilts, old furs, blankets, and a few pillows, all collected over the past months to assemble a more comfortable lounge space. I lay there, staring at the ceiling, directing my thoughts away from Leningrad, when the door swung open.

As I sprang to my feet, Daniil covered the distance between us in a few long strides, the tight set of his jaw accentuated in the lamplight. "Did you poison that Russian man from the garrison, the NKVD commissioner? Sokolov?"

The soldiers. Had they located the young man—Sasha, Nadya's lover—who had come to the garrison seeking her? The Fritzes must have confronted Daniil about what I'd done to their men and the commissioner, told him of their intention to arrest me, even threatened him in an effort to extract my location from him. But Daniil was here, alive, unharmed—

A tight grip found my shoulders, followed by sudden urgency. "Answer me, Mila."

I jumped, then let out a slow breath to calm my pounding heart while he relaxed his hold. "Of course I poisoned him. How did you—?"

"Shit," he said through clenched teeth before turning away, running a frustrated hand through his hair, and slowly walking out of the light and into the shadows. "Why the hell didn't you talk to me first?"

"We've never discussed any of my assassinations prior to carrying them out."

"Because you were supposed to be assassinating the enemy."

"That's exactly what I did, and if you're going to criticize me for your own misunderstanding, the least you can do is face me. I was going to tell you as soon as the Fritzes stopped searching for me. Sokolov was a collaborator."

"No, Mila, he wasn't." Daniil returned until he stood centimeters from me. Instead of the anger I was anticipating, his eyes were bright with something close to fear. "She sent him there to lend false support. He was spying for her."

Her. This time, it was my turn to step away. It was an obvious conclusion—that the man had been cooperating with the soldiers under false pretenses, as I was. But the thought had never occurred to me. And there was only one *her* who belonged to the NKVD and was powerful enough to order a commissioner to do her bidding.

The dead Fritz on the railway platform and the body the villagers had presented to me were the only evidence of her presence I'd ever seen. It seemed her work against the fascists hadn't ended. Now I had interfered with everything. I was the traitor. I had committed the greatest sin possible, and there would be no forgiveness.

"Yuri told me today," Daniil said, a little calmer now. "He knows you're loyal to our cause, so he figured something had gone wrong."

"No." I shook my head. "No, he . . . Sokolov knew my name, told me to get out . . ."

"Maybe Yuri told him about your mission, so he wanted to scare you away without revealing his own. He probably didn't like the idea of a young woman facing the dangers of infiltration."

"I'll decide what dangers I face." Silence fell before I continued more softly, even though I knew the answer to my next question. "Does Orlova know?"

"According to Yuri, Sokolov sent her a report before the poison's effects set in. It included mention of your presence at the garrison." The muscle in Daniil's jaw twitched. "She already knew about you, since I asked Yuri to tell her about your infiltration after the mob attack."

I swallowed past the dryness in my throat. "Even without Yuri's report, Sokolov mentioned me in his own. It's not your fault, and besides, it doesn't mean much," I said, clinging to the desperate, useless need to dispute him. "Why suspect me of killing the Soviet when there were hundreds of Nazis at the garrison, too?"

"Because more than a dozen men were fatally poisoned that night, and the soldiers would have killed the Soviet alone. And Orlova knew you were working with poison." Daniil stepped closer to me and spoke so softly I almost didn't hear him. "Mila, the NKVD is looking for you."

Only once understanding swept over me did I realize I had buried myself in Daniil's arms. He said nothing, simply held me close while I pressed against him, too numb to cry or panic or do more than listen to his racing heartbeat and drink in the lingering scent of cigar smoke.

Perhaps Babushka was right all along. Perhaps this wasn't my fight. But I'd made it my fight, no matter how poor a competitor I'd turned out to be. Now I had to face the consequences.

Swallowing back the terror, I lifted my head. "What has Fruza said?"

"She's away in Polotsk, so I haven't told her," he replied as he released me. "I imagine she'll want to take disciplinary matters into her own hands—which won't happen if the NKVD gets ahold of you first."

Meeting Fruza in Polotsk would be foolish; it was still too close. The NKVD would surely search for me there.

"I need to get out of this region," I said softly. "At least until the NKVD search lessens. Then I'll go to Fruza myself."

After I shoved my poisons aside to make room on the table, Daniil spread a few papers between us. He'd already spoken to Yuri about making plans, though we were both sworn to secrecy about receiving his help. The notes included information about train schedules and routes, details on each city, trustworthy contacts, and theories about where Orlova might concentrate her search. Daniil reviewed the list, discussing the benefits and risks of each location.

"Moscow is the heart of Orlova's territory," he announced, coming to the final option. "NKVD presence will be heavy there, but they'll search the Vitebsk Region and its surrounding areas more closely because those are the places you'd be more likely to hide." He tapped his pencil thoughtfully against the paper. "What if we sent you elsewhere? Farther west, maybe. We also have the Fritzes to consider, but if we found a way to—"

"Moscow," I said with finality. "That's where Orlova is, so she'll never expect me to go right to her. Once I get there, I can figure out where to go next."

Daniil grabbed another paper containing a list of hotels. "Here." He pointed to the location, wrote down the name, address, and room number, tore off the scrap of paper, and handed it to me. "Be on the first train in the morning. Yuri will meet you at the railway to supply you with papers, money, anything else you'll need to travel safely."

I nodded even as my chest tightened. After spending all these months desperate to escape this region, suddenly I was leaving the farm, my grandparents, this old shed, the Young Avengers. Daniil. And I didn't want to leave a single one.

"My grandparents," I managed at last. "If the NKVD knows who I am, they'll know where I live."

"Yuri volunteered to come here tonight to look for you. That's how he bought us more time, and that way, your family will remain safe."

I let out my breath. "Will you tell them?" I swallowed hard as forming words became difficult. "Don't tell them why I've had to go, just . . ." I paused again, because I didn't know what to tell them. What did you tell people you would probably never see again?

Though I hadn't finished, Daniil nodded. "Once you're on the train, Yuri and I will do our best to handle the NKVD, then I'll meet you in Moscow and we'll figure out the safest place to go."

At this, a different feeling crept into my chest, the one that always prompted me toward him. When I gave him an inquisitive glance, he passed a hand through his hair.

"A Soviet under my command killed another Soviet; for that, Fruza will want my head and yours. We might as well face her together. Once we find somewhere safe, I'll contact her with our location and say we're surrendering ourselves to her, then she'll decide how to proceed." He refocused on his notes. "Spend tomorrow night in Moscow. If I haven't arrived by noon the next day, go on without me. You'll have to develop your own plan, but promise me you'll contact Fruza once you're settled."

I didn't respond; the inflection in his voice matched how it had sounded that day in the garrison. The day he had given me such an unusual look, concern and affection and terror wrapped into one.

The old flutter rose into my heart before I pushed it down. We had gone through this already; I was at peace with it, even if I still longed for something different between us. But we had made our choice clear, regardless of our feelings. This war had destroyed us before we had the chance to begin.

Besides, when it was safe, I was going back to Leningrad. He would remain here. Assuming we both survived the results of my treachery. Why wish for something bound to end?

With my plan in place, I started for the door. Daniil gave me no time to reach it. He caught my waist, pressed me against the tall, sturdy post running from floor to beam, and kissed me.

Unexpected, thrilling, intoxicating as I urged him nearer, kissing him fiercely until it was my turn to hesitate. If this was simply impulse, if the NKVD caught me, I was not going to contribute to further heartbreak for either of us.

Silence fell. I touched my fingertips to the scar on his forehead, washed silver in the darkness. One hand wrapped around my waist while he brushed his thumb across my cheek and jaw. Down my throat. Traced the curve along the base of my neck. The desires fear had suppressed now found their way to the surface; his eyes gleamed charcoal in the moonlight spilling through the window, no longer hindered but certain.

Yet there was one certainty neither of us could guarantee. Not in the midst of war.

"I can't say what the future will hold," I whispered in response to his searching gaze, pressing my hand to his cheek. "If it were in my power, I would promise you a thousand tomorrows."

"We can only promise today." Daniil turned his head to kiss the inside of my palm. A little shiver traveled down my spine.

"Today," I agreed softly. "And every single today until we reach tomorrow."

His hand curved along the back of my neck while the other found my chin, tilting my head upward. I kissed him with every longing of my heart. Everything I had held inside these past months, each hope and desire, now infused and drawing us in to one another. I wrapped my arms around his neck, tangled my fingers through his thick hair, succumbed to his lips, his tongue, his fingertips.

This, that I had honed and crafted for so long, balancing every dose, trying to be patient, fighting to work through everything that nearly destroyed its delicate balance. This, my finest work—no, *our* finest work. This, that we had forged together.

As every breath matched his and every kiss deepened, I forgot everything but him. His fingers ensnared in my hair, the taste of smoke and salt on his lips, the beard against my skin when I caressed his cheek, the beat of his heart in time with mine. All of it, united and unfaltering. In a life laced with poison, he was my antidote.

My time to forget would be all too short; morning would carry it away like the sun washing across the sky until no evidence of darkness remained. For now, I was present, fully and completely, with the way my whole body tingled, wanting—*needing*—him. My soul ached for his. It was an ache far too strong to satiate; the more we came to know one another, the more the yearning both eased and intensified. Perhaps it would never be satisfied, but I permitted it to expand and constrict, to rise and fall, to find fulfillment and yet seek more, always more. I focused on today and everything I dared to believe it might bring.

Today was all that was promised, but I hoped for today and thousands of tomorrows.

PART 3

There is no sphere of our life where the
Cheka does not have its eagle eye.

—G. MOROZ IN *IZVESTIA*, 6 NOVEMBER 1918

Svetlana

~—~

August–September 1918

Chapter 42

Moscow, 30 August 1918

I paced the length of the bedroom next to Kazimir's, my cell for more than a month since he had accused me of treachery, taken my pistol, and forbidden me from working with the party. My only company had been Vera and Fanya, who tried to visit me once a day but did not always manage it. As for what Kazimir intended to do with me, he had not said, and Vera insisted he had not confided in her. Life imprisonment, perhaps, though many were clamoring for my execution. If the party pressured him enough, I was certain he would do it.

Whatever Kazimir's plans for me, they no longer mattered. He had kept me alive these last weeks, so I would be gone before he had a chance to carry out further punishment. The day of Lenin's scheduled speech in Moscow had arrived. The day Vera and Fanya—despite their feelings about the matter—had promised to help me target him, to stop the increase of Bolshevik power, to encourage Orlova to come for me at last. Then I would go to Kiev. To Tatiana.

A little shiver went through me as I paced. Fanya watched; she had given up trying to make me sit down.

When the door opened, I hurried to meet Vera. "Did you get it?"

She presented my Browning. This pistol, my steadfast companion, its loyalty unwavering. Two tasks left for us to fulfill. Blinking past sudden tears smarting against my eyes, I tucked the gun into my waistband.

"I bribed a boy to deliver a message to Kazimir as if from another SR contingent, asking for a meeting to discuss the Bolsheviks," Vera said. "He's leaving now. I'll make sure the route to the back exit is clear, but the hotel is quiet today, so we shouldn't have trouble. Be ready when I return."

When she was gone, I field-stripped my pistol, giving it a thorough cleaning and inspection, then filled my pockets with the extra cartridges and magazines Vera had brought. Fanya did the same. Though I had not asked her to join me, she had insisted.

We had spent this entire revolution side by side. It was only fitting we finish it that way.

Once ready, we sat on the bed. The feeling in my stomach wasn't the usual knot of tension. It was a rush—warm, almost giddy. I closed my eyes, savoring it.

How often did Tatiana wonder what had happened to her parents, or what had put her in Saint Anne's Foundling Hospital? Soon she would know the truth. When we were settled somewhere entirely our own, I would teach her how to load a pistol and aim at her target; tell her how, with the help of a dear uncle who had given his life for the cause, Mama had defied her class, joined the revolution, and saved it from the brink of collapse. My life had been oppression and bloodshed; together with my daughter, ours would be freedom and hope.

I looked to Fanya beside me. The day of the bomb plot, we had sat on our bed in our dingy apartment in Kiev, each loath to break the quiet. I had given birth days prior and was still in so much pain, so fragile, the emptiness taking up all the space inside me even as I kept it enclosed, sealed away until the work was done.

"Did you build the bomb?" I asked, giving Fanya a teasing nudge.

She laughed. "After today, if I have to spend another decade in a katorga with you, there will be hell to pay, Svetlana Vasilyevna."

* * *

WHEN WE REACHED the Serpukhovsky District in south Moscow, the sun was bright, its heat relentless. The Mikhelson Armaments Factory stretched down the street, four stories of weathered bricks consuming most of Partiynyy Pereulok. The surrounding buildings were weak and tired, pummeled by missiles from the revolution.

Fanya, Vera, and I sat on a bench in the small square across from the factory. Streetlamps lined the quiet little park, while a group of sparrows perched in a young oak and hopped through a patch of grass. None of the surrounding trees or shrubs were large enough to obscure my line of fire once I assumed the position I had in mind. Across the square, on Pavlovskaya Street, a dilapidated building stood tall, with boarded windows and crumbling bricks—perhaps a hotel at some point, close enough for me to see and hear during the speech. The perfect location.

I tilted my head toward the decrepit establishment. "There."

Vera pulled her gaze from the sparrows that had migrated to the sidewalk, then nodded. "I'll go back to stall Kazimir in case he returns. Get a message to me when this job is done, and after you've faced Orlova, assuming you succeed."

It was the only part of our plan that left an ache in my

chest—the uncertainty of what awaited Vera at the hotel once my absence was detected. "Are you sure you want to go back?"

She nodded again, drawing a resolute breath. "He'll listen to me."

True enough; he would believe her if she feigned ignorance of my scheme, and I would not allow Vera to acknowledge her awareness and give up her place with the cause for my sake. When I spoke, I hardly trusted my voice. "I appreciate everything you've done." Cries echoed in my head, the newborn shrieks fading as every step carried me farther from Saint Anne's Foundling Hospital. Now every step carried me closer.

Vera's hazel eyes gleamed as she looked to me. "We will meet again," she said softly, as if saying so aloud would guarantee our lives beyond the revolution.

Then she rose, turned, and strolled across the square to Pavlovskaya Street, scattering the sparrows as she went.

Fanya let out a breath, softening the deep lines across her brow. "I'll be with the crowd."

"You don't want to wait with me?"

"And miss a front-row seat to the best show in Moscow?" Though her manner was light, the unspoken message was clear. We always stayed together during missions.

"Your eyes?"

She stared at the factory while a slight wind carried her murmur to me. "It gets worse each day. I'm nearly blind."

It was no use suggesting she wait for me at Hotel Petrov or anywhere else. When Kazimir discovered my absence, neither of us would be safe, and we needed to stay together. After this, we planned to meet outside an old bookstore a few blocks away, then find somewhere to stay until I was finished with Orlova, then go to Kiev.

Another breeze swept over us, cooling the warm droplets on my skin, stoking the steady burn inside me as it waited to be unleashed. The usual knot settled in my stomach, so I took a breath.

"If I'm caught—"

"I'll go straight to Kiev."

My rehearsed speech fled from my mind, replaced by the final touch of tranquility I had been missing. Still, I had to be certain.

"I realize I have no right to ask this of you. And that I've effectively banished both of us from our contingent."

"The revolution was over for me the moment I blew up the café. You helped me remain a part of it anyway." She fell silent before holding my gaze. "Finish this if you feel you must, Sveta. No matter what happens, Tatiana won't be left alone. I promise."

A swell rose into my throat, so I swallowed hard; I clasped her hand, letting the gesture communicate what my words didn't. One simple statement was all I managed.

"You are a dear friend, Fanya."

Her eyes shone, but a different light joined, the same one reflected in her gaze before we set off the bomb in Kiev. Our actions were grave, necessary, yet nothing would be the same after this.

With a newfound weight in my chest, I made my way to the abandoned building.

I circled the exterior and found a broken window in the back. It was as if the place wanted me inside. After sweeping a few stray shards of glass away, I climbed through, while a rat scuttled into the shadows, chittering in annoyance. Dusty, stale air settled, thick with decay and rot, and I coughed to relieve my lungs. The building creaked. Perhaps warning me away, perhaps inviting me farther in.

Around me I found a broken coffee table and a decrepit armchair, an old clock with its hands frozen in time, and a front desk. A lobby, if this had once been a hotel as I'd surmised. I crossed the wooden floor and ascended the stairs, flight after flight, until I lost count and the steps ended with a single wooden door. I pushed it open.

The door squealed in agitation and sent a cloud of dust to assault me. Once again, I coughed, and waited for it to settle, then I stepped across the threshold.

The attic. Worn planks beneath my feet; tiny sets of tracks through the filth; cobwebs draped along every surface like strands of lace. Miscellaneous pieces of furniture—a broken headboard, a yellowed mattress, a stained rug, stacks of books, a young lady's portrait, a small desk with an old typewriter, a paperweight carved in the shape of an eagle. Across from the door was a single window, tall and narrow.

Each step sent up a fresh cloud of dust. When I reached the window, I used my sleeve to clean the dirt and smudges from the pane, but the view remained cloudy. Instead, I cracked it open—difficult, until it succumbed with a little shriek. Fresh air poured inside, so I drank it in.

Below, I had a clear view of the square, where Fanya remained, and Partiynyy Pereulok, where the front door to the factory stood about halfway down the block. Before the door, a small stage and podium had been set up for his speech, as though waiting to hail a hero.

I moved out of direct sight to wait. My Browning was loaded, as always, but I checked to make certain.

The first few bullets were Lenin's, the next for when she came for me. Those were reserved for Orlova.

* * *

THE HOURS PASSED. I stayed in position, hardly moving. The single thought of my mission consumed me, while every beat of my heart reminded me of my target.

At last, the crowd gathered below, each person difficult to distinguish from this height, but I had seen him countless times in newspapers and on propaganda posters. I would recognize him when he came. Maybe I would fire before he had the chance to address them.

No, better to wait. That would show him exactly what I thought of his speech.

As the crowd began to shift, a black car turned onto Parti-ynyy Pereulok. My finger drifted toward the trigger, while the heat inside me threatened to spill over; I quelled the urge. Now was not the time. I kept my eyes on the car as it stopped in the middle of the street.

The door opened, revealing a bald head and thick dark mustache. Again, the heat pulsing through me encouraged my finger closer to the trigger. I resisted. When he stepped onto the pavement, a roar rose from the crowd while he buttoned his dark three-piece suit jacket, adjusted his tie, and placed his flat cap onto his head. He lifted his hand in a wave before disappearing into the factory, passing Red Guards stationed by the door.

A breeze encouraged a few wisps of hair to fall into my eyes, so I pushed them back. I stayed to the side, hidden from those below, but pressed closer to the window.

Lenin didn't stay indoors long, too eager to deliver his speech to his horde of adoring subjects. He stepped up to the podium amid a steady ovation while the onlookers moved as one entity, surging closer. Poor Fanya, trapped among them. When the applause died, he spoke.

"We Bolsheviks are constantly being accused of forsaking the slogans of equality and fraternity."

Such whining. If he found the accusations offensive, he should have been open to a Constituent Assembly—a true chance for equality as opposed to single-party rule. I waited while he droned, but I had a mind to interrupt the speech multiple times. Each time, I stayed my hand.

"And our task today is to carry on our revolutionary work . . ."

How much longer would I have to endure this? Beads of sweat gathered along my brow, and I wiped them aside while his bellows floated through the window to assault my ears. At last, Lenin raised his voice in an exuberant cry, a clear finale to his proclamations, a call to arms.

"We have only one alternative: Victory or death!"

Finally, something we agreed upon.

The crowd cheered while I took aim.

Lenin moved through the crowd as it parted to make a path to his car. His driver opened the door and stepped back, waiting for him. I pulled back my slide. When it snapped, I released the fire inside me. The one that never missed its target.

Victory or death.

Three smooth, quick shots, and the world below erupted. Even from this height, I saw the places of impact—his coat, his chest, his neck. Blood as crimson as the Bolshevik flag poured from the wounds while he collapsed amid the scattering crowd's screams. Red Guards swarmed into the masses, seeming to believe the shots had come from the crowd. I waited, prepared to fire again if necessary, longing for the pronouncement of his death, when the door behind me screeched on its hinges.

Fanya must have decided to join me, to celebrate our victory together.

No, not Fanya. A man.

His frame took up the entirety of the narrow doorway as he stepped from the shadows, the smell of cigarette smoke joining the gun smoke around me. Shaggy black hair, thick beard, piercing eyes glowering at me as they never had before, the usual ember glow caught between his lips. Even if I hadn't been stunned into silence, he left me no time to speak or react.

Kazimir leveled his revolver at me and fired.

Chapter 43

Khimki Forest, 31 August 1918

When I woke, my entire body was stiff and sore, but the heaviest ache was concentrated upon the left side of my scalp.

Where his bullet had struck.

Was this death? As much pain and misery in the second life as in the first? My mother had always talked about eternal rewards; I supposed my reward was the everlasting discomfort of my death blow. If so, I accepted it along with the pain and misery accompanying it. All the agony in the world had no power to take away my accomplishment.

The thought sent a flicker of warmth over me. I opened my eyes, blinking and pushing through the fog inside my mind.

If this was hell, it was unimpressive. Not the flames of eternal damnation but a tiny, decrepit wooden structure and a pitched roof overhead. An izba, perhaps. The logs forming the cottage resembled spruce; on the far wall was a large white pech; across from it, a small bed. Shelves lined the walls; in the center of the room, chairs surrounded a square table, where an oil lamp rested, providing light in addition to that from a single window. Through the filthy pane, I glimpsed blurry outlines resembling a forest.

Ropes secured my wrists to a chair's armrests and my ankles to its legs.

I wasn't dead. What kind of incompetent fool failed to assassinate his target and chose to kidnap her instead?

The chair was constructed of a light wood—perhaps also spruce—but dark stains surrounded my arms, the seat, and the floor around me. Countless measures of blood had been spilled here. I tugged on the bonds; with a little work, they would loosen.

A whiff of rose and honey, evidence of a scented oil, blended with stale traces of blood, vomit, and piss, so pungent and cloying I fought a gag. I shifted, acutely aware of the emptiness against the small of my back. That bastard had taken my pistol again.

"Kazimir." A croak, but I continued, undeterred, until my voice regained strength. "Where are you? Get in here, Kazimir, I know you can hear me!"

As I shouted and thrashed against my bonds, the ropes cut into my skin with every movement. A few rope burns would not deter me. I would gnaw through the ropes if that was what it took, and by the time I was finished with Kazimir, he would be wishing I had assassinated him instead of Lenin.

When the door swung open, bringing a sudden burst of light, Kazimir said nothing.

"What the hell is this?" I asked through my teeth. "Is it so difficult to shoot me properly?"

A muscle in his jaw twitched. "How many times did I warn you not to sabotage the revolution?"

I opened my mouth to retort but stopped, caught on one word. *Sabotage.* Did he consider fighting the Bolsheviks sabotage?

Meeting my incredulous gaze, he answered the unspoken question. "The Bolsheviks take particular interest in the surviving family of those executed alongside Aleksandr Ilych Ulyanov, Comrade Lenin's brother, and learned my father was among the condemned. After the uprising, they helped me realize a successful revolution and avenging my father meant working with the Ulyanov family, as he had."

Each breath fell shallow, painful. At last, the abrupt shift in his leadership made sense, the way he promoted propaganda and organized meetings but had ceased taking aggressive action against the Bolsheviks. His allegiance had changed. All this time, he had accused me of being disloyal when he was the real traitor.

"Uncle Misha and your father had mutual friends. You always told me that those connections led you to the Socialist Revolutionary Party."

"And now the Bolshevik Party is the only remaining hope," he snapped, then he grabbed my shoulders. "If you wanted me and what was best for this revolution, you would not have fought either one." He tightened his grip as his voice softened into a sudden break. "I wanted success. I wanted *us*, Sveta."

My heart twisted as he turned away; I had wanted the same more than I had ever admitted, though not at the price of my ideals. Not even for him.

"Kazimir," I said softly, "there's something you—"

"I would have executed anyone else without a second thought. Not you." Harsh again as he paced, passing a hand through his hair and over his beard. "What more could I have done to secure your full loyalty?"

"You have been lenient, and I'm grateful." He had not mentioned Vera or Fanya, so surely that meant he was unaware of their involvement, and if he had known about my plot, he would have prevented it. Someone at the hotel must have uncovered it, someone who had not interfered but had told him after I'd broken out, claiming to have heard I'd gone to the speech; for fleeing imprisonment and defying orders, the baron's daughter would surely be executed. "Please listen—"

Kazimir caught my chin, looking at me with eyes that saw only the aristocracy, then jerked me into a firm kiss, tasting of ash and betrayal.

"You have proven you won't stop. Not even if I grant you mercy. So do not expect mercy or anything else from me ever again."

When I twisted aside, blinding pain coursed through my head. It had no time to pass before a cloth smothered my nose and mouth—damp, with a slightly sweet taste and oddly metallic odor. Though I screamed and hurled muffled curses, everything faded.

* * *

Khimki Forest, 5 September 1918

I lost count of how many days it continued; I spent them unconscious or left in horrific isolation. It was as though Kazimir hated being in the room with me. I knew nothing of his plans for me, nothing of my friends, only that my chance to find Orlova was gone.

The drug-induced haze lifted from my mind as I roused. Kazimir sat at the table with a cigarette, refusing to look at me.

I swallowed against my dry throat. Now that he was here, I had to make him listen.

The door swung open, accompanied by a new voice—clear, distinct, shrill with desperation. Unmistakable. "You were supposed to get there, Kazimir!" As he rose to meet her, she gripped his forearms, shrieking. "You were supposed to get there!" She looked to me as her voice fell to a tremble. "Before she fired."

No, it was not possible.

I stared into those familiar eyes, bright and hazel.

"Traffic was heavier due to the speech, but I went exactly where you told me to go—and what the hell were you thinking?" he retorted, though something beyond rage tainted his own voice—guilt, fear, perhaps both. "This is your fault, Vera, not mine. You lured me out of the hotel, let her go, and then sent me to stop her, all to prove a fucking point."

"Because when I told you she mentioned a desire to assassinate Lenin, you said we needed to leave her imprisoned while we worked harder to bring her into the party, so you had to see for yourself that she won't change. Now do you realize she was never going to stop?"

"You're both Bolsheviks?" I demanded, prompting them to look at me. Then in an unsteady whisper, "You, too, Vera?"

I wanted her to say no. It was too late for Kazimir; he had already confirmed the truth. And indeed, the truth had shattered us. I had always known it would, though this was a truth I had never anticipated. So much had been taken from me—years in a katorga, precious time with my daughter, the uncle who had cared for me, the man I loved. Now Vera had to assuage my concerns, to assure me we would endure. Ours was a friendship built from perceptions and revolution and mistrust. Fate would not be so cruel as to permit us to overcome so much only to destroy us.

But I knew not to put my faith in such impossible hopes. Fate was the pistol pointed always at my chest, firing one bullet, then another, until all that remained was an empty magazine and an unrecognizable corpse.

The silence was deafening, broken only by my sharp intake of breath when Vera nodded.

"My mother and Kazimir's were sisters," she said, moving a chair closer to me and sitting down. "After Bloody Sunday, the Bolshevik Party recruited survivors, so I responded to an advertisement. At first they just laughed—a little girl with no-where to go, offering to join a political party? But I wanted justice and retribution, as did they, so they took me in."

"When you lost your families, why didn't you and Kazimir try to locate one another?"

"By Bloody Sunday, my aunt and uncle were already dead, so I thought the Old Regime had killed my cousin, too, until a mission took me to Moscow. I learned he was alive with a contingent of Socialist Revolutionaries, and my superiors gave me permission to infiltrate to win his loyalty. Until then, he thought I'd been killed alongside my parents."

The bonds around my wrists and ankles felt tighter with every passing moment. "Why did you keep your familial tie from everyone?"

"So party members would not fear favoritism between us. I joined the contingent a couple years before you returned; then, after the uprising, I told Kazimir my loyalty was with the Bolsheviks, as his should be." She exchanged a glance with him. "We hoped to show you the same. It was the most direct path to vengeance."

It was all so outlandish, so impossible; betrayed by the two I had trusted, both Bolsheviks. I succumbed to an uncontrollable burst of laughter. "You thought Lenin was the best path to vengeance?" I leaned forward as far as my bonds allowed. "I shot that bastard three times. If given the opportunity, I would kill him again." Sitting up taller, I locked eyes with Vera. "Defend your dear comrade's honor. Make me a martyr."

Fanya was on her way to Kiev now, surely. She must have realized something had happened to me. My daughter would have an adoptive mother to love and care for her. Someday, Fanya would tell her about her birth mother, a woman who had given her life for her country and cause to give Tatiana the life she deserved.

Vera leaned closer. I waited to relish the click of her revolver.

Silence hovered between us until she spoke with painstaking clarity. "You misaimed."

It was as if she had struck me.

It was a lie, an effort to unnerve me so I wouldn't face death proudly. She accepted a collection of newspapers from Kazimir—*Delo naroda, Izvestia,* and the two Bolshevik papers, *Severnaia kommuna* and *Krasnaia gazeta*—then opened them to show me the concurring headlines.

An assassination attempt. *Attempt.* The man was not dead.

No, it wasn't true. I never missed. I never failed.

"Comrade Lenin is expected to make a full recovery," Kazimir said as if the headline hadn't burned itself into my mind.

Suddenly I was fighting to break free of the ropes again while shouts and curses tore from my throat. I lost all control, numb to everything except *you misaimed* and *a full recovery* as they filled every corner of my being, taunting me, torturing me.

A sudden, sharp pain struck my cheek, so hard it knocked out my breath while a loud smack sounded in my ears. I slumped back into my chair, wanting to curse her, unable to do more than stare. My friend had betrayed me, now held me captive; had she just struck me, too?

"When you insist on being irrational, you leave me no choice." Vera glanced at her palm before letting it fall, and I spat out a mouthful of blood. "I gave you every chance to change your ways, but you were too obsessed with me to see reason."

Her words were the missing piece, the final clarification.

Me.

My shallow, shuddering breaths disrupted the quiet, piercing as a gunshot. The gravity of the truth contained the fullness of my own incompetence, of how entangled I was in this web of deceit.

"Did I not tell you?" Vera prompted. "Most people know me by my surname."

The surname I had so diligently sought these past months; the surname that could not belong to my friend.

"Orlova. Vera Fyodorovna Orlova."

Chapter 44

Khimki Forest, 5 September 1918

Knowledge was the most dangerous weapon of all. I had loaded my enemy's gun and presented it to her, and there I sat—unarmed, awaiting the death blow. She had everything she needed to bury the bullet in my skull.

Vera knew everything. Kazimir, my daughter, my plans against Orlova. She had led me down an unending labyrinth of deception; now I was lost, never to emerge.

"Did you know it was her?" I asked Kazimir. His cousin was not simply a woman with the same surname, but *the* Orlova. "Did you know during our discussion about her after I returned from the katorga?"

He shook his head. Lying to me even now. He had made love to me, betrayed me, shot me, all while honesty remained impossible. Now we faced the decaying remnants of what we had been. We confronted one another with more honesty than ever before, and still he shied away from it. From me.

"You forbade me from targeting her." I wanted to claw the truth from his throat, to hear that he had known, had intended to let her have me all along because I was nothing to him beyond a tsarist whore. Not that I was a woman he'd chosen to love, then chosen to betray. "If you didn't know who Orlova was, why protect her?"

"I was serving the Socialist Revolutionary Party and chose to protect my contingent from the reprisal such an effort would have brought upon us. It was for the party's safety. And yours. Not hers." He toyed with the pack of cigarettes in his hands. "Vera joined the contingent under the name Volkova and told me she had been briefly married to a revolutionary named Volkov who had been killed. When Orlova's attacks started, I knew it had once been Vera's surname, of course, but I had no reason to believe my little cousin was the same woman. I didn't know Vera was Orlova until after the Bolshevik uprising."

I gripped the arms of my chair to suppress a scream of frustration.

He had indeed truly cared for me. He had betrayed me. And he had let Vera kill Socialist Revolutionaries whose views he had once shared, men and women who admired him, trusted him, believed in him. Perhaps he had helped her do it as he was helping her now. Even if he had fought for none of those he now opposed, a part of me clung to the belief that he would fight for me.

But a larger part of me knew he would not. His mouth pressed into a thin line; his dark eyes never meeting mine; the deep lines across his forehead; above all, his silence; each another bullet slicing into me.

"Uncle Misha," I managed at last, looking at Kazimir. "She killed him, and you're working for her? After all he did for you?"

Something crossed his face—guilt, perhaps regret. "I didn't know Vera was responsible until she told me she had never been married, and that she was a Bolshevik working under her real surname. I wish it hadn't been necessary."

Necessary. The ache in my head spread to my chest.

Vera circled the room slowly. "Not quite the Petrov family estate, is it?" she asked with obvious contempt. "This is where I grew up. Where my mother cooked, sewed, and foraged and my father hunted and traded." She trailed a finger across the table. "I have learned much over these last few years, but it has never been difficult to bring people here. Perhaps Misha brought me good fortune; he was easiest of all. All I said was I had information pertinent to the revolution and requiring utmost caution, and he followed me here."

My breaths sharpened, though I swallowed the fury threatening to spill over. Vera took her seat across from me.

"Kazimir deserved a leadership role, and I needed his help to eliminate the contingent after I won him to Bolshevism. Misha was an obstacle."

"So you killed him." I paused to banish a tremor. "You of all people should know what it's like to lose your family."

She visibly flinched before glowering. "Do people respond to anything but violence? I tried peacefully protesting once; did it do any good?" she asked bitterly. "Look at what these endless party disagreements have caused. Even after the revolution, if countless parties remain active in the government, it won't end. With one party in control, there's no cause for dissent, no need to suppress it with violence. That's all I want—for everyone to see reason and understand."

"Is that what you want? For me to see reason?" Blood rushed in my ears as I dug my fingernails into the bloodstained wood beneath my hands. "Was invading my family's home a reasonable way to win me over to your cause?"

"I told you, that was not meant to upset you." The hardened edge in her eyes softened as she placed a hand over mine—a grasp I tried to break, though my bonds prevented it. "Kazimir and I hoped that, if we could reason with you regarding the estate, then you would be open to discussion regarding political allegiances when we offered you a chance to work with us."

Nothing we had experienced together had been under honest circumstances—not Kiev, not Petrograd, not my family's estate, not our days at Hotel Petrov, not a single moment. All along, she had stayed hidden from me. I had wanted a friend and had found a liar. An assassin. A Bolshevik.

I leaned closer, holding her gaze. "Are we going to finish this? An evenly matched fight to the death? Or are you going to kill me while I'm as defenseless as those who sat here before me? Take me to the Cheka, perhaps? Whatever you choose, I expect you to look me in the eyes until I draw my final breath, you cowardly bitch."

Kazimir straightened in his seat, as though interested in this answer himself.

Vera was on her feet again, facing him with sudden fury. "Sveta is Comrade Lenin's attempted assassin now that you didn't stop her, but *I* volunteered to infiltrate the Meshchansky District contingent, and because my superior believes *I* failed to uncover the plot, this is all my fault."

Kazimir's jaw clenched, as if he knew exactly what those words meant. She was already pacing, addressing no one in particular.

"Hours of beatings and blame, but I accepted responsibility for failing to uncover the scheme, because if he had known the truth, he would have killed me. It still ended with a gun to my head—empty, though I was unaware until after he had pulled the trigger."

I shuddered, fury dissipating as my heart twisted. "Why not hand me over?"

"No need." Vera paused with an unsteady breath, as if pushing away the burst of rage. "The perpetrator was in custody moments after the shooting. If I hadn't already extracted her confession prior to my own interrogation, I'm certain the pistol against my head would have been loaded."

She had not extracted my confession. I had been here with Kazimir. Yet the look Vera directed at me was solemn, expectant, perhaps waiting for me to speak.

When understanding came over me, my breath caught as I looked to Kazimir. He did not look back.

"Where is Fanya?" My voice rose, bonds biting into my lacerated flesh. "Where is she?"

He set different editions of the SR and Bolshevik newspapers and various copies of *Izvestia* into my lap.

A gasping sob clawed my throat. She had been caught with her Browning and accused of shooting Lenin, and she had taken full responsibility, even after a few days of interrogation. She had been executed with a gunshot to the back of the head.

"Why didn't you stop this?" I shrieked. "She was innocent, nearly blind! You knew I had shot him, you had me moments later, and still you let her die."

And then words failed me. I was left with nothing but the aching knot in my chest, though I knew exactly what she had been thinking: *Let me take the blame for a change, Sveta. Go to Kiev. Be with Tatiana.* She had given her life for our cause, for everything we had endured together, for me and my daughter. Unaware I, too, had been caught.

Kazimir presented me with a final copy of *Izvestia*, then stepped outside. After the attempt on Lenin's life and Fanya's execution, Sovnarkom established a new decree. Its title was splashed across the headline: "On Red Terror."

"This decree grants sweeping power to the Cheka so we can suppress future dissent. The Socialist Revolutionaries at Hotel Petrov have already been executed. All due to your actions and Fanya admitting guilt." Vera gave my hand a little pat. "We owe a great debt to you both."

Red Terror. Everything I'd fought to prevent, I'd set into motion. And now Fanya and the members of my contingent were dead.

"You let me assassinate your party members in my efforts to find you," I said as Vera took her seat. "Why not face me outright?"

"Kazimir and I had agreed not to approach you about joining the party until it was safe to do so. When you told me about your assassinations, I thought I could discourage you; instead, you grew more persistent until you settled on Lenin." Her eyes darkened, as though frustrated with herself, then she drew a steadying breath. "Fortunately, you failed to kill him."

I recoiled as if the bullet had gone into my own chest.

I had no time to reply before Kazimir entered with another man—Sergei, who refused to meet my glare as he shuffled inside. Another traitor, it seemed.

When Vera nodded toward me, Sergei passed a hand over his beard and lifted his eyes to mine. "After my arrest," he explained, "Orlova came to me in my cell. That's when I discovered she was Vera. She offered me the chance to work for her in exchange for my life."

Filthy coward. No wonder he had suggested we stop fighting the Bolsheviks; his fear of execution had driven him into her service. Sergei swallowed hard and looked to the floor.

Vera stood and glanced from me to him, a look that made me press my back against my chair. "A local Cheka has been established in the Vitebsk Region. Through them, I've taken the liberty of seizing control of a farm outside Obol."

Seizing control likely meant *killing the farm's former inhabitants.*

. "From this day forward, you and Sergei will reside upon the property, tending the farm and living as husband and wife. A formality, nothing more," she added quickly. "No need to share his bed unless you wish it."

Banishment and a forced marriage? Pure insanity.

"No." I shook my head in vehement refusal. "*No*, I won't do it."

"We have no choice, Svetlana," Sergei mumbled, focusing intently on the bonds surrounding my ankles.

"No choice?" I repeated with an incredulous laugh. "I will die as a patriot before I live as a coward."

Though he winced, his mouth remained shut.

"Kill me and let me give my life for my country." I turned back to Vera as I struggled. "If you don't, I'll tell the Cheka I shot Lenin and—"

"And I will send them to Kiev."

Shock and rage debilitated me. Would my friend order the Cheka to kill my daughter, a little girl, because of her aristocratic blood? The room was thick with silence, aside from the strike of a match as Kazimir lit a cigarette. He sent Sergei outside.

My wrists and ankles bled from rubbing against the tight bonds, but I was numb to the pain. Numb to everything.

"Kazimir," I whispered. "Let me speak with him alone."

I had to tell him the truth, to make him see beyond parties and revolution to what I had wanted when all of this was over. Had I obeyed orders, I would have demonstrated my loyalty to his position, the party; by defying him, I had confirmed his and Vera's fears. I was volatile. Untrustworthy. Not one to concede to Bolshevism under any circumstances. The *us* he had envisioned had centered on my loyalty to him above all else.

I looked at him, but he focused on the opposite wall, ignoring my request for a private audience. Smoke curled around his cigarette.

"Shoot me." Perhaps a demand, perhaps a plea. I didn't know anymore.

"You are my dearest friend. I'm doing all I can to keep you alive and safe. And the time Sergei spent in Cheka custody will seem merciful compared to the time he will spend with me if he fails me."

"If you want to keep me alive and safe, then listen to me and let me do the same for you. No matter how much you've done for them, the Bolsheviks will kill you if they find out about this; you know that. Do not go back." Surely she recognized that I was not attempting to change her political loyalties, simply reminding her of the truth. "The Cheka can assign anyone to be Orlova; it does not need to be you."

Her eyes sharpened. "I have granted you mercy, and I can rescind it at any moment. And those loyal to me can be found in every local Cheka in every region, and they will not disobey my orders. Do not forget that." Only a momentary surge of anger, then Vera brushed a graying wisp from my forehead and continued with quiet resolve. "When you leave this place, you will tell no one who I am. You will not interfere with the revolution and will relinquish everything from your former life, erasing all connections to your political affiliations. Including your daughter."

Those words were a bullet to my racing heart. I surged against my bonds, as if pure wrath could break them.

Before I could protest, she shook her head. "I cannot permit you to impart your ideals on a little girl."

"Kazimir, listen to me!" I shouted even as the words broke. "She's—"

"He knows." Vera motioned for him to come closer. "About Kiev. Saint Anne's. Tatiana Kazimirovna."

The ropes cut more deeply into my skin with every passing moment. "Everything I have done has been for myself or for Tatiana," I said softly, though Kazimir did not meet my gaze. "Not the bourgeoisie. For our future."

He released a thin stream of smoke. "Why should I believe you when you've proven you can't be trusted?"

"Why is the aristocracy all you choose to see in me? Hold my birth against me, if you wish; if you hold it against Tatiana, keep me from her, harm her—" I swallowed hard, voice trembling with terror and fury. "I swear on your father's grave, I will kill you."

He had adopted that look—impassive, maddening, so far from me.

"I'm not asking to be with you. Not now, not ever again." My eyes smarted as I heard my newborn's cries fading in the distance, felt the cold gale stealing her lingering warmth from my flesh, pressed on as each arduous footstep took me away from her. "If you ever wanted me, cared for me, *loved* me, do not punish our daughter."

Kazimir finished his cigarette and met my gaze, his own raw, aflame with hatred.

"I have responsibilities to my family and party. Those do not include you or your child, dvoryanka."

Then he went outside and slammed the door.

It was so forceful I flinched before turning to my final, desperate hope. Despite the sorrow and pain glimmering in her gaze, Vera remained unflinching, leaving me no chance to protest. "I wish it had not come to this. But what you've done cannot be excused."

A choked sob forced its way from my chest. Small, despairing. Broken.

Twelve years' worth of separation now stretched indefinitely. I wept for myself, everything I had tried and failed to achieve for my country, everything I had wanted for my future, everything I had done so terribly wrong. Most of all, I wept for an innocent little girl left in Kiev, wondering.

My plans disintegrated. An empty casing with no bullet inside, worthless and useless.

Vera lifted my chin. Wiped a tear. Blinked back her own before speaking, firm and unyielding. "If you ever violate my terms, the girl will be held accountable. I will see to her death myself, and I will ensure you are present to listen to every scream." She tightened her grip. "Am I clear?" After I nodded, she released me.

"Let me write to Tatiana. Have Sergei approve the letters before I send them, if you wish, but please, Verochka . . ." I swallowed hard, though nothing released the strain on my voice. "Let me write to my daughter."

Vera reached into her skirt pocket, then lifted a glass vial containing a dropper and a deep crimson liquid. She held it within my view.

"Sveta, how can you write if you can't see?"

Mila

March 1943

Chapter 45

Moscow, 14 March 1943

Though the German attempt to conquer Moscow had failed during the first months of the invasion, I felt no safer from the Germans, the NKVD, or Orlova. Not during war.

In the middle of Sverdlov Square, a faded, rusted German airplane lay like a fallen corpse, unworthy of burial and left to rot, surrounded by rubble and debris. Some buildings crumbled or suffered from gaping wounds or had been reduced to charred remains; others had escaped destruction but stood in solidarity alongside their comrades. Gaunt forms sat on street corners or wandered past me, most bundled in rags, worn shoes, old coats, and thin shawls. My stomach tightened with every step. If this was what had happened to Moscow, what had happened to Leningrad?

I made my way down Gorky Street—formerly Tverskaya Street but renamed after a famous writer, himself a revolutionary. I halted to allow two men to pass in front of me, delivering sacks of buckwheat to a grocery store. The sight was a small comfort, knowing some stores remained in operation and people had access to food. As for my home, the siege still raged.

No time to dwell on Leningrad. I was a traitor now, a Soviet guilty of Commissioner Sokolov's murder. Every minute on the street left me exposed for the NKVD to find. Better to get to the hotel, my destination for the evening before Daniil joined me so we could flee together, then locate Fruza. According to my directions from Yuri, it wasn't far—near the Red Square. All I had to do was stay on my current route.

Pigeons scuttled underfoot while I adjusted my coat to better conceal the dress beneath, faded blue, boasting countless dirt and grass stains. Over the past few years, new clothes had been the last thing on my mind, even if I'd had the funds for them.

Mila Lvovna, no longer the young woman from Leningrad, just a local farm girl. Perhaps that was who I was now, after all.

When I reached the Red Square, the Kremlin was covered in wooden structures painted the same rusty brown as most ordinary rooftops. A clever plan to disguise it from enemy bombs. The Cathedral of Vasily the Blessed soared above the square, its vibrant domes filling the cloudless sky in bright whites, reds, blues, greens, and golds. This cathedral and its grandeur, this square, the Kremlin, the Moskva River—this was what I had missed about life in a city. This city had endured every struggle and hardship, wounded but never broken; someday, it would be whole and fully alive again. After the war, perhaps Daniil and I would return to explore, then I'd show him Leningrad—or whatever was left of the place I once called home.

A sudden flush rose to my cheeks. Why consider life after the war when we might not live to see it? The future resided in tomorrow; the present was today, and today was all we could promise one another. For this today, we were apart. If we were going to live to be together again, we had to live past Moscow. And then past my treachery. Still, I mulled over the idea a moment longer, its brightness vibrant as the cathedral domes.

The evening light faded, painting the sky in colors like those atop the cathedral. Daniil would board the last train tonight and arrive in Moscow in the morning. One night by myself.

But after last night, what a lonely night it would be.

His callused fingers and soft lips against my skin, coaxing the breath from my lungs and the dress from my shoulders; my hands shaking in time with my heart as I unfastened the buttons on his shirt, trailed my fingers through the dark hair on his chest. Fully revealed to one another, lamplight spilling across our bodies to mingle with moonlight and shadow, pools of liquid gold, silver, onyx. The way we fell onto the pallet, warmed by furs and blankets and the heat drawing us ever closer to one another, surrounded by the sweet smell of hay and the faint spiciness of his cigars. Each moment absorbed me fully until I knew only him, us—bodies intertwined, hearts beating as one.

A breeze swept over me, chilling as the cool air that had come between us when I had disentangled myself from the blankets—from him—this morning and dressed in cold, rumpled clothes, chasing the warmth from my skin. The heat of his lips against mine before we parted, one quick kiss—two, three—then I left all warmth behind, venturing alone into the dark, icy morning.

He'd ordered me to leave without him if he didn't come, but I had no reason to consider such thoughts. The NKVD wouldn't catch him; neither would the Fritzes. He would be here.

I felt for my amulet, then my pocket, where I had a pistol from Yuri and an assortment of poisons. My feet thudded against the pavement as I returned to Gorky Street and proceeded toward my refuge. On Sretenka Street, I stood before my destination—a simple brick structure, relatively unscathed from battle though scarred by time. It could have been an empty wooden barrel for all I cared, so long as it meant safety. I glanced at the hotel name on my paper, then at the faded black letters on the building, confirming it was the right place.

Hotel Petrov.

Once inside the small, quiet lobby, I cast a final glance over my shoulder, making sure no NKVD agents were following me, then crossed the black-and-white porcelain tiles to meet the woman seated behind the desk on my right. She was rather unimpressive—thin and slight, round eyes wrinkled around the edges, light hair streaked with white. Perhaps a bit younger than Babushka.

After examining my new false identification and a hotel reservation under the name, both prearranged by Yuri, the woman opened a book and picked up a fountain pen. She scanned her entries until she touched the pen to the proper one.

"Fifth floor, room number twenty. Follow me."

I had no time to oblige. A man's bellow sounded outside, his words unmistakable.

"Find her! Search everywhere."

My heart rose to my throat. I gripped the edges of the counter and glanced over my shoulder, glimpsing the dark street through the glass windows. Shadows moved outside, getting closer. As my breaths sharpened, I lifted my eyes toward the woman's in a silent plea.

One look at me, then she stood and beckoned me with a wave. "Quickly," she murmured.

I darted behind the desk. She pushed her chair back, giving me space to duck into the small alcove, then she resumed her position. And not a moment too soon, because the door burst open.

Hugging my knees against my chest, I made myself as small as possible and bit my lip to slow my breaths. I huddled beside her sturdily booted feet, close enough to study a few tiny cracks in the leather. When I looked up to glimpse her face, she kept her eyes forward, unassuming, unafraid, and waited.

Footsteps came closer; I bit my lip harder. After a moment, they stopped.

"This young woman is wanted by the NKVD, and I have received a report that she's been spotted in Moscow." A flutter of paper accompanied the authoritative voice, indicating the man had probably set a paper with my information upon the desk.

A report that I had been spotted. If what Daniil had learned was true, Orlova had every single NKVD agent on the lookout for me. The public had surely been alerted, too. Who had reported me? I had been so careful, hadn't spoken to anyone . . .

"Have you seen her? Mila Lvovna Rozovskaya." He went on to describe me, as if the old woman were too incompetent to read the document for herself.

I pressed my back to the desk. She knew exactly what I was hiding from now. She wouldn't protect a stranger from the NKVD. Not at risk to her own life.

But when he was finished, she shook her head. "I'm afraid I can't be of assistance."

My relief didn't last. A pair of large, leather-gloved hands reached over the desk, gripped her collar, and jerked her closer. She braced herself against the desk while I flinched.

"Trouble with your memory, Babushka?" he asked derisively. "Or are you simply hard of hearing? I said Rozovskaya is wanted by the NKVD."

He didn't vocalize a threat, but he didn't need to. Everyone

knew the NKVD well enough to know the torturous punishments they inflicted. I dug my fingernails into my palms.

After a moment of excruciating silence, she spoke, her voice
calm. "I assure you, if the girl comes, I will make sure she falls
into the proper hands."

A satisfactory response. It had to be.

When he released her, the woman smoothed her blouse,
maintaining her composure while her heart surely raced, if my
own was any indication. Another flutter announced the man
had snatched his paper from the desk. The footsteps retreated,
then ceased after the door closed.

If the NKVD knew I was here, I needed to get out of Moscow. But they didn't know I was at this hotel; since they had in-
quired once, they had no reason to return. They would search
the city, probably expecting me to run once I realized they had
located me. If I stayed, waited for Daniil, and left with him
tomorrow, it might outwit them.

The woman waited, perhaps ensuring the NKVD agent
wasn't coming back, before she motioned for me to follow her.
By the time I had crawled out and risen to my feet, she was
already leading the way.

When we stepped off the elevator onto the fifth floor, my
room was directly across from it. Inside, the space was clean
and simple, with a window framed by curtains, a sturdy
wooden bed frame, a small desk, and a beautiful Chelaberd
rug across the floor. After the woman shut my door, I went
to the window, making sure the curtains were closed, then
tucked the gun beneath my pillow. Just in case the NKVD paid
me another visit tonight.

No, they wouldn't, because they had already investigated.
As far as Orlova knew, I wasn't here. The gun was simply a

precaution; Yuri was keeping an eye on the situation from Obol, and tomorrow Daniil would arrive. Then we would be gone. One night alone in a safe space, that was all. I could manage a single night without letting my imagination run away with me.

When the woman returned, she brought a small cart laden with two trays of bread and soup. Right away, my eyes gravitated toward the bottles of wine and vodka.

"You look as if you need some," she said, following my gaze before pouring drinks. "You also look as if you need some company." As she brought the trays to the bed, a bit of the turbulence inside me settled. "To a successful evening." She lifted her glass in a toast, giving me a knowing glance.

A narrow escape; nevertheless a success. A tiny smile found my lips. I raised my glass in response, then we drank.

Steam rose from my bowl while a pleasant array of lemon, sausage, tomato, pickled cucumbers, cabbage, onions, and spices filled my nostrils. Not as plentiful as the *solyanka* I ate prior to wartime, and not as good as Babushka's, but both food and company were incredibly satisfying.

The woman refilled our drinks. "Are you traveling alone?"

"For tonight," I replied, examining the icy vodka in my glass. "I'll have company tomorrow."

I expected her to press me about the NKVD, but she didn't. It was the safest approach. The less she knew, the better for us both.

When I shifted and let out a shaky breath, she regarded me with such an odd look, as though she understood and yet was curious to uncover more about me. She was of the revolutionary generation; perhaps she, too, knew what it was like to hide from her enemies. Though brief, the look struck me. As if a single glance held the ability to strip away all my secrets. Undeniable power and purpose resided in those eyes—sharp, hazel.

Once we were finished, we deposited our trays onto the cart. With a full stomach and two glasses of vodka inside me, my mind was more at ease, ready for sleep. Ready to see Daniil tomorrow. A pleasant buzz tingled inside me, this one not from the meal or the alcohol.

Still, my imagination refused to be silent. I glanced at the woman. "Do you think the NKVD will return?"

She shook her head. "Not unless I send for them."

I let out a breath and stepped away, giving her space to rotate the cart, open the door, and push it into the hallway. As I waited for her to depart, I studied the Chelaberd rug with its geometric pattern resembling an eagle's wings and talons.

I was still admiring the rug when the door closed, followed by a little chuckle.

"Well, Mila, it's been delightfully fun to watch you squirm."

I looked up to find the woman had not left. She stood by the closed door, facing me.

"That little display with the NKVD in the lobby was even more effective than I anticipated. I couldn't have you feeling too comfortable, could I?" Her small, grim smile disappeared. "Not after what you've done."

In a singular, fluid motion, she produced a Nagant M1895 revolver from her waistband and leveled it directly at me.

The pleasant warmth that had overtaken me fled. I stared at her, unable to breathe. Had her exchange with the NKVD been a prearranged act, simply to frighten me? Who was she to possess the authority to orchestrate such a scheme?

She regarded me with the same intrigued look that had so

easily fooled me and prevented me from recognizing what lurked beneath the surface. The combination I now found inhabiting her bright gaze—intentionality mingled with complete mercilessness—revealed the truth even before she said it.

"Did I not tell you my name?" She adjusted her aim, focusing on my head. "Most people call me Orlova."

Poisoning Sokolov had been a mistake, all of this had been a huge, terrible mistake. Now was my time to tell her, but my voice betrayed me and fled. Even if I'd been close enough to fetch my gun from beneath the pillow, I remained on the Chelaberd rug as if its talons had come to life and gripped me in their clutches, holding me captive.

Another second of horrific silence, then Orlova fired.

Chapter 46

Khimki Forest, 15 March 1943

My head had throbbed when I'd knocked myself out in the garrison to fool the Fritzes; that pain was nothing compared to the one greeting me when I came to my senses this time. This one felt like I'd hit my head against the shelf a hundred times before finishing off my work with a knife to the skull.

When I tried to touch the source of the dull, aching sensation, my hand didn't move. Surely I hadn't consumed one of my poisons—again.

As I pried my eyes open, my vision was cloudy, arms refusing to budge. I needed whey to stop this before it got worse; fortunately, I kept some in the shed. But as I took in my surroundings, I realized I was not in the old shed.

I was—well, I didn't know where I was. A little log cottage, perhaps someone's old izba. The single open room held a pech, bed, table, chairs, and oil lamp. The sole window was so filthy I had to concentrate to make out the blurred outlines of trees. Cobwebs grew in every corner; layers of dust and dirt covered the table. A bottle sat on the counter with a small cloth beside it, and I squinted to make out the label.

Chloroform. Once a popular anesthetic. Only a few drops required, administered by inhalation; a different sickening sweetness filled my nostrils now, as though an attempt to mask the rank, foul stenches surrounding me.

Had I swallowed hallucinogenic mushrooms? Suddenly the space felt tight, crushing. I tried to rush to the door, but my body remained on a small wooden chair. Whatever I'd taken would get the best of me if I didn't purge, so I tried to shove my fingers down my throat. Nothing moved. My wrists and ankles were bound to the chair's armrests and legs.

When I gasped, testing the strength of my restraints with a quick pull, movement revealed an unusual stain on the light brown wood. Mottled, various shades of red, brown, even black, carrying down to the wooden floor—except only the planks beneath my feet displayed the odd variation of color.

Not a design choice. Bloodstains.

With another sharp cry, I strained against my bonds while the pain in my head intensified. Moscow, the NKVD, the bullet that had grazed my scalp.

The bullet she had fired.

"Calm yourself, dear girl. It's no use."

I stilled. Her footsteps sounded against the floor as she walked from behind me and repositioned her chair to face me. Her revolver was tucked into her waistband.

I succumbed to a shuddering breath. *Mila, you stupid girl.*

No wonder Orlova had remained inconspicuous for so long, considering the woman before me appeared nothing like a ruthless assassin. She crossed to the small table and picked up a pen and slip of paper. After jotting something down, she brought the message to me and unfurled it.

"What do you think? Legible?"

Two simple words in a graceful red script: *Orlova. NKVD.* The paper she would leave with my body, as with all her victims—shoved down my throat, waiting for someone to extract to identify the person responsible for my fate.

I found no strength to do more than stare.

After folding the note, she grabbed a pitcher, filled a tin cup with water, and permitted me to drink. Had she found my poisons? Laced the water with arsenic? Death by poison sounded better than death by her hands.

It was wishful thinking. Poison wasn't her weapon of choice.

The ensuing silence was my opportunity to beg for my life. No words came. I thought only of the murdered Fritz in Obol—eyes blood-red, skin torn and slashed. While she put away the cup, I lifted my hips toward my bound hands, trying to access the vials and capsules in my pockets. One suicide pill, that was all I needed.

No matter how I adjusted my position, I couldn't find the proper angle to reach my belongings. I fell back into my seat.

Daniil was probably at Hotel Petrov in Moscow by now, perhaps suspecting I'd left without him—or he was in NKVD custody, if Orlova had been expecting him like she had been expecting me. If he had visited my grandparents, he would have lied about where I'd gone. No one knew where I was, and they never would. Not until Orlova hauled my body back to Obol and tossed me in front of the garrison.

After putting the cup away, she inspected a small vial, about half full of a liquid that fell between crimson and deep purple. Whatever else made up the concoction, the color was one I recognized: belladonna. Toxic if ingested. If dropped into the eye, results included dilated pupils, blurry vision, and possible blindness.

This time, instead of the Fritz's mutilated corpse and blood-red eyes, I imagined my own.

After tucking the vial into her pocket, Orlova crossed the room toward me. Her fingers curled around a long, thin dagger that glinted in the flickering lamplight.

"It was an accident." I pressed my back into the chair and watched her come nearer, nearer. "If I'd known your agent had infiltrated on your behalf, I wouldn't have poisoned him, but I didn't, I swear I didn't."

"Even if you'd been as ignorant as you claim, you remain responsible. Now," she said as she reached her seat and adjusted her grip on the blade, "tell me about your plot to kill Kazimir Grigoryevich Sokolov."

I nearly felt his tight grip on my wrist, heart pounding as I stared into his face, the set of his mouth beneath his thick beard, eyes like two ink stains seeping into me. I shook my head in earnest refusal. "Not a plot. I thought he was a collaborator, and—"

A scream swallowed my words when the dagger's stinging bite met my arm in a series of expert slices. Blood bubbled from the wounds and soaked into my thin sleeve.

Truth or lies made no difference. There was only one truth, harsh and undeniable: This was far from over. An ongoing dance of accusations and pleas, blows and screams, blades and blood. A brutal finale.

Orlova brought the dagger's sharp tip beneath my chin; though her touch was light, she used it to draw me closer. "Lie to me again, and I will leave you here until I find Tatiana."

My voice broke as I tightened my grip on my chair. "Mama? How do you—?"

She struck again and sprang to her feet, while I flinched, expecting the next blow. "Your grandmother told you I was going to send Kazimir to the garrison, didn't she? Ordered you to kill him when you saw him? You let Svetlana use you for her own retribution."

A laugh sprang from my throat, whether from fear, pain, confusion, or all three, I had no idea—though I shouldn't have laughed at the woman armed with a blade. "What? Babushka wasn't involved."

Orlova pressed the dagger into my forearm, eliciting my strangled shriek.

"I didn't know who that man was, and I swear it on my life and my mother's and my grandmother's!"

Whether she believed me or not, she removed the blade. I slumped back, unable to look at my wounds, unable to hold her piercing, thoughtful gaze as it searched me. When her hand neared my face, I recoiled; she brushed her thumb against my cheek and wiped a single escaped tear. A quiet statement followed.

"No need to protect her, Mila. Not after what she did to your mother." When I slowly lifted my head, heart rising into my throat, Orlova leaned closer. "No one told you? Your grandmother chose fighting in the revolution over her illegitimate child, left the baby outside a foundling hospital, and never came back."

Lies. Mama had admitted Dedushka was not her birth father, but she had grown up on the farm outside Obol with my grandparents.

Except Mama had never told me she had been raised in Obol. She had told me nothing about her parents or childhood. Just vague resentment toward her mother.

As for Babushka, she had never revealed anything about her daughter—perhaps because she didn't know her daughter at all. But was I supposed to believe my grandmother—

the woman who demanded I stay away from the Fritzes—had taken part in the revolution?

Though I shook my head to dispute all counts, no words came.

Why was I listening to a murderer who had kidnapped me and tied me to a chair? True, she had intimate knowledge of my family, but it was too distorted to make sense. And despite her assumptions, Babushka and I hadn't conspired to kill Sokolov, and killing him had been a terrible decision on my part. That much I knew.

Orlova glanced at the clock on the far wall. When she got up, I closed my eyes, combatting the sting of my injuries until something thick and coarse forced its way between my teeth. With a sharp breath, I struggled, but she had already knotted the rope behind my head.

"It's not for long. He should arrive any minute now."

He.

She had summoned a man.

As my mind conjured all the terrible reasons she might summon a man, she presented a black cloth. "This won't be for long, either." She folded it, placed it over my eyes, and tied it securely. "Just for a little more fun."

Fun. If I had learned anything about her definition of that word, it meant something horrible and twisted, something she knew that no one else did. Something that never appeared as it seemed.

I heard her take a seat with a satisfied little sigh. Moments later, the door swung open. A pair of boots sounded across the wooden floor, each step painfully slow compared to my racing heart.

"You are the man I sent for?" she asked. "Good." Her skirt

rustled, indicating she had gotten up, then her footsteps drew closer to me.

I yelped around the gag when something closed around the nape of my neck—her hand, I realized once my breaths slowed.

"This is the young woman who assassinated Commissioner Sokolov."

Another foreign object found my cheek, cold and thin and solid. Sucking in a breath, I drew away, though not far enough. The dagger—I presumed it was the dagger—remained against my skin while I bit down hard upon the rope.

The dagger was vicious, but this blindfold was agonizing. Darkness surrounded me, unhurried yet intentional, consuming me with every passing moment.

"I've had little success getting proper answers from her." The blade's sharp edge moved beneath my chin, pressed harder into my flesh, drew a whimper through my clenched teeth. The grip on my neck tightened. "Make her talk."

Orlova removed the blade and released me. Neither eased the stiffness in my shoulders.

Her steps trailed away, then disappeared, as the door closed behind her. The man's approaching footsteps joined my shuddering breaths.

When I felt his hand on my head, I pulled away, protesting as much as the gag permitted—though, to my marginal relief, he removed the blindfold. Even as I writhed, I blinked, taking in the blurry colors of the NKVD uniform, Orlova's bloodstained dagger she must have placed in his hands, and as my vision cleared, his face.

Daniil's face.

"It's me," he was whispering urgently as he removed his cap and knelt to my eye level. "It's me, Mila. You're safe."

He placed the blade on the floor, showed me his empty hands, didn't touch me, perhaps for fear of startling me further. As my breaths slowed, I stared at him.

"Orlova contacted Yuri with a request for one of his men. She wanted someone stationed in Obol so he could . . ." Daniil faltered. "Take you back with him when she was finished with you. Yuri gave me this uniform and directions to the location she provided." He paused, searching my gaze. "I should have stayed with you from the start."

Slowly, he picked up the dagger, glancing at me to gauge my reaction. When I made no objection, he carefully cut one wrist free.

"Take off the gag," he said, turning to my next wrist. "We'll be gone before she comes back. I didn't have time to contact your grandparents, but I asked Yuri to get in touch with them."

I didn't move as life returned to my stiff muscles and joints. Daniil was here; Yuri had sent him; Orlova had requested another man, had silenced me, impaired my vision.

Just for a little more fun.

As Daniil freed my second ankle, I ripped off the gag and caught his shoulders.

"Yuri is loyal to her, only her. He sent me right to her—he must have told her where I'd decided to run, because she was waiting for me, and he did the same with you. She must know you helped me."

Daniil opened his mouth, but I tightened my grasp.

"It's a trap. Please, Danya, please go before—"

He held my face between his hands, halting my pleas. I clung to him, words fading into hiccupping breaths while his eyes gleamed golden in the light. He brushed a few sudden tears from my cheeks.

"I don't care if she has the entire NKVD waiting for me. I spent so long keeping myself from you. Not anymore."

When he kissed me, fiercely and desperately, I lost myself in him, in the way today tasted of hope and devastation, comfort and fear; of a tomorrow that was never, ever guaranteed.

Daniil kept his pistol on the closed door while I crossed to the window, but the moment I pushed it open, a bullet struck the side of the house in warning. I slammed it shut; this was a game, more of her fun. She had left me alone with the man I loved, had let me believe we had a chance of escaping while all along she had been guarding the exits, awaiting her opportunity.

The door swung open. A gunshot rang in my ears, followed by Daniil's sharp cry.

My own cry joined his, and I rushed to his side as he clutched his bleeding bicep. He fired once before Orlova dodged the missile and turned her gun toward me.

"My next shot will go into the girl's skull."

Daniil had already stepped in front of me; he held up his pistol in surrender, grimacing since it was the same arm the bullet had struck. In response to her expectant gaze, he placed the gun on the floor and kicked it closer to her. While she tucked it into her waistband and picked up her dagger, blood seeped through his fingers as he applied pressure to his injury. I covered his hand with mine, glaring at her.

"You had no reason to bring him here. He did nothing wrong."

"Did nothing wrong in helping a wanted criminal evade arrest? You mean in the same way you did nothing wrong by killing Kazimir, supposedly because you *misunderstood*? Both remain unforgivable acts of treachery and classify you as enemies of the people."

"I thought I was protecting the resistance!" I shouted, on the verge of furious tears. "But you're right; I did kill a Soviet, so I'll accept the consequences. If that means you want my treachery to be intentional, fine. I'll admit I conspired against you and the NKVD and assassinated Sokolov to sabotage your infiltration, but only if you leave Daniil and my family alone."

When he opened his mouth, Orlova shifted her aim to him, though her eyes remained on me. "Sit down."

Swallowing past my dry throat, resisting the urge to reach for my poisons, I crossed the few meters toward the blood-stained chair and cut ropes. Once seated, I expected her to bind me again; instead, she turned the gun back to me and looked to Daniil. His arm bled profusely, face pale, gaze darting from me to the pistol aimed at my head.

The dagger lay on the table beside her where she had placed it. A perfect distraction. If I lunged for it, her attention would turn to me, giving him time to overpower her.

Another crack of a gunshot, another agonized cry. Daniil dropped to his knees, blood pouring from his thigh. I sprang to my feet, but she had already stashed the pistol in her waistband and traded it for the dagger.

Maybe I screamed for her to stop. Maybe I screamed his name. Or maybe I just screamed and darted forward while Orlova caught Daniil's hair, forced his head back, and drew her dagger across his throat.

As he gasped and choked, I fell to the floor beside him, scarlet blood covering us, unaware how fiercely I was sobbing until his shaky hand found my cheek. And his eyes, those beautiful, rich brown eyes rimmed by such full lashes, glistened as his breaths grew shallower and his mouth formed the phrase his voice was unable to summon. A phrase I had imagined passing over his lips someday, between kisses, while the spiciness of his favorite cigar filled my lungs and his beard sent tingles across my skin.

I clutched the hand on my cheek, pressed my lips to his palm, then held it against my pounding heart, echoing the phrase with every beat. The tears left no room to speak, but I nodded and managed a whisper.

"Very much."

Daniil blinked slowly, while a single tear slipped across the bridge of his nose. A choked breath escaped, and the hand clinging to mine relaxed its hold.

As the sobs ached to my core, a familiar grasp found my hair, igniting the pain of my gunshot wound. Still, I held his hand to my chest, waiting for the dagger to slice my neck; instead, a cloth covered my face.

I clawed and scratched, digging my nails into the unyielding grip smothering me until everything darkened. As the world slipped from my reach, all that remained was his hand beneath mine, pressed forever to my beating heart.

Chapter 47

Khimki Forest, 15 March 1943

When I woke, I was tied to the chair again. Everything ached—my head, throat, chest, stomach, my bound limbs. My eyes were swollen, face tight; then I saw Daniil slouched against the wall beneath the window where we might have escaped. Clothes soaked in blood, the slash across his neck.

A gasping cry sprang from my throat. I turned away. Vermillion stains covered my own clothing and skin. His blood and mine, indistinguishable, united.

"Quick and merciful. Far better than the death my comrades would have granted."

I hadn't noticed Orlova sitting in her chair, watching me. She nodded toward Daniil.

"Justice requires a high price, doesn't it?" She placed a bloodsplattered hand over mine; I didn't struggle, but I pictured that same long, deep slash across her neck instead of his. "It's a necessary lesson to learn. One your grandmother must learn as well."

This again. Babushka supposedly using me in a plot against Sokolov, that she had abandoned my mother in favor of the revolution. It made just as little sense now as it had when Orlova had started spouting her claims. The only difference was I had no strength left to dispute her.

She was convinced she was right. She had killed Daniil. She had poisoned me with a toxin far more potent than any I had ever utilized; for this one, there was no antidote.

When she caught my face in a strong hold, I gripped the arms of my chair. As she tilted my head back, Orlova lifted her glass vial with the belladonna mixture.

"Not this time," she said, more to herself than me. She set the vial down and picked up her dagger. "This time, Svetlana needs something to keep."

Her slender fingers curved as she tightened her grip, forcing my chin higher until I gazed directly at her. Directly at the tip of the blade hovering centimeters from my eye.

It was like when I found the proper balance of chemicals and everything combined into a single, deadly force.

I spat in her face and was rewarded by her furious cry; when her grip loosened, I twisted my head and broke her hold. At once, I bent over my right wrist, where the hag must have gotten careless, because the rope felt slightly loose. I caught it in my teeth, tugging and chewing while attempting to work my hand free; my efforts lasted mere seconds before a sharp pain against my shoulder opened a wound. When I gasped, Orlova caught my hair and wrenched me upright.

"Dear, treacherous girl. The fault is not entirely yours, I know. She knew what she needed to do to protect you and your mother."

She leveled the dagger before me once more—the last thing I would ever see, her cryptic words the last I would ever hear. Then I gave my right arm a swift jerk, a final attempt to pull free, and my hand slipped from the rope.

I caught her wrist and pushed against it while she resisted, but she was strong, so strong that she started to overpower me. Her long fingers brought the stained blade nearer; my screams pierced the air and mingled with her sudden, bright peal of laughter.

When she released me, my chest heaved in a sobbing breath. "You are just as relentless as your grandmother," she said, her eyes dancing with sudden eagerness. "Very well."

With deadly ease, the hilt of her blade collided with my jaw—quick, unexpected, unbearable agony. Her hands found my wrist, then my ankles; each time something strained against my lacerated skin, then released. I had to resist, to break free before she fulfilled her intentions, but I choked on blood, coughing and spitting. At last I looked from both freed wrists to Orlova, who dipped her head toward the door.

"It's not locked."

The air tasted as metallic as the blood in my mouth. She wouldn't let me go. Or would she?

"Remember, Mila, I have been doing this for many years. And if you make it through that door, into the forest where I spent my childhood, I will have no trouble finding you."

No, of course this wasn't mercy; she was simply a madwoman. Yet perhaps her deranged new game was the opportunity I needed. If she wanted fun, I would give her fun.

I still had my poisons.

While she toyed with her dagger, I rose; my injuries flared in protest. Gasping, I doubled over and clutched the chair, as if too weak to proceed; instead I slipped my free hand into my pocket, closed it around a vial, and pushed off the stopper as I lunged for her.

She wasn't just strong; she was quick. Before I could toss the poison into her eyes, she knocked my wrist aside. The vial flew from my hand, where it shattered against the floor. I had no time to reach for another, to wrestle the dagger from her grasp, to do anything before she caught my arm and slammed me face-first into the rough wooden wall. Upon the debilitating impact, the sharp edge of her blade pressed against my neck.

"I'm afraid you will have to do better than that."

While she extracted my vials and capsules from my pockets and tossed them aside, I held still, wincing every time another glass broke, announcing another ruined poison. My heart pounded against my chest, more painful with every beat. She had destroyed my poisons. She had destroyed the man I loved. And no matter how I fought, she would destroy me.

None of Orlova's victims had survived; why should I be the first?

She gripped my injured shoulder, and I gritted my teeth against the agony while she leaned closer. "Shall we keep on? Or shall I carve your eyes out?"

Though my breaths trembled, I infused every bit of terror and fury into a final jeer. "Let's see you try, you merciless old bitch."

She had already raised her blade.

Amid my struggles and screams, she gripped my hair, forcing my head back, then the door banged against the wall. Light flooded into the room, bringing a new voice charged with rage.

"Vera!"

When Orlova turned her head, I managed to knock the dagger from her grasp. It clattered to the floor while I looked toward the doorway, where Babushka stood with a Browning pistol leveled at Orlova's chest.

"Get your hands off my granddaughter."

Orlova—or Vera, since Babushka somehow knew her name— didn't obey.

"After all I did to protect you, Sveta. Even that was not enough."

Whatever she was implying was lost on me. Babushka didn't relax her set jaw; she merely adjusted her aim.

I was well accustomed to my grandmother's anger—often directed at me—but this was different. She was like arsenic, unyielding and merciless. Her petite frame seemed to swell and fill every corner of the space; the arm leveling her gun was sturdy and steady.

"Mila?"

"I . . . I'm all right, but she . . ." My voice shook, so I swallowed hard, eyes on the pistol centimeters from my head. "She has a gun."

Babushka didn't look surprised; she never looked surprised by anything. She tossed a newspaper to the floor, one I hadn't noticed her holding. Its headline publicized Sokolov's death. "Did you expect me to hear about this and not guess what you would do next?"

"My terms were always clear. Have you come to tell the truth about what you've done with her?"

"I already told you in my letter," Babushka retorted, her voice tight. "Tatiana is in Leningrad, the same place she's been since she left Kiev on her own accord. How could I have gotten her out of a siege?"

"Then explain why my men were unable to locate her. Or her body, if there's one to be recovered."

Mama, no longer in Leningrad? This was Fruza's doing, surely—except she was supposed to send word if she managed to help my parents. And I had received no word from her. If

Fruza wasn't responsible for my mother's disappearance, what had happened to her?

"Twenty-five years," Babushka said through her teeth, her voice level, dangerous. "For twenty-five years, I have never violated your terms. Why would I start now after spending so much time protecting my family from you?"

"Protecting them, or plotting revenge? Using this war to sneak your daughter out of Leningrad *was* clever, I will admit, and I'm impressed you managed it. And, when I inevitably found out, you expected me to send Kazimir against Mila, then used her to fulfill your vow to kill—"

"Wait!" I shouted. "Why do you exchange letters?" When my grandmother said nothing, I went on in a strained whisper. "You informed on me? To her?"

Though Babushka swallowed hard, her voice didn't falter. "Full, detailed reports. Those were the terms. I had to agree before I could write back to your mother and grant permission for you to stay with us."

All those letters my grandfather had sent and received. They hadn't been attempts to contact my mother or exchanges with neighboring farmers. Those letters—together with Yuri probably reporting on me, as well—had told Orlova everything about me and my work.

"If Mila does not leave here alive, Sergei will go to the NKVD," Babushka said, tightening her grip on the pistol. "They won't spare either of us when they learn you've been harboring Lenin's true attempted assassin. And that you were aware of my plot."

Each claim returned to my mind—the revolution, my grandmother, Mama. And now this, an attempt to kill the leader of the Bolshevik Party. It was impossible, had to be; but most impossible of all was how to distinguish the truth from the lies.

Orlova pulled me in front of her, pressing her pistol to my back so I faced Babushka. "Why should the NKVD hear the whole truth and not your own granddaughter?"

I had felt the weight of the unspoken truth behind every *Stop prying, Mila*. Charged yet fearful, shielding a reality my mother did not hold full knowledge of yet refused to face. I had spent so long desperate to face it; now I had to find the strength.

"Is it true, Babushka? Did you choose the revolution instead of my mother?"

She drew a breath before responding. "It was only supposed to be for a time."

"Time spent pursuing me when I wanted her cooperation instead," Orlova added.

First Lenin, now Orlova? How many had she targeted? I was the granddaughter of an assassin. Our family was blood and carnage, destruction and death, not the family we might have had, the one we might have become.

Babushka did not deny the accusation; she held her aim steady, suddenly appearing so old. "Tatiana believes I left her at the foundling hospital because I was an unfit parent, being unwed and unable to see."

"Unfit? You might have at least given her a believable excuse. You would have learned how to manage, I know you would have, and your eyesight didn't hinder your ability to carry out an assassination attempt!"

I waited for Babushka to rage back at me. To tell me I was stupid, that I knew nothing of her life or her choices, of how an assassination attempt was the work of one moment compared to the lifetime of parenting a child.

"Don't you see, stupid girl?" The words contained an unusual amount of warmth as she offered me a half smile. "I wasn't always blind."

It was like finding the proper balance of chemicals—all at once, everything fit together, and the poison was real. The man my grandmother had tried to assassinate was the one Orlova had spent her life defending.

"You must understand, Mila, your grandmother was dangerous. To the Bolshevik Party, to herself, and to her daughter. I should have known never to expect loyalty from an aristocrat." The words dripped with loathing, though my grandmother didn't react to them.

An aristocrat? I fought to envision Babushka as the woman Orlova had described. A noblewoman. She had spoken French to Reuter, the soldier who had attacked and regularly stolen from us. I had assumed she had learned by working for a noble family, listening to them; had *she* been noble?

"When she tried to sabotage the revolution, I granted her mercy. I let Sergei write letters to Tatiana for her; I have kept in touch with her all these years to ensure she didn't pose further danger to the Soviet Union, her daughter, or you; and I have kept all of this from the NKVD aside from a few trusted comrades who have helped me." Orlova swallowed hard, pushing down the strain in her voice. "It wasn't fair to leave you in Leningrad to fall victim to the fascists, so I permitted her to accept your mother's request to send you to Obol. All she had to do was adhere to our agreement."

Was I to trust the woman who planned to murder me? Or

the grandmother who had lied to me, hidden her past from me, and destroyed our family?

"Given your numerous breaches to our agreement, I must hold Mila responsible for your choices, Sveta."

Silence followed, heavy and charged, poison spreading through the bloodstream.

Babushka appeared surprisingly calm, though the flutter of her chest said otherwise.

"Put down your gun. You can't shoot me without hitting Mila."

"Can't?" Babushka laughed and lifted her chin. "You underestimate me, Vera—no, you overestimate yourself. Isn't that why you let me attempt to kill Lenin, because you were certain you could stop me?" The pistol was an extension of her, so easy, so natural. "Go on, then. Stop me."

The gun's pressure against my back intensified amid Orlova's shaky breath. "Kazimir needed to know . . . It wasn't supposed to happen . . ." Another faltering breath, then her voice was sharp, frenzied. "You simply cannot give me up, can you? First at the price of your daughter's life, and now your granddaughter's." Her fingers locked onto my hair like talons, sending a stabbing agony across my gunshot wound while the pistol barrel found my temple. "Didn't I promise to let you listen to their screams?"

Her hold tightened, drawing forth my cry even as I managed a gasp, a command, a plea. "Don't listen to her, Babushka."

These were old friends, old rivals, both poisoned by time, by their choices, far more than the blood coursing through their veins. Maybe my grandmother did not have the power to save me, nor I her. Maybe we were going to die here. But if we were going to die, we were certainly not going to surrender.

"I know you, Orlova." The name was a curse upon my grandmother's lips. "All these years, you have wanted to kill me as fiercely as I have wanted to kill you." The unmasked truth, naked and ugly and brutal. Then she continued, all hostility stripped away. "But I also know you, Verochka."

Orlova's reply was so uninhibited, full of such anger and pain. "I am not confessing to the NKVD, Sveta, and neither are you. Not after all I have done in this career, and not after everything I did to protect you. To trust you."

Sorrow passed over Babushka's face before her steely resolve returned. "Then you must decide, because you will have time for only one shot: me or Mila." She let her challenge spread across the room, neither her aim nor her voice faltering. "I may have missed Lenin's heart, but I will not miss yours."

With a furious shriek, Orlova shoved me aside so forcefully that I collided with the floor amid the crack of gunshots. My landing drove the air from my lungs, but I reached for Orlova's dagger, lying centimeters from me. Little use against a gun, but my only option.

As soon as I caught the blade, the air fell quiet.

On the floor, maybe a meter away, Orlova had one bullet through her chest, one through her neck, and one through her skull. Pools of blood surrounded her body, seeped over the old stains that darkened the floor. The streaks of red crept closer, eager to claim me as this place had claimed so many before me.

"Mila? Mila, answer me."

I turned away from the corpse, rose to my feet, and opened my mouth to tell her where I was, but she had already found me.

Babushka cradled my face, traced her thumbs across my

cheeks, over the bridge of my nose, across my lips and fore-head. Her breath quickened slightly with every cut, every bump, the bandage on my head from the gunshot wound, be-fore she moved to my shoulders and arms, finding the slashes from Orlova's dagger. Once finished, she kissed both my cheeks, sighed, and pulled me into her arms.

A sudden sob escaped as I nestled into her and let her hold me close.

"She's dead," I managed, because I needed to hear the words to make them real. "And Daniil . . ." Another sob bubbled up my throat. Babushka tightened her grasp.

Something damp seeped through my dress and onto my stomach, so I lifted my head to locate the source of the sensa-tion. A crimson stain.

I hadn't even felt the bullet. With a shaking hand, I sought the wound but found none even though fresh blood coated my fingers. Blood that wasn't mine.

Babushka pressed her hand against her waist, where deep burgundy soaked the ivory fabric of her dress. At my sharp in-take of breath, she frowned. "None of that." She turned toward the door, somehow leading the way.

I caught her the moment she swayed.

March 1943

Chapter 48

Vitebsk Region, 17 March 1943

Svetlana

The first time I had journeyed from Vera's hideaway in the Khimki Forest near Moscow to the Vitebsk Region in Byelorussia, Kazimir had tossed me into the backseat of Uncle Misha's old Mercedes with Sergei; he hadn't drugged me. I was already dazed. Weak. In such horrific pain. The white-hot agony of the liquid had felt as if it had gnawed away at my eyes until nothing remained but empty sockets.

I had assured Vera it wasn't necessary, implored her not to do it, begged as I had never begged for anything. Nothing changed her mind. The eyes that had set their sights on Lenin would never again locate a new target. Neither my state of awareness nor my pain alleviated the hallucinations brought on by the belladonna.

The things I saw. The things I heard.

Pain while my vision blurred, colors and shapes smearing. I blinked, tried to clear it, then a timid whisper broke through my shuddering breaths.

"Mama?"

"Tatiana?" A hazy outline, impossible to discern. The little girl I had seen in Kiev?

The little voice rose to a tiny, sobbing cry. "Where is my mama?"

"Tanya, darling, I'm here now. It's all right . . ."

"Mama!" This time a shriek of pure terror as the small figure shrank away from a new one, also indistinguishable. Only a flash of hazel eyes.

Tatiana was supposed to be safe. I had sworn to abide by Vera's terms, had conceded to every demand, all to protect my daughter. She could not do this. I shouted, I protested, I thrashed; then I was floating, falling, drifting through open air and sky and sea as a mellow voice murmured of safety, a bed, that all was well.

All was not well. All would never be well again.

I blinked. The figures were gone. The voice—Sergei's?—was gone. I lay in bed while warm fingertips caressed my bare skin, drew me into a muscular frame so familiar, so *needed*. Kazimir. He trailed kisses down my neck, between my breasts, along my stomach, every touch a whisper of his love for me, for our daughter, for us.

Then he held me down, his pistol against my forehead, eyes blazing with pain, fury, betrayal.

He pulled the trigger.

I screamed. I felt no pain, no blood, nothing, as everything blurred again. His outline remained, so close I nearly smelled him, nearly felt his lips against my forehead, gentle this time, nearly heard a few words, shuddering and soft.

"How did it come to this, Sveta?"

Then his voice and image faded, leaving me with confusion. Pain. Darkness. The little voice whispering, *Mama?*

Guilt was a darkness that would never lift.

* * *

My INJURY WAS not going to improve. I had seen enough gun-shot wounds in my lifetime to be certain of that.

The pain in my side flared as I lay in bed, gripping two letters—Vera's accusing me of trying to bring Tatiana to Obol, and a little scrap folded inside her note. As though whoever had tucked her letter into its envelope had added it without her knowledge. This note, when Sergei had read it to me, contained directions to the izba and a few simple lines.

You said every choice you made was for yourself or her; I trust that has not changed. Should you ever need to reach this location, I will not stand in your way, dvoryanka.

No signature. Those few, infuriating words from the man so consumed by his own pain and bloodlust, he had refused to trust me and rejected our daughter. A man so convinced of my treachery, he had left an innocent child alone in Kiev, at the mercy of a regime that would have killed her had they known aristocratic blood coursed through her veins. A man who had chosen our child twenty-five years too late.

I had not asked Sergei to burn this letter, as I had the others Kazimir had written to me throughout the years. Letters containing phrases like *forgive me* and *you must understand* and *I never wanted her to hurt you.* Letters that made me wonder if some of my hallucinations from the belladonna had not been hallucinations at all.

Still, apologies meant little after what we had done. Our sins had blackened us like bloodstains, their traces impossible to remove.

If Kazimir had lived long enough to see Vera carry out her

revenge, would he have helped me beyond giving me this note? Had he been ordered to kidnap Mila, or perhaps Tatiana once she had been located? Both? And, once Vera had them, would he have stood by even if I arrived and tried to stop her? Ever loyal to his cause, and his cause alone.

No, he was not so coldhearted. Even if he had followed his orders, surely he would have protected our daughter. Our granddaughter.

I crushed the note in my fist. Tatiana Kazimirovna, abandoned by one parent and spurned by the other. Twenty-five years Kazimir and I had spent apart, cursed by our own choices and betrayals yet no more deserving of the lives we might have found. No punishment was severe enough—not blindness and separation, not loneliness and death. These two shattered souls had atoned for nothing.

Sergei and I had followed Kazimir's directions to Mila. At my insistence, he had stood guard near the commandeered car, armed should more members of the NKVD arrive, ready to assist if necessary, while I confronted Vera alone.

On the return journey down the hidden dirt path leading from Vera's izba through the forest, then along winding roads to Obol, I'd been sprawled in the backseat again, this time with Mila pressing ripped fragments of her skirt against my injury and fussing at Sergei each time a bump jostled me. Sergei had carried me inside and placed me in bed, just as he had the first day we'd begun our lives together. Mila had insisted on the pech—prattling about folktales and spirits—but I chose my bed. Neither the pech nor household spirits held enough power to help me.

This was the same bed where I'd spent my first weeks here—at first out of necessity, too weak to do much else until my condition improved. Then, when Sergei had attempted to coax me from this room, I hadn't obliged.

How useless everything had seemed.

After tucking the letters beneath my pillow, I passed a hand across my eyes. Sometimes the feeling returned, the heaviness that had bound me to this bed. I felt it encroaching again, slinking closer, preparing to strike. Even a bullet held no power to chase this enemy away.

Why the feeling had returned now, I wasn't certain, but I didn't always know. The reasons varied. A thought of Tatiana, of how much she surely resented the mother who had forsaken her. A fight with Mila, often caused by everything I was bound to keep from her. Though so much had been restored, pieces remained unresolved. And I was running out of time to remedy them. The largest piece of all had always been my daughter, now trapped in Leningrad, dead, or somewhere entirely new. Perhaps I would never know.

Sighing, I closed my eyes, then I slipped my hand beneath the cotton bedcovers and found the bandage across my side.

The coarse, rough fabric had gone soft. A familiar stickiness met my fingers while a sharp, metallic scent rose to my nostrils. Bleeding again.

I peeled the blankets away, though it took some effort. Apparently Mila had convinced herself that I was certain to recover if she buried me beneath linens. After I removed the numerous layers, the tang of blood sharpened. Wetness seeped down, puddled along my waist, soaked into the bed, crept up my back.

I grabbed the edge of my solid oak nightstand, worn by my grasp over the decades. Gritting my teeth, I pulled myself into a sitting position and swung my legs over the bed. The injury extracted its revenge. With a gasping cry, I pressed my free hand against the stab of agony.

Damn you, Vera Fyodorovna.

Once I'd combatted a wave of lightheadedness, I lowered my bare feet to the wooden floorboards. Gripping the nightstand tighter, sliding my fingers against grooves and notches in the wood, I stood. One more jolt of pain. I hunched over, tightening my hold until my arm trembled with exertion, then the worst was over. Beads of sweat trickled down my neck and back; the hand clutching my side was damp and sticky.

Under normal circumstances, I could walk to the end of the nightstand, take four steps forward, turn left, and take about six more until I sensed the dip in the floor where the boards sagged in front of the tiny linen closet Sergei had built at my request. I shuffled forward until my fingers found the end of the flat wooden top. Extending my free hand, I took a step, then two, half my usual stride. Everything started to spin, faster and faster, though I pressed on until my hand slammed into the wall and my body followed.

Steps pattered down the hall, drawing my attention away from the sudden pain coursing up my wrist. Quick, purposeful—Mila's pace. She had a terrible habit of visiting me at the most inconvenient times—such as when I was not being the amenable patient she wanted me to be. Perhaps I could return to bed before she caught me ignoring her instructions again.

The doorknob jostled. When the hinges squealed, Mila's sharp breath followed.

"How many times do I have to tell you not to get out of bed?"

Her feet thumped against the floor, then I felt her hand in mine. Once relatively smooth and unblemished, now rough and callused from farmwork, cooking for the Wehrmacht soldiers, and foraging. Her free hand rested against the small of my back, where the damp fabric stuck to my skin. She had surely noticed but didn't pull away. With her guidance, I returned to bed.

I waited in silence while her footsteps pattered this way and that. She let out a little huff of exertion, then an unmistakable squeak of hinges reached my ears. She had opened the heavy wooden trunk at the foot of my bed. Fabrics shuffled against one another, and I didn't need eyesight to picture the disarray Mila was leaving in her wake.

"You'd better fold those."

"Do you want a clean nightgown or not?"

The lid shrieked and slammed, then more footsteps, then the creak of my linen closet and more flutters of fabric.

I pressed my palm more firmly to my side; the warmth oozed around my fingers. "Are you getting your bloody hands on my clean linens?"

"I'm using the hand that doesn't have blood on it." Her voice was muffled. She was probably diving deep into the cabinet, selecting pieces to replace the soiled ones. "And if you don't want blood on your bedding, don't get up and aggravate your wound."

"You and Sergei didn't listen to me and bandage it properly, so when it started bleeding again, I had to address it."

"Now it's our fault that you're disobedient?" The humorous lilt brought a small smile to my lips.

A gentle thump, indicating a sheet had descended to the floor, then the cabinet door swung shut. Mila left the room before returning moments later—a clinking bowl, a slosh, a telltale splash, a quiet curse.

"Just a little water. I'll clean it up," she added hastily. "Let me change your bandage first."

Sighing, I pressed my fingertips against my temple. "No need. You've done enough."

"Too late. You already complained about it, so I have to change it."

When I felt her hands on my knees, I expected the same chaotic frenzy to peel the nightgown above my waist; instead, her movements were cautious. Once she lifted my skirt, cool fingertips pressed against the hot skin of my abdomen.

She went about her work. Each time dried blood or torn skin refused to loosen its hold, Mila gingerly eased the bandage away while I clenched my fist and did my best not to wince. At last, cool air swept over my midsection, then a cold dampness settled against the injury. The accompanying sting was like a fuse meeting dynamite, destroying everything in its path. When I screamed and pressed my fist into the bed, Mila sucked in a breath, though she didn't lessen the pressure.

"Almost clean," she said apologetically.

My response was a growl in the back of my throat. Why did she and Sergei insist on such pointless treatments? The result was unchangeable. It made no difference whether the injury remained clean or not.

"There," she announced at last, as though she had done me a great service. "Now for the new bandage."

"Leave it," I replied through my teeth, but of course she didn't listen.

Mila would do as she pleased whether I protested or not. It was what she had done ever since coming to live with us.

I lost the energy to argue as she bandaged my injury, changed my clothes, and switched the linens. Once finished, she departed, promising to come back, and I listened to her bustling about in the front room. When she returned, a fragrance of lemon and mint met my nostrils.

Mila poured our tea and offered me some of the thin rye crackers she had made the other day; then the mattress creaked and sagged by my side, indicating she had taken a seat. I reached for her, finding what I sought at once before she moved from beneath my touch.

"I'm fine."

"Did I ask if you were fine? Come here."

Though she muttered under her breath, she obeyed. This time, it was my turn.

The marks along her arms, once slick with fresh blood, had taken on a rough protective layer. When I reached up, my fingers met the fine hairs along her scalp and traveled to the left side of her head. Her injury was in the same place as mine from so many years ago—such a skilled shot, grazing the scalp just enough. She had removed the bandage this morning. The scab stretched into her hairline, a few centimeters in length. Soon we would bear twin scars.

"Babushka?" A note of fragility crept into her tone, one that slipped out on occasion before she pushed it away. This time, she didn't fight it. "How did you know she had found me?"

Since we had returned to the farm, Mila had not spoken of that day. Neither had she asked of my experiences from all those years ago, beyond what she had learned during our confrontation and whatever Vera had shared prior to my arrival. The girl's boundless curiosity had fled, destroyed by a single bullet and thin blade.

Vera alone with Mila, demanding answers impossible for her to give, buried deep within the truth she had always sought but never received. My fingers itched, longing for a trigger; I took a breath to settle the urge.

How had I known? Because I felt Vera's presence everywhere. In every whisper on the wind, screech of a soaring eagle, creak of the floorboard, ache in my head. Because when the newspapers announced prominent NKVD Commissioner Kazimir Grigoryevich Sokolov was dead, I knew he had infiltrated the garrison. I suspected a certain resistance member had perceived him a traitor and taken justice upon herself, and I knew what conclusions Vera would draw. Because Mila had fled from a woman who reveled in pursuit and being pursued. Because I knew Vera Fyodorovna Orlova, and I knew her fun.

"Refill the teapot," I said at last.

"Why? We've only poured one cup each."

"Because we're going to be here for a long time. If I'm going to do most of the talking, I want tea."

The bed squeaked, the pitter-patter of feet faded. Secrets and lies had held this family in their clutches for decades, yet now their grasp had loosened. Now perhaps we might escape— unless we were bound forever. Perhaps the shackles of deception were so unassailable, not even the truth could break them.

With an unsteady sigh, I closed my eyes and examined my bandage while I waited for her to return. Though the wound was no longer bleeding, it would become its own living thing again in time—hot, spreading, pulsing. Fully alive, beating as fast as a certain careless girl's heart as she turned her back on the aristocracy and found her way to a hotel in Moscow.

* * *

By the time I finished my story, the wound was bleeding again. I said nothing to Mila.

Throughout my tale, she had said surprisingly little. And when I was finished, she slipped from the room.

I drank the last of my tea. Another headache had settled over me—a common occurrence following the bullet to my head—reminding me always of Fanya. How many hours I had spent in this room mourning her. Mourning everything I had cost us. My revolution; my only true friend, who had seen me from the start of my revolutionary work through life imprisonment and beyond; a woman who had deceived me and taken everything from me; the man I had never been able to resist, might have been able to love all my life, though all of it too distorted, too damaged, too late. Most of all, my daughter.

And yet, so often, I missed those days during the revolution. Sharing tea with Fanya. Fighting for my cause. Slipping from my bedroom, wandering down the dark hall to the room across from the elevator. Giving myself permission to forget everything but Kazimir, to be impetuous for one night.

Reality in those days had been false, warped into something impossible to recognize, so buried was I in deception. Why had I spent so much time over the past twenty-five years longing for it?

Today, though, I didn't long for it. Perhaps because an unusual calm had begun to make its presence known following my conversation with Mila. It hadn't overtaken me yet, but it had begun a tentative exploration, like my initial fumbling efforts to load a gun or Mila's indiscreet cuts in my belladonna plant for her studies of poison. Clumsy attempts perfected themselves, given time.

Boots thudded down the hall, drawing nearer in an unhurried stride. Sergei's.

"Mila said you asked for me."

Wood scraped across the floor as he fetched the small chair from the corner and dragged it beside the bed. The chair gave an indignant creak, announcing he had settled into it.

"Was she all right?" I asked softly.

"Yes, I think so. She went outside."

To the old shed, I imagined. The same place Sergei had hidden my Browning since Kazimir had returned it—likely without Vera's knowledge—after bringing us here. Sergei had assured me it was only hidden for my safety. It hadn't taken me long to find it. I slipped into that old shed so many times without him noticing, learning to navigate my pistol and my targets without my sight. I defended my daughter with my obedience, but if the time ever came to defend her with my old methods, I intended to be prepared.

Sergei's voice broke the stillness, perhaps prompted by my silence. "She was fine, Sveta. She looked relieved."

Faint traces of lemon and mint tea hovered in the air, soured by antiseptic and blood. Each breath drew a twinge of pain to my side. My long talk with Mila had left me little strength for more words, but I gathered my remaining energy.

"Seryozha." I shifted positions, then grimaced when my injury objected. "You have been trapped here with me long enough. With Vera gone . . . you don't have to stay."

He had every right to loathe me, to resent me, to wish me dead. To leave me. Yet every part of me longed to beg him not to go. A moment of silence, as excruciating as the wound in my side, then his gentle voice.

"It has been a long time since being here with you has felt like a punishment."

Of course I knew his feelings for me, and mine for him; still, a little relieved breath passed over my lips. More than two decades together. I, loathing him at first; he, terrified I would rebel and get us killed. When he learned of Tatiana, it eased his fears. He knew I wouldn't jeopardize her and swore he wouldn't, either. He even wrote to her for me, though I rarely received a response.

And he read the letter revealing I had a granddaughter named Mila who needed a place of refuge.

"You were willing to die that day, when Vera revealed what she had in store for us," Sergei said. "Whatever the cause required of you, you were proud to give it. I always thought I would be the same." The words ended with a bitter edge, tinged with regret and shame. "I wasn't willing to die. And I wasn't willing to fight for you, either."

I took a slow breath before responding. "If you hadn't kept us alive, Mila would still be in Leningrad, likely with the entire Gestapo chasing after her."

His faint chuckle, then a wistful silence fell over us.

The man doomed to be my warden had become my comrade. This had been his punishment, earning his life yet giving up his freedom, forever shackled to my sins. Perhaps cowardice had driven him into Vera's service, but he had willingly atoned for it each day—my friend, my caretaker, a man who fought for the protection of me and my family as he had once fought to preserve his own life. A man who respected me as he had in a small, frigid apartment in Petrograd. He loved me with the purest of sacrificial loves.

I wiped a single tear and broke the silence with an unsteady murmur.

"You'll care for her until the war is over?"

"And for many years after, if she permits me. Even when she's caring for a family of her own." I heard the smile behind his words.

When I reached toward the location of his voice, his large hand, hardened and strong, enveloped mine. These hands had worked alongside one another for decades and bore the scars to prove it. And though my eyes were unable to show me how time had treated Sergei, I imagined skin wrinkled from years dedicated to this farm, blond hair thinning and whitening, pale blue eyes clear and mild.

A familiar touch on my cheek, then a forehead pressed lightly against mine, always letting me know he was near. I tilted my head up, finding his lips. One kiss, gentle and comforting, then he released me.

"I need you to do something for me."

Each word became more difficult as the pain spread and my lungs constricted, so I paused, drawing strength from the peaceful feeling as it forged its cautious path inside me. So many of my wrongs were impossible to right; others, I now had the power to remedy. I owed Fanya, my daughter, the revolution, and myself the truth.

I spoke slowly, assuredly. "I need you . . . to contact . . . the NKVD."

Though it was all I managed, it was enough. Fanya had sacrificed her life for me; now was my chance to erase the blame that had been placed upon her name. Hers was an undeserved punishment, one that had tormented me these past decades. How cruel it was that I had finally been granted the ability to address it only to be robbed of the time. Still, I had managed to share the truth with Mila; Sergei would help me set the declaration of Fanya's innocence into motion; perhaps I had time to locate my daughter if she remained alive. To explain even if I never expected her to understand. Little by little, this cursed wound intensified its hold on me; soon enough, it would seize me completely.

Until then, my efforts were under way. For now, that sustained me. The unusual peace expanded, a bullet settling into its chamber. Waiting.

Chapter 49

Vitebsk Region, 19 March 1943

Mila

After almost two years of living with her, I hadn't known my grandmother at all. My grandmother, a former aristocrat, had taken an active part in the revolution. My grandmother had been a political prisoner. My grandmother had tried to kill Vladimir Lenin.

I had taken a brief trek through the forest, attempting to forage before giving up and returning to the shed. Shifting in my seat, I reached for my gloves; as I did so, my eyes found one of the long, thin scabs across my forearm.

And then I was bound, bleeding, Orlova's voice in my ear—clear, distinct, her dagger leveled before me.

This time, Svetlana needs something to keep.

I passed a hand over the eyes I'd almost lost, reassuring myself they were still there.

Perhaps I'd feel her eyes on me for the rest of my life. Or maybe just until I grew accustomed to the fact that she was dead and the NKVD wasn't actually hunting me. The papers had reported Sokolov's death, not that he had been assassinated—leading Babushka to believe Yuri's story of an NKVD manhunt had been Orlova's doing, encouraging me to flee. Part of her fun.

I was safe, but the urge to flee remained. To flee from the knowledge of everything she had done. Everything she had taken. Orlova had kept my mother from her family after Babushka's choices had separated them in the first place.

My mother—a loyal Soviet—was the daughter of an aristocrat who had then become a Socialist Revolutionary. Perhaps my grandmother's political views had differed from those that had triumphed, but she had joined the fight for equality, leaving everything behind. Even her daughter. For what she had done to our family, I should have resented her as much as Mama had all these years. And I did.

Yet Babushka had believed in her country and her cause so fully that she had dedicated herself entirely to both. And I knew that urge. My cause had seized control of me, a power impossible to combat, too mighty to overcome. The more it consumed me, the more I wanted to be consumed. If it had been wrong for my grandmother to permit her cause to do the same, then it was a fault we shared.

With a shaky breath, I pushed my tangled hair from my face and touched the scab on my head, located in the same place I'd found Babushka's faded scar after the Fritzes had struck her. Using a temporary head bandage, a large overcoat, a shawl, and a headscarf to disguise myself from any Fritzes still hunting for Nadya, I'd gone to Obol yesterday, then a second time this morning, and picked up everything I thought might be useful. Anything that did not require Katya to jeopardize her family, swearing her to secrecy regarding my return. As far as Fruza needed to know, I was still on the run. Now my collection of toxins and chemicals lay before me, and I had no idea where to begin.

In working for the resistance, I'd seen plenty of horrific

injuries. A bullet wound on my grandmother's body was far more difficult to bear. The gaping hole. The angry red flesh. The bloody bandages. And her face, sallower every passing day, eyes dull, voice weak.

The story she had shared made it impossible to focus. I pushed my notes away, left my materials scattered on the table, and stepped outside. Squinting in the bright morning light, I shielded my eyes and traversed the familiar path. A cool breeze swept across my skin while a few clucking chickens strutted ahead, then scurried out of the way of my quick strides. When I reached the door, I paused, drawing a breath. Facing what was on the other side required all my strength.

The main room was abandoned, indicating my grandparents were likely together in the bedroom. I had a direct line of sight down the hallway, where the door was open.

"Did you contact them?"

Though her voice was soft, it found my ears as I neared the threshold between the main room and the hall. I stopped. They would hear me if I came closer.

A creak of a bedspring, a little groan from Babushka, then her tight voice continued. "What did they say?"

I suspected this wasn't a conversation meant for me to overhear. All the more reason to listen.

"These things take time, Sveta. My report is being processed, then I'm sure Fanya's innocence will be declared."

Fanya. Babushka's friend, the woman arrested by the Cheka and killed for my grandmother's crime. I strained my ears to hear better.

"And they do intend to convict me?"

Dedushka's response came low and even. "I can't imagine

the NKVD will do anything else for Lenin's true attempted assassin."

My heart slammed against my chest; I had no time to process the information before my grandfather's boots sounded against the floor. I hurried to the table, tidied the remaining hard-boiled eggs and blini from breakfast, and began washing dishes. Dedushka passed through, saying something about being outside if I needed anything. I nodded, unable to speak around the weight in my throat, then the door closed behind him.

I dropped my dishrag and pressed my wet hands against the counter to stop them from shaking.

She had asked him to turn her in, and he had complied. After he had spent all these years fighting to keep her—all of us—safe.

Fury latched onto me, deadlier than any poison. I left the half-finished dishes submerged in soapy water. Outside, the sun struck me once again, but I narrowed my eyes against it and saw Dedushka emerging from the stable. My eyes never left him as I sprinted toward him, arms pumping, strides lengthening. By the time he noticed me and opened his mouth, I was already yelling.

"How could you?" My shrieks overtook us, and I didn't know if I wanted to hit him or fall at his feet, but I didn't have a chance to do either. He caught my shoulders while I struggled and shouted. "Can't you see she's been through enough?"

"Mila, stop." Dedushka's usual calm, far too calm. "She asked me to—"

"I don't care!" All at once, my voice caught, rage fading into desperation. I grabbed his forearms. "Please. Please don't let them arrest her."

My grandmother had spent her entire life sacrificing for her beliefs; perhaps it was selfish of me, trying to prevent her from doing so again. It was impossible to change who she was. She was a patriot who belonged to her country, a revolutionary who belonged to her cause; but most of all, she was Babushka, who belonged to me.

"Listen." Dedushka tightened his grip slightly. "I didn't contact the NKVD."

I blinked hard to control the torrent of tears threatening to spill over. "You didn't?"

He shook his head, relaxing his hold. "She asked me to do it so she can claim responsibility, but I didn't. The NKVD won't be merciful, and she's been through enough." A faraway look crept over his face. "Besides, Fanya never revealed accomplices, knowing Svetlana would have gladly come forward. I suspect she had a good reason to give her friend a chance at life beyond the revolution."

I poured all my gratitude into my embrace, breathing in the combination of grass and hay on his skin. "Why did you lie to her?"

"Don't tell her, or she'll put a bullet between my eyes." When he spoke again, the twinkle of mischievousness was gone. "If she thinks I've done her bidding and it brings her peace, so be it."

I wrapped my arms around his neck, rose to my tiptoes, and kissed both his cheeks.

* * *

I SPENT MOST of the morning and afternoon with Babushka. She had told me about her political activism; now was my chance to tell her about mine.

Once I'd finished, her face was as impossible to read as always. We had only one point remaining to address. The one I had avoided despite how it pressed upon me, inescapable and crushing.

"That man, Commissioner Sokolov." My mother's father, my grandmother's lover, my grandfather; now my treachery felt even more severe. "He gave you a note that helped you save my life, and I . . ." My voice broke. "I killed him."

Babushka was quiet for a moment. "You did. And he did send me a note as a precaution when he learned Tatiana was no longer in Leningrad."

"He knew who I was. In the garrison. He told me not to come back."

She remained quiet, pensive. "He did not wish to harm you," she murmured, sounding relieved. "As to whether he would have followed orders or helped us if the time had come, I hope he would have protected his daughter and granddaughter."

His threat had disguised a warning. Comforting, in an odd way, though not when I thought about the gun he had held to my chin or the mushrooms and arsenic I had given him.

"One honorable decision does not excuse a thousand selfish ones. Not for him. And not for me."

At her soft yet emphatic statement, I imagined my grandmother with the man I'd met. His physical features hadn't been lost on me, despite his age—maybe that was how it had started. An impulsive tryst fueled by passion. But the memory of his unyielding grip still sent a shiver through me.

"Will you help me write a letter tomorrow?" Babushka prompted. "For your mother, for when you return to Leningrad."

I found her hand and gave it a little squeeze. "Of course."

Neither of us acknowledged the fact that, according to Orlova, Mama was not in Leningrad. I might not see her again to
deliver this letter. I folded my hands into my lap and stared at
them, suddenly unable to bear the glimmer behind my grandmother's eyes—evidence of an old, lasting wound far more severe than the one across her midsection.

"And your young man, Daniil."

His name alone tightened an ache in my chest. I hadn't wept
for him since that day. After settling Babushka in the car, Dedushka and I had found a sheet, wrapped Daniil, and brought
him with us. I hadn't wept while shoveling the grave I insisted
on digging myself, or while placing him in it, or when sharing
the story with Katya. Perhaps I had mourned him with everything I had, and now nothing remained.

"You loved him."

Not a question. An affirmative statement, slightly above a
whisper, prompting tears to return. Reminding me I hadn't
finished mourning him at all. I took a slow breath, fighting to
keep them contained.

"Very much."

Babushka didn't press further, but she placed a hand on my
forearm.

Silence stretched over us, then I rifled through the bottles
on her nightstand until I found her painkillers. After pouring
a glass of water, I offered both to her. She didn't react.

"Take your medicine."

Babushka blinked slowly, as if distracted, then accepted the
pill. I placed a hand behind her head and raised her a little
higher so she could swallow more comfortably. Once she was
settled, I pulled the blankets away to check the bandage.

"Leave it alone, Mila," she murmured.

This woman had endured political imprisonment, beatings, gunshots, and blindness-inducing eyedrops. She was more resilient than anyone I knew, yet her attitude toward this injury baffled me. Ignoring the protest, I changed the bandage. Keeping the wound clean was one of the most important parts of the healing process.

Babushka stayed quiet as I worked, aside from the occasional grimace or groan. None of her usual complaints. Perhaps she was resigned to the fact that her frustrations wouldn't stop me, so resisting was useless. Or her attitude was prompted by something different. Something more disconcerting. The bullet had torn through her resolve as surely as her flesh.

No, impossible. My grandmother had won much more difficult battles than this; she had spent her entire life fighting. She wouldn't stop now.

* * *

AFTER RETURNING TO the old shed, I sat at my workspace with my notes and materials. For a long time, I watched the little flame flickering in my kerosene lamp.

Babushka hadn't attempted to get out of bed in the past two days. The hands resting on her quilt were thin and bony. Her face drawn. Her pallor like white arsenic. None of her medications or treatments had done much good. I had wanted to experiment, to develop something to help her improve. Instead I did nothing. A faint creak announced the door had opened, though I barely noticed when Dedushka appeared by my side. Neither of us spoke, the silence crushing while we stared at the bottles, powders, and vials.

At last, he cleared his throat. "Mila, come inside." Slow and cautious, sensitive yet emphatic. Almost pitying. He didn't continue, but I knew what that inflection meant. The words I didn't want to hear.

The sobs came all at once, fierce, choking. Dedushka coaxed me into waiting arms; soon his shirt dampened beneath my cheek.

Babushka hadn't given up; she simply understood she wasn't going to improve.

The truth had lurked inside me all this time. Each time it fought toward the surface, I smothered it by providing care, dispensing medications, performing every curative measure. My mistakes had led to this. The reality of what I'd caused was laid bare before me, as hideous and destructive as the tear in Babushka's skin.

At last, he brushed a tear from my cheek. "The man who swore allegiance to Orlova and conceded to guard your grandmother did so because he had seen so much death, so much suffering. And I'd be lying to you if I said he was no longer controlled by the terror of those experiences, because he still told Vera everything she wanted to know about you." He traced the scabs on my forearms as if his own hands had put them there.

"Cowardice comes in many forms, but so does bravery. You did what was necessary to allow Babushka to know her granddaughter, to honor my mother's request, and to protect me as best you could." I covered his hand with mine and blinked past my lingering tears. "I hold nothing against you, Dedushka. And I never will."

This time I brushed my thumb over his cheek, sweeping

away a tear before it disappeared into his beard. He kissed my forehead and let himself out, closing the door behind him.

Wiping my eyes, I picked up the brown bag containing the new medications I'd gotten this morning. I was about to throw everything away when I noticed two slips of paper in the bottom.

I picked up the first. Katya's handwriting.

Mila,

I was instructed to report your return, and I can't disobey direct orders. As a result, I was asked to give you the following message. Please understand.

Katya

Part of me had expected as much, nor did I fault her for it. I already suspected who had written the next note.

Saturday, 20 March. 8:00 A.M.

F

Tomorrow. She was coming here, I assumed. Maybe I should have been afraid, but I wasn't. No more running. Besides, not even the fear of whatever fate Fruza had in store for me was enough to make me leave Babushka.

I collapsed on my pallet. Coming back to this shed was one of the most difficult things I had forced myself to do. Being here, all I thought of was Daniil. That night. How the crease between his brows had lessened while the tension in his shoulders gave way to a little slouch. How the fire in his eyes had dulled to an ember, one that brought me into its steady heat. Welcoming his lips against mine while everything else vanished. This place was the pull of my heart toward his.

Now every tomorrow had been stolen, leaving me with a today that was unbalanced and impossible to remedy.

I had to live without him. And soon I would have to live without her.

Chapter 50

Svetlana

Every day, Mila bustled about my room—bringing tea, prompting me to accept medication, treating my injury. If dedication alone held curative power, she would have healed me ten times over. I wondered if she knew how little good her efforts did, or if blind devotion to her task prevented her from seeing anything else.

Every day, I told myself to ensure she understood the severity of my condition. And every day, something held me back.

Perhaps because I knew what would happen when she found out. Everything would change. No longer would she treat me as she always had. She might try, but she would dote on me, choose her words carefully, ask if I was comfortable. She would never say the word. To mention it was to bring it to fruition. Death was an unapproachable subject with the dying. As though others assumed we failed to realize what was occurring inside our own bodies.

Dying was exhausting enough without the needless, incessant mourning. No one would grieve in front of me, but its presence would taint everything. Every touch, a final farewell; every statement, a eulogy. So I refrained from bringing it up.

Mila had the rest of her life to mourn. As for the rest of mine, I intended to spend it as I had the last two years: with this stupid girl—or, rather, young woman.

The door to my bedroom swung open. For an instant I nearly felt the kitchen table beneath my forearms as I waited in tense silence, the rush of summer heat sweeping across my skin as the front door creaked, bringing with it a new gait across my wooden floor. The quick steps, so familiar to me now, announcing my daughter's daughter had indeed come, did exist, was not a figment of my imagination or another of Vera's schemes.

Now as she entered, Mila hummed an absentminded tune. Judging by the location of her voice, she was approaching the linen closet, likely to put away the blankets she had washed yesterday. The cabinet door creaked, confirming my suspicions. When it slammed—too hard—Mila's ditty turned into a frustrated mutter.

"I hope you weren't asleep," she said, louder this time.

"Not anymore after that racket."

"Liar. You weren't asleep at all."

A wisp of a smile found my lips. One the pain in my side quickly chased away. I clenched my jaw and adjusted my position to fight it; instead it worsened, prompting a little groan deep in my throat.

The sound of liquid filling a glass reached my ears, then a gentle touch alighted on my shoulder. With Mila's help, I sipped the water she offered me.

The gesture took me back to Kiev moments after giving birth. Tatiana, her little face red from screaming while I held her against my chest. Myself, too exhausted to do more than cling to the tiny life I had brought into the world. Fanya, wiping sweat from my brow, gathering bloody rags, lifting my head so I could drink the water she brought to my lips.

An ache settled in my stomach. It had found me so often over the years; each time, I permitted it to linger, to remind me of everything that might have been.

My daughter had built a life for herself—a home, a husband, and a child. I had done nothing to assist her, aside from entrusting her to the foundling hospital and abiding by Vera's terms to keep her safe. At least I had managed that. And when Mila arrived, it was as though Vera had sent her to taunt me. Here was a girl who knew everything about the child I'd lost, but broaching the subject meant revealing the complexity of our family's secrets. My part of the bargain would have been compromised. Somehow Vera would have found out.

Maybe my daughter's life had been a happy one, maybe not. But she had Mila; for all her foolishness, there was something to be said for the girl. Surely Tatiana recognized it as well. And now Mila understood what had brought me here. Someday, perhaps she would share my story with the girl who had always been left wondering.

Now I was the one left without answers. Wondering where my girl was. If she was still alive.

A little clink indicated Mila set the cup on the nightstand. She repositioned my pillow, smoothed the hair from my forehead, and pressed her lips to it while the clock chimed eight times. The heat of a tiny, shuddering breath met my skin before she drew back. The patter of her feet, the gentle click of the door, then silence.

I touched the bandage on my side. Instead of the usual dampness, my fingers found a hard crust. Dried blood. Perhaps my body had no more blood left to give.

A small sound captured my attention. Mila always claimed my hearing was superior to hers, despite my protests to the contrary. Without sight, I paid more attention to my other senses, naturally. She never paid attention to anything, so it was no wonder she was so astounded when I heard things she missed.

I easily deciphered what it was: The front door opening. A murmur of voices. Impossible to tell how many, though one sounded male—Sergei. The voices faded, then the door closed and it was quiet, indicating everyone had gone outside.

Perhaps I fell asleep, because the next thing I knew, Mila's voice was at the foot of my bed. "Babushka, I've brought a visitor."

Did she mean Sergei? I hardly classified him as a visitor. And she had never sounded this excited prior to bringing him to me. Her pace departed, back to wherever she had left him. The murmur of voices again, the voice I had picked out as Sergei's, Mila's eager lilt, words I could not discern. Her footsteps drew closer, joined by another's. Not Sergei's. His gait was shorter, heavier than this one.

This was a new pace, one my heart recognized. Quick, confident strides, purposeful like Mila's. Like mine. The same gait I had witnessed many years ago from a small alleyway in Kiev, when a young girl had led the way for her comrades.

This time, when the little ache found my stomach, a vibrant heat came with it. The footsteps paused once they passed through my doorway.

"Tatiana." It wasn't a question, because I knew.

Alive, somehow. And, seemingly more impossible, here.

A shaky breath, then footsteps again, this time retreating.

They stopped abruptly, perhaps halfway down the hall. A sharp whisper. One I wasn't meant to hear, though Mila should have known better.

"Wait, Mama. You have to talk to her."

"I have nothing to say, and I never should have come." Tatiana attempted to match Mila's tone, but hers was shrill, tainted by rage and something else. Fear?

"If you don't go back in there, I'll drag you in myself."

The threat brought a faint smile to my lips before Tatiana's indignant protest followed. "Do not talk to me that way, Mila, and if you keep prying into matters that don't concern you, I'll drag you back to Leningrad, siege or not, and—"

"Stop stalling."

The footsteps returned, though one set sounded like a stumble. Mila must have fulfilled her threat. They stopped at my bedside; then I heard the small chair scraping across the floor, drawing closer. The bed creaked, proof Mila had assumed her usual place. Silence, then a little huff, then the chair settled as Tatiana sank into the seat that had been supplied for her.

Someone had helped Tatiana flee from Leningrad, had brought her to Obol, leading Vera to assume I had found a way to reunite with the daughter she had forbidden me to raise. This, the reason she had written those terrible words that Sergei's shaky voice had read to me little more than a week ago: *I am writing to remind you of our terms, of which you are now in violation, as Tatiana can no longer be located in Leningrad. Kazimir is now stationed at the Wehrmacht garrison in Obol and will remain there until further action is taken.*

Those words and their implications, *further action* meaning action against Mila.

I drew a shaky breath. None of it mattered anymore. Kazimir and Vera were dead, Mila was safe, and my daughter was here.

I pictured Mila waving a hand, urging her to speak, and Tatiana, unmoving, staring at me. Perhaps she expected this bed to contain the hateful crone she had always envisioned. Instead, I was an aging blind woman, once strong and capable for my age, now frail, slipping away.

She would not be the first to speak. What would she say to someone she had resented her entire life?

I lifted a hand toward her. After a whisper that sounded like encouragement from Mila, I felt a flushed cheek beneath my fingertips.

Though it required significant effort, I traced her features, creating her image in my head. Skin bearing a few marks, nearly indistinguishable—likely small, old scars; brittle hair pulled away from her face. High cheekbones; rounded chin. Straight nose, similar to mine. Full lips with a gentle curve, similar to Mila's. But the cheekbones were hollow, bones sharp. She was thin. No surprise, given what I had heard about the siege in Leningrad, though a knot formed in my stomach.

I envisioned her clearly now. She still looked so much like the girl I had seen in Kiev. So much like I had at her age.

Gently, I lowered my hand and rested it on my abdomen.

"Brown eyes, like yours," Mila supplied for me. "Dark hair, but lighter than the grips on your pistol."

I released a little breath as the pain from my gunshot wound flared. "Were you expecting me to be dead before you got here, Tanya?"

A short bark of laughter. "I wasn't certain I cared to find out." Though her tone was tart, Tatiana's shuddering breath followed.

A familiar hand clutched mine. Even as it trembled, Mila

gave me a little squeeze, as though assuring me the news hadn't come as a shock. It seemed she was more aware of my condition than I anticipated.

"I should have listened when you told me to leave the garrison before it got worse," she said softly. "If I had—"

"None of that."

She didn't regret a single moment of her time at the garrison. Of that, I was certain. Perhaps she regretted what had befallen me, but not joining the resistance against my will. Not giving everything to her cause. It was impossible for her to regret such choices when the same blood ran through our veins. She wouldn't be my Mila if she did.

Tatiana cleared her throat. "Well, I hope Mila hasn't been too much of an inconvenience." Her chair creaked when she shifted, as though every passing moment frustrated her more than the last. It was strange for her, I supposed. A dying mother she had never met. A daughter she hadn't seen in almost two years. The three of us, blood relatives, yet strangers.

I tilted my head in Tatiana's direction. "What has she told you?"

A little breath escaped, then a whisper. "Everything."

For a moment I forgot the pain in my side.

She knew.

In the ensuing silence, something in the room shifted. It occurred beside me, where Tatiana was seated, like the turmoil inside her had reached the brim, preparing to spill over. I braced myself to accept the brunt of its force.

"I want to thank you." The words came quickly, perhaps fearing they would refuse to cooperate unless she rushed them, then she continued more slowly. "For saving Mila's life. And for saving mine."

Perhaps I had done everything in my power to keep them safe, but such actions deserved no praise when I had endangered them in the first place.

"I won't say I understand, because I'm not certain I do. Not completely. I spent my entire life thinking you never wanted me, and I . . . I wish I had known you were protecting me, that's all."

How often I had made the same wish. Every day, I longed to tell her the truth. And every day, I wondered what might have been if I had not left my daughter outside a foundling hospital in Kiev. If we had found a way to remain together while I finished what I had started. She was what I had wanted most of all, a desire I had never viewed with full clarity until my mistakes were impossible to reverse. Self-inflicted wounds cut deepest of all, yet their scars were the most resilient.

I was hers, and she was mine. Perhaps that would have been enough.

"You owe me no thanks, no love, no forgiveness. But know that if I could have given you an explanation, I would have, though I don't expect it would have improved your opinion of me. Vera never . . . ?" My words faded, partially because my voice was too weak to cling to them any longer, partially because I feared the answer. "You've been safe?"

"Yes," she murmured. "I've been safe."

The pain in my side dulled, while a slight headache settled in from the old gunshot wound. A hand fell over mine—light, uncertain.

"You did well." A pause, then a tentative whisper. "Mama."

I clung to the word as strongly as I had once clung to the pistol that never left my side. The word felt different, unexpected, but as it slipped into my grasp, I adjusted my grip, finding the proper fit. *Mama*, molding to me, settling until it felt like it had been part of me all along.

When I clutched my daughter's hand, she held on more tightly, and Mila, who had never released me, traced her thumb across my skin.

Not once in twenty-five years—perhaps in my entire life— had I ever felt at peace. Now calm settled over me, easy and effortless as my finger resting against a trigger. My sights had remained on this target for so long; at last, I had found my mark, and the peace stretched to every corner of my being. Because I never missed.

Chapter 51

Vitebsk Region, 23 March 1943

Mila

The castor oil plant's vibrant buds were already starting to bloom. I brushed my fingers over a spiky pink bulb—with gloves on, of course. My first day here and my introduction to Babushka's tight grasp had taught me that lesson.

A few days ago I had assumed I had seen this place for the last time. I had gone to the door on Saturday morning, heart racing, expecting Fruza alone on the other side; instead she had presented me with my mother, turned around, and left.

After returning from Moscow, I had tried to contact Mama through every means possible, desperate to make her aware her mother was in critical condition, hoping she was still in Leningrad, despite what Orlova had said. Suddenly here she was—my arms around her, hers around me, Fruza retreating in the distance, having freed my mother despite not sending word, which explained why Orlova had been unable to find her. Allowing us these final days together.

As I watered the plant, the fresh pink scars on my arms caught the sunlight falling through the window. Even in memory, the bite of Orlova's blade stung just as sharply. The scream constricted my throat, fighting for release, but I kept my mouth decidedly closed, combatting the ever-present past.

Calm yourself, dear girl. It's no use.

A sudden wave of fury washed away the croon. I reached for the amulet around my neck. Holding it to my eye level, I focused on the smooth glass. I knew poisons: The way arsenic had debilitated me. The way each toxin in this amulet wreaked havoc on the human body. The way it had safeguarded me against the Fritzes, despite a few close encounters.

With it, I had warded off every enemy. Now I poisoned the voice, the memory, all of it, until they were so incapacitated they disappeared from my mind. Then I took a deep breath and tucked the vial beneath my blouse.

When I let myself outside, a frigid breeze greeted me while I lifted my face toward the sun's warmth. Clouds, fat and lazy and gray with the threat of rain, meandered across the azure sky. I looked toward the old shed in the distance. Surrounded by slush and mud, it appeared even more decrepit than usual.

My feet had no trouble along the path, the same route I'd traveled countless times—day or night, sun or rain or snow. I propped the shed door open, allowing the cold inside. Slowly, I crossed to the wooden post. Dappled sunlight fell across its knots and grooves. I pressed my fingertips against the golden patches, warm as his fingertips upon my skin.

For as long as I could bear, I clung to his voice, his presence, his memory. Then I fetched my poisons from the shelves before locating one more item: the wooden box I had knocked over one day, leading to my inadvertent discovery of Babushka's Browning.

Inside, I found magazines and cartridges, so I pulled out a

few and produced her pistol from my pocket. After we had returned to the farm, she had entrusted her most prized possession to me, making sure I knew exactly how to clean and handle the weapon. Now I put my knowledge to the test.

After field-stripping and loading the gun, I studied it, picturing my grandmother as a young woman handling it with ease.

Babushka, the revolutionary. How many people had she killed with this weapon? Though the thought never ceased to baffle me, it wasn't difficult to imagine. I had seen her wield this pistol. I had seen her fight.

Gripping the gun, I lifted it toward the far wall. Despite having kept up my skills to satisfy Daniil and Fruza, I had never used a gun for more than target practice. The fit didn't feel quite right—not like my poisons—but it wasn't unnatural, either. When I closed my eyes, I recalled Babushka leveling the gun at Orlova's chest, so I adjusted my hold until it matched the image. I scanned the wooden planks on the wall. Found a target. Fired.

The crack pierced the air; when it died, I inspected my work; the large knot in the wooden wall, my designated target, had a hole through it. I traced it, imagining a similar bullet tearing across my scalp.

"Not bad."

Turning, I found Mama, eyes alight with interest. I offered her the pistol. "Do you want to try? I can help."

She examined the gun, then I stood close, lining up my sight with hers, and covered her hand with my own. She stood steady, certain, the concentrated silence not forcing us apart but coaxing us to act as one. Drawing a slow breath, filling my lungs with the gun smoke that still lingered in the air, I applied slight pressure to her finger; she took the direction. Together, we squeezed the trigger.

A piercing crack resulted in a hole directly through the knot's center. An even more precise shot than my attempt. With a smile, I released my hold, while Mama's lips curled slightly in triumph.

After being apart for so long, being reunited with my mother felt no different than before. It was much like being with Babushka during those early months. Sometimes we had moments of camaraderie, such as this. More often, we didn't. And, like with Babushka, I never knew which moment would present itself at what time.

She followed me back to the table, where she surveyed my poisons and medications. "Yours?"

I nodded. When she reached for a vial, I smacked her hand. "Not without gloves."

Sighing, she crossed her arms, protecting her hands from potential attack. In silence, I returned the remaining cartridges and magazine to the box, suddenly unsure what to do or say. At last, I cleared my throat.

"How is Papa?"

"In Chelyabinsk by now, I suppose."

What was my father doing all the way in the Urals? "He left Leningrad? And the Kirovsky Zavod?"

"Much of its production moved prior to the siege, and Lev received orders to relocate when a land corridor opened outside Leningrad. We were about to leave when Fruza's contact arrived and said you had sent for us, so we agreed he would go there and I would come here."

It was almost harder to grasp than the thought of Papa in Chelyabinsk. She could have stayed in Leningrad, though I had listened to countless radio reports: Mama's paper-thin skin, skeletal features, and thinning hairline were enough to confirm every rumor of hardship and violence. She could have gone with Papa. Instead, she had come here. To her mother's. To me.

When I blinked, a few sudden tears escaped. A gust of chilly air swept into the shed, so cold I felt as if it might turn the moisture on my cheeks to ice.

"I never thanked you," I said quietly when I had steadied myself. "For sending me here. You saved my life."

She said nothing, simply stared at a deep crack in the tabletop.

"I'll be gone tomorrow," she murmured at last, addressing the fissure. "To join Papa."

A dubious laugh sprang to my throat. "Thousands of kilometers away?" When she didn't acknowledge me, I caught her forearm. "Mama, you can't. It's too far, especially when you'll be traveling alone and the Fritzes—"

"I will not stay here." She broke my hold as sudden intensity banished the vacancy behind her eyes; then, so soft I almost didn't hear: "I cannot stay here." Without awaiting a response, she exited and closed the door behind her.

A stab of disappointment found my chest. To her, this place was the mother she had never known, the family we might have been, everything she had been denied. Yet it was also a chance to stay with her daughter throughout the remainder of a war that had done nothing but tear us apart. A chance she did not want to take.

I had just finished cleaning up my materials when the door

opened. In the doorway stood a young woman, dark hair in a tight bun, icy blue eyes on me as she toyed with her pistol.

Despite my heart thudding in my ears, a sense of relief accompanied it. At last, this would end.

"I'm only going to ask you once to surrender your weapons."

Drawing a slow breath, I shook my head. "I'm not armed. The pistol is on the table, and the poisons are on the shelf."

"Good. Let's make one more thing clear." Fruza strolled forward until she stood a few meters between me and the door. "You do not leave here until I'm finished with you. Perhaps not even then."

She had already granted me far more mercy than anticipated. Now it was time to atone for my wrongdoings.

"How did you manage it?" I asked. "Finding my mother and bringing her here?"

"It was a fruitless effort until January, when the land corridor opened up. I had a hell of a time contacting anyone I knew in the military, NKVD, or otherwise, but one connection led to another until I located her, got her out, and brought her here." Fruza turned her pistol over in her hands. "Coinciding with your return from Moscow was a happy coincidence."

Maybe she would send me away. Toss me into a cell. Sentence me to some form of hard labor. Shoot me. Whatever her decision, it didn't matter. She had brought my mother to me and Babushka's daughter to her.

Fruza strolled back and forth as she continued. "Comrade Rozovskaya, you killed an NKVD agent, putting the validity of my organization in jeopardy. You ran from them and from me, and now one of my most dedicated men, Comrade Tvardovsky, is dead." She paused, taking note of my wince. "I have every reason to execute you."

She held my gaze, as though testing whether I would dispute her or not, but she was right. Inadvertent or intentional, treachery deserved the most severe punishment.

"He was like a brother to me." A little quaver; no longer the Young Avengers leader, simply a young woman grieving her loss. That, more than anything, brought the tears to my eyes.

"Nothing I say will ever be enough," I whispered.

"No," she agreed, though softly. "It will not." Another breath, then her voice regained its strength. "I'm also told Sokolov's infiltration was simply a cover for his real intentions: He was at the garrison under Orlova's orders, prepared to do you harm at a moment's notice."

My heartbeat pounded in my ears. "How did you find out about that?"

"I've been watching this property since I picked up your mother in Obol—the same day I realized you fled—so I was aware of your return prior to Katya's report. I happened to see you leave for the village one morning and decided to pay your grandmother a visit. She told me what she knew and showed me letters as evidence."

I almost smiled. Of course Babushka had tried to protect me one last time.

"That brings me to one conclusion." Fruza stepped closer and arched a knowing eyebrow. "If a man threatens one of my girls, the bastard deserves to die."

Sokolov's piercing dark eyes flashed inside my memory as I stared at her. "What are you saying?"

"You eliminated a threat against my Young Avengers—one directly from the NKVD, an organization whose interests are aligned with ours in opposing the fascists—and you saved the NKVD the embarrassment of having this agent's treachery exposed to the public eye. As for Orlova's death, that was not your responsibility, nor is it something the NKVD will want publicized, either. That is what I will be reporting to my Komsomol superiors. I imagine all of this will go away quietly." Fruza tucked her pistol into her waistband. "And as long as you work for me, I expect you to continue fighting the patriotic war."

* * *

I STAYED IN the shed for some time following Fruza's departure, listening to faint peals of thunder while droplets pattered on the roof. Now, as I emerged, a few lingering clouds were all that remained of the inclement weather, while dappled sunlight fell across the grass and treetops. The sweet perfume of recent rain clung to the air, mingling with sodden earth.

Mama stood a few meters away beneath a birch tree. I joined her, staring at the mound of overturned earth, and at the wooden planks Dedushka had put together for a marker.

She had died shortly after Mama's arrival. As though their reunion had been the permission she needed.

A breeze rustled the leaves above us and carried the scent of fresh earth to my nostrils. The tiny sprig of belladonna, the one I'd planted beside the grave, waved gently in the breeze.

When the wind disturbed her hair, Mama tucked it behind her ears without taking her eyes off the grave. I had so many questions for her—how she felt now that she knew her mother's story, what she had endured in Leningrad, if she insisted upon going to Chelyabinsk after leaving here. The voice in my head quickly silenced me: *Stop prying, Mila.*

I reached for her, then retracted my hand.

The crinkle of paper broke the stillness. Mama pressed a worn, thin note into my palm.

20 September 1918

My darling girl,

My husband, Sergei, is writing this letter for me because my vision is severely impaired. When you were born, I was unwed. Placing you into another's care was the most compassionate thing I could do.

I do hope you will forgive me for many things. Most of all, for my inability to be the mother you deserve.

Svetlana Vasilyevna Petrova

"I have hated that note for the last twenty-five years. Almost as much as I hated her," Mama said when I handed it back. "It was easier when I assumed my parents were dead, or when I imagined they were alive but assured myself that they must have had a valid reason for leaving their daughter outside a foundling hospital, a detailed explanation I would surely receive someday. Then, when I was twelve years old, I received this. My entire life has been silence, excuses, lies." A strain crept into her voice, so she took a breath before continuing more quietly. "I never needed a perfect mother; I only needed mine."

Some decisions were the results of fear, others of love; when prompted by both, they became a creation entirely new. Perhaps selfish, perhaps courageous, perhaps something in between. Whatever it was, it was what we had become. The heart and soul that had been obscured for so long now glimmered, light piercing through the shadows that had hidden us from one another. My mother's heart and soul, my grandmother's, mine, different and yet the same, each necessary to eradicate the secrets, to counteract their poison.

I studied Babushka's name etched into the marker: *Svetlana Vasilyevna Petrova*. And, in the mound of earth I had dug beside hers, on the marker I had made: *Daniil Ivanovich Tvardovsky*.

From the corner of my eye, I glanced at my mother. Her eyes glistened. She crossed her arms over herself—perhaps for protection against a cool gust, perhaps for a reason unknown. As the breeze rustled my skirt, I smoothed my hands over it. The Browning in my pocket clinked against the vials of poison.

At last, I took a breath. "I need to go to the village, or I'll be late for my meeting. I'll be back in time for dinner."

"Still fighting the Fritzes?"

"The war isn't over yet, is it?" I responded with a little smile.

Though Mama narrowed her eyes, I didn't miss the faint light in them, mischief and intrigue. She *was* in a direct bloodline of assassins, after all.

I reached into my pocket and took her by the wrist. When she opened her palm, I placed Babushka's Browning into it. She arched a quizzical brow, so I nodded to the pistol.

"Keep it."

"Don't you need it?"

"I'm much more suited to poisons. Besides, she's your mother. She would have wanted you to have it." Especially if Mama intended to travel all the way to the Urals.

Her hand wrapped around the grip, then she rested her finger against the trigger. Easy, natural. A perfect fit. I toyed with my amulet while she tucked it into her waistband.

I turned my eyes toward the forest. For so long I had felt as if returning to what I had once known would erase everything that had been buried for decades and conjured anew by this unknown place; the yearning no longer seized me so fiercely. Not now that this place felt as much a part of me as the blood in my veins, the scars on my skin, and the poisons around my neck. I knew these aspens, spruces, and oaks, aglow with lingering raindrops; the tall pine with the old eagle's nest; the underbrush thick with mushrooms, roots, berries, and belladonna. I knew the decrepit shed and tiny farmhouse. And I knew this tall birch tree and the two who rested in the ground beneath it. So much had driven my family apart, nearly destroyed us; yet ultimately those same imperfections had brought us together. Ours was a home no flaw or secret or scar was powerful enough to eradicate.

"Be off to your meeting," my mother said with sudden briskness, breaking the quiet. "Tell your friends I appreciate their help in getting me out of Leningrad." She started down the path toward the house.

As the distance stretched between us, suddenly I was hurrying after her, a cry breaking free. "Mama!"

She halted, seeming startled into stillness by my haste. I wasn't certain what had prompted me to stop her, only that the urge had grabbed me and refused to relinquish its control.

"If you . . ." My voice was quieter this time, pushing past the tightness in my throat. "If you want to stay . . ."

Though I was unable to finish, the urge renounced its hold, as if it had done enough. When it departed, a fierce ache took its place—a longing I recognized but always suppressed, because it always ended in disappointment.

This time, I didn't suppress it. We were a family torn apart by secrets, fallen classes, betrayal, revolution, suffering, war. Our past was ugly, but it was ours. Maybe the exposed truth held the power to sustain us, to nourish the bond we had tried and failed to curate.

My mother looked beyond me to the graves before meeting my gaze. Her eyes didn't hold their usual indifference; rather, they reflected the same longing and curiosity roiling around inside me. When she spoke, her voice was soft, unable to shield a sudden break.

"Perhaps."

Without awaiting my reply, she continued toward the farmhouse.

A flicker of warmth rose in my chest. I watched until the door closed behind her, then I proceeded down the path, past the old shed, and toward the village.

Perhaps. It was all the certainty one could promise during these times. Not a thousand tomorrows, not even all of today; simply a *perhaps*, borne on the wind of an icy breeze. Yet, for all its uncertainty, *perhaps* came laced with the hope of a different tomorrow. For those who had always been left wondering, *perhaps* felt certain enough.

Acknowledgments

Every novel presents new and unexpected challenges, but the second published novel is a unique experience because the author is very new to actually being an author—how to write one book while promoting another, perhaps work on a deadline—all those challenges that might not have been part of the first novel. This was certainly true for me, and it can add a lot of pressure and worry; fortunately I had an incredible support system to help me through it, and I owe them the biggest thanks. To my editor, Lucia Macro, Asanté Simons, and everyone at William Morrow and HarperCollins—marketing, publicity, design, production, audio, foreign rights, and everyone in between—you are all an integral part of this journey. I'm so grateful to have you by my side.

My fantastic agent, Kaitlyn Johnson, for your patience and guidance; I'm so fortunate to work with you. My incredible critique partner and wonderful friend, Olesya Salnikova Gilmore, for providing invaluable insight into Russian culture, helping me uncover this book's potential, and never giving up on me or this story. Marina Scott, for your encouragement and faith in me, and for being an additional pair of eyes checking cultural sensitivity—one can never have too many! Amanda McCrina, your feedback was an immeasurable help, as always. My #HFChitChat family on Twitter for giving me a place to celebrate historical fiction, especially my hardworking co-hosts—Olesya Salnikova Gilmore, Janna G. Noelle, and Syd Young. Halley Cotton for knowing all there is to know about mushrooms. Cristin Williams for helping me with the French language.

Most of all, to my family and friends for supporting me every step of the way: from helping me with research, to telling friends about my books, to setting up events, and so much more, your love and support means everything to me and makes such a difference. Finally, to my readers. Thank you for allowing me to share this part of me with you, and for giving me the gift of doing what I love.

About the author

About the book

Insights,
Interviews
& More . . .

Meet Gabriella Saab

Janie Long Photography

GABRIELLA SAAB is the author of
The Last Checkmate. She graduated
from Mississippi State University
with a bachelor of business
administration and lives in her
hometown of Mobile, Alabama.
She is of Lebanese heritage and is
one of the cohosts of @HFChitChat
on Twitter, a recurring monthly chat
celebrating the love of reading and
writing historical fiction. ∾

Historical Note

I have said it before, and I will say it again: please read this author's note for more insight regarding the real history and real people who inspired this novel, but wait until after you've read the book.

If you have finished the book, you may proceed.

I came across the inspiration for this story when I was researching my debut novel, *The Last Checkmate*. In doing so, I stumbled across a young woman named Zinaida Martynovna Portnova, a member of the Belarusian resistance who poisoned Nazis. How could I pass up the opportunity to tell her story? Since I'd been considering a dual timeline for this novel, I started researching women in the Russian Revolution to see if I could find another interesting figure to use as inspiration for a second storyline. Sure enough, I did: Fanya Kaplan, who was executed for an assassination attempt against Vladimir Lenin. I also discovered Vera Figner, a noblewoman who left her family to join the revolution. From these women, my characters Mila and Svetlana were born, and I included a fictionalized version of Fanya Kaplan as well.

I had access to some excellent research resources, some named below, but much of this history was difficult to uncover, and reports often conflicted. Though Mila's life is significantly modeled after Zina Portnova's, and Svetlana's after Vera Figner's and Fanya Kaplan's, sometimes I blended ideas from conflicting reports or developed my own thoughts to craft these characters and this novel. It *is* fiction, after all. ▸

Historical Note *(continued)*

Zina Portnova was born in Leningrad to Belarusian parents, and her father worked at the Kirov Plant. In the summer of 1941, then-sixteen-year-old Zina went to visit her grandmother in the Vitebsk Region of Byelorussia—now Belarus—and, shortly after that, the Nazis invaded the Soviet Union. I took creative liberty by including the Vitebsk Region in the early days of the occupation. When a group of soldiers seized her family's cattle and struck her grandmother, Zina was infuriated and resolved to join the resistance to free her country from Nazi oppression. A fictional version of this account motivates my character Mila to seek vengeance and justice by joining the resistance.

In Obol, Zina joined a resistance group that was organized by the Komsomol, a name derived from the Russian name for Communist Union of Youth, or All-Union Leninist Young Communist League. Zina's group was led by Yefrosinya Savelyevna Zenkova, who was rumored to have gone by the nickname Fruza. According to accounts, she was born into a peasant family in Ushaly, located in the present-day Shumilina District, and was asked by a group of partisans to establish a Komsomol presence in Obol in order to report on Nazi activity in the area and use the railway to gather insight on matters such as troop movements. Since Zenkova was only eighteen at the time and all her members were teenagers and young adults, they were named the Young Avengers. This group spread propaganda, gathered information on Nazi troops, and participated in acts of sabotage against them, and Zina Portnova joined them at age seventeen.

In 1943, Zina secured employment as a kitchen aide in the Nazi garrison in Obol, where she began poisoning the soldiers. In this book, you may recall a scene where the garrison soldiers become suspicious due to an outbreak of a supposed illness, so they accuse Mila of poisoning their food. To prove otherwise, she eats from the dishes she prepared, including those laced with arsenic— though she knows it will make her sick, even kill her if her body absorbs a large dose. Her risk pays off, and the men believe she is telling the truth regarding her innocence. She purges the poison at her first opportunity by drinking whey, and although she still gets very sick, she survives and returns to work.

As unbelievable as it might sound, this was taken out of Zina Portnova's real life: Multiple accounts claim she really was accused of poisoning the soldiers and did eat contaminated food in front of them to prove she was, in fact, *not* poisoning it. The Nazis let her go. Though she survived, reports say she went into hiding for a while, then re-infiltrated the garrison later. Rather than having my character hide, I wanted her to be able to return to work, so I lessened the severity of her poisoning and had her devise a way to place blame on her coworker, a woman named Zina—and yes, I named my Zina after the real Young Avenger.

Following Zina's capture by the Gestapo, reports vary about what happened next. Some say Zina took her Gestapo interrogator's pistol, shot him ▶

5

Historical Note (*continued*)

and a few others, and fled before being caught in the woods. Others claim she shot a few men and was caught after her gun misfired. Either way, she was recaptured and tortured, then possibly killed during interrogation or taken to the woods and executed on January 15, 1944. According to reports, all the Young Avengers, except Fruza, were eventually caught and executed.

On July 1, 1958, both Zina Portnova and Yefrosinya Zenkova were declared Heroes of the Soviet Union—a posthumous award for Portnova, while Zenkova lived until 1984. You may have noticed that a fictionalized version of Yefrosinya Zenkova also appears in this novel. Much of Fruza's character is as true to the limited research on her as I could find, and much of Mila's is heavily based on Portnova's life. *Stalin's Guerrillas: Soviet Partisans in World War II* by Kenneth Slepyan was a fascinating account of the partisan experience, though I condensed and simplified the Young Avengers for story purposes.

Once I had the idea for my World War II character, I wanted to tie in the Russian Revolution, a fascinating and pivotal part of Russia's history. *Caught in the Revolution* by Helen Rappaport was an incredible read, providing so much insight into the circumstances leading up to the overthrow of the Romanov family and the Bolshevik Party's ascension to power. Svetlana Petrova's character is a composite of the real Fanya Kaplan, featured in this story as a secondary character, and Vera Figner.

Fanya Kaplan's real name is not actually known. Various sources refer to her in different ways, including Fanny Efimovna Kaplan, Dora, Feiga Haimovna Roytblat, Feiga Khaimovna Roytblat-Kaplan, and Fanya. An article titled "The 1918 Attempt on the Life of Lenin: A New Look at the Evidence" from *Slavic Review,* Vol. 48, No. 3, credits her as Feiga Khaimovna Roitman, later Fania (also spelled "Fanya") Kaplan. Going by this source, I use Feiga Khaimovna Roitman as her birth name and combined Fanya Kaplan with one of her other listed patronymics, Efimovna, as the name she adopts after marriage; the Pale of Settlement was one of the few areas where Jews and other minorities were permitted to live, so marrying someone who resided outside of it was necessary to achieve permission to leave.

According to this article, Kaplan was born in 1887 to a Jewish family in a Ukrainian province, Volhynia. Most likely she married a man named Kaplan who lived outside the Pale and adopted his name, then she settled in Kiev in 1906, joining a few other anarchists who were planning an attack on the governor-general. When an explosion went off in her hotel room and killed a maid, she was arrested and a Browning revolver was uncovered in her room; she insisted she knew nothing and did not reveal accomplices. She was charged and sentenced to death, but after her age—nineteen at the time of the arrest—was taken into consideration, the sentence was lessened to life imprisonment in the Nerchinsk katorga.

Within the Nerchinsk katorga, conditions in Maltsev, or Maltsevskaya, were not as severe as in other prisons, so women often studied, but the lack of ▶

activity had an impact on their mental health. For Kaplan, this led to severe headaches and temporary loss of sight that became more and more permanent. In my story I increased the severity of conditions in Maltsevskaya to include hard labor and had this be the cause of Fanya's health problems.

By 1912, Kaplan went completely blind but learned to read Braille and care for herself, and she familiarized herself with others by touching their faces; she transferred to Akatui Prison, where a doctor recommended electric treatments at a prison hospital. These helped to restore her sight somewhat. She was released from Akatui in 1917, following the overthrow of the imperial government, which lifted the sentences of political prisoners; for simplification purposes, I kept my character Fanya in Maltsevskaya and liberated her alongside Svetlana. After years, even decades, of imprisonment, the women in these labor camps and prisons had formed close bonds, which I wanted to illustrate by having Svetlana and Fanya remain together following liberation.

The real Kaplan was undergoing more medical treatment when the October Revolution took place in 1917, not in Moscow with the revolutionaries, as my character is. Kaplan went to Moscow in February or March of 1918 to rejoin some of her friends from prison and began considering political terrorism against the Bolsheviks. Little more is known about what she did until the attempt against Lenin's life.

On August 30, 1918, testimonies conflict: some say a witness saw Kaplan shooting Lenin, yet other evidence says no one actually saw who pulled the trigger outside the Mikhelson Armaments Factory that day. Red Guards arrested all suspects, including Kaplan, though accounts of her arrest differ. Some say her nervous, odd behavior was what drew attention to her; then, once in Cheka custody, she admitted she shot Lenin but refused to provide further information. Most sources report that her execution took place on September 3, 1918, in the Kremlin courtyard.

Some historians speculate that Kaplan was an anarchist and not affiliated with the Socialist Revolutionary Party, as no evidence proves one way or another where her political affiliations fell. And with so many conflicting reports about the assassination attempt against Lenin, it is impossible to know if Kaplan really was responsible; given her vision problems, many find reason to doubt. Could a woman who was nearly blind carry out such an attempt, or was she caught and falsely accused, so she accepted blame to protect her party members? I thought this was fascinating, and, of course, it got me wondering: What if someone else had carried out the attempt, but Fanya accepted the blame for it?

This started my idea for Svetlana's character, while Vera Figner provided much of her background. Through Figner's *Memoirs of a Revolutionist*, I dove into a firsthand account of this woman's fascinating life, in which she left the nobility to join a revolutionary party. Of course, it left me with so many questions: Did other revolutionaries trust that her heart was with their cause? Did she regret breaking ties with her family? Why were ▶

her convictions so strong? How far was she willing to go for her beliefs? Such a woman made for a complex, difficult character with so many layers, which was so much fun for me as a writer.

In 1852, Vera Figner was born to a noble family in Kazan and dreamed of becoming a lady in court. She attended the Rodionovsky Institute until 1869 and then returned home, where she lived in the country and, as a result, rarely interacted with anyone outside her family. Her uncle was a "thinking realist" who began sharing his ideas with Vera. He expressed negative opinions about the wealthy and encouraged freedom from class and religion, universal education, equal rights for women, and utilitarianism. Gradually, Vera became what she called a "repentant noble" and no longer aspired to the comfortable life her class promised; she wanted to attend university and do good for others. Instead, her parents presented her to society and she married, but she adopted more radical views and eventually separated from her husband.

Figner was part of the People's Will, which later developed into the Socialist Revolutionary Party. She began spreading revolutionary ideas, though some people were suspicious of her due to her aristocratic background. At last, she and her party members concluded that terrorism was necessary to effect change; one man attempted to assassinate Tsar Aleksandr II and failed, so Figner dodged investigations and continued to support attempts to assassinate the tsar.

After more failed assassination attempts, the revolutionaries managed to mortally wound the tsar; Figner escaped arrest while a few others were caught and executed. The government began enticing people to turn in revolutionaries, so many became spies and informed on their friends. Figner was ultimately betrayed, arrested, held in the Fortress of Saints Peter and Paul, then transferred to Shlisselburg. Her mother entreated the government for mercy, so Figner was released in 1904, after twenty years of imprisonment.

Because neither Figner nor Kaplan were Bolsheviks, this gave me the opportunity to explore some lesser-known political sides of the Russian Revolution—namely, the Socialist Revolutionary Party, one I learned about mostly through *Captives of Revolution* by Scott B. Smith. Most people know the Bolsheviks ultimately claimed control of the government, but I was fascinated to learn more about the various parties vying for political power. As briefly mentioned in the story, the Socialist Revolutionaries did indeed attempt to link Bolshevik violence with the violence of the imperialist Old Regime. I learned about the Bolshevik secret police from *The Cheka: Lenin's Political Police* by George Leggett, and this organization evolved into the NKVD and later the KGB. Vera Orlova is fictional but is inspired by real women who worked for the Cheka, many of whom were notoriously ruthless; Vera also represents countless Bolsheviks who were unflinchingly devoted to their cause, and many of these were people who had suffered terribly under imperialism. I did my best to clarify the views of each party, but politics were simplified and condensed for story purposes.

Many of the other events in the story did happen, including the execution of ▶

Historical Note *(continued)*

five men condemned for the attempted
assassination of Tsar Aleksandr III—
among them was Aleksandr Ilych Ulyanov,
Vladimir Lenin's elder brother. This
served to increase Lenin's motivation
toward revolutionary pursuits. The
Khodynka Field tragedy in 1896, the
Bloody Sunday massacre in 1905, and
the execution of more than seven thousand
Soviet civilians, mostly Jewish, at the
Gully of Petrushino between 1941 and
1943 did happen as well, unfortunately.

Aside from the liberties mentioned
here, I attempted to stay true to all names,
events, dates, and places, although allow
me to note that all dates are listed in
accordance with the Gregorian calendar
for simplification, to the best of my ability.
Soviet Russia changed from the Julian to
the Gregorian calendar in February 1918,
right in the middle of my timeline, which
might have created unnecessary difficulty
for the reader. The October Revolution of
1917, for example, is remembered
historically in accordance with when it
took place on the Julian calendar, since
that was the calendar used at the time, but
if you refer to the chapter in which it takes
place in this novel you will notice a
November date in keeping to the
Gregorian calendar. Lastly, since the
characters in this novel are Russians living
during the revolutionary and Soviet eras,
all names and places are spelled in
accordance with Russian transliterations,
to the best of my knowledge.

I hope this clarifies some of the history
included in this story, and, as always,
I hope it encourages you to learn more
for yourself. Any errors in history or
setting are entirely my own. ∾

Further Reading

Nonfiction
Memoirs of a Revolutionist (1927)—Vera
 Figner
*Natasha's Dance: A Cultural History of
 Russia* (2002)—Orlando Figes
The Cheka: Lenin's Political Police
 (1981)—George Leggett
*Lady Death: The Memoirs of Stalin's
 Sniper* (2018)—Lyudmila Pavlichenko
Caught in the Revolution (2016)—Helen
 Rappaport
*Stalin's Guerrillas: Soviet Partisans in
 World War II* (2006)—Kenneth
 Slepyan
Captives of Revolution (2011)—Scott B.
 Smith

Fiction
I Was Anastasia (2018)—Ariel Lawhon
The Huntress (2019)—Kate Quinn
Red Mistress (2020)—Elizabeth
 Blackwell ∽

Reading Group Guide

1. Compare and contrast the women in this story: Svetlana, Vera, Fanya, and Mila. What similarities and differences do they share as young women active in their causes? How do Mila and Svetlana compare and contrast in their youth, and what changes do you find in the woman Svetlana was versus the woman Mila knows as Babushka? Do you think Fanya, Svetlana, and Vera were true friends to one another or not? How does Vera change when acting as Orlova, and does her role shift or change as her years working for the Cheka—then, as it evolved, the NKVD—progress? What similarities do you find in all these women throughout their lives? What differences?

2. Sight is a key theme and symbol utilized throughout this story: Fanya suffers from deteriorating vision, Orlova blinds her victims, and Svetlana loses her eyesight. Discuss the message this represents in relation to the choices these characters make—those related to their political views, family life, romantic interests, etc.

3. Discuss the politics in the story— the imperialism of the Old Regime, the Socialist Revolutionary Party, the Bolshevik Party, Nazi Germany, and the USSR. What did you learn about these parties and their conflicts? Do you think the Russian Revolution

resulted in a government the people wanted or expected? Discuss positive and negative outcomes of the revolution. Do you notice any similarities or differences between Adolf Hitler and the Nazi Party versus Vladimir Lenin and the Bolshevik Party?

4. Svetlana falls in love with Kazimir, Mila with Daniil. Do you think these were healthy relationships? Why or why not? How do both men seem similar and differ? What do you think both women saw in their love interests? If their lives had turned out differently, do you think either relationship would have lasted? Discuss Svetlana's relationship with Sergei.

5. Mila fights her battles with poison, Svetlana with a pistol. What do these weapons and approaches say about these women?

6. One of Svetlana's most difficult decisions is her choice to place her daughter, Tatiana, in a foundling hospital for safety until the revolution is over. Do you agree this was the wisest choice, and do you think this choice was made from motherly concern, obsession with revolutionary participation, or a combination of both? How did this decision impact her emotionally and psychologically, and what effect did it have on Tatiana? How did her broken relationship with her own mother impact the way Tatiana parents Mila? ▶

Reading Group Guide *(continued)*

7. What do you think family means to these characters, especially Mila, Svetlana, and Tatiana?

8. What does the novel's title, *Daughters of Victory*, mean to you? What triumphs do these characters experience? What failures? Do you feel these characters are victorious? Do you think *they* feel they are victorious? Do you think the concept of victory and what it means to them changes throughout the course of the story? ◠